MW01181788

Other Books by Austin Reams

THE MORNING TREE

Did Jesus write a gospel in his own hand? His disciples say so, and one of their own has stolen it.

Days after the crucifixion, a centurion, Ras is tasked by the disciples of Jesus to find the missing scroll of the man from Nazareth who would be called the Christ.

Although sunlight can kill him, Ras, a man of war, searches from the wastelands of Galilee and Judea to the secret dungeons of the temple in Jerusalem.

But Ras has been deceived. People are not who they seem to be. A hidden truth is revealed under the morning tree at the tip of a blade: to serve Jesus with violence is to destroy his teachings ...

Available for order on-line through Mimbrez Publishers
www.mimbrez.com

THE SUPERUNKNOWNS

THE SUPERUNKNOWNS

A

Novel

AUSTIN REAMS

MIMBREZ

MIMBREZ PUBLISHERS
P.O. BOX 13508
OKLAHOMA CITY, OKLAHOMA 73113
WWW.MIMBREZ.COM

ACKNOWLEDGMENTS

My deepest love and gratitude to my wife, Ling, and our children, Sophia and Lara. Many thanks to my itinerant readers, Ling, and Ann Barnes, who read the first draft of this work. To my father for teaching me that I can do anything I set my mind to, whether true or not, and to my mother for showing me the importance of art. Thanks to Teresa Deering and Debbie Tyler for their support. I would like to express my sincere appreciation and honor to the kenshi at Sen Shin Kan Dojo in Oklahoma City, including Sensei Bryan Mosley, Luis Angeli, Shaw Furukawa, Mil Mang, Zane Aleson, Claire Delpirou, and many others in the Southwest Kendo and Iaido Federation, and All United States Kendo Federation, for lessons in the way of the body, sword and mind. Special thanks to my editor, Kate Gilpin of Words Into Print, for her hard work and understanding.

FOREWORD

The next time you're in a coffee shop, airport, checkout line, traffic light, stadium, concert, or any public gathering, take a moment to look around. Count the number of people using an electronic device, and ask, *Who's in control here?*

For Sophia and Lara, always.

And for Ling, who saved me.

Reports that say that something hasn't happened are always interesting to me, because as we know, there are known knowns; there are things we know we know. We also know there are known unknowns; that is to say we know there are some things we do not know. But there are also unknown unknowns — the ones we don't know we don't know. And if one looks throughout the history of our country and other free countries, it is the latter category that tend to be the difficult ones.

United States Secretary of Defense
Donald Rumsfeld

The medium is the message.

Marshall McLuhan

I will see you again in mountains.

Chia Tao (779-843)

From "Seeing Off a Man of the Tao"

THE SUPERUNKNOWNS
BY AUSTIN REAMS (C) 2016

Subject............	Edith Nobutora Song
Facility..........	29 Palms
Sublevel..........	Talos
Level.............	6
Age...............	17
Height............	5'10"
Weight............	120
Complexion........	Fair
Eyes..............	Green
Hair..............	Black
Occupation........	Student
Home..............	Okla.City
Parents...........	Rory Lawson Helen Song (Deceased)
Remarks..........	DANGER UNKNOWN

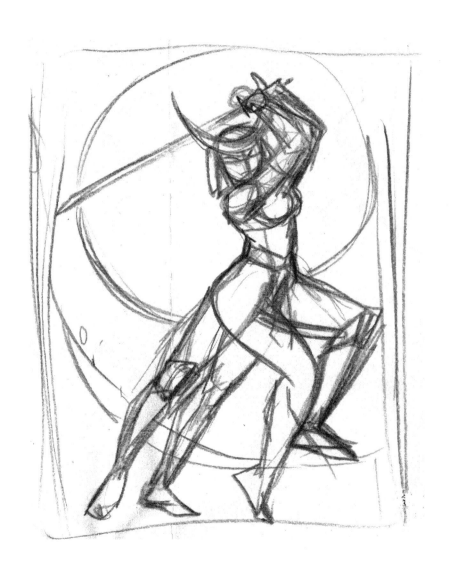

Subject...........	...Irene Nobutora Song
Facility.........	...29 Palms
Sublevel.........	...Talos
Level............	...7
Age..............	...17
Height...........	...5'10"
Weight...........	...120
Complexion.......	...Fair
Eyes.............	...Blue
Hair.............	...Black
Occupation.......	...Student
Home.............	...Okla.City
Parents..........	...Rory Lawson Helen Song (Deceased)
Remarks.......	EXTREME DANGER

Chapter 1

OUR ENGLISH TEACHER PUNCHED IRENE IN THE FACE ON A CLEAR day. Mr. Gaddis wasn't really a teacher. He was a Marine colonel. We weren't supposed to know that then. I know it now. I know a lot of things I'm not supposed to, if I ask the right questions.

Tuesday. Senior English literature class. First period. Mr. Gaddis limped in and scanned over our heads with a sigh of ownership, like a farmer taking inventory of his crops.

A sadistic grin dug into his pock-marked cheeks. He pulled at the neckline of his secondhand tweed jacket, out of place on military shoulders. I don't know why he bothered to wear such clothes that morning. No one would see him for the military man he was. Just the same old teacher, no one would notice. Except some things can't be overlooked.

"Pop quiz," he said. As if we'd be having a party.

Silence. Wide-eyed students stared into empty space over their desks. They waved their hands and fingers through the air. Some even talked over each other. Not with each other. A constant murmur filled the room. I hate that sound. Comes with the most intense feeling of loneliness. Being in a crowded room with people, friends and family even, who don't know I'm there. High school is suffocating enough. To bear it alone in a crowd is another thing entirely.

Lipstick-shaped cylinders hung around most of the students' necks from fiber optic hoops. The crystal Citizen Bands glowed green in active mode. Truckers once called them "CBs" a long time ago. Talked to each other on the road. *Breaker, breaker*, and all that. The new CBs were way different. Everyone could talk to everyone, see anything, all the time. Tied up the brain into a pretzel. *Cerebral Bands*, Papa used to call them.

My classmates. I knew what they were seeing. A pristine room. Minimalist features. Clean white walls. Ms. Croucher in a plaid dress and gleeful smile pacing around stainless steel desks. Warm sunlight filtered in through the windows. Everyone dressed in pressed school uniforms. A CB lie. I knew it, and a few others knew it too. Aariti and Margaret. Mr. Gaddis knew it all too well. The dealer of lies.

He pressed an invisible button in mid-air. CBs flickered and went clear. Students gasped and groped into empty space.

"Where'd it go? Where'd it go? Where'd it go?" someone said from the back.

"I'm Mr. Gaddis," he said. "Your new teacher."

The students gawked at him like aliens had landed. In a way, that was exactly right. A harsh and foreign landscape with unknown people. Grimy walls. Rusty desks. Scuffed tiles. And a stranger. Still, none of that mattered. A strong dose of truth is not enough to make change. But it sure does hurt.

"Hey!" another said. "Turn it back on!"

"Your wish is my command," Mr. Gaddis said. "So long as you know who's boss now." He pressed his finger to the air again. CBs warmed from clear to green around the students' necks.

For those with CBs, the landscape of the classroom washed back to utopia. Ms. Croucher replaced Mr. Gaddis, better dressed and groomed than the man standing before me in the tweed jacket. Mr. Gaddis waved his arm. Five questions hovered above the desktops. "Answer these questions," Mr. Gaddis said as he paced around the desks like Ms. Croucher had been doing just moments before.

To the few of us without CBs, the grizzled and drab Mr. Gaddis stayed put, scowling at the front of the room. He produced CBs and glasses and offered them to Aariti and Margaret. "Put them on, ladies," he said.

Girls don't sweat like boys. At least not as much. Some of us put off excess water in other ways. Not Aariti. Sweat formed around her brow and below her ears. I could already smell it. Her eyes darted from Margaret to me, and to Irene, so fast and erratic she looked possessed. I shook my head. She understood the message. *It's no use.* She took the glasses from Mr. Gaddis and slid them on. The light of the CB brightened when Mr. Gaddis hooked it over the crown of her head, saying, "Now there's a good girl."

Mr. Gaddis held the glasses out to Margaret. She slapped them out of his hand. People who lose their tempers are sometimes less scary than those with no reaction to anything. It's like they have no feelings, no remorse, no empathy for pain. Happy or angry, the same expression. They could witness a murder in cold blood or sing happy birthday. Makes no difference to them. Either way, their faces stay placid. A steady heartbeat. Even loving eyes. That's

3

how Mr. Gaddis was. We all felt it, I'm sure. He dug his fingers into Margaret's hair at the back of her head and held the glasses to her right eye. "You're going to wear these one way or another, sweetie," he said.

Margaret had a mental touch in common with Mr. Gaddis. She knew crazy, the stubborn kind that would walk into a burning building because someone told her not to. But sometimes she also knew when to pick her battles. She put on the glasses with an air of boredom, glaring back at him with pale belligerence and a nasty finger gesture. From her perspective, Ms. Croucher paced the spotless room and at the same time she could still see Mr. Gaddis surrounded by grimy decay. Such dual vision would be short lived. Not even a well-intentioned sociopath could resist CB distractions for long. Her eyes betrayed the inner battle. Pupils dilated and contracted wildly. She could maintain clarity for a while, then, in no less than twenty-four hours, even she would give in to the blissful sheen of beautiful false reality.

Mr. Gaddis slipped a CB over my neck and dropped a pair glasses in my lap. "Until we can have your special contacts fitted," he said, and turned to Irene, sitting two rows over at the front of the class. "Here are your CB and glasses, Irene." He held out the CB to her as if feeding a wild beast through a barbed wire fence, sounding almost apologetic, betraying his doubt.

Irene didn't take the CB. A smirk hinted at the edge of her mouth. She tapped her knee against her aluminum cane, knocking it against the desk. The sound said, *Go to hell!*

Mr. Gaddis rubbed a meaty hand over his face. He tossed the CB on his desk. "Irene," he said. "Be a good girl now and take your CB!"

4

She hummed a familiar tune. Something quaint from a government infomercial.

He gritted his teeth. He nodded his head, and the veins in his neck pulsed. "Irene. *Have ... you ... seen ... your ... father ... lately?*"

Irene's blue eyes burned into him. "*He's ... dead ... you ... jerk!*" She went back to tapping and humming.

Mr. Gaddis took a small step and glared at Aariti over Irene's head.

"I hear Aariti had a close call just the other day. Got caught on the other side of the fence with wildlings, no less. Guess you helped save her. Her father must be eternally grateful." He sighed. "Yes, and what of her parents? Short on their house payments, I hear."

Hearing her name, Aariti's eyes searched blindly. "I don't need this, Irene," she said. "My *parents*. Thanks for everything, Irene, but ... but there's a time and place ... " She bowed her head and massaged her temples, slipping back into distraction.

Mr. Gaddis held his hands out to me. "You want to talk some sense into your sister?"

"She won't listen to me. Never has, never will."

Irene snickered through her nose.

Mr. Gaddis stuck out his jaw. He took another step toward Irene.

"Irene, Irene, Irene," he said. "You're going to put your CB on ... or your friends, your *family* ... "

Gaddis kept on. Every direct and veiled threat enumerated. Irene just stared a tunnel into the floor. The expression of arrogant amusement drained from her pale face. No longer listening, all

5

sound drowned out by tinnitus. She was mesmerized with two wispy flames – blue and green – conjured from the floor like intertwined souls released from bondage.

A low hum vibrated through everything and everyone in the classroom. Mr. Gaddis held out his forearms to fend off a blast. The flames fell on me and Irene. A bubble of blue light swelled around Irene, pressing outward. Something shocked me and I jumped out of my desk, trying to kick out what felt like an electric snake buried in my nerves. Something popped and green mist dissipated after blue.

Mr. Gaddis lowered his arms. He bumped into the front of Irene's desk, gaping with an open mouth at the windows at the back of the room. I could see the same thing he was seeing – there was nothing out there. He hurried down the center aisle of desks and pushed the window open. Leaning out, he searched the sky.

I gathered with Aariti and Margaret behind Mr. Gaddis. The girls had torn off their CBs so they could see.

"It's gone!" Mr. Gaddis said. He stepped back from the window, pressing a finger to his ear, listening and nodding to a distant voice. "Yes, it's gone," he said. "By all reports, it left."

He turned to Irene. She leaned heavily against her cane, looking mournfully at the windows. Her confidence crushed. Replaced with fear.

"It's gone," Mr. Gaddis said. His eyes glinted with predatory hunger.

He rushed forward and punched her on the bridge of her nose. Irene's cane slid across the floor as she crashed backwards into his desk. She lay there motionless, her lame legs twisted underneath her hips.

6

Mr. Gaddis wrung out his hand in pain. He held a finger to his ear again. "She's here. Come and get her!" He gulped. "Really? It's really him? Excellent! *Three* for one."

Boot heels roared down the hallway outside the classroom.

Chapter 2

Martin was having a bad day. So he believed. And so he was.

Looking back on him now, I just wanted to shout, "Wake up!" He was so close to seeing the truth. But like someone drowning in two inches of water, close to being rescued isn't close enough.

Even if I could get a message to him in the past, he wouldn't have heard me. Can't explain what's real and what isn't to the blind, only point the way.

He sat on his hands, palms down, rocking back and forth, tapping cap-toed Italian shoes made from cognac leather, which matched his sandy hair and pale skin. Charcoal wool suit, grey overcoat and burgundy scarf -- he spiffed to the nines in the real world. Most others looked like they'd been sleeping in their clothes for a week.

He gave a thousand-mile stare over the top of his daughter's coffin. I've seen that look before. Everywhere, in fact. Everyone has it. Not looking anyone in the eye. Seeing but not seeing. Hearing, not understanding. His eyes jumped to a blue jay that lit on a bare cherry blossom limb, holding the sight for a moment. Something inside him was stirring. A little bit of light from reality piercing the darkness. The shock of death, or joy of life, does that sometimes. Only the strong tear the rest of the way through. His pupils went wide again, unfocused and wandering.

Christy, his sister, sat to his left, nursing a hangover. She looped her index finger through the air, conducting an invisible orchestra of blogs, shopping networks, and news feeds. To anyone seeing her through CB eyes, she appeared fancifully dressed in a sleek pant suit, knee-length overcoat, hat, and sunglasses. All black. To my view, she wore a stained white cotton nightgown with blue and pink print flowers under a full-length down coat with tube socks and flip flops.

"Sit still!" she hissed. Her vague gaze shifted toward him, not on him.

His eyes searched the deserted cemetery without finding. "What difference does it make?" he said. "We're alone. We're *always* alone."

"No, we're not." She pointed to a tower of digits hovering a few feet off the ground to her left. "See the counter! Thousands tuning in. And *we're* the only two here. *You're* the one who wanted to come *in person*. We should have attended from home like everyone else."

"They're not here. Not really. Just ghosting us on a sub-channel so they can pretend to care." He was right. Most linking to the funeral muted their feed while they worked or shopped.

Every few seconds another virtual bouquet popped into view around the casket, blocking the view. Martin waved his index finger.

The flowers blew away in with a soft whump, a collapsing tower of ashes.

"Why'd you do that?" Christy said. "People will think you're not grateful."

"They won't notice. Besides, I came to *see* her. With my *own* eyes. Not false sympathy!"

"You know how badly she was injured. You don't want to see that."

Martin rubbed eyes with the heel of his hands. The light of his CB pulsed. Everything at the graveyard – land and air – became flooded in a light red. A green "Answer" and red "Decline" button appeared in front of his chest mid-air. He punched decline. The red hue faded.

Meaningless chatter poured out of Christy. And a loud bizarre murmur of words, slurs, and grunts, like a mixture of demon possession and drunken elation. Some words and phrases were pieced together. None of it made sense as a whole.

Martin patted the back of his hand on her cheek. "Catching up on gossip?"

She stopped and looked around, bringing her focus back to the tombstone landscape. "Sorry. Forgot to mute the verbal."

Actually, no one ever mutes verbal. She was the typical sort. Scanning shopping networks, video product reviews, weather updates, opinion channels, the whole bit. During meals, showers, church services, and even sleep. All the time. In a state of constant distraction, people like her keep talking over others who don't even notice. Every gathering – at dinners, church services, buses, classrooms, restaurants, offices, hospitals, everywhere and all the time -- sounds like a loud party, no matter the occasion. The thing

11

is, no one is talking to anyone that's actually present, and they're all talking over each other, without hearing each other.

His CB lit up again. Words blinked across the clear sky: "National Emergency! Pick up now! – R."

"Damn it!" He punched the "Answer" button. A ghostly image of Rachel Bluewater swelled to life on the grass, her hands on the hips of her wool pants, tapping her black heel on unseen linoleum. Like Martin, Bluewater looked the same in real life, too.

"This had better be good," he said.

"We have a meeting!"

"Now? I'm at Brandy's funeral!"

"It's starting, now, with the defense secretary. Just follow my lead."

Bluewater's legs walked, but her body staying put, like performing a 1980s moonwalk, not that she'd know about that. Even if she had, she'd certainly have forgotten it by then. She pulled out an invisible chair. Her mid-section disappeared. An elongated conference table materialized, surrounded by suits and uniforms. Darkness fell around the table.

"Where's the president?" Bluewater said.

Anna Style, the Secretary of the Navy, swiveled in a chair on the opposite side of the table, shooting a devil-take-it look at Bluewater. "The president is being taken to her undisclosed location." She spoke with an air of newfound power, the sort previously denied and suddenly given to one with a desperate desire. And she liked the taste.

"As Director of National Intelligence, I am to be in constant contact with her. It's the law. So tell me where she is. Now!"

"This is different," Style said. "The president signed

Readiness Exercise 84. It's *Martial Law*, now. So it's lights out until she's safe."

Martin crossed his arms. "She suspended the Constitution?"

"I don't believe it!" Bluewater said.

"Can you believe objects as big as cities are floating around in the skies?" Style said.

"Don't be ridiculous. Those are only scattered reports from a few nuts out there," Bluewater said. "Probably just a System glitch."

Secretary of Defense Richard Freight materialized at the head of the table. A thick beard grizzled his jaw from ear to ear. Narrow viper eyes met everyone present, one at a time, piercing and challenging. "The president's plane is missing," he said. His kind enjoys giving bad news with indifference, as if showing no feelings demonstrates power, a way to get others to react, and in doing so, identify enemies.

Bluewater stiffened. "Where was it last seen?"

A bald aide in a white smock appeared to Freight's right. "On its way to McConnell Air Force Base," she said.

"I was asking the secretary," Bluewater said.

Freight waved off the aide, who dematerialized. He nodded to Style.

Style reiterated an update at the same time she spoke. "We're scanning the area between D.C. and Kansas," she said.

Martin's fingers noodled through the air. "I don't see it on the System," he said.

Bluewater leaned back, waving a contemptuous hand. "I don't see a lot of things. My access has been restricted."

"The System automatically restricts access once Rex84

is triggered," Style said. "Only the president, vice president, and defense aecretary have full access now."

"And the president is *missing*," Bluewater said. "Where's the vice president?"

"His helicopter went down on the way to Mt. Weather."

Martin closed his eyes. "Who else was on board?"

Style coughed. "The speaker of the house, president pro tem of the senate, secretary of state, and secretary of the treasury."

Bluewater turned to Freight. "Well, if they're all gone, that would leave you in charge, *Dick*. Congratulations." The scorn in her voice made the accusation plain. His promotion – no accident.

With a blank face, he said, "Rest assured, *Rachel*, we're looking for her. We still have a situation here." He waved his hand. A large floating screen of squares appeared in the blackness around the table, blinking blue, red, and green, and then cycling through several video images of blue skies over various backgrounds of buildings, fields, trees, and mountains.

"Someone explain to me why people around the world are reporting UFOs when no one can even see them!"

"There's nothing there," Martin said.

"I know that!" Freight said. "So tell me why hundreds of thousands are reporting UFOs across the country. Explain why the System can't *see* them!" His anger seemed to drain the power of his digital presence, which swelled brightly when he said "see" and dimmed out before fuzzing back.

"Every day hundreds of thousands of people report seeing dragons and unicorns, angels and demons, you name it," Martin said. "I'm sure someone out there says they got a gnome infestation. There's every kind of crazy report if you look hard enough. That's no reason for a national emergency."

General White, Director of the National Security Agency, shimmered into view on Martin's right.

"What have you got, General?" Freight said.

"A platoon of Talos units right under one of those things in California," White said. "Their CBs still show nothing. Just blue skies. No UFOs."

"That's 'cause there's nothing there but blue skies, bub," Martin said.

Bluewater stared a hole into Martin. She must have regretted bringing him along. Sort of like she'd invited a drunk ex-boyfriend to an engagement dinner. But she still needed someone to back her up.

Freight nodded his head to White. "Give me a rundown of stats."

White, a short Korean-American with pock-marked skin and a flat-top, wiggled his fingers in the air. Another bald aide in a smock materialized from the chest up in the middle of the table. "Sundogs appeared around the sun at exactly 10:01 a.m. Pacific Standard Time. The atmospheric phenomenon was followed by scattered reports of UFO sightings. With the same statistical average per capita for each sighting zone, massive UFOs were reported coming from the sundogs around San Francisco, Santa Fe, Oklahoma City, and near the Grand Teton Mountains in Wyoming."

"How many reports outside those sight zones?" Martin said.

"Zero." The talking head faded.

"That's all we got," White said.

Martin fingered his temple. "It's obviously a virus or

something," he said. "The fact that limited sightings are coming from the same locations just tells us that's there's a common glitch in the System in those locations. Not that there are really UFOs arriving. I mean ... give me a break! What's wrong with you people?"

Freight's stoic gaze held Martin. At moments like that, seconds can seem like minutes, each moment of silence more accusing that the last. Finally, he said, "Well, you'd be the one to know about System glitches, eh Martin?"

Martin was surprised. It wasn't the reaction he'd expected; it made no sense to Martin, not then anyway. Freight smirked, knowing Martin had no idea what he was talking about.

Martin pointed an unsteady finger at the screen. "There's nothing there! If this weren't a hoax, more than a billion – everyone -- should be reporting them. The President is missing! Find her! That's our priority! Not this hoax!"

Freight studied Martin. "I'm sorry for the loss of your daughter, Martin. "Brandy" was her name, wasn't it? The grief must be terrible."

Martin ground his heels into the dirt at the cemetery. Everyone has their breaking point. From the look on Martin's face, I wondered whether he might actually jump over the table and grab Freight by the neck. Maybe if he could actually have touched him, he would have. Instead, he calmed himself and pointed at the screen. "There's nothing there!"

A wry smile stretched over Freight's chin. "Just before I came to this meeting, I saw one in the sky. You think I imagined it?"

Martin shook his head slowly. Not a response to the question. Just naked disbelief.

"Good," Freight said. "Now, everyone get on this and figure

out what these things are. Report *directly* to me if you find *anything*. I don't care how insignificant."

The conference room popped out of view, revealing the cemetery. Looking over Brandy's casket, Martin saw a shimmering half halo around the mid-morning sun. On its edges, sundogs swelled.

A holographic priest walked behind the casket and began a sermon. "Our Father, who art in heaven."

Martin got to his feet and took a tentative step, looking through the priest to the morning sky.

Huge disks emerged from the halo around the sun, floating into the blue ether of the morning sky.

Martin threw a disgusted glance to Christy. Her fingers were playing with the air. The priest kept talking with programmed conviction.

Martin approached the casket and laid a hand on the warm aluminum. He looked into his reflection, a more haggard image than his System self.

"I love you, Brandy. I love you. I won't forget."

He didn't know that he already had.

Chapter 3

It was November and cold when Papa died, almost two years before the Sundogs arrived. I'd like to forget it. Make it not true. Make something else true by asking it into existence. Like a child crying, *it's not, true, it's not true, it's not true*, over and over again like really, really meaning it would make it not true. Of course, it wasn't true. But even falsehoods have a way of being true when everyone else believes them.

Just knowing the truth isn't enough to alieve addiction to lies. I see addicts every day -- doctors, lawyers, politicians. Housewives, teachers, bus drivers, waiters, and so on. They all know there's something wrong with the way things are. Deep down, they know the world is not as it seems, that CBs show them a world at odds with the truth. Most people have never known any other way to think or act. They don't remember a time without CBs. To them, a world without a CB-view is impossible, even scary. To think that life as seen through CBs is not real is simply unacceptable. Suggesting otherwise would threaten reality as they know it. So they cling to the lies in the world around them, drawing reassurance. Something they're willing to fight for at the expense of truth.

I know people like that because my sister was once one of them. Not where they think there are, not doing what they think they're doing. Not seeing, not knowing, not really. From the outside – from reality – they seem confident, even happy. Placid arrogance washed over their face. As if they thought they knew a juicy secret but won't share it. It's enough to piss me off sometimes. Then I remind myself, they're oblivious, helpless even. And I feel sorry for them.

Irene was oblivious. I didn't feel sorry for her, though. She knew better. She knew all about CB lies, but bought into them anyway. I was pissed. And so was Papa.

Irene squared off with her opponent, both in full dark blue kendo protective gear. A referee yelled, "*Hajime!*" An irate-orangutan growl blared from the blackness behind the metal grille of Irene's *men*, a part of kendo armor covering her whole head. The glinting eyes of a snake sparkled at her foe. The space around her body hummed with power. Then I saw it, the pulsing green glow of a CB just under her chest protector.

I could see Papa out of the corner of my eye. His rippling jaw, grinding teeth. I'm glad he wouldn't look at me. I didn't want to see the fury.

Aariti nudged my side. "She's wearing a CB!" she hissed.

I know, I mouthed.

It was the national kendo competition. The downtown convention center, which held over ten thousand people, was mostly deserted with just a couple hundred people. Most stadiums like that were abandoned, some collapsing on themselves. Large gatherings

20

were out-of-the-ordinary sights. Sports, music concerts, anything with a big crowd, were attended from home, via CB, even by the players and performers. In those days, the government mostly used convention halls to process migrant workers, military draftees, and environmental refugees -- one of the lies people told themselves, including myself. Back then. They were all just prisoners.

Irene was one of them, too. A prisoner of lies. Instead of a grungy stadium, and drab spectators, she saw herself fighting in an immaculate traditional dojo in a gleaming Japanese sixteenth century castle. She and her opponent were dressed in perfectly white kendo outfits and protectors. Even the audience appeared to be wearing traditional kimonos.

Sure, Papa was angry about Irene. In part. I didn't know then what he knew, though. In less than twenty-four hours, he'd be sorted in the same convention center as a prisoner. Destination: a debtor concentration camp up north. He was scared, too. For me and Irene. For what was to become of us once he disappeared for good, a fate worse than dying. Gone and forgotten, for real. With the help of CBs. He worried less about whether we would remember his face and more about whether we would forget everything he'd taught us.

Papa's pensive eyes wandered over the small gathering of quiet people. No one talking over each other. No one wiggling their fingers in the air. No CBs. They actually watched and saw with their own eyes. All except one. Irene. Papa's weary attention fell on her, heavy with sorrow. Even now, I didn't know exactly what he was thinking, but I had a pretty good idea.

The loss of a child must be unbearable. To actually see it the day before a parent's own death, an unspeakable horror. Papa

21

must have known the CB would take his place after he was gone. She would forget him. She would forget everything he'd taught her to protect herself from the unknown. There was nothing he could do about it.

"*Do!*" yelled Irene, the guttural howl of raw malice blasted her opponent's mid-section at the tip of a bamboo sword. All referees raised red flags. Point for Irene. A tear drew a line down Papa's cheek.

"Go, Irene!" I said. Papa shot a burning look at me. His eyes said, *Cut that out!* Margaret whispered in my ear. "What is wrong with you?" Cheering like that was totally out of line in kendo. I wanted to crawl under the bench.

Irene blasted another point. "*Kote!*" Three red flags went up. She had won the match.

Papa's stoic blue eyes regarded Irene. His left cheek twitched and he was grinding his teeth. Something else was bothering him. Not just Irene's CB.

After dominating the second match with two head strikes, Irene's final match came. The women's championship. Her opponent was Pepper, a blonde from Dallas who studied kendo at a large dojo in an upscale North Dallas Prefecture. Like Papa, Pepper's parents wanted to protect their kids' minds from CB vagaries. And here was Irene, wearing a CB during a kendo match.

Irene and Pepper circled around each other, tapping the tips of their swords, testing for an opening. Pepper flicked a wicked swipe at Irene's forearm. "*Kote!*" she said. Close, but no point. Her stance was all wrong. She didn't follow through.

Irene lunged at Pepper's head. Blocked. Clashing, their swords crossed. She eased her leverage, then tensed back, making an opening. Her sword snapped on Pepper's temple. Irene's yell was loud and proud.

I knew Irene well enough to see she had relaxed ever so slightly, expecting a point. The judges just watched. Nothing. She didn't yell "*Men*" when she landed the hit. Realizing this, Pepper struck Irene on the forearm with a strike, screeching, "*Kote!*" The judges raised their white flags. Point for Pepper. Irene mumbled something under her breath. *Uh oh.* That's when I really started to worry. Papa rocked on the bench and clenched his fists.

Pepper lunged for a head strike. When she yelled, "*Men*," Irene responded "*Do*," and cut hard against Pepper's side. Point for Irene.

"I guess you saw it *that time!*" Irene said. And loud! Even though I knew it was her voice. I knew she'd said it. I still couldn't believe it. A cloud fell over the faces of the referees. If there had been any sound in the stadium before, any rustle or murmur, it had all frozen with an equally cold silence, the sort that falls over a crowd at the gallows. The referees huddled with the presiding referee. Irene's point was nullified for uttering an offense against referees.

One minute to go. Her shoulders ridged, Irene was determined to score. If time ran out, Pepper would win. And if Irene didn't make two consecutive points for the win, the match would go into overtime. They crossed swords and butted chests. Irene lunged time and again. Pepper blocked each one. When they stepped back from a clash, Irene yelled with a blow to Pepper's *men*. No point was given. Given what had happened, the referees would be more demanding of Irene.

Pepper lunged in hard at Irene's head. Irene blocked it. Pepper rebounded with a hand strike. Irene blocked it. With less than thirty seconds to go, Irene unleashed a blinding forearm strike. The match went into overtime.

As Irene and Pepper faced off once more, time slowed. There were moments like that in my life, when what's happening seemed unimportant, but for whatever reason, it was burned into my memory more permanently than other times. As I watched Irene and Pepper bow, the green light from Irene's CB swelled. I could see the reflection in her eye. I thought, *That's not Irene. And so, who is that?* In that split second, I surveyed the crowed of CB-less people. Other than Papa, they're the only people who see me. And I felt naked. My self, the real me, exposed for everyone to see. I wanted to run out of there. Just for that moment. I wanted to put a CB around my neck and just go away, somewhere where I could do all of the looking and no one looked at me. A shudder hit me. Repulsion. Remembering the horror I was inviting upon myself. Sort of like someone wondering what it might be like to commit suicide. Curiosity followed by horror. Even healthy people do this. Try on insanity to see what it feels like. For most, then comes the cringe. I remembered myself and pushed the thought away. I knew, deep down, that ideas like that were dangerous. CBs were dangerous. There was no such thing as using them part-time because there would be no turning back. And in this moment, my chest gripped my heart. I didn't care whether Irene won. I worried whether I could ever get her back.

The first to make a point in overtime would win. I was grinding my teeth to Papa's rhythm. As Irene and Pepper circled, the attention of the convention hall was drawn in like a whirlpool. Bamboo swords slapped, animalistic screams -- the only sounds. I'd watched her fight for championships many times before. This time I felt like there was much more at stake than a trophy or status. This seemed like a duel of death.

I've reviewed the following moments in time slow and fast, from every angle. It looks the same each time and still doesn't make sense, despite everything I can know. A brilliant white flame appeared at the crown of Irene's head, blazing to life like a stove match. I grabbed my neck and bolted to my feet with a half raised arm, expecting the referees to stop everything to prevent a kenchi barbeque. Margaret pulled me to my seat, saying, "What's gotten into you?" It seems I was the only one could see the fire. Thinking it best to keep the brush with madness to myself, I pretended not to see the obvious.

Pepper miscalculated, giving an opening to Irene. She took it. As cleanly as it could be executed, Irene struck Pepper over the top of her head with textbook precision. What followed was an abomination.

Irene dropped her sword, fell to her knees, and yelled, "Yes!" pumping her right fist down to her side in celebration. The judges had half-raised their flags for Irene but stopped. Pepper already looked defeated. She could have easily scored a point against Irene as she sat there unguarded on the floor. Realizing no point was given, Irene jumped to her feet and yelled, "What do I have to do to win -- shoot her?"

That kind of behavior was the epitome of *wrongness* in kendo etiquette. It was a slap in the face to everyone present. It was roughly the equivalent to the President of the United States farting into the microphone during her inaugural address, and then saying, "Hey, smell that!" It is unheard of. It is unthinkable. It is something that would never, never happen. Yet Irene did it.

Unflinching, the judges restrained their shock. They

conferred with the presiding referee, then with the director. Irene had committed a cardinal sin – insulting a referee – twice. The penalty, a point to the opponent. Pepper automatically won. Irene stomped out of the court in a huff, seeing a CB-world-scape as she crossed a majestic Zen bridge out of the Osaka castle. She probably thought that performance looked noble and dramatic, like a princess escaping a mad ball. To the rest of us stunned onlookers, she scurried pitifully in a clump of tattered knots and matted hair over the scuffed floor, through the peeling hallways, to the darkness of the women's locker rooms. Paying no mind to the blatant offense, Pepper and the referees bowed to one another, ending the match and the finals.

Papa slammed his bag in the overhead bin of the bus and fell into his seat. Irene was slumped against a window at the back, a hood over her head, faint green light seeping out.

The electric hum of the bus helped me zone out a little. Out the window, I could see the Wild through the barbed wire fences beyond the elevated highway. Metal junkyards were scattered across deserted neighborhoods with dilapidated roofs. Unruly weeds burst through cracks on every street. Rising columns of smoke smoldered from bonfires in the middle of intersections. Many of the houses had been burnt down long ago or blown away by tornados. Police cruisers no longer ventured there. I let my imagination get carried away about the Wild sometimes. The CBs never mentioned it, and even though I was one of the few who even noticed it, I still didn't know much about it. We didn't live there, and certainly didn't go there, ever.

I saw a girl walking alone in the middle of a quiet street, her light blue down jacket smudged and torn; her pants, filthy and baggy. She looked up as our bus passed. She was pale, with stringy

26

hair. No CB, either. *She could be me*, I thought. A sudden feeling of connectedness fell over me for the simple reason that we saw the world for what it was, not what CBs showed us.

Irene shared no common thread with such strangers. Her eyes, following the same landscape as mine, saw rows of happy homes, painted fences, and trimmed grass along smooth sidewalks framing weeded green lawns; instead of a wandering figure in the street, a well-groomed wife strolled on a sunny day.

The bus stopped at Aariti's place last. "Thanks for everything, Mr. Lawson," she said, stepping off. Papa just nodded. That unnerved me -- the silent treatment, worse than a lecture. I knew we were in for it once we got home.

We got off the bus after him. He didn't even glance back. I could hear Irene shambling behind me. Papa let us in through the side entrance. The lights in the *dojo* flickered on. Painful silence pressed against my chest with the dread of what he might do or say. I just wanted to scream to make him tell us what he was thinking, no matter what it was. Parents seem to know that saying nothing is even worse; makes kids suffer more for their transgressions. Here I didn't even do anything. Irene was on the hook, not me.

The wood floor was empty except for a shrine at the front. The stillness of the place just made me cringe. We bowed as we entered. Irene went for the exit to the kitchen. She dropped her bag against the wall. If petulance had a sound, under those circumstances, that was it.

"Where do you think you're going?" Papa said from the middle of the *dojo*.

Irene talked with back turned. "To bed," she said. "It's been a long day, *Pops*."

She was really asking for trouble with an attitude like that. She was putting my neck out, too. Whatever happened to her was going to happen to me.

"Suit up for *keiko!*"

"Are you kidding?" Irene said.

Before I could say, *He's not kidding, Irene*, his eyes swelled to dinner plates, pupils completely black. He rushed in at Irene and stopped in front of her, leaning into her face. In a loud voice, he blared, "I … said … *keiko! Both of you!* He snapped the CB off her neck and tossed it on the floor.

Facing Papa, we lined up sitting on our knees, full protective gear to the right, swords to the left. Papa called out, "*Mokuso!*" Placing my left hand over right, palms up, tips of thumbs together, I closed my eyes, expecting him to immediately yell, "*Yame!*" That's what usually happened. We'd meditate for a split second, then make a few quick bows, and suit up, as if it was all one long motion. I peeked at him, sitting stubbornly serene. I shut my eyes for another split second and then just stared at him wide-eyed. I almost said, *Time! Hello? Like, that's enough!* It was part of some point he was trying to make, I figured. Eyes closed again. Time drew out on my thoughts like a slow blade, stabbing to my heart. Before succumbing to some kind of outburst, I tried to clear my mind of the day's events, forget about my concerns, let go. No luck. The image of Irene's match kept coming back; the pitiful thought of her tromping out, pretending she was living in a princess samurai fairytale. As other thoughts arose, I tried to swat them away. Images of Papa, the homework due Monday, even Mama. Hunger nagged before a dose of drowsiness. My mind swung from one idea to the next like a monkey. When I noticed my thoughts again, I returned my focus to my sitting, being in the moment. After about forty-five minutes I almost tore my hair out.

By the time Papa finally said, *"Yame!"* my legs had gone completely numb. I wanted to stand and stretch. I figured Papa would make me sit for another forty-five minutes if I did. We bowed to each other, suited up, and got to our feet with swords at our sides. My sleepy legs weaker than I'd realized, I fell to my left knee after trying to take a step. Papa glared at me as I massaged my calves. If Irene had a problem, she wouldn't show it, not to save her life; she had too much vested in that day's belligerence.

While I sparred with Papa, he told Irene to squat on her heels and wait. I circled around, keeping my distance, trying to get the circulation flowing. I kept eyeing Irene's CB on the floor, trying to stay away from it like a land mind. Sometimes Papa did things like that, played mind games in and out of the *dojo*. Even as we clashed and crossed swords, I wondered whether he'd thrown the CB there just to distract me, make me fret about it. For a split second, I dreamed that it was watching me as much as I was watching it, that there was no difference between the two, that my reality of fighting Papa was secondary to the CB-world's version of it. And then I thought maybe he'd put it there for no reason at all. I was just distracting myself, putting him on a pedestal too high. He snapped his sword on my wrist. *"Kote!"* he said. Point for Papa. He had been toying with me and I'd been making it easier for him.

Then it was Irene's turn. Watching Papa and Irene circle each other for several minutes, squatting on my heels, my pain returned. I burnt a hole in the CB until the green light singed a hologram on my retina. Papa and Irene didn't even brush against it. Five minutes passed and another three minutes before Papa finally slammed Irene in the head. "*Men!*"

I could barely stand when I faced off with him again. The thought occurred to me to just let him make a hit, but that just meant more squatting. Fight or suffer. Suffer or fight. I steeled my resolve to win and make it all stop because nothing would please me more than to go to bed and drift off to sleep listening to *The Cure*. I unleashed a flurry of swings to Papa's head. He parried them and responded with a hard blow across my mid-section. I looked at the clock as I squatted again. Only five minutes had passed. *Aw, come on!*

Pain, pain, and more pain. Now Irene and Papa circled for more than fifteen minutes. Irene had always been Papa's perfect little girl, the obedient kendoist. Now her blind loyalty had boiled to the surface in a slather of raw animosity. Each of her desperate blows showed the depth of her resentment. He circled around with her and easily unleashed a blow on her head, the venom in her face plain. Her yells sounded like cuss words. A couple of times, I was pretty sure they were.

The eastern sky glowed light orange to my bleary eyes. My pain turned to stark numbness. I fell back over my haunches, landing on my knees. Papa yelled "*sonkyo*," prompting me back to squatting. Once facing off with Papa for another match, it seemed we would be there for the rest of Sunday. My mind let go of the pain. I had forgotten about the embarrassment of Irene's match. My mind and body were steeled into the core of my training. The sword -- the only thing. I didn't even see him anymore. Just an obstacle. From instinct and training, my arms flinched and I lunged forward. I heard a sharp wrap and the sound of my own yell, "*Kote!*" It took me a few seconds to figure out what had happened. I blinked. I'd scored a

30

point on Papa. It was nearly ten o'clock in the morning.

We lined up, bowed, kneeled, and placed our protectors aside. After meditating again for five minutes, Papa spoke to us in a smooth tone. "I've done everything I can to teach you the way of this life," he said. He pointed at two samurai swords – a *katana* and shorter *wakizashi* – hanging on the wall behind him. "If you understand kendo, there's nothing you cannot see.

"Irene, your conduct today was against every fiber of kendo. The sword follows the hand, the hand follows the spirit. Through your actions you showed I am an abject failure as your father and as your teacher. Everyone saw that. Even more, you failed yourself. I've never been more disappointed. Not because an eldest daughter dishonored her father. Not because she let her teammates down. Not because she did this in front of kendo masters from around the world. You've failed to transcend the only true opponent in kendo – yourself."

His voice dropped. "I've taught you everything I know. There are hard times coming. Soon you'll be tested. You'll have to ask yourselves whether you've learned anything. I hope you have, for your sake and mine. Life is not about winning or losing! You've heard me say: 'Victory means survival, defeat means death.' There's no room for pride in that! Winning is a *selfless* act! Celebrating victory is the opposite. Remember this: there is no self. Now wipe down this floor. As you do, repeat and mediate to yourself: 'What is nothing?'"

Papa bowed and left the room. The next day, he was dead.

Chapter 4

Ms. Croucher was giving out our reading assignments, her blonde hair, with streaks of gray at the temples, knotted in a bun. She kept her white shirt tucked into a plaid navy skirt, starched and clean all day. That was just before the System was updated, before people stopped caring about how they looked. I try to remember Ms. Croucher as she was then, preferring not to think of her as a slob.

A holographic picture of e-books hung over our desks. As a class, we were reviewing summaries of books we'd be discussing that quarter. The Principal, Mr. Smith, entered, wearing a tweed suit that matched his salt-and-pepper mustache. He shot Irene and me an uncertain look as he drew Ms. Croucher out into the hall with his index finger, whispering hurriedly. Looking back on them, watching them talk and interact like that, outside the CB world, it seemed almost foreign.

"Irene, Edith, please go with Mr. Smith to the office," Ms. Croucher said.

I knew something was wrong when I saw *Lao Lao*, my mother's mother, standing in Mr. Smith's office. Not only was she supposed to be in China, but a golden flame was burning in a ball over the crown of her head. And I don't just mean yellow. The halo of fire had a metallic look to it, like a 24-karat softball burning in mid-air. If Irene saw it she didn't show it.

Since we were kids we had butchered her Chinese family title -- "La-La." We'd visited her a few times in China when we were little. She came to the States for our birthdays. Other than a few phrases and random words, she couldn't speak English. We were eleven the last time we saw her, when Mama took us abroad with Papa for the Lunar New Year. Mama got sick on our way back home. We thought it was just fatigue. It was something else. The cancer. Six months later she was dead. La-La came for the funeral. That was the last time we had seen her, when someone close had died.

Funerals and births once brought families together. Weddings and graduations, too. Once CBs came along, families drifted apart. Attending such events virtually, fathers, daughters, mothers, sons, brothers, sisters and so on didn't interact in person. They drifted apart in reality, believing they'd been brought closer together by interconnectedness of the System. But personal relationships are meaningless without eye contact. Assigning social functions to an impersonal world of digital algorithms inclines one to illusions and eventually to manipulation. At that time, when Papa died, things were changing. And very fast. Whether someone had died, divorced, disappeared, or was simply forgotten; it was anybody's guess. But no one was questioning. Just accepting spoon-fed lies.

When we saw La-La, we knew without asking. It was Papa.

34

"What's going on?" Irene said. "Where's Papa?"

Mr. Smith asked us to sit. Irene refused, so he simply told us in a matter-of-fact tone that our "Dad" had been killed in a bus crash on the way to work. The whole thing had burnt up on impact with an eighteen-wheeler. Irene and I locked eyes for a moment. We nodded at him with no emotion. We knew what he wasn't telling, the lie he'd wanted to accept himself.

"I'm sorry," Mr. Smith said. "No one survived." He wiggled his stubby fingers at his sides like that somehow showed he really meant it, like we were supposed to say or do something else in response. For a second, I thought he was going to say, *I mean it, kids! Your dad's dead! Did you hear what I said? Dead!* He knew damn well Papa wasn't dead. But it was one of those lies worth fighting for. If Mr. Smith didn't believe our papa was dead – really, really dead – then where was his wife, or college son who died in a freak lightning accident, for that matter? He couldn't question the things that propped up his paper tiger world. The answers would crush his sense of reality. His way of life would come apart, force him to challenge everything. And that path led only one place – the Wild. Or a colony.

I wondered whether he could see the sympathy on our faces. Looking confused, he sighed, and with a tone of *I-give-up*, said, "Your grandmother is here. She's going to stay with you for a while."

As Irene gave La-La a warm hug, Mr. Smith fidgeted with a new CB around his neck.

That night I cried into my pillow until falling asleep. I didn't hear a peep form Irene.

35

Chapter 5

MOST PRISONS DO ONE THING — KEEP PEOPLE IN WHO WANT OUT. Some prisons keep people from getting out who don't want out because they don't know they're in. Those are blind prisons and, it seems to me, they are the worst kind. People caught in them will even fight to stay in even though it's really just hell.

The problem is spotting blind prisons. Sure, barbed wire fences and armed guards are good clues. Short-term memory, a quality of all blind prisons, soon wipes away those red flags. So the best clue is any sinking feeling of incessant repetition. When the alarm goes off in the morning, and you slide your feet out of bed to the ground, just for a second, before you take a shower, eat breakfast, fetch a cup of coffee, and take the same route to work, you feel like you're running in the exact same circle, like it's never-ending, and every day is the same. You feel, deep down, something is very wrong. There are no exact words to describe it. You don't know what it is, not exactly. Heck, you don't have time to think about it. So you move your feet toward the shower. Forget the quest, even though it's still buried back in your brain somewhere. You're supposed to forget. You've been trained to forget, to be obedient. You don't ask questions about things you know don't make sense. You follow. You don't ever step out of line. You don't speak up about anything unless calling an alarm about someone else breaking the rules, even though those rules don't make sense. You're rewarded for enforcing those rules on others, since you know punishment follows speaking out, questioning, or breaking the rules, heaven forbid.

Looking in on people in blind prisons, it's easy to criticize. We see how simple it would be for them to escape. We want to just tell them, *Look, here's the exit! It's not locked! Just turn the handle and walk out and you're free!* But it's like telling an addict, "Just say no." Meaningless words. You may as well give a maze rat a GPS. He won't know what it's for.

By the time Papa saw the walls and barbed wire fences it was way too late for him to do anything. Like most lab rats, he and the other prisoners were smart enough to know they'd been taken to a bad place. I used to blame him for not seeing the signs. Now that I've had time to ask some questions, and think on it, he couldn't have guessed what was happening to him. Not alone. Not without a little help. From me.

When Mr. Smith was telling us Papa was dead, Papa was arriving at Freedom Colony, Kansas. An orange sunrise warmed the side of the aluminum bus as it approached a twenty-foot tall concrete wall. A beautiful morning sky looks the same at a beach resort as it does at a slaughterhouse. Only the mind sees a difference. Rusted oil and gas tanks were dotted here and there among flat wheat farms for miles around. Whippoorwills and wind were the only sounds.

The unassuming beauty of stillness masked the quiet horrors of the place.

A metal section of the wall slid away on a rail. The bus passed an empty guardhouse with a rusted "Welcome to Freedom" sign, and after meandering across a barren gravel road, it stopped at a "High Voltage" gate. Obvious clues for Papa that his new job wasn't what he'd been told. He looked around in a panic for a second and took a deep breath, calming himself. Fear can make a dangerous situation worse. He'd told me as much more than once. Better to stay calm. A woman in the seat behind him tried the window. It didn't budge. Many of the other passengers were asleep or distracted, not paying any attention. That's what not paying attention will get you – a life of blissful incarceration.

The gate slid back and the bus went on to the next sign which read, "Minefield." Amazing that someone didn't try to break through the glass at that point. An automated gate let them through. The last gate was unmarked. Even without asking, one had to assume something worse than buried bombs or mere electricity. By the time most buses had made it that far, often at least one or two people would refuse to even get off the bus or try to sprint back to the first guardhouse. None of them ever made it. You can check into Freedom Colony but you can't check out. Of course, plenty of people wanted to cancel their reservations upon arrival, before the place became a blind prison for them. But soon they'd be clawing to stay in, not leave, they would even fight to keep others in; the only real security measures needed in such a place.

The bus stopped and let out a tired hydraulic hiss. Papa got off first with a large duffle bag over his shoulder like he was ready to start swinging it at someone. Several other men and women followed with carry-on-sized roller luggage, as if they'd gone on vacation or something. The door closed when the last person stepped off. Wind whistled though the fences. The morning sun seemed to shrink in the crisp air of a clear day. The new arrivals stood in a crude line, gaping at the surroundings, flipping up their collars and crossing their arms for warmth. You could see it in their faces. They were scared, afraid they'd just made the biggest mistake of their lives, getting on that bus. They were right.

In the distance, down a long cobblestoned causeway, people were walking along rows of off-white buildings, each circled by chain-link fences. Each building was thirty-one stories, each story smaller than the last, tapering up like a Mayan pyramid. Glass blocks were uniformly set around the walls of each level. The grounds between each building were open and mulched, devoid of vegetation. With the exception of a few big-box structures scattered around, they were the only possible living quarters. Not a very welcoming sight to those who thought they were there to work off some debt, especially when most had been told they'd been transferred to an office near a beach.

Around the walls, beyond the layers of fences, taller and narrower pyramids loomed overhead, topped by octagonal pillboxes, searchlights and antennas. Heavy caliber gun barrels pointed out from the darkness of long narrow slits. At the end of the causeway, a monotone building stretched for a half-mile. Other than those approaching, there were no other souls in sight. With all those ominous buildings of accommodation, and the absence of people, the whole place had the feel of a roach motel.

Dressed in gray uniforms, with black-lined breast pockets and collars, the heels of four guards echoed through the expansive grounds. Assault rifles rested across their chests. Their helmet straps squeezed the blood from their faces. Papa turned to a red-headed woman standing next to him. She shifted her weight back and forth in maroon patent leather heels, her plaid skirt wrinkled. She gripped the handle of her luggage and looked at Papa with scared blue eyes. She didn't have to be a genius to know that something was terribly wrong, that someone had lied about something along the way, because she had not signed up for a prison tour.

"I'm starting to think the Wild wasn't such a bad option," she said out of the corner of her mouth.

Papa nodded and looked out over the layers of fences. He steeled his jaw sideways at the guards. "I thought that the moment I left home." He gripped the CB in his pocket, probably wishing he could call me and Irene, tell us things had gone wrong, it was all a mistake. But he'd been cut off from us once he'd boarded the bus. Normally, he only used the CB to communicate with us when needed, only with framed glasses, older technology, that showed limited text and video. He didn't wear the CB otherwise. Just kept it in his pocket, often rolling in into a sheet of tin foil to keep it from tracking him. Of course, he'd forbidden us to use them with contact lenses at all. We could use CBs with glasses just a little bit. So Papa was pretty shocked when Irene showed up at the tournament with CB lenses.

That's the thing about evil. It sneaks up on you. You know something is wrong but sometimes it gets a toe in the door. Once that happens you start to rationalize that a little bit of evil is necessary, pretending to cling to ideals of goodness. When the System first started to take over, at first some people tried to self-limit CB use. They'd only wear CBs at work, or at school, or only when they needed them to send a message. Some, when they found themselves consumed with the CB world at all times, tried to quit. That didn't work for most. They just unplugged for a while, and when they tuned back in, their trained brains were voracious. Once an addict always an addict. They had to communicate in work, school, marriage, leisure, travel, paying taxes. There was no avoiding CBs completely. Most eventually submitted. The only real option to escape CBs was the Wild. Poverty, crime, flooding, tornados, no electricity or heat – not a real option – at least, that's what everyone believed.

Holding a diamond formation, the lead guard said, "Halt!" Smiling over the new arrivals with a look of ownership, he said, "Welcome to Freedom Colony, Employees!" His voice was boyish with exaggerated conviction. His body belonged to an athletic fifteen-year-old. So did his face, ravaged by acne. His rough cheeks and rosy nose suggested hard drinking. He tapped the air in front of him and called out names alphabetically, reading from a holographic list. His black eyes scanned over the new arrivals. A bulletproof vest pressed awkwardly into his gray military uniform. He seemed to be suppressing some fear of trouble, not unheard of on new arrival day.

The redhead answered to the name of Sarah Roberts. The Korean said, "That's me," to "Employee Richard Chen." A black man in his late fifties, wearing jeans and a striped sweater, responded to "Employee Joe Johnson". And so on.

Papa exchanged uneasy glances with the band of unexpected inmates.

Richard, in jeans, loafers without socks, and a casual sports coat, said, "Employee?" Like Papa, everyone else had packed for something other than Alcatraz. Calling them "employees" had the feel of a joke roll call where the term "Sergeant" is used for military draftees. A shivering white guy in his mid-twenties had on Hawaiian shorts, flip-flops, and a baby-blue knit shirt, with a light gym bag tossed around his shoulder. He responded to "Employee Doug Masterson" by running to the bus and banging desperately on the door. The bus engine revved up and pulled away. Another man, Fred Kindrick, in an overnight backpack and hiking shoes, shuffled after the bus waving his arms, "Hey, stop!"

"Sorry, it's on a schedule," said the name-calling guard. "Another'll come along shortly. You can be on it if you like but you still have to be processed before you leave." He held up his arms with a smile. "Now, don't worry, you can still go back home if you want. Trust me, though. After you hear what we have to offer, you'll want to stay." A guard behind him smirked.

Papa raised his hand. "What's your name?"

The guard guffawed with a red face. "How rude of me." He turned sideways to the other guard. "Now wasn't that rude of me," got nods from them. "Please, Employee Lawson, Call me Mr. Rusty." His tone said, *How dare you ask me a question?*

"Is this Freedom Colony?" Papa said.

Mr. Rusty put his hands on his hips. "Another very good question," he said, with a grin and a southern drawl that said, Now you're pushing it, mister! "Yes, yes, it is. This is Freedom Colony. I'll give you the fifty-cent tour once you're processed." And there was that grin of his again.

Chapter 6

When Mr. Gaddis punched Irene in the face, it had been nearly two years since Papa had died. We still didn't know for sure what had happened to him exactly. Deep down we figured he hadn't been in a crash. Like a lot of other absent people, he wasn't dead. Whereabouts unknown.

You might think it horrible of us to do nothing. *How can you just sit there and accept that kind of lie?* you might say. Truly powerful lies, the kind that shape our world, move the masses to act or not act, bring revolutionary change, or prevent it, force themselves on us until they're intertwined with our very existence. We rely on them as the oxygen we breathe, and so we defend them with our life. To deny them, to openly challenge them, is to cut off our own legs. Go to the so-called police and say Papa's not really dead, or worse, talk about it on the System, and we would have found ourselves without a house, dumped out into the Wild with the rest of the have-nots, or even in a Colony like Papa.

It killed me later that we didn't know how badly he needed

us, and he didn't know how much we needed him. It had been a bad time since he had left, especially for Irene, and things were going to get worse for all of us. There was some comfort in knowing later that I was helping him in a small way, if only with my mind, my most powerful source.

After Mr. Gaddis had bashed Irene to the floor, soldiers in dark grey exoskeleton suits and assault rifles poured into the classroom, their eyes and faces shielded by dark visors.

Mr. Gaddis pointed at Irene and me with a mechanical elbow. "One and two," he said, and crossed his arms in satisfaction.

Robotic hands grabbed Irene from the floor and snapped her to her feet. A soldier hooded her with a black nylon bag. I screamed. "Irene!" A hood was yanked over my head. Thick plastic bands were snapped around my wrists and ankles. Several hands took me by the ankles and wrists. At moments like that, when you'd think I was focusing on the pain in my side where I'd been kicked, or the loss of circulation in my legs and arms from the bands, I mostly thought about the strange plastic smell inside the bag around my head, worrying that it was poisoning me. "*Help me, Papa!*" I thought with all of my being.

Someone was screaming. I heard Irene whimper. A diesel engine rumbled nearby and loud metal doors slammed. Hands tossed me onto a metal table and strapped down. More slamming followed the clang of latches.

"Irene?" I said, crying. No one answered. I heard muffled men's voices outside. I recognized Mr. Gaddis; he chortled with gloating satisfaction. I cried some more. "La-La!" I thought I heard someone yell my name, and Irene's, too. I said, "Papa?" with barely a whisper.

A woman's voice next to me said, "Your *papa* can't hear you."

A hand grabbed my forearm. A needle sank into my arm. Lights out.

Papa.

Chapter 7

WHY DON'T COWS FIGHT LIKE MAD ON THEIR WAY TO THE slaughterhouse? Are they really that stupid? Why don't the condemned kick and scream on the way to the execution chamber? Why do people stand for a firing squad? Why not just run like hell, even with a blindfold on, or even just fall down, refuse to cooperate with their own murder? I think it's because every sentient being has an inherent irrational feeling of hope. Even in the face of impending doom, they think that somehow, at the last minute, something or someone is going to save them. *Death isn't really coming*, they think. *Not this time.* We all think that we're going to live forever, unchanged from the way we are now. Our identity is permanent and cannot be destroyed by death, and certainly not by technology.

Thoughts like that are what must have kept Papa and the other Employees strolling down a well-kept austere sidewalk leading from the causeway to a round concrete building with a white geodesic dome. Stupid cattle see the same kind of sites on their way to becoming packages sold by the pound at the meat market. A black-on-white "Processing" sign hung over the double-door entrance. That meant nothing to these Employees, just as a "Killing Room" sign means nothing to ignorant cattle.

Knowing what it really meant, to me the sign seemed to peer down over Papa and the other Employees with a foreshadowing horror as he passed under it into the theater hall. Stair-stepped rows of plush velvety recliner seats formed a semicircle around a sunken stage, the scene of executions. Folding tables with white plastic tops lined the curved wall at the back of the room. Bored men in green smocks and hair nets loitered there.

Mr. Rusty pointed. "Find your names on the tables. The nurses will check your CBs and contacts. Drop your things and find a seat near the stage."

Employee Masterson shook his gym bag as if testing its weight. "I'll be leaving on the next bus so I'll just keep this with me."

"I'm sorry, Mr. Masterson," Mr. Rusty said. "Since you've come to a secure location we have to check it for contraband and whatnot. Sorry. Rules are rules." Mr. Rusty shrugged apologetically. Probably because he had called Doug by his common name, instead of the ominous "Employee Masterson," Doug tossed the bag on the table with a nod.

Papa took his time finding his table as he scanned the room. He probably felt like a mouse in a cage. There were only two sets of doors opposite each other; both closed and no exit signs. He must have already known by then that he wasn't leaving with permission. His chances of escaping after stepping off the bus were no better or worse. *Let your opponent make the first move*, he taught us. So he'd wait to see where the first strike would come from, and it wasn't hard for him to figure that out.

"Employee Lawson?" said one of the nurses through a surgical mask.

Papa nodded, went to the nurse, and set his long nylon duffle bag on the table. Wearing latex gloves, the nurse waved a black light over Papa's eyes.

"Where are your contacts?" said the nurse mechanically.

"Took 'em out," Papa said. "No need to wear 'em when my CB stopped working."

The nurse quickly produced a set of contacts for Papa, which must have been unsettling, since they had to be biometrically fitted to each person to work properly. Papa turned white as he slowly put in each contact.

"Where's your CB?" the nurse said.

Papa fingered the CB out of his pocket and held it up. Before he could say, "Stopped working," he noticed its green glow had returned. With a goofy smile, he said, "Go figure."

"Put it on, please."

Papa nodded, looped his CB over the crown of his head and turned to the theater. On the way to the middle aisle, he let the CB slide forward off his head to the ground. Picking it up, he wound the cylinder between his fingers and squeezed until it cracked through the middle. He slipped it back on and found a place in a middle row half-way down to the stage. Seated and reclining, he looked up at the inside of the dome, a huge screen that covered all peripheral vision. Richard took a seat in the front row. Sarah sat in the row directly in front of Papa, a little to his right.

And thus came a tall slender woman to the front of the theater for a self-introduction. Anyone meeting her for the first time would feel right away that she was more a creature of some abnormal circumstance than a product of anything normal or just. Her black hair was slicked back into a bun. Her bony frame was clothed in a light grey wool suit with pressed creases in the pants. A narrow black silk necktie divided her white oxford shirt. The image of the *Talking Heads* in a retirement home came to mind, but without any soul. Her papery skin puckered against sharp cheeks on either side of an angular nose. Red lipstick over thin lips. Stepping onto the stage, she turned and faced the Employees. Her left hand clutched her right wrist.

"I'm *Pilgrim* Coralee," she said with a smoker's voice. "Just Coralee to y'all." The word "pilgrim" rolled off her tongue like a razor slash, as though it had a malicious meaning, the sort of person who'd burn the falsely accused for witchcraft. "On behalf of everyone at Freedom Colony: Welcome!" Her lips flattened with a smile revealing blazing white teeth. "Now, if there's anyone in charge here, that would be me." Mr. Rusty coughed from the back of the room. "Well, of course, Mr. Rusty is the Master of Guards. I believe you've met him. But anyway, I think you'll find there's no need for bosses around here. As you'll see, we're one big family. We all work together. We're all on the same team, see?"

Papa frowned.

"So when can we get outta here on the next bus?" Richard Chen said.

"Now, now, Mr. Chen. Be patient. After we give you a grand tour, you'll be free to go. First I'd like to show a short introductory film about Freedom Colony, so you know what you'd be missing." Coralee winked at Sarah as if they shared a secret. Sarah shot an unsettled look at Papa.

Coralee continued. "I see y'all have your new CBs and glasses on. *Good.* No time to lose." She walked to the back of the room. "Get ready to be *a-mazed!*"

A holographic cylinder screen rose from the stage to the ceiling and rolled out across the domed screen. At first, there was nothing but static. The tower swelled to green and morphed into blue. It cycled through the primary colors and then flashed faster to a constant flicker. High and low pitched sounds repeated. All the lights went out. The sounds slowed to a deep moan.

Then the lights came back on. Papa didn't see any of the light show, since his CB was cracked. He'd closed his eyes and meditated the whole time, blocking out the erratic sounds.

The room went noisy, too loud to ignore. It sounded like a crowded dinner party, with chaotic talking and laughing, had barged into the theater.

From the corner of his right eye he could see Sarah blankly staring at the ceiling. She looked dead, her eyes dropping and body limp, except her mouth was moving a hundred miles an hour, laughing and talking some politics.

Coralee came back down the center aisle and stood in front of Richard. She waved her hand in his empty face, and then slapped him hard. "Still want to leave, you shmuck?" she said.

No response. Richard sat comatose.

"Rusty?"

At the back of the room, Mr. Rusty waved his fingers through the air, browsing the System. "He's at a cocktail party with his wife and two friends in Santa Fe."

Coralee gleamed with joy at Mr. Rusty. She snapped her

fingers at Richard. "I knew it!" she said. "You closed your eyes, didn't you?"

Richard sat up and spun around, a fearful expression in his eyes. "What the hell's going on here?" he said.

Coralee stepped back as one of the guards came from behind and hit him in the stomach with a stun baton. Richard convulsed back into his chair, frothing at the mouth.

Coralee signaled to a nurse. "Give him the usual treatment and take him to his apartment. Let me know when it's done. I want to see his rehab video myself."

Coralee went up the aisle to Sarah.

Sarah was spitting out phrases like, "President Hernandez doesn't care about health," "the system's just broken, *broken* I tell you," and "I don't believe anything she says," and so on. Coralee slapped Sarah, and then caressed her cheek. "What about you, cutie?"

No response. Sarah just continued with her political diatribe, happily oblivious. "If she raises our taxes once more, I ain't voting for her, not even if she wins the primary," Sarah said. Her voice had the conviction of a liberal talk show host; her body looked dead.

"What?" Coralee said, holding her palms to her cheeks with mock shock.

"That's right!" Sarah said.

"You're staying!" Coralee said. "Great news! Was it my charm? Well, yes, we'll talk more about it later." Coralee was the sort of person who deeply enjoyed the sound of her own voice.

"Mama, I had my eye on her," Mr. Rusty said.

"You chose first last time, sweetie."

"But Mama, no, you did!"

"We're getting a large group of new Employees from Los Angeles next week. There's always some juicy ones to choose from there. You have dibs … I promise."

Unaware of the gloating over her, Sarah went on about politics as Coralee fast-walked back up the aisle.

Before she passed him, Papa started lecturing casually about kendo, pretending he was in the *dojo*.

When Coralee reached the top of the aisle, she turned and said, "Now all of you Employees -- back to your tables -- now!"

Sarah leaned forward as if she had a board down her back and stood as she continued to talk, her head hanging slightly forward. Papa did the same and returned to his table with the others. The male nurses were still waiting.

"Now strip!" Coralee said. "Everything off but your CBs."

Without any pretense of modesty, the Employees disrobed, tossing their clothes to the ground. Doug kept talking about some wave he'd missed. Fred was trying to sell a tent to someone who was already buying a backpack. All the new Employees down the line of tables were going on about one thing or another, completely unaware of their real situation, save Papa.

The nurses gave each of the Employees a standard physical, a series of shots, and drew vials of blood. Coralee strolled down between the tables and Employees, inspecting their personal belongings and biological appendages with the unhindered zeal of a teenager in a peepshow. Ignoring the incoherent chatter, she examined each Employee up and down, her eyes especially pausing on their privates.

She stopped at Papa's table. *Katana* and *wakizashi* swords sat on the table next to his clothes. "Goodness," she said. She picked up the longer sword and faced Papa. He was counting in Japanese with a shout as if leading a kendo class.

"Those were in his bag," the nurse said, without a glance at Coralee, as he examined Papa's ear.

"Pray tell, why did you bring *these* toys to school?" she said to Papa. He went on counting.

She clumsily unsheathed the *katana* and held its blade between his legs. Without flinching, he went on counting.

"Rory Lawson," she said. "I mean, Employee Lawson. Maybe my question was a little too … *artful*. Now, tell me … Employee Lawson … what is this?"

Papa said, "A *katana* sword," in a monotone voice, and went on counting.

Coralee lifted the point of the sword to his neck. "Well, you're not going to need this little needle here, I shouldn't think." Kneeling at Papa's feet, the nurse looked up, with more of an expression of curiosity than concern, probably wondering whether Coralee would put on a show and skewer him right then and there.

Papa kept counting.

Coralee tossed the sword on the table. To the technician, she said, "Bring those swords to my office."

Mr. Rusty sighed. "I wanted the long one." He thumbed to another guard. "I told Nevel he could have the short one."

"I'll make it up to you," Coralee said. "I *promise*. Remember? Los Angeles!"

Mr. Rusty shrugged. "I've got no use for suntan lotion and dildos."

Coralee stopped in front of the Sarah, regarding her full and healthy body with glowing eyes. "This will wait."

56

Chapter 8

Incarceration stokes the ego. Although most try to avoid it, once bagged and tagged, more often than not, you secretly revel in the attention it brings. Imprisonment garners a sense of meaning to an otherwise dreary life. The arrest confirms you are "wanted," not so bad sounding when said out loud. On a subconscious level, it has a better ring than "unwanted." The trial proves "beyond a reasonable doubt" there is meaning to whatever you did, even if very bad. Then comes imprisonment, where your worth is confirmed on a daily basis. Food, shelter, bedding, clothes, and a daily schedule of activities are even provided. And should anyone want to talk to you about your badness, your purpose is validated. Who in their right mind would want to give all that up for anonymity without meaning or perks? Nobody. So, we delude ourselves with thoughts of escape. In truth, we have no intention to flee. Instead, we cozied into purpose of any kind, and forget freedom as best we can, a meaningless endeavor when undertaken alone.

I woke up prone on a bed. My face was wet from slobber on

a stripped and stained mattress, feeling inside and out like I'd been manhandled. No broken bones, nothing torn or otherwise violated. I'll take a little good news in a sea of bad news any day.

My right hip screamed in pain from the horse that must have kicked me. I forced myself up on the bed, wiped my mouth, and rubbed my butt. On all fours, I looked under my chest to my knees. All of my clothes and jewelry were gone, replaced by a neon orange jumpsuit. A metal zipper ran up from the cuff of the left leg hem, across my hips and stomach, and up the middle to the right side of my neck. A nylon tag-- "Edith Song-- was sewn in over my heart.

Another prison indicator-- marking the incarcerated with ownership-- names, numbers, colors. What difference is there really between stripped prison jumpsuits and branded corporate knit shirts? Nothing-- it's all about control.

My bleary eyes fumbled over the room with indifference. A kitchen window opposite the bed revealed a bright summer day. *Not very cell-like*, I thought. I rolled my hips and flung my feet to the cold floor. With both hands, I patted the foam futon bed. Track lights hung from a mock ceiling, giving the room a sterilized feel.

I sized up the small countertop built into kitchen area on the other side of the room. There was a small sink, and cabinets without doors on either side. A white table stood near the sink with four metal office chairs on a white laminate floor made to seem like wood. The window-- the colors crisp and bright-- crowded the table.

I tested weight on my swollen feet and hissed-- ankles raw from the cuffs. Staggering to the table, I plopped into one of the cold hard plastic chairs, my sore butt smarting. *This must be what a tiger feels when it's tranquilized and tagged*, I thought. Not that you can find a real tiger anymore. The thought made me feel like an endangered species. Another reason for pause.

Out the window, past the white linen drapes, a grove of Bradford pear trees swayed, flakes of their blooming white blossoms fluttering like snow across warm green grass, spreading in every direction. A few white clouds meandered through the soft breeze of an electric blue sky. Despite the warm day outside, I felt a chill behind my ears and scalp. A reminder that nothing is as perfect as it seems. As I watched the trees move, they hesitated, and then resumed in a familiar sway. Too familiar. I blinked and rubbed my eyes, feeling the CB lenses in my eyes. I pried out the lenses, holding them with my thumb and index finger. Where the window had been, a brushed metal wall stared me down. I examined the lenses-- they were clear. The one's I'd been wearing before had been light auburn.

"Nice," I said, my voice weary with defeat. I flicked the lenses over my shoulder.

I went to the false window, leaned against the sill, and rubbed a hand over the metal wall. A dome the size of an overturned pasta bowl bulged from its surface. It curved outward like the back of a ladybug. Where a ladybug's black dots would have been, there were several deep holes the size of large buttons. Surrounding the metal bug were evenly spaced quarter holes. I stuck my pinky in one of the holes, twisted, slipped it out, and held it to my nose. Oil.

Turning to my left, I raised my eyebrows. "You've got to be kidding me," I said.

A round metal vault door, big enough for a small car, was set into the side of the wall. No visible hinges. An alphanumeric keypad was bolted to the door, displaying several key and card slots. A spoked wheel hung in the middle of the vault. I resisted the impulse to spin the wheel like the captain of a pirate ship, or bang frantically on the sprawling buttons, screaming, "Let me outta here!' Not my style, I guess. Besides, I had to have something to do later, if I got desperate or bored.

A red leather lounge chair, bolted in the center of the room, faced the window. I tried out the chair and put up my feet. The leather farted as I sunk in, enjoying the modicum of comfort. I clasped my hands behind my head and surveyed the room again, pretending I owned the place. Short angled walls jutted out between the living area and futon, and the kitchen and the vault. I realized that the room was round. Remembering the metal ladybug in the window, a chill shot up the back of my neck. *A bug in a killing jar.* The place was a cell, nothing less, and maybe more-- an execution chamber.

I sprang out of the chair and paced the room. I went to the small bathroom behind a thin sliding door. No lock. A small sink, shower head, and toilet-- all stainless steel. A metal shower head hung next to the sink. Hot and cold knobs were attached to the pipe. More of those iron ladybugs stuck to the wall. One in front of the curtainless shower, the other under the mirror. A large drain was drilled in the middle of the room.

A brushed steel mirror was studded into the wall behind the sink. Seeing myself, a shudder ran through my spine. My shoulder-length hair was a matted mess. Someone had tried to wipe away mascara by smearing it around my eyes like a kabuki mask. A bar of dry orange glycerin soap gleamed on the sink next to a bottle of black hair dye, as if screaming, *Use me! Alice in Wonderland* came to mind.

I smiled into the mirror and said, "*Somebody* doesn't like my hair color." My straight black hair was shoulder length. Bangs cut ruler-straight across, an inch of the ends bleached platinum blond, as were the ends over my shoulders. My roots had grown out snow white about an inch-- not my natural color. Assuming there was a team of lab coats watching me from a remote dark room, I flipped the bird at the mirror.

The entire room jolted, followed by small vibration swelling from the floor, turning into a violent shudder. The ground moaned like a sinking aircraft carrier. I held onto the sink. "What is this, a funhouse?" I said. Everything stopped. I looked into the mirror, waiting. No aftershock. I turned on the faucet and washed my face. I leaned against the sink, letting the water drip off my bangs, hiding the concern seeping into my face. *Why were my bangs growing out blonde?* It actually worried me more than imprisonment.

Behind me, the vault door came to life with a celebration of bangs, clicks and hums. A mechanical female voice said, "Disarmed! Ready to arm!" The door swung open. La-La stepped in like she was walking across a minefield.

Chapter 9

Stripping buck naked in public doesn't expose much about
people, as it turns out. Inner secrets know where to hide. Clawing
after them from the surface drives them deeper. Exposing outer
vulnerabilities makes you more committed to the lies that got
you there in the first place. That's how Coralee used nudity – she
entrenched newcomer minds with false realities by marching them
around in their birthday suits.

Papa followed other bald headed Employees from Processing
out a back door to the large causeway that led down a staggered row
of the pyramid buildings. These new Employees carried on one-way
conversations, talking over each other with droopy eyes and the
perky naiveté of a fresh recruit. Papa kept on like he was teaching
a kendo class. He was awake, though. I could see it in his eyes. A
nervous glance here and there, careful not to let his chin follow. He
was still trying to figure out his next move, how to get the heck out
of there.

Nikki Benton, a late-twenties hipster, led the way. She'd

been dressed in heels, nylons, a thigh-length wool skirt, and a mock turtleneck – all black. She could have either been a librarian or Betty-Paige-cultist. Her nose ring and flaming red koi and green Buddha tattoo—inked from her left shoulder blade, down the middle of her back and butt, stopping half-way down her hamstring—suggested it wasn't the former, unless she was from Seattle. In fact, she'd owned a failed high-speed nail and hookah saloon in downtown Oklahoma City, where many evacuees wound up after the mass exodus from the coasts. "Gloss or semi-gloss," she was saying, followed by a diatribe of local gossip. Who was sleeping with whom and so on. A monotone voice from the new implant in Papa's ear told him to follow Nikki.

It must have been painful for him walking down the causeway, raw skin exposed to a straight north wind with a twenty-five-degree chill factor, especially since he was aware. The rest of the new hires ignored the pain, a testimony to the power of the System. Shivering is an uncontrollable response of the body. When your core temperature gets too cold your body will shiver, no matter what. Papa was the only one shivering. He clenched his jaws between ramblings to keep his teeth from chattering. It was only a matter of time before he would be found out.

The previously deserted causeway had come to life. A few other Employees, men and women of all ages and races, in lime green jumpsuits, streamed along in a river of people. All of them had shaved heads, and none of them noticed the line of nudes yammering away, engaged in intense one-sided discussions. Everyone on the causeway—Papa's newbies included—moseyed along with lids hung low over glassy eyes while their mouths babbled on with anger, happiness, anxiety, euphoria, fear—the gamut of emotions.

Nikki stopped at a chain-link gate. An "Apartment Block 8" sign hung overhead. Papa kept his eyes ahead, resisting any temptation to gawk at the squat pyramid beyond the fence. Chatting about some celebrity who'd cheated on his wife, Nikki punched a few numbers on a keypad. If she was faking it, she was doing a great job. The gate buzzed open and they passed through to an automated turnstile door that poured them into a chilly concrete foyer with austere features—no pictures on the walls, no seating, no lighting except the ambient aura seeping in through glass bricks in the walls.

The voice in Nikki's ear said, "Go to the elevator." She complied. "Press the up button." She did. To Papa, the voice said, "Enter the elevator and press 29." Receiving similar instructions, the others followed, pressing their own floor buttons. "Wait." It was crazy loud in there, what with all the state-sponsored nudists talking over each other. I chuckled through my nose a little the first time I conjured the scene. But the more I watched the more horrified I felt. If there are levels of hell, blabbering on in a cramped and freezing elevator with a bunch of other oblivious naked strangers has to be one of them.

Stops on Levels 14, 23, and 24 let Nikki, Doug, and Sarah out into the cold. For a moment, if you couldn't see her slack face, Sarah's cheerful voice, talking about her daughter's high school graduation, brought a positive ray of light as she walked away, a feeling quashed by the image of her bare behind slouching alone down a dark hallway as the elevator door closed.

Exiting alone on 29, Papa followed the walkway that hung over the Level 28 passage below. By design it was nearly impossible to commit suicide by jumping from the building. He rightly assumed that he was still being watched by circuit video cameras that covered most of the space throughout Freedom Colony. If a new hire had made it that far without being detected, more often than not, once let off alone from the elevator, they would let out a sigh of relief and take a look around. Sure enough, down below, Nikki was getting caught. "Ha! Got one!" a voice yelled over an intercom. Papa kept going and talking. If he hadn't stopped shivering, he probably wouldn't have made it any further.

Room 2911 was situated on the northwest corner of the building. Entering without a lock, Papa found a lime green jumpsuit laid out on a thin stripped mattress over a concrete slab bolted to the cinderblock wall. A metal toilet hung from the opposite wall. No toilet paper. No furniture. No paint. A single row of three glass blocks in the upper side of the outer wall near the ceiling allowed enough light for movement. Not a place for reading, chess playing, nail biting, hacksawing, or anything else a prisoner might do requiring attention. Definitely not a place to live.

Completing the kendo class in his mind, shouting numbers in Japanese and giving instructions in English, at the prompting of the voice in his head, Papa pulled on the green jumpsuit and lay down on his back on the slab. "Sleep," the voice said. He went silent and let his eyes fall all the way closed. At least he had made it through the first day without getting caught. He breathed slowly. I knew him well enough to see he was counting each breath silently, like he'd taught us to do. Probably he was working out his options, trying to figure out a way of escape. If it were me, I would have been tempted to just wait a couple of hours, then to jump down the outside levels to the ground and make a run for it. Knowing what I know now, it never would have worked.

Chapter 10

WHEN LA-LA STEPPED INTO MY CELL, IT STARTLED ME TO SEE another vault door behind her. My chest caved with a feeling of hopelessness. *There's no getting out of here*, I thought. That's part of the illusion of most blind prisons, in one form or another—the uselessness of resistance. The barriers to escape are made known to us. You'd think they'd be hidden so we'd be caught by hidden pitfalls upon escape attempts. Wardens show us the fences, barbed wire, and guns because they know we'll conjure those images to rationalize inaction, make us think there's no way out. We give in to incarceration, accept it, learn to embrace it, love it even, to the point where we think it was our idea to begin with. Helps us rationalize the unreasonable acceptance of our new purpose.

La-La locked her elbows together like a human cannonball waiting on a burning fuse. A jade Buddha hung from a gold necklace pulled taut into crossed arms. The sleeves of her black cotton sweater were scrunched up to her elbows, revealing a dzi bead bracelet on her left wrist. I remember those amulets of hers from Mama's cremation. La-La wore them to funerals and hospital visits. *Real encouraging*, I thought.

"La-La?" I said.

I went to hug her but she gave me a speak-to-the-hand sign. I stopped. She nodded, her eyes following an invisible object across the floor, listening to a voice in her ear barking orders in Chinese. As she took baby steps, her left hand clutched the necklace, while she tested the floor with the balls of her feet. I glanced at the metal ladybug on the steel wall in the false window, then searched around the room and shrugged my shoulders. *What the heck is this place? A prison,* my mind said, the answer coming before I could think it. Whatever it was, it had to be booby trapped. Once satisfied she wasn't going to be blown up, or whatever was worrying her, she rushed in and hugged me.

"Edith, Edith, Edith!" she said. Her Chinese accent made me more desperate to escape. Images of her steaming kitchen with hot pot soup, drunken chicken, and green tea came rushing to mind. I wished I could just go back to China with her, forget this crazy world, and start over in some humble village, making dumplings from a street market, or selling bonsai trees out the back of a humble Zen garden.

"La-La! What's happening?"

She took me by both shoulders. "Edith, listen."

As if a cat had spoken to me, the hair on the back of my ears stood at attention. It was the closest she'd ever come to putting an English sentence together.

"Do what they say," she said. The words sounded forced, practiced. "Answer questions. Go home."

She squeezed my shoulders. I felt bad for her. She was probably more scared than me. I knew she'd give her life for me and Irene. She was just doing what she thought would help. Whatever they'd hoped to accomplish by sending La-La to me, it was working, softening me up, making me want to cooperate, giving me false hope that there was a way out. You know, there are people who spend a lifetime studying how to manipulate prisoners, make people play ball with all methods of mental and physical torture. Makes you wonder what they could accomplish if they'd use such know-how to encourage people to love each other.

"I'll do it, La-La," I said. In Chinese, I told her I loved her. I knew that much just from listening to Chinese pop rock. "Answer questions." She smiled and nodded eagerly. "See you home."

"Home," she said. She grabbed her necklace and placed her other hand on my shoulder. "Mama proud."

I wiped more tears from my face. I missed Mama more than ever. In the back of my mind, somewhere buried in my unconscious, something I didn't want to admit, I wondered whether the people watching were telling her to talk about Mama. *Yes*, my mind said, *Yes. They'll use everything like that against you. Keep up your guard.* I hugged La-La again to hide the knowing stoic look that fell over my face.

"Martin come," she said. "Answer questions, okay?"

"Martin?" She was just repeating the words fed to her hear. I nodded, holding her hands.

She squeezed her necklace again. "*No mind.*"

"Okay, La-La. Never mind. Go home."

She held my face with both hands. "No. Mind," she said, emphasizing each word slowly. There was a stark intensity in her

69

eyes I'd never seen. *No mind.* Her black pupils swelled and engulfed her brown eyes. She was trying to tell me something urgent, not repeat something whispered in her ear.

I didn't know it then, but she had been told the room would be flooded with nerve gas, causing instant paralysis, followed by sudden death, to us both, if I did not agree to cooperate.

"Never mind," I said, smiling.

She sighed and dropped her arms.

Chapter 11

Most people don't need to be reminded to piss. Prisoners do. They live in a world of reminders. Without them, everything falls apart. A prison cannot survive without efficiency. And obedience.

The voice in Papa's ear said, "Use the toilet."

Sliding off the concrete bed, he went to the toilet and did his business, making imagined conversation about manufacturing flat screens. He was doing a pretty good job of making up all of that stuff. The fear of losing the will over his mind must have been strong inspiration.

Following directions of the voice, he left the apartment and made his way to the lobby, joining a group leaving Apartment Block 8. The causeway flowed with thousands of green jump suits, men and women, young and old, all shapes, sizes, and ethnicities, heading toward a T in the pathway. Man, it was loud! Broken monologues barked across the Colony. Papa just shouted nonsense, taking the opportunity to brainstorm how to get out while coming up with faked dialogue. Sooner or later he'd be found out. Anyone watching him from a video could double-check his made-up gibberish with where he was projected to be in the CB world. He didn't know where he was supposed to be, so they'd quickly realize he was faking it.

The pathway to the left led to a rectangular building a half-mile long and ten stories high, a large white "Factory" sign painted on its side from the ground floor to the roof. The causeway to the right led to a low square building about a quarter-mile long, the sign above the wide-open doors—"Cafeteria". Another quality of a blind prison is simplicity. Prisoners—smart and stupid—must be able to follow simple rules and comprehend simple messages. Signs like those scattered around Freedom Colony were basic enough for Employees to comprehend without distraction from their CB-world responsibilities.

A blast of air hit the top of Papa's head as he passed into the cafeteria with the crowd of green suits. The voice said, "Go to Line 8." He followed other Employees heading to a cattle chute. "Line 8" hung from the top of a pole attached to its entrance. The line passed an inclined ledge hanging from a stainless-steel wall where cafeteria trays were spat out through a long slit. Something like oatmeal mixed with nuts, chopped carrots, and corn had been slopped on the trays, a disposable spork tossed into it. As he took a tray, mimicking the other Employees, he followed the voice toward a set of empty tables at the other end of the expansive room.

He met a line of Employees coming the other way. His wandering eyes connected with those of a passing guy, who abruptly blurted out, "I've got a live one here!"

A siren blared. Everyone in the cafeteria stood and encircled Papa without missing a beat, chanting, "Live one! Live one! Live one!" *Talk about creepy!*

As it turned out, the guards took turns pretending to be Employees. They'd walk among the green jumpsuits, most of whom wouldn't even notice the guard. Heck, they didn't notice each other, since they didn't even know where they really were. None of the Employees looked at anyone straight in the eye. Their eyes didn't acknowledge anything. The guard would usually spend most of his time looking people in the face, trying to get eye contact, a sure sign that the Employee was awake, or at least getting there. A pretty dull job, but the guards lined up for their turn. There'd be a year's pay bonus for each "live one" they found, which was rare, so they typically shared a third of the bonus with the rest of the guards. There'd be celebration that day at Papa's expense, and it was all for Papa's own good, just saving him from unemployment, or worse, termination.

Chapter 12

WAITING IS A HUGE PART OF ANY PRISON SYSTEM. GIVES TIME TO worry. At first you feel relieved and confident. You might even be confident in the illusion of your escape. But the longer you wait, the more you question yourself. And worry, wondering what's coming next. Your imagination gets the best of you, thinking of all the bad things that can happen. Pain, torture, loss, pretty much anything. Towards the end of a long wait, you start to get anxious about getting out, doubting escape, thoughts pressing you toward the inevitable loss of hope and acceptance of a new purpose. Along the way, you dwell on what's going on outside your cell, what you're missing out on, what's coming apart, who's looking for you, who's suffering because of your absence, or who's getting away with what they've done to you. And you become desperate to get out. Maybe willing to do anything to get out, which lends itself to your submission, driven further by self-worth gained from being locked up in the first place. It's all by design. Pretty much like any eight-to-five job.

After La-La left I snooped around my room for a couple

hours. The drawers in the kitchen and bathroom—all empty. Standing on the kitchen table, I pushed up the ceiling tiles, half expecting to see surveillance cameras, wires, bombs, what have you. Nothing but a curved metal ceiling up there with more of those ladybugs. I shrugged—weird—figuring there must at least be cameras in the false kitchen window. And if there were—big deal. Like most people, I was already under a constant microscope. CBs had turned everyone into a walking talking video camera, taking everything in around them, processing it into the System, available to everyone. Besides, what was I going to do if I found hidden cameras? I'd promised La-La I would cooperate and I wanted to go home.

Bored, I examined the vault door. Its keypad had the typical upper- and lower-case letters and numbers, but with symbols I'd never seen before. It beeped when I strummed the ten-key pad. I felt like the vault was watching me. When I hit it with my fist, it squawked. Clenching my jaws, I waited for an intercom voice to say, *Cut that out!* Nothing.

The red recliner beckoned me with its apparent cushiness and smell of new leather. Regarding it with fists on my hips, the more I looked it over the more it seemed desperately out of place. No one would want to sit there and watch a video of a false spring day in a metal cell unless they were on drugs. I circled around the recliner, got down on one knee, and tapped the white wood floor with the back of my knuckle. The sharp smell of glue still permeated the air. Everything was new, probably made to suit me. I paced around the recliner. *That's probably what they had in mind—put me on drugs, and once I was sedated, start in with their questions.* The idea came to me like a joke, a nervous reaction to something not far from the truth. Like the entire room and vault door, the recliner was one of many restraints for me to see and accept. That's exactly what they wanted.

I plopped into the recliner. Just as I was about to fall asleep, the vault door clattered again. From the corner of my eye I could see this unassuming guy with glasses and wavy blond hair come in. Wearing herringbone tweed slacks, he had a leather briefcase in one hand and a crumpled paper sack in the other. I guessed he was in his early forties—pretty close, as it turned out. The collar of his white oxford shirt was unbuttoned, with both sleeves rolled up to his elbows. Reminded me of a typical politician stumping for votes, putting on fake blue-collar airs in designer duds. A complete pretender.

"You must be Martin," I said.

"I am *he*," he said with a shrug and a grin, setting down the paper sack on the table as the vault door hummed closed. He noticed my eyes shoot at the door before it closed. Trying to look casual, he half held his hands up in a mock surrender. "I thought we would have some lunch before we chat," he said, with a forced grin.

Now I can usually get a pretty good read on people, picking up on little signs of fear, nervousness, deception, compassion. I'm not always right, but more often than not, I am. He reached into the sack and set out a large platter of assorted sushi, nigiri, and sashimi, and two cups of soup in styrofoam. "I hear you like this kind of stuff," he said. His ring finger was trembling. Just that one. He was scared for some reason. *Could it really be me?* Not likely. Maybe there was something about the room. La-La was scared, too. Such ideas just made me more worried.

I let down my feet and cat-stretched out of the chair. "La-La told you, I guess?"

Yes.

He pulled out a chair. "Please, have a seat." Despite knowing he was afraid, I still felt like a lamb in a cage with a lion. I hesitated.

Martin took his hand off the chair and combed it through his hair, presumably to hide his trembling. "I'll be honest with you, Edith. I don't want to be here, either." He sat, snapped off the green rubber bands around the sushi containers, and pried off thin plastic tops. One of the many things I've learned—the best deceptions are those with a little truth mixed in. Sort of like a double fried cookie made with organic whole grain wheat. One percent of it is good for you—enough to justify eating it—the rest of it will rot your gut.

I huffed and dropped into the chair with crossed arms. "Well, then let's get out of here."

He handed me a pair of chopsticks with a smile that said it obviously wasn't going to happen.

I glared at him for a moment before snatching the chopsticks. "Here I am, anyway," I said. "Y'all got us. Good for you! Now what do you want?" I went for a piece of red tuna nigiri and stopped. I palmed the chopsticks with hands together and closed my eyes. After praying, I snagged the sushi and plopped it in my mouth.

Martin snapped a piece of spicy salmon and watched me for a moment before taking a bite. "You knew we would have questions, Edith." He spoke with about as much urgency as an automated time and temperature announcement.

"La-La said you have some questions, and if I answer them, you'll let us go."

"If you answer *all* of my questions—*truthfully*—you can go home *today*."

"Really?"

No.

"Yes, really," he said.

"Do you promise?"

"I promise."

He's not your friend, I thought. *Don't trust him. Remember that.*

I pinched a slice of salmon and said, "I'm going to hold you to your word, Martin." After chewing, I snapped the chopsticks down, grabbed the plastic bowl, and gulped the miso soup. I slowed before finishing. It was cold. Wherever he'd gotten the food, it'd been a long way away. My stomach turned, knowing I was a long way from home.

He held his own bowl to his nose, peering at me over the rim. "What did you pray for, Edith?"

The answer came to my mind—*to go home safely today with La-La and Irene*. I held a tuna nigiri in front of my face and looked at him square in the face. "Is this part of the test?"

"There's no *test*, Edith, I just have some questions after we eat."

"I prayed for my La-La and sister."

He nodded and took another sip from his bowl, keeping his eyes on me. "Why not pray for your dad?"

"*Papa*? He's dead. They didn't tell you?"

No.

He repeated the word "papa" and nodded at the table, committing it to memory. "Okay." He swirled the soup in the bowl. "Your papa died in a bus crash, right?"

No.

79

An awkward silence passed. "Yes, that's right," I said.

"Do you remember the day he last left your house?"

"Yes." I thought about what happened at the kendo tournament, Irene's behavior, the flame over her head, the grueling match with Papa back home, cleaning the *dojo* floor.

"Do you remember where he was going?"

"I believe he was going clean out his office. He'd lost his job. The factory was shutting down."

"Do you remember what your papa took with him when he left the house?"

"A bag of clothes and two samurai swords."

"Did that seem strange to you?"

"I don't know why he took the swords. I figured he was going to sell them. We needed the money." This whole line of questions surprised me. I thought he'd be asking about the UFOs right away.

Martin nodded. He took a sip of his soup. "Have you ever heard from him again?"

Yes.

Blood rushed to my cheeks. "What kind of question is that?"

"Just answer the questions."

"No, of course not."

"What about the swords?"

"I assume the swords were destroyed or lost in the crash." A lie. In fact, we had seen one of the swords again. I doubted there was any way he knew about it.

"What about the *wakizashi* sword Irene has?"

Oops. "That's a different sword." The fact that he knew the sword's proper name worried me.

"Where did she get it?"

"I have no idea. You'd have to ask her."

He nodded and smiled. "Your grandmother told you I would be asking you some questions."

"You know she did."

"Yes." He reached down and thumbed open the two locks on top of his heavy briefcase and pulled out a small metal box, placing it on the table. Inside the briefcase flaps there was an embossed image of George Washington over classical lettering -- "I cannot tell a lie." He pointed to it and said, "Can you say as much?"

"Yeah, except I didn't do it and I don't have a hatchet."

Martin gave me a wry smile.

"I'll tell you everything I know and I will not lie," I said.

"*Good,*" he said with weighty emphasis. "I assume your parents raised you to know the difference between right and wrong?"

"Sure."

"They taught you *not* to tell lies?"

Yes.

"Yes."

"Without exception?"

"Well ... I guess ... there could be an exception right?"

"Like what?"

I felt like there was a smart-ass tone to his voice. The nigiri started to smell rank. I frowned, and said, "Well, like, I guess if your life depended on telling a lie, or you needed to exaggerate to get out of trouble."

"Have you ever told a lie to *get out of trouble?*"

"Probably."

"Give me an example."

I put down my chopsticks and crossed my arms. "Once my seventh grade teacher asked me if I'd cheated on my math test. I told her 'no.' But I guess that really wasn't a lie because I'd actually cheated on the history test."

"That's a great example, Edith, because, *really*, it was a lie. Do you know why?"

"No."

"Because you weren't *candid*. Have you ever heard that word, 'candid'?"

"Sure."

"What does it mean to you?"

I shrugged. "Frank."

"That's pretty close. It also means *straightforward*. For our purposes it means you should answer each question completely and honestly. And it means you should offer any other additional information that could be relevant to the question."

"Like what?"

"You should have told your teacher about cheating on the history test. That was obviously what she was after. Another example: if I ask you whether you had a burger for lunch today, the answer is 'no,' but you should go ahead and add the rest. 'No, I had miso soup and sushi for lunch.' Got it?"

"Got it."

"Or if I asked you, 'What happened to your papa after the last time you saw him?' what would you say?"

I nearly said he'd died in a bus crash. A different answer popped into my mind – *He went to the Freedom Colony, Western Nebraska*. There was no audible voice, or voice in my head. The information was just there, all of a sudden, within my knowledge. I could even see an image of the place in my mind's eye. My eyes widened and I felt my heart clench.

"Edith?"

"He'd dead! Understand? Dead! Is that too hard for you to understand?" I always wanted to believe he was alive. We didn't see his body at the funeral. They said he was too burnt. I fantasized he had survived somehow. The wrong body had been cremated. After the *wakizashi* blade showed up at our house in the mail, my mind went wild. Now I had a piece of information I didn't have before. *Freedom Colony.* I didn't know where it came from. In my heart, however, I *knew* it was true.

"I'm sorry for your loss, Edith," he said with a tone that sounded anything but.

Chapter 13

PAPA! HELP US, PAPA! HELP!

Unknown to me at the time, I'd developed an ability to send messages to others. After Papa had left, I'd called out to him for help when we'd been going through tough times, especially Irene. Somehow, he heard me.

Papa woke up standing and disoriented. His face was sweaty. A chill flushed his cheeks as though he'd walked into a cool room from a hot summer day. His right hand was pushing against a large sliding metal door, rolling upward. In his left hand he held a white cord connected to the lip of the door just below his right. The position was similar to the grip on a samurai sword ready for a strike.

He dropped his hands and stared at them blankly. Searching from side to side, he said, "Edith?" *Help us, Papa, help us*, he whispered. He was alone in a long white concrete hallway dozens of yards long. Behind him waited a large hand-guided pallet jack loaded with stacks of shrink-wrapped cardboard boxes. The voice in his ear said, "Proceed." He cupped his hands over his mouth to vomit but stopped it by shivering, swallowing hard, and clenching his teeth. Willing himself to focus, he grabbed the pallet jack's handle and pulled it into a large storage room.

It had been two months since he'd left. The Sundogs hadn't shown up yet. They would, though. Sure, they would. After being caught the last time, Papa had been strapped down and plugged into the System, and good. He'd been walking around blabbering like the rest of the Employees, getting in the groove of slack-eyed, droopy-necked obedience. They kept an eye on him for a couple of weeks, making sure he'd been turned. That's all it took to see someone wasn't faking it. Without the help of the CB System, a human body just couldn't put up an act for that long. Sooner or later a person would shiver, make eye contact, sweat, or piss. When an Injured Employee like Papa was under the microscope of observation, it was simply impossible for him to play-act the gibberish talk without being found out, since he could never know what he was supposed to be saying. The guards did, though. He'd been completely rehabilitated with the Workers Compensation treatment. His observation period proved its success with flying colors. Being put under the blanket of oblivion of employment at Freedom Colony must have been something of a relief. Not that it was a good thing. Certainly not. Just that he didn't have to fret about Irene and me, nor stress about getting out. Waking up was a massive slap in the face. A painful reminder of the scope of his pain and worry. Asking a few questions along these lines, I realized that many people who wake up unexpectedly actually turn themselves in. They want to go back to the false reality of no concern or responsibility, where cause has no effect. When Papa heard my voice, though, turning himself in was out of the question.

He remembered why he was there, and why he had to get out.

Rows of stacked boxes lined a huge storage room. The voice was still there, in his ear, giving orders. Papa went to the last row near the outer wall next to several loading docks with closed doors. He pushed the pallet into place and eased it down with the hydraulics. He probably wanted to sit down and clear his head, try to figure out what was going on. He was right to keep moving, like everyone at Freedom Colony, because he was being tracked all the time. Everything from meals, showers, and well, you know – *everything* -- to widgets finished on an assembly line and the number of pallets pushed back and forth, had to be done efficiently, on time every time. The voice would know the instant he disobeyed directions. For all he knew, there was a red light over Coralee's desk right then reading, "Live One!" with a close-up video shot and cross hairs over his face.

Papa drew the stacker out of the room, left the door open, and went through a maze of hallways and sliding doors to the large factory floor. Overhead, boxes sped over a spaghetti of metal rails suspended by wires. A sea of green jump suits lined the factory floor for hundreds of yards. The place reminded me of an Irish *Devo* concert, everyone yakking it up, carrying on conversations to different rhythms. With green gloves and smock hats, they all sat in lines behind long tables, piecing together CBs and placing the finished product into a small red tray. Their droopy eyes glazed over with exhaustion, Employees pushed the trays down to a large conveyor at the end leading upward where the CBs were automatically packaged mid-air. The boxes were stacked and shrink-wrapped onto pallets. Several other pallets of CBs waited for Papa to pick them up.

A worker—a guard—on the assembly line searched Papa's

face as he loaded the pallet. Papa kept his eyes forward. Returning the way he'd come, Papa whispered a passage from *The Book of Five Rings.*

When he returned to the storage unit, several of the sliding bay doors against the outside wall were open. Two men were pushing pallets up ramps into trucks. Two others were standing around doing nothing. They were all dressed in white jump suits and hardhats labeled "Contractor" at the front. Papa could see right away they weren't Employees, since they were talking to each other, making eye contact. And well, there were the other blatant signs. One of the loafers had his black galosh up on the bumper of the truck, smoking a hand-rolled cigarette.

One of the contractors pushing a pallet moaned. "You ain't supposed to do that, Reggie," he said. "Smoking is illegal."

"Yeah, but so's unemployment. Anyways, nobody cares as long as you pick up your butts and pull your load on time."

Papa neared. Reggie pointed at him and said, "Hey, you! Take that *right* into the truck there! We're gonna be taking it in anyway."

Instead of turning, Papa went straight to the truck ramp.

Reggie flicked the butt at Papa's feet. "Well, get a load of this! We've got a live one here." Turned out Reggie was just playing. He often did that to Employees, cussing at them, even throwing a light punch to their cheek from time to time. Reggie would receive a bonus if he ever caught a live one. Papa was his first catch ever.

"We're splittin' this one, ain't we?" the other Contractor said.

"Yeah, yeah, sure, sure," Reggie said, meaning *no way.*

Papa awoke with a headache from a strapped-down head

against a red leather recliner, wireless thumbnail electrodes stuck on his temple. His wrists and ankles were secured and two larger belts hugged his hips and upper body. He examined the soft cuff on his right arm with frantic eyes. A thin rubber band ran tightly around his chest. Two of his right-hand fingers were socketed into short black tubes. He could barely budge his head left or right. Two other sweaty guys were also strapped down on either side of him. One said, "Hello?" The room sounded cozy—sound-proofed with egg-carton foam across the walls and ceiling. Probably realizing that screams were the only sounds to keep in, Papa's breath slowed into resigned, sweatless terror.

From behind, Coralee strutted in front of them and turned on her heels with the tips of her fingers together in a cage under her sharp chin. She was enjoying her dark revel. Such a gluttonous show of revenge is tolerated in some places. Victims' family members witnessing a state-sponsored execution, for example. But if you ask me, it's still just revenge by another name. Those with unmitigated power shouldn't be allowed to indulge in an impulse that leads to more suffering. No wholesome person who tastes this indulgence feels satisfied. Just leaves empty feelings and more pain. Good people who witness their enemy hanged, electrocuted, or put to sleep like a sick dog inevitably say something like, *Justice was done but we'll never feel the same, nothing will bring so-and-so back*. That's because it serves no real purpose for the pure in heart, save the suffering in the soul. Sociopaths are the only ones who find real satisfaction in it, the kind of dark happiness to be scared of. Coralee had that kind of black eyes, filled with gleeful malice. She enjoyed revenge in all its forms and tastes.

"You're here because you're distracted," she said. "Distraction leads to wandering thoughts, and thus, inefficiency." Her bony index finger uncurled and pointed to the ceiling. "Your only purpose is to be efficient. Obviously, any lingering subjective ideas must be rooted out. Now, I *know* you want to be efficient. So I'm going to give you another opportunity. One ... more .... chance."

"Just let me go home," wailed the guy on Papa's left. "I'll forget about this place, I know I can. My wife needs me. My kids. We'll leave our house, the Prefecture. We'll go to the Wild."

"Sweet, but sorry. Not an option, Mr. Green. You've got to pay off your mortgage and consumer debts. You could never pay them off in a single lifetime, so ... "

The black guy on Papa's right said, "You're going to kill us?"

Coralee guffawed and shook her head. "Oh for heaven's sake, stop! Of course not! We're going to *employ* you!"

"This isn't employment," Papa said. His voice sounded pretty relaxed for someone strapped naked to a gurney. "This is slavery."

Her skin stretched back, revealing her false white teeth, as she said, "Oh, darling. This is nothing new to you. What do you think was going on before? Why do you think it's so easy to process a person into an Employee? In a matter of seconds? You were *already* processed. Most of you were already *employed* when you got here. You're with me, here ... now, probably because you were bad Employees. You were inefficient, lacked focus. You were slowing things down, interjecting too many of your own subjective ideas into daily life, and mucked things up. Like a virus. And it's still a problem for you. But I'm here to help you."

"We don't need your *help*," Papa said. "Release us. Let us go back to our families."

90

Coralee dropped her hands with the dejected frustration of a toddler. She was accustomed to following orders. To her, the confident and smooth tone of his voice sounded like something to obey. She slowly pulled her hands behind her back, holding them in a knot of swollen knuckles.

"I don't think you understand, Mr. Lawson," she said. "There's no family for you to return to." Anguish flushed over his face. She waved her hand. "No, no, no. I don't mean your families are dead. I *do* mean that *you* are. *All* of you. Your wives, husbands, lovers, buddies, co-workers, doctors. Everybody. They think *you're* dead. You all died from an accident, illness, or what have you. At least, that's what all of your families believed at first. After the initial disappearance, they slowly forget about you, you know, to make it less painful for them. By now, you're all dead and forgotten to your families and the world. I'm afraid it's irreversible. Your families and friends wouldn't know you if you returned. They'd call the police if you set foot in your old homes. And let me tell you, there'd be no changing their mind. No, you cannot go back, not to your old life, not ever. Besides, your debts are too great. You'd never pay them off in a lifetime. You don't want to be turned out into the Wild with nothing, do you?"

The guys on either side of Papa erupted in mixture of shouting and tearful wailing.

Accustomed to such outbursts, Coralee talked over the racket. "Now, you three are here because you've all taken a Personal Day or two. We can't have that around here. This is your last chance for full employment. Think about this before we begin. Everyone you knew believes you're dead now. No one is looking for you. No one is coming for you. If anyone is thinking of you, and that's a big if, it's in the past tense. You can still help the ones you love, though. It's a selfless act. Give in to employment. By working and letting go, you're saving the lives of your families. Isn't it better to drop this corpse you're dragging around? Isn't it easier to forget about the pain of loss, your ego, your selfish expectations, your attachments? Make it easy on yourself. Accept it. You're not leaving. You're not going home. This is your home now. Accept it for the sake of others and your own freedom."

As Coralee walked out, she said, "Remember this: no one has ever left Freedom Colony unemployed." *No Employee had ever left alive,* she meant.

Chapter 14

WHILE I FLYSPECKED MY NEW CELL, IRENE STRUGGLED AGAINST leather straps, cringing from the screeching sound of a record needle on a warped record. Projected letters and words flashed and turned against a dark background of strobe lights flickering in primary colors. Grainy black and white video flashed on the wall: a dead rat, its open bowels eaten away by maggots; a pruned grandmother puking in a boy's face; a nest of shiny baby bats churning in guano; a shaved cat with tubes coming from its pink stomach; an infant eating a greasy steak with both hands. *Gross!*

Chaos stopped. Brief silence. Then soft amber lights slowly warmed the rounded floor base. Irene was panting like a marathoner. Her panicked eyes probed the room. A soft New Age hum swelled with the rising sound of trickling water. Her heart rate slowed. The sweat from her brow evaporated. She let her eyes fall halfway shut, on the verge of sleep.

In her ear, a smooth male voice said, "What is your name?"

"Irene Song," she said.

"Who is your sister?"

"Edith Song." I'd never heard her say my name so sweetly. So that's when I knew she was faking it.

"Who is your father?"

"Rory Lawson."

"Where is your father?"

With the smoothest, loveable tone, she said, "He's dead, you jerk!"

Irene's belligerent grin grew across a holographic screen in the darkness aside a large conference table. Colonel Gaddis muted the sound and swiveled around with a toothy scowl. Two broad-shouldered military men in desert fatigues—Gaddis' sidekicks—menaced still and stoic at the opposite side of a long conference table near Martin. Secretary Freight's fuzzy image sizzled with snowy reception at the head of the table.

Gaddis wiped sweat off his brow and rubbed his stubby fingers dry as he spoke. "I've never seen anyone so completely immune," he said, sounding impressed.

"How many times has it been now?" said Freight.

"Six," Gaddis said.

"Six," Freight said, drawing out the hiss at the end.

Martin broke the pregnant silence. "More than eighty-five percent succumb to the first treatment. Holdouts normally have a complete mental breakdown before the end of the third time, or were already mentally imbalanced to begin with. A fourth go-around causes seizures or aneurysms about forty percent of the time. No one has ever made it through a fifth round. Never."

Anna Style, Secretary of the Navy, joined the conference, her seated image tuning into the chair next to Martin. "Seemed like it was having some effect for a minute there," she said.

"Don't be ridiculous—she's playing with us!" Gaddis said.

Secretary Freight's slanted eyes flashed and drew a malicious bead on Gaddis. "Drop the mind games. This one needs brute force. She's practically asking for it. Everyone eventually caves. It's a matter of time and biology. Start with waterboarding, every which way you can do it. Simple but effective. If that doesn't work, get medieval on her—thumbscrews, blowtorches, razors, pull teeth— whatever you've got. Just get some answers! Make her tell you what she knows about the Sundogs!

"What about the other one?" Martin said.

"Edith," Gaddis said, flicking my name from his fingers.

"This one's not as stubborn," Freight said, who plainly didn't know me as well as he thought. "With a few mind games, she might tell you everything. See what the polygraph ruse turns up. Her father. Use him."

Jerk.

"They figured him alive once they got that sword," Style said. "He's scheduled for termination. Using him could be a home run. Give her hope of saving him as a way to motivate, get her to react."

Witch.

"There's more to it than that," Freight said. "Ask what she knows about him. Don't tell her the answers. See how she reacts. One of these girls knows more than she's letting on and it could be her. If she knows about her father, then she should know about the Sundogs, too, and a lot of other things, if you just get *her* to ask *your* questions."

Martin frowned. "What do you mean, 'ask my questions'?

Why do you think she knows anything?" he said. "She's just a girl."

"Just ask her!" Freight said. "Ask her and see! Trust me, she *knows!*"

Boy, was he right.

Chapter 15

ON THE DAY THE SUNDOGS ARRIVED, AIR FORCE ONE LANDED at McConnell Air Force Base. The wedge-shaped stealthy craft taxied into a cavernous hangar. A side hatch opened from the back. A gangplank of stairs displaying the presidential seal slid to the ground.

Twenty-four secret service agents armed with automatic assault rifles poured out of the aircraft and formed a perimeter around the plane. Even to me, they seemed like way too little protection. Bullets weren't the biggest threat. President Sophia Martinez pumped her knees down the metal stairs in tan patent-leather high heels. Six armed suits followed, more of way too little. Two platoons of Marines had taken defensive positions at the entrance to the hangar. It didn't matter how many guns were put at hand – the president still didn't understand the real danger.

Robert Green, her chief of staff, clung to her elbow, a swarm of assistants in tow with briefcases. Air Force Lieutenant General Cindy Reddy met the president at the bottom of the stairs. For a woman in uniform, she had style, wearing her chestnut hair in tight European braids around her head.

"Madam President, the conference room is waiting as you requested," Reddy said.

Agitated senior blue-uniform types grouped nearby. The Marine Corps commandant, General Nolan Bishop, stood several paces away, flicking ashes from a Blue Pall Mall cigarette to his side. He took a long drag. Glowing coals glinted off his black eyes.

President Martinez cruised past General Reddy toward an open door inside the hangar. "Have a secure connection available. The Speaker of the House and the vice president will join us, with the Joint Chiefs, from a different location."

"The Speaker?" General Reddy said, shuffling behind the president. She glanced over her shoulder at General Bishop, smoking with a knowing stare. "But I was told …"

General Bishop shouted after the president. "Madam President, forgive me, but I've taken the liberty of moving the conference below ground … for your safety." He flicked the cigarette over his shoulder and pointed after it without looking. "A Sundog is approaching from the west."

President Martinez turned toward the strange sight visible through closing hangar doors. A few strands of her long black hair came loose. She pulled her blazer closed with trembling hands. The curved edge of something as large as a floating city emerged from a rolling thunderhead, bearing down on the base.

"What is the world coming to?" she said.

Chapter 16

POLYGRAPHS HAVE A LOT IN COMMON WITH TORTURE. THE inquisitor shows his subject—the victim—the tools to be used to look inside the soul and see the truth. He explains how the machine works, shows and handles the instruments of veracity, and convinces you that the machine does, in fact, work. That's where most of the similarities end. The instruments of torture—water, electricity, fire, sharp objects, pliers, and such—actually can and do drown, shock, burn, cut, and rip. So the victim of torture knows exactly what's coming, no matter what. But the instruments of a polygraph don't actually tell whether the victim is lying. A polygraph is essentially a ruse to convince the victim that the machine can pry into her mind, and once so convinced, the test is used to mentally squeeze out hidden knowledge. In other words, the victim is essentially tricked into telling all. In many instances, but not most, an experienced polygraph-giver can detect signs that a person is more of a Pinocchio or a George Washington. It's all subjective, and anyway, governments have the final say on whether you pass the test. If the powers that be don't have a warm fuzzy feeling about the test results, you fail. Too bad, so sad. No appeal. And with that in mind, it's not really a test per se, since the final result is actually subjective.

Martin wound two elastic tubes around my upper chest and clipped them around my back. I held my breath as he fiddled with the clasps of the tubes, wishing he'd just get on with it. He clipped two plastic tubes on my left ring and middle fingers. Green lights on top of the devices blinked. He toyed with a blood-pressure cuff, frowning as if he'd forgotten how it worked, and clicked it around my arm. He stuck electrodes on my temples after priming my skin with a cold lotion from a tube. Before smacking them on, he showed me they also had green lights. Wires ran from all these devices to sockets on a panel sewn in the side of the chair. *Wires.* It seemed a little old school to me. Unnecessary. *What were they for?*

Electricity.

After hooking me up like Frankenstein, Martin stepped back. With his hands on his hips, he said, "Feel comfortable?"

"No."

"No, of course, you don't. But do try to relax." He was so melodramatic, the way he held his fingers to his chin, as though sizing up a painting in progress. I didn't know it then, but the test had already begun. It had begun the moment they'd put me in there. He, and those watching, were already able to follow my pulse, breath, temperature, and brain patterns. By asking me questions they knew the answers to, they could establish a basic normal pattern for how I responded when I told the truth. Anything outside of that pattern would suggest deception, to them anyway.

He reached into his pocket. "Oh, I almost forgot," he said. *I doubt that.*

He handed me a contact lens case. "Please put these on, they may come in handy."

The lenses were a slightly darker green than my own color. "I *so* missed them," I said. I held my lids open one at a time and dropped in the lenses.

He returned to the chair at the kitchen table, putting him at my peripheral vision. My chair faced the false window.

"You're lying," he said.

"Well, I'm exaggerating, of course. Anybody can tell that without a machine."

"Yes, but the machine also told me." He reached his hands up, holding one over the other, and twisted an invisible ball over the kitchen table. The window screen fuzzed back to life. Vital-sign monitors were stacked one on top of each other, replacing the spring view of swaying trees. Separate bouncing lines tracked horizontally across the screen, marked "Brainwaves," "Perspiration," "Blood Pressure," "Heart Rate," and "Respiration." The first two lines were turning pink.

"See the screen, Edith?"

"Yes."

"The two tubes around your chest measure your rate of breathing. Those clips on your fingers measure heart rate and perspiration. The one around your arm—blood pressure. And the two on your head—brainwave activity. The last one monitors the neural activity in different cortexes of your brain. When you lie, some areas are more active than others than when you're telling the truth."

"Is that so?" I said, my eyes glazing with boredom.

No.

Exactly, No. Sure, my heart rate and so on were being monitored, but that machine wasn't reading my mind, other than to detect that my brain was working.

"Did you say something?" I said.

"I was saying this is a standard polygraph, or 'lie detector' test," he said. "Detecting deception is scientific. With this, I can tell whether you're being truthful or deceptive." He got up and pointed at the monitor over the window screen. "Just now, when you exaggerated about missing your lenses, your brainwaves in the anterior, dorsal, and parietal cortices of your brain spiked. So did your perspiration—you sweated more."

I sighed. "You sound like a weatherman."

He shrugged, returned to his chair, and touched a few invisible buttons over the table. "Do you *understand* … with this machine … I can tell whether you're telling the truth?"

I nodded.

"I need an audible answer."

"Yes."

"One of those tubes on your finger and the electrodes on your temples are more important. *Liars* may learn to control their breath and keep their blood pressure and heart rate constant. But *no one* can control their sweating or control their brainwaves. The perspiration monitor is most sensitive. It picks up on sweat that you wouldn't even notice."

I examined the devices on my finger and shrugged. "Okay." Boy, was I a sucker!

"Let's get started."

He asked questions about my birthdate, where I was born, my Social Security number and City Passport, and where I went

102

to kindergarten through present. I felt impatient, frustrated. I expected him to know all that stuff already, to get to the *good* stuff – UFOs, paranormal activity, exploding tanks, samurai swords, the riot! I belted out my answers, sometimes before he could finish the question, like I was on a game show, thinking more answers given, the closer I was to home.

When he finally got to his *real* questions, they weren't what I expected.

Chapter 17

Knowing where to look for a twelve-year-old in hindsight, I found Tabitha in the Teton Mountains.

"Morning, Tabby!"

Tabitha dropped the screwdriver. Screws bounced across the floor. "Aw, Lenny…" she said. She took off her green Red Sox cap and tossed it on the desk. Like me, she had a soft spot for pop culture relics, only she had never seen a game nor heard of Fenway Park. A yellow flame burned with golden translucence over the crown of her head, visible only to some, like me.

Lenny stepped into the shipping container and knelt down with her, swollen fingers hovering over the rotting plywood. He wanted to help but could only pretend.

"Sorry, little darling," he said, squinting. "I couldn't see these if they were as big as rocks." He tipped up his Giants ball cap, and wiped his brow with a red paisley handkerchief. A rash ran from forehead to cheek where his thick white beard began. "I just wanted you to know … there's a new load. Should be to the dump in fifteen minutes."

Tabitha shot a look at the digital clock above her work bench. "This'll wait." She pushed her chair under the desk and hooked the ball cap from the desk with the right stub of a forearm ending about six inches above where her wrist should have begun. She flipped the ball cap on with her left hand and pulled down the curled bill. "Let's get."

Clutching a backpack, she hurried down a narrow dirt walkway between two metal shipping containers, her strawberry blonde ponytail wiggling behind her. She took the handle of her faded plastic Radio Flyer wagon and peeked inside one of her dad's shipping containers. Esau was pushing a plane over a bare wood table. He was short and stocky, with a bald head ripe for a new shave.

"Hey, Dad!" He jumped, pushing the plane to the floor. "We're going to the dump."

"Sure thing, Tabby," Esau said. "Be back before sunset, though. Your mama's cookin' something special." He leaned to the side. "Oh! I didn't see you there, Lenny. You come, too, if you're hungry."

"Sure, sure," Lenny said. "Can I bring anything?" He always said that. Esau knew Lenny couldn't cook or see much. So he was always hungry. Lenny was as good as family, but if Esau didn't press him to come for dinner, Lenny would probably starve himself.

"Just yourself," Esau said.

"Come on!" said Tabitha, waving for Lenny to follow.

They arrived at the dump as the flatbed wagon arrived. Four longhorn steers pulled a twenty-foot galvanized metal container along a rutted dirt road. The driver stopped next to a long sun-bleached row of rusted sheet metal tables supported by chopped timber legs twined together in X's.

One of the wagon guys opened the container with bolt cutters, climbed inside, and tossed a gleaming white cardboard box to a woman with long red matted hair. A grey graphic was embossed on the top of the musty boxes—a sphere, halved through the middle, with a "C" and a "B" centered on either half. "Looks like more of those 'C-Bs'," she said, making quotation marks with her fingers.

A woman behind the table groaned. "Well, at least we'll be home for supper."

The other guy in the container threw out several more boxes onto the mud behind the wagon. He yelled out from deep inside the container. "Yep, they're all CBs! Nothing else."

Working double-time, the team of men and women unloaded the container in fire-drill fashion. The CB boxes were tossed to people at the tables, who slid them down to four people who threw them into a large pile.

Tabitha took one of the boxes and opened it on her knees. Inside, a CB, bound electrical plug, and connective wire were shrink-wrapped and placed side by side in the package.

"Take a look at this," she said with a whisper.

Lenny leaned over her shoulder. Though he saw little more than a blur, he nodded and said, "Umm, hmm."

"It's an older one—got two holes at the end instead of one. Hooks up to something."

Years ago, when the camp had found the first few containers of CBs, each box had contained only one CB and charger. Campers wore them for a while like jewelry. Their charm wore off after more than a dozen containers of them had been found.

"Don't you know what this means, Lenny?"

"Say little angel, you look like you've got a halo over yer head," Lenny said.

"It means…"

The soil under her feet vibrated with a low hum. The metal wagon pushed away from her like a polar-opposite magnet. The bulls went crazy and yanked against the yolk. The yellow flame swelled into a transparent sphere around Tabitha. She stood and closed her eyes with her arms stretched out to her side. "Lenny?"

"Yes, Tabby," He said his voice shaking.

"Do you feel that?"

"I don't feel nothing, Tabby. But you're all yellow."

An amber outline grew from her right forearm where her palm and fingers should be. "Lenny, Lenny, Lenny!" She gasped his name as if she'd been thrown into ice water. "I can feel my hand!"

As Lenny touched her shoulders, a loud thunderclap boomed and threw them to the ground. A Sundog bigger than the Teton Mountains approached from above.

Chapter 18

EVIL TAKES ROOT WHERE WISDOM DOES NOT. I STILL DON'T KNOW whether there really is such a thing as good or bad. Look at nature. Is a weed bad per se? It grows the same as any other plant, using sunlight, water, and nourishing soil, the main exception being that a weed survives and prospers by competing for resources, choking out other plants to survive. Like a sociopath, it will to do anything to get its way at the cost of others who would otherwise propagate in balance with their surroundings.

Jeremy Westcroft was like that. A weed. As a Sundog arrived in the Bay Area Prefecture, he sat at his kitchen table, his flopping black bangs dangling over a bowl of oatmeal. A jet black ball of smoke, burning without light, churned with malice over his head.

"I don't know what you've been up to, Jeremy," his father said. "Someone from Homeland Security contacted me this morning first thing." Mr. Westcroft twisted his fingers through the air.

A holographic image appeared in the middle of the kitchen table. A plain-faced guy in a dark grey suit, blue shirt and green-

and-white-striped tie was saying, "Mr. and Mrs. Westcroft. Please accompany your son, Jeremy Westcroft, to the Homeland Security Office in San Francisco no later than 10:30 a.m. today." Those government types all looked the same to me, monochromatic and soulless, indifferent to others. The address and directions followed.

"We have just enough time to make it there, Bucko," said Mr. Westcroft. "Now get your butt into your room and get ready."

"Why should I go?" said Jeremy. His hands lay palms down on either side of the bowl in front of a plate of white toast. The black flame slid off his forehead to the table. He was mesmerized by the malignant blackness as it danced around a steak knife next to a stick of butter on a coffee saucer. Fiddling with the System, his dad didn't notice.

His mom hunched her shoulder and bowed her head over the sink. "Just go, Jeremy," she said with a sigh. "Just go, for my sake." More than anything, she wanted her abusive husband and devil of a son to get out of the house, give her some rare peace at home.

"He's going, all right," said Mr. Westcroft. He straightened his navy blue tie and pressed his palms over his high tight hair.

"It's probably nothing," said Mrs. Westcroft. "They're just following up from before. Just checking in."

"It better be!" said Mr. Westcroft, clenching his fist at Jeremy. "Maybe *they* can teach him something I can't. Now Jeremy! Get your butt up out of that chair and go pack your things."

Jeremy pushed the chair back and eyed his father from under his hair. "Sure thing, Pops," he said with a grin.

Mr. Westcroft rushed at Jeremy and caught him in in the neck with an open palm, slamming him against the kitchen wall. His mother screamed, shaking her hands on either side of her face.

Jeremy slid to the floor.

"That's the last time you call me 'Pops'," said Mr. Westcroft.

Coughing, Jeremy got up with robotic movements. Resisting the urge to rub his throat, he dusted off his black trousers. "It certainly is," he said, wheezing. "It's the last time for a *lot* of things." He turned and went to his room stoically, leaving his parents alone with the dark flame.

The décor was minimalist—a spotless white desktop, empty shelves, and a cream bamboo dresser. His black backpack was hooked on a swivel desk chair. A single framed black and white poster—a classic photo of a Notre Dame gargoyle menacing at the distant Eiffel Tower—hung over his desk. It hardly looked like anyone lived there. In a way, that was true. Like most other people, his life existed mostly in the imaginary System world, courtesy of the CBs, where he'd learned to flourish by living off others.

He eased the door closed and sat on his bed. He held his head in his hands and ground his teeth. The room vibrated with a deep hum. From the kitchen, his mother yelled, "Earthquake!" An aura of curly black smoke formed around him. He lifted his eyes to the gargoyle and gritted his teeth. "*Pops, Pops, Pops! Now you do as I say!*" he hissed. "Go and slit Mom's throat with that steak knife there and then put it into your heart as hard as you can. Do you hear me? As hard as you can!"

A thunderclap blasted him from the bed against his desk. Gathering himself from the floor, he heard a loud scream and gurgling from the kitchen. A heavy thump followed another.

Jeremy went to the kitchen. His parents were dead, sprawled in swelling pools of blood.

Chapter 19

MARTIN PUSHED HIS GLASSES UP THE BRIDGE OF HIS NOSE. "EDITH, let's talk about the day the Sundogs arrived. Do you remember that day?"

"Yes." I thrummed my fingers on the leather armrest. He was finally getting to what I thought he wanted to talk about.

"Tell me what you remember."

"Okay. It was a Saturday morning. I'd slept in, as usual. But I could hear Irene messing around in her room through the wall."

"What was she doing?"

"She was at her desk dictating stories to a flat screen on the wall over her desk."

"She had a, flat screen? I didn't know they made those anymore."

"Yeah, Papa was a general manager at the factory making them. He could get them for below cost. No one was buying them anyway. Obsolete since the CBs came out. Papa didn't like us to use our CBs much. He was okay with the screens. He let us have them in our room but he still limited our time. We just couldn't have them on after 10:00 p.m., for more than two hours a day, or before we finished any homework. He was more laid back on the weekends."

"What was Irene dictating?"

"Stories, mostly. She's a big storyteller. Ever since we were babies. According to Papa, Irene babbled more than me. By the time we were toddlers, Irene was making up her own stories, usually based on something she'd already heard Papa read to us at night. Irene just jumbled them around a little. After Mama died, when we were in first grade, Papa stopped reading to us. Irene started making up her own stories."

"Do you remember any?"

"Well, back then, she'd repeat this story about a samurai warrior princess who had all kinds of supernatural powers. She was usually fighting off some demon, searching for her parents, or something."

"Why do you think she liked telling stories?"

"Growing up, Papa usually put us to bed. Both Mama and Papa worked full time, but Mama was usually home later than Papa. So, he put us to bed. He read to us every night."

"Did Irene have any favorites?"

"Definitely. The *Journey to the West* … you know … the one with the Monkey King? Papa had a children's version."

"What about later, when she started writing her own stories?"

"They were usually along the same lines—a mix of martial arts and science fiction. She loved the old-time movie superheroes from late twentieth century. The *Star Wars* and *Matrix* trilogies were her absolute favorites. She also loved old Hong Kong martial arts and older Japanese samurai movies. She watched *Inframan* and *The Seven Samurai* about a jillion times. She had movie posters all over the wall next to her flat screen. Several of her pen and ink drawings were there, too. She was pretty good. She's old fashioned, really, using real paper and ink, instead of computers. Irene said the characters were more real when she could feel them."

"So, on the day the Sundogs first came, Irene was dictating a story?"

"Yeah, she was in her room talking to the screen. Sometimes she'd stand there in front of it, swinging a kendo sword, nunchucks, or just her cane, spitting her story out as fast as she could. She'd play out the scene, looking pretty goofy, if you ask me.

"On that day, she was working up another one of her stories. I could hear the floor creaking, so I knew she was acting it out again. I lay there listening. It was about a samurai girl who could fly, and had an array of hand-held weapons. Her sword blasted through anything she swung at, moon-shaped blades shot out of her black-gloved fists and exploded. And she had powerful swords, of course. She could stop bullets and throw things around at will. All this sounded familiar to me, a mix of her favorite movies. She was working herself up into a frenzy about some fight scene. It was a good story and everything, except she was loud, and *I'd been sleeping. Hello?*

"I love post-modern music, as much as Irene loves her old movies. I'll listen to just about anything from the late 1960s to mid-2000s. I'm especially into New Wave stuff from the 1980's the most—Simple Minds, Missing Persons, Flock of Seagulls, Berlin, the Pretenders, Blondie, and so on—and some other hair and metal stuff—you know, Poison, Motley Crew, Winger, Metallica, Pantera, AC/DC, Iron Maiden, and so on—the usual."

Martin raised a soft fist in the air, and said, "Rock on. I like PoMM, too."

"Like who?"

"The Beatles on Monday morning, the Rolling Stones on Friday night."

"Cool," I said. *Gag me with a spoon!* I thought. I just wanted to laugh at him. He had no idea what music was about. "Yeah … anyway … Almost everyone at school had earbuds and the prescription lenses put in surgically. 'Not until you're a citizen at twenty-one,' Papa would say, 'then the choice is yours.' So I had to listen to my music through the old-style headphones. Wireless earbuds sound pretty good. I used to like them better. But then I actually preferred bigger, wireless headphones; the ones that cover my ears. They look cool and the sound is *mucho primo*. I ordered them with credits from a place in India still making them."

"The shipping must have cost more than the headphones," Martin said.

"Papa paid it. I guess he was just happy I had an interest that kept me off the CBs. Anyway, as I was saying … that morning … I could hear Irene working up one of her stories. So-and-so samurai girl was battling so-and-so demonic guy. Superpowers galore clashed—colorful lightning—arrays of glowing hand weapons—arrows, bullets, bombs and projectiles. There were fabulous, detailed costumes, which was my favorite part … not that I'd admit that to Irene.

"The only thing I wanted to tell her was 'Be quiet!' I rolled out of bed and dialed my headphones into a pair of wireless sound-plates on my wall. Papa's factory made those, too. I twisted a fat knob on the side of my headphones. The sound blared— *No More*

Words, by Berlin. I went to my closet and fingered through T-shirts and skirts. I pulled on a Blondie T-shirt I'd cut into a halter top.

"It didn't take long for Irene to push open my door with her cane. 'Turn off the music!' she said.

"I could see her from the closet in her maroon and black plaid flannel shirt and jeans. She had terrible fashion sense. A throwback to 1990s Grunge—her favorite music—the only kind of PoMM I can't stand. Her face was red and sweaty.

"I strutted out of my closet with my hands on my hips, screaming over the music. 'Keep your voice down, I can't hear my tunes!" I said. "Besides, it's Saturday! You're in there blabbering away, swinging your cane around like a wild child. I can't sleep!'

"Irene dropped her cane and held her hands to her ears. 'It's so loud I can't even think!'"

Martin raised an eyebrow. "She walks without her cane?"

"Well, yeah, sort of. She can cross a room on her own, but she'll need to take a rest about every fifty feet. I hate to see her walk. She used to be fine, like me. Now, when she walks, she yanks each leg across the floor, her hips and back twisting back and forth, as she tries to keep her balance with her cane. It makes me hurt just watching her wrench around like a crab.

"So, when Irene threw down her cane, I knew she was mad. And so was I. I said something like, 'That's the point, isn't it? Just stop!'"

"'Just put your stupid headphones on and shut up!'" she said. 'That's how you are all the time these days, anyway! You tune everything and everybody out like a shield!'"

"Shield? Do you realize how silly you sound? I tune *everything in* I want to hear, cowgirl!'"

"'You think you know everything!' Irene said."

"'I know everything I want to. Like I know you have a crush on *Simon*!' And he doesn't even exist!"

"Irene held her hands to her ears. 'Shut up! Shut up! Shut up! Just shut up!'"

"'That's what I'm saying,'" I said. I shot her with an invisible six-shooter and tipped the invisible brim of a ten-gallon hat. She blocked the shot with her forearm just as a deep vibration shuttered through our room. The two things were so well timed, for a moment I thought she'd caused the shaking. My headphones fell off the wall peg. The floor was moving like a funhouse. Just as I was about to lose my balance, a globe of blue and green light swelled and exploded around us. Irene and I were knocked to the floor away from each other. I fell on the bed. She caught herself in the doorway and collapsed on the floor. A mixed aquamarine dust dissipated through the air."

Martin calmly twisted an invisible Rubik's cube in the air. "Is that *exactly* what you said to each other?" he said.

No.

"Yeah, as best as I can remember."

Word for word, Martin repeated what I'd just told him. Everything I said was being recorded and transcribed to his screen as I spoke. "Is there anything else you or Irene said, just before the explosion?"

You know it's true! It's true, it's true! It's true!

The information was there, although I did not hear a voice. I'd actually forgotten I'd said it. After being reminded, by who knows what, I remembered I'd said it to Irene. I hesitated, glancing at the vault to see if someone else had entered. It was just Martin and me, and all the other untold white lab coats who were watching us from another room, of course.

"Are you okay?" Martin said.

"Yeah, I think I also yelled something else at her, just before the hum and bang." I told him what I'd said.

"And what did you mean by that?"

I shrugged. "I guess I meant it's all true."

"All of what?"

"Everything. Not just what I said about Simon, but what I'd said, and everything about the stories she was telling and everything."

"The stories she was telling that morning, or all of her stories?"

"All of it."

Chapter 20

WE'VE ALL SEEN HORROR MOVIES WHERE THE GOOD GIRL IS DOING exactly the wrong thing, walking into the woods by herself, not looking behind her, calling out into the darkness, "Is anyone there?" Well, yeah! The killer is right behind you stupid! What's wrong with you?

That's what President Martinez was doing when she stepped out of the freight elevator into a glassy black tunnel. Danger had been creeping up on her for a long time, so methodically and so slow that she hadn't noticed. Pretty much the story of most people back then. Distracted and numb from a constant barrage of overstimulation from CBs. Few recognized that they'd effectively given their minds over to systematized slavery. And those in power understood least of all. "They are watching you," people used to say, referring to a vague conspiracy of "them," including governments, corporations, or Masons, pulling everyone's strings. But as it turned out, "they" had become subject to their own methods of control.

Green, the president's chief of staff, whispered to her as

they followed General Reddy through the corridor. "I've never see anything like this, have you?" Six Secret Service agents walked with the president, ahead and behind. General Bishop and the other brassy-looking uniforms followed in a cloud of silence.

"There's something like this out at Mt. Weather," President Martinez said. "I'd heard there were some new bases. I had no idea they were this deep. The tunnel led to a small light rail train. "I certainly didn't know McConnell had an underground *train station*, of all things!" Tracks descended into blackness down another corridor. A smaller tunnel ran sideways from the train into the opposite wall. "Where on earth do they go?"

"Madam President, there is a secure conference room at the next level down," General Reddy said. "We'll have to take the train."

"The next level down?" Green said. "We've already taken two long elevator rides down. How many more levels are there?"

One of agents stepped close to the president, his finger on his ear. "We should wait for the rest of my team, Madam President. I don't have any contact with them at this level."

"I would certainly agree with that," said Green.

"Madam President, there's no need to go any farther without the others," General Bishop said. "We have a conference set up through here." He pointed to the smaller tunnel opposite the train.

"Why wasn't I informed of this?" General Reddy said.

General Bishop shrugged. "Just following the president's orders. Besides, we'll wait in there for the rest to follow while she checks in with Secretary Freight. Then we'll go on down to the central command station at the lower level."

Don't do it, Madam President! No! There's no use yelling at something like a television, of course. The good guy always looks in the closet where the killer is waiting.

The president nodded. "Let's go."

General Bishop led them through the small tunnel opening to a domed room the size of a small hangar, an oval conference table in the middle. Three rows of folding chairs lined up behind it.

"I'm sorry we couldn't arrange for something more formal," General Bishop said. "Here, we'll put you in touch with the other branches of government at Mt. Weather and the secretary's bunker at the Pentagon."

"Very well," the president said.

General Bishop pointed to a table at the left of the entrance. "Secure glasses and CBs for everyone. We've rerouted a new connection, just to be safe. You won't be able to see or hear anything without them."

As Green reached for a CB, he did a double-take at the side of the room opposite the tunnel entrance. Forty armed Marines, all of them dressed with visors and helmets, in exoskeleton suits, formed two staggered rows.

"What's with the goon squad?" Green said.

"Security, as always, security," Bishop said.

"I wasn't notified," Reddy said.

"Marines aren't your jurisdiction," Bishop said.

"They are as long as they're on my base," Reddy said.

"It's fine," the president said. She signaled to the agents who followed close to her back as she approached the table of CBs.

The president took a pair of glasses and a CB. The agents followed, fidgeting with the butts of their assault guns.

"Your agents need new CBs, too," Bishop said.

"They don't participate in conferences," the president said.

The president took a seat, slipping the new CB around her neck. She tossed the old CB on the table, popped out her old lenses, and put on the glasses. Green remained standing, holding the back of his chair. He cast an uneasy glance at the line of soldiers.

Reddy touched Green's elbow and whispered, "This level is mostly occupied by the Marines, anyway. Bishop is just being cautions with everything that's happening. He's also showing off his toys a little … for an audience with budgetary powers."

Green relaxed and sat next to the president.

Reddy joined Bishop at the back of the room.

"It'll be just a moment," Bishop said. "First, they'll test the system and then the conference will begin."

From the perspective of the president, a large tubular screen rose from the middle of the table. When it turned purple, everything in her vision washed purple, turning blue, and ran through the primary colors, flashing faster with high and low pitched sounds.

When the color cycle stopped, the president went off, talking like she was giving a formal speech. Two of the agents looked over their shoulders. Five of the Marines had edged in closer, to whom one of the agents said, "What's up?"

Reddy interrupted with chatter, talking to her husband, outlining her schedule for the rest of the day. Her conversation was certainly out of place during a presidential conference on national security.

The president kept talking. Not about UFOs, though, nor was she connected with anyone at Mt. Weather. She was going on about her support for the farm bill making its way through Congress. His assault weapon raised, one of the agents turned on Bishop.

"Now!" Bishop said. "Now, now, now!"

The line of Marines drew stun guns. Coils of wires with high voltage barbs hit the agents. As they collapsed, an agent fired a single shot, ricocheting through the room. The president went on with her speech. Green wore a placid smile, watching girls play volleyball on a virtual Maui beach.

Chapter 21

ROUTINE IS THE GATEWAY TO OBLIVION. YOU HAD GREAT DREAMS and aspirations before you started doing what you're doing now. You've been doing the same thing every morning. Getting up, putting your feet on the ground, taking a dump, brushing your teeth, looking in the mirror, and losing track of the daily progress of age and decay in the person looking back while those dreams and aspirations slip away with every-day concerns of commute traffic, staying on schedule, paying utility bills, buying and consuming. Day in, day out, the same blind efficiency. And where are you going? Nowhere. That's the point. You're wasting your life serving someone else's plan when all along you thought you were doing it for you. Along the way, you have brief moments of clarity. You may even resolve to change, make resolutions. Quickly forgotten. And they're supposed to be. False hope in self-renewal allows you to accept the status quo.

That was Papa's state of mind in the first year at Freedom Colony. In and out of funk. Sometimes faking it. Sometimes completely absorbed by the false CB world. He'd gotten pretty good at false chatter even when being mentally aware of his imprisonment. Other times he'd take a vacation from the internal battle against his horrible existence. Accept the false life shown to him through contact lenses. There were times he'd go weeks and months being lost in happy ignorance. But the System wasn't perfect and he'd sharpened his mind with kendo. When something seemed out of place, or the false world didn't mesh with the reality he'd buried deep in his mind, he'd snap back to full awareness – met by utter suffering – reason enough to give in again.

After a year of living this way, Papa was pulling another load of CBs through the maze of storage rooms, having a lively conference with a flat screen parts supplier who didn't exist. He turned into an expansive concrete hallway and met Coralee face to face.

He obeyed the voice to "stop and hold," still yammering on about rechargeable lithium batteries. Hands limp at his side, he stared through Coralee with indifference. "We'll need at least five thousand by Monday," he said, and, "We don't guarantee anything for workmanship ... No, no warranties," and so on. Gave me the chills the way his lifeless face spoke with spirited wit.

"How are we doing, *Papa?*" Coralee said, her grin cracking her lipstick, smeared beyond the corners of her mouth. She had a mirror – a fact that made me question her sanity.

"That'll be fine," he said. "Good talking to you, too. Okay, okay, okay. Next time. Yes, drinks! Sure, sure. But this time I'm buying. Bye, now."

Like a wound-up pitcher, she drew her fist behind her ear, holding it there with a grin, and hit him smack dab in the center of his nose. His head snapped back and forth like a flagpole in a storm.

She wrung her hand. A steady flow of blood came out of his nose and over his lips and dribbled down to the front of his green jumpsuit. Coralee watched this like a six-year-old waiting anxiously for a cherry bomb to explode on an anthill. Licking his lips would be a telltale sign that he was a *Live One*. A red line veined into his mouth and drooled out to the floor in a watery mix of coagulation.

"Well, Well," she said. "Look at you! I'd say you're doing just fine. Fine as wine!"

She manhandled his face, squeezing his cheeks and patting his forehead as she tapped her pumps like she was waiting for a frozen steak to thaw. Whatever she was looking for, she didn't find it. She stomped her heel and stepped back, waiting to see if he'd shift his weight or sigh, other signs of unauthorized awareness.

A mean grin stretched under flat eyes. "I forgot to tell you some news. Employees get so little mail here, after all. It's hard to keep up with family and friends. I know, I *really* do know. From time to time, I try to help people make the connection, keep abreast on current events."

She held a silver case of hand-rolled cigarettes out to Papa. "Smoke? ... No ... I guess not." She thumbed a small gold lighter and drew the gas flame into the cigarette tip with a long drag on the filter.

"You have two daughters. Edith and Irene. What *beautiful* names. *Really.* It must have been difficult to leave them behind for *this* place." With her index finger she tapped ashes on Papa's slip-on canvas shoes. "Still, I can see you like it here."

"*Irene*. Now there's a tough one. I hear she was quite

athletic. Into sword fighting and martial arts. Stuff like that. She *was,* anyway. Too bad, though. Irene's come down with some kind of bug. Got it from a flu shot, no less. Nearly completely paralyzed." Coralee shook her head and took another drag, studying his face for the slightest twitch. "I hear tell she spent two weeks in the hospital. They sent her home after a couple of weeks, expecting her to die, poor girl. She didn't, though. Like I said, she is tough. Tough, tough, tough.

"You probably know that, though. She got better. A little. She went to physical therapy for a bit. Then your insurance ran out. You know, I do think she could have benefited from a few more months of treatment. A few weeks is all they'll allow these days. She tried to do some self-therapy at home, I hear. She's tough, all right. Tough. She pretty much beat the disease. Now she's walking with a heavy limp. Got a cane and everything, like a polio victim. What is she, about sixteen now? She'll have her first prom soon. It'll be tough being the only pretty young girl who can't dance. *I'll bet she needed her papa through all that. I'll bet she cries for you at night.* Even though she *knows* you're dead." She flipped her half-smoked cigarette in Papa's face. "She's tough, though. Tough, tough, though."

I'm still trying to figure out a way to go back in time to smack her bony face. When I do, this part of the story will end differently.

She elbowed past him. The sound of her heels faded and the voice in his ear prompted him forward. A tear ran down his check to his lips. He licked it off.

Chapter 22

GREAT THINGS HAVE A WAY OF FINDING ORDINARY PEOPLE. LIKE seeds scattered across a rocky mountain, some find their way into the cracks and take root, slowly wedging their growth into grainy weaknesses, following moisture, before taking hold in an otherwise indomitable environment. Some seeds of greatness fall into the hearts of those with great potential but squander it. Others find the least likely person and, for good or evil, explode exponentially.

Greatness does not necessarily mean good. Hitler was great, if it has something to do with his effect on people and the world around him, no matter how hideous. In many ways, he was quite average. Not the kind of person you'd expect to change the world. He wasn't so smart, really. When I went back, asking the right questions, peeking in on his true history, learning the otherwise unknowable, it was amazing how every dark opportunity opened up to him at every turn, as if his rise to power, and resulting pain and suffering, were unavoidable. And this bothers me because it makes me wonder whether I can prevent bad things from happening. A question with no answer.

Yes, I've tried to change history. There's nothing I can do to prevent World War II, the plague, global warming, or other horrors that have been. Like Papa's past, no matter how much I try, changing it is not in my power, at least not as far as I know. Maybe I just haven't asked the right questions. More likely than not, it's another superunknown. There might be an answer, I just can't, or don't, know it. Yet.

While I don't really believe that there's such a thing as inherent good or bad, many of the great people on the righteous side of things also seem to have had every opportunity materialize to aid them in their rise to virtual sainthood. Gandhi and Martin Luther King Jr. come to mind. The more questions I asked about these two, knowing some things to go on in hindsight, I saw how perfectly things came together for them, like preordained cause and effect.

Little Miss Tabitha was like that, though she wasn't a Mother Teresa exactly. More like Amelia Earhart with a rocket launcher and an ammo dump of paranormal karma.

Lenny yelled after her. "Keep going, girl! Don't wait on me! Keep going!"

"Come on! Come on! Come on!" Tabitha said, waving her stump. The Sundog had arrived in Lizard Creek, bearing down on them from Teton Mountain crests.

Korea, Tabitha's mom, was waiting for them at the edge of camp. Tabitha huffed into her arms.

"I was so worried," Korea said, her curly red hair falling over Tabitha. "What is this world coming too?"

Lenny reached the entrance out of breath. "We ... were ... in

"... the ... dump," he said, wiping sweat from his cheeks. "Saw ... it ... coming."

Korea held Tabitha by the shoulders. "Go find your father. He's hollering through the whole camp for you."

"I'm getting a video of this!" Tabitha said. Before Korea could say anything, Tabitha darted between two containers.

Lenny looked over his shoulder at the Sundog with a sigh. "I'll go fetch him," he said.

"Walk, Lenny, walk!" Korea said. "Tabitha would have a heart attack if you had one."

Korea poked her head into Tabitha's metal container. "Honey, come to the smoke cellar now! Everyone's going to wait this out until we know what's going on with that huge thing ..." she pointed over her shoulder, "... floating ... up there."

A long wooden desk lined one side of the inner wall. Rows of shelving above were filled with all sorts of ancient electronic stuff: DVDs, VCRs, receivers, equalizers, game consoles, tape decks, and flat screens; all of it found new-in-the-box. Despite being over seventy years old, and radioactive, the devices worked, preserved from the elements by the sealed containers in which they'd been unearthed over several years by the residents of Lizard Creek.

Korea yelled. "Get out here! Now!"

"Found it!" Tabitha said. She turned on a halogen light bulb at the end of a hanging wire and pulled up a chair at her desk. She manhandled a large video recorder, twisting it every which way until she pushed the right button and it popped open. From the shelves, she found a shrink-wrapped VHS tape. "This is it."

As Tabitha bolted out of the container door, Korea grabbed her by the nape of her jacket. Tabitha pushed the stub of her right arm against Korea's forearm. "Mama, please, let me! I've been dreaming about this. I swear to you – *dreaming* about that thing up there. Please, please, please, let me video it." Tabitha wiped tears from her freckled cheeks. "Come with me, Mom. We'll stay right here at the end of the container. Just you and me this time! Please."

Korea ran her fingers over Tabitha's short ponytail. "I had a dream, too, Tab." Korea winked. "Okay ... but promise me we'll stay right here. Not any closer."

"Yeah, right here, Mom. I promise. Right here."

Chapter 23

WHILE HIS PARENTS BLED OUT IN THE KITCHEN, JEREMY STROLLED down a deserted sidewalk, his sleeves rolled up and with a knowing grin, toward a small gathering in front of the Speedy Night Market. Psychopaths take great pleasure in testing new ways of suffering on others.

He took a seat on a bus bench catty-corner from the market. Leaning forward on locked elbows, he watched a small group of people craning their necks up at the massive UFO floating over the city. Crowds of people on the sidewalk streamed around the gawkers. Oblivious to everything around them, few of the passers-by noticed the group of distracted people. Even fewer saw the UFO.

Some in the small group punched invisible buttons in the air between them and the UFO. They were trying to take pictures of the thing. When they searched for their photos on the System, they found nothing but clouds and blue skies.

Their voices carried to Jeremy.

"I can't see it in the video."

"Where is it?"

"I don't know."

"I keep uploading. All I see is blank sky."

"It's there," a man in a suit said. "I can see it! Right there!" He rubbed his eyes and looked back up. "Am I imagining things?"

The Sundog was much wider than the Marin Prefecture. Bigger than the greater San Francisco Bay Area Prefectures combined.

After several minutes, some lost interest and went away.

"Must be a glitch," a pizza deliveryman said.

"Yeah, the System's been pretty buggy lately," a biker said.

People were moving back into the flow of the crowd, either assuming the Sundog was a virus, a hoax, or a prank, or just not caring.

Jeremy stared intently at a tall bald man in a dark blue business suit, who was still trying to take photos with his CB, holding a coffee mug in the other hand. Jeremy's eyes swelled like he was about to pass a grapefruit. In frustration, he said, "Just do a head plant, you idiot!"

The bald man shuddered like he'd been hit by lightning. Without any hesitation or preparation, he jumped up and out at an angle, curled in with his hands back in a diver's tuck, still holding his mug, and dove into the sidewalk head first. No one around him noticed. The crowed just moved around him like schooling fish, giving the same indifference to him as everything else. He rolled around on the pavement half-conscious, people stepping over him.

The bald man sat up, blood gushing down his face. He wiped his cheeks with a kerchief. "Someone help me," he said. "Help!" As if shocked out of the System by the screaming, a heavy-set woman in jeans and a 49ers jersey stopped in her tracks behind him. Instead of noticing the bloody man at her feet, she looked up in shock and fiddled with her CB. "What the hell is that?" she said.

Under his breath, Jeremy said, "Hey, 49ers. Strangle Baldy."

A chilling stoic glaze fell over the woman's face. Like a robot carrying out instructions, without pause, she grabbed the hoop of the bald man's CB, and yanked as hard, twisting her fist to cinch it tight. The man dug at his neck. Apparently shocked out of the System by the macabre spectacle, a tall kid in a school uniform jolted to a stop. "What the hell are you doing, lady?" he said, and pulled at her curly blond hair.

"That's not how it's done," Jeremy said. "Punch her in the throat a few times as hard as you can." The basketball kid went blank and complied. Sure enough, the 49er lady stopped, gasping for air as she clawed at her collapsed windpipe.

"Hey, kid! Run out in front of that bus," Jeremy said.

The kid found the oncoming bus. With cool resolve, he did as he was told and died instantly, crushed on the street by heavy tires.

Jeremy's smile grew, muttering directions under his breath. The people he found in front of the Market exploded into bloody chaos.

Chapter 24

Gaining the subject's trust. Making them think that they are passing the test with each answer. These are key steps of any polygraph. After an hour of questioning, I wanted to cooperate, subconsciously accepting the idea that telling all would help me get out, that I would be rewarded for cooperation. Submission is the way to satisfy any desire, an idea that I was beginning to accept, if even just at the subconscious level. But a voice kept me from falling completely into blackness.

Martin's eyes bounced back and forth like he was watching a high-speed tennis match. I assumed he was reviewing the results of my first lie detector test. Minutes passed, which is a long time when you're wired up to a leather chair in a steel vault. I stole a look at him from the corner of my eyes. A bead of sweat rolled down his right temple and onto his lip. He ignored it. He was nervous for some reason.

"Edith?" he said. My legs and arms jolted. "I have a series

of simple questions I'd like to ask you. Let's review them first just to make sure you understand each question, Okay?"

"The sooner we get this over with the better," I said.

"You got it. Now, on this first run, let me know if you have any questions, to be sure you understand. After we go through this first set – call it a test run -- I'll ask these same questions three more times. Answer each of these questions quickly and succinctly. Just give the first answer that jumps into your mind. Okay?"

I nodded.

"I need an audible answer, please."

"Yes."

"Okay, what is your name?"

"Edith Nobutora Song."

"What is your sister's name?"

"Irene Nobutora Song."

"What is your *papa's* name?"

"Rory Jackson Lawson."

"What was your mother's name?"

"Helen Song."

"What year are you in school?"

"Senior."

He asked for my home address and prefecture I.D. I told him.

"Who is your favorite musical group?"

"Berlin." It really wasn't, I just blurted it out because I'd already mentioned it to Martin.

"Have you lied to me today?

"No." My stomach ached like it'd just been hit with a pound of meat loaf. Actually, I'd just lied to him about Berlin. I felt out of

140

control, losing confidence. I worried my little lies would keep me locked up.

"Have you ever stolen anything?"

"No." Another knee-jerk response. I swallowed phlegm at the back of my throat. My mind raced with uncertainty, thinking: *Well ... wait a minute ... didn't you steal nail polish from Margaret Mathers in third grade? But that wasn't stealing was it? I sort of just borrowed it.* I searched my past for other times ....

"Have you ever cheated on a test?"

"No." *Well, what do you mean, 'cheat,'* I thought.

"Have you ever smoked marijuana?"

Surprised, I hesitated, but told him the truth. "No."

"How did your father die?"

He didn't.

My heart nearly came out of my throat. The answer came to my head again. I couldn't help hesitating. "In a bus crash," I said.

Then he asked, "What do I have in my shirt pocket?"

A gold locket with a photograph of your four-year-old daughter, Brandy.

I frowned at him. Was he talking to me?

Nothing.

Did they insert ear buds into my ears while I was a sleep?

No.

I would have noticed ear buds in my ears. My hip hurt again, and I finally said, "How should I know?"

Martin yawned and stretched his arms as his fingers toyed with something invisible on the System over his desk. "I know some of these questions may seem unimportant to you, even strange. Several of the questions give me a baseline for honesty. For example, when I ask you for your name and address, I see how you react when you're telling the truth. And I know you don't know what's in my pocket. So, when I ask other questions, like whether you've ever cheated on an exam at school, I compare your reactions. Understand?"

"Yes."

"Did you understand all of my questions?"

"Yes."

"Good. Now, make yourself comfortable and let's run through these questions again."

I didn't feel comfortable. I'd been hooked up for over an hour with a sore butt. I reminded myself I just wanted to go home, out of this place, to see La-La and Irene, have some hot cocoa and forget everything, just move on. When Martin asked the questions again, I felt surer of my answers, more confident I would be walking out soon. The tone of my voice sounded steadier. I started to believe all of my answers, even the little white lies.

After asking the same questions three times, he gazed blankly at the space in front of him for several minutes. I examined the tube-clips on my fingers. The lights blinked randomly. I held out my arm, looked over the large plastic ring; it was cutting off circulation, making me sweat. I assumed the electrodes, or whatever they were supposed to be, were still attached to my temples, although I could hardly feel them. The silence of the room was oppressive, the only sounds my own breathing and the faint rustle of Martin's shirt. I closed my eyes and listened. The more I thought about it, the more convinced I was there should be more background noise; there wasn't any.

Mama had taught Irene and me how to meditate when we were kids. We cleared our minds and just focused on one of the five senses. Sometimes, when I just listened, I was surprised at how noisy a still house was; the central heating system, the creaking of the walls, humming from electronics, the wind. Now, in this vault, or whatever it was, there were no sounds from plumbing, no distant doors shutting, no muffled voices, no central heat and air, no nothing. My chest tightened. I'd assumed I was still in Oklahoma City, maybe at Tinker Air Force Base, but actually, I had no idea where I was.

Where am I? I thought.

29 Palms

Martin was still fiddling with thin air. *I don't see any palm trees around here*, I thought. Sounds like a beach resort. *What is 29 Palms?*

A deep underground military base.

How deep is it?

No answer. Instinctively I thought maybe I wasn't being specific enough. *How many feet is this room below the surface above?*

Three thousand two hundred forty-eight feet.

I could feel my heart pounding against my chest. For a moment, I thought I might throw up.

"Are you okay?" Martin said.

"I'm fine," I said, gripping the armrests with both hands. "I almost dozed off, and kinda snapped back, you know?"

"Sorry to take so long, Edith. I just wanted to confirm the good news."

"Can I go home now?"

"Not yet," he said, shaking his head. He crossed his arms and straightened his back; reminded me of Papa when he was proud of something I'd done. "But you're on your way. You did very well

143

with those first questions. Looks to me like you're being straight with me. If you keep this up we'll make a short day of this. Sound good?"

"Sounds great!"

"I still have a few more questions, as you might imagine."

"About the Sundogs?"

He nodded.

"Ask me anything, but I still don't know anything."

"We'll see."

Chapter 25

WE WERE CHOSEN AND I STILL DON'T KNOW WHY. I STILL DON'T who "we" all are, although I'm sure there are others. I don't know if there was some reason for the fire to land on us. I've asked, and like many other questions, but not most, there's simply no answer given. No response. As if the question is invalid. Without meaning. Makes me question my own existence. When I ask, *Do I exist?* I get nothing. It's not like I am nothing. Just empty. Not permanent. Ever changing. Not knowing but not without meaning.

Looking back on things, knowing what I know now, I see Nicholas Tosa, my love, stepping off a bus in front of the Walatowa Visitor's Center at the Jemez Pueblo. "Drive safe," he said to the empty automated passenger bus. From his parentless upbringing, he had a dry sense of humor. The double-swinging doors flipped closed. The steering wheel turned and the bus drove down Highway 4 toward Los Alamos.

His shoulder-length black hair whipped in the gusty wind. He carried a soft-case guitar bag with a built-in backpack to the opposite side of the road from the Visitor's Center. Red-faced rock bluffs ran along the highway, a stoic monument to all human activity that had come and gone from the deserted valley. To the west, thick clouds curled over the tips of low mountains presiding over a landscape of dry brush and dry creeks.

Sure enough. When I looked back, I saw he had the fire, too, a burning white-hot flame over his head. He was unaware of his shimmering blue-rimmed halo, though he could probably see it if he could just take a look over his head. Of course, he couldn't. He'd not been around a mirror in some time. Society discarded such things long ago, replaced by the false CB reflections. Most other people couldn't see his fire either, unless they had it, too, or the fire was about to come to fruition.

He crossed the dusty road to a curved platform supported by thick cedar beams. Extreme weather and sun had faded the turquoise paint from the ornamented flat-slatted roof. He threw his pack to the top of the platform, and climbed up, pushing up from a crumbling wall on the back side. He sat down next to his pack, unzipped a pocket, and took out a blue paisley handkerchief. He folded it around his nose and mouth, and tied a knot at the back of his head. With the blue blaze over his head and the mask, he reminded me of some kind of crazy Hell's Angel without wheels. His guitar was his ride. Took it with him everywhere he went, taking every opportunity to practice his chops.

Scanning across the road, he read the Visitor's Center sign aloud: "Welcome home." The west side of the adobe building had collapsed with the roof. No need to for urban renewal, since tourism had been replaced by virtual travel. People vacationed in their minds, courtesy of the System.

He grabbed a Plexiglas case from his pack and opened it with a click, pulling out a pair of wrap-around sunglasses with gradient smoky lenses. When connected to the System, the glasses were meant to surf web pages, make video calls, watch movies, listen to music -- the usual. It could all be accessed with a series of eye movements and blinks from a small screen projected inside the lenses. Before tourists stopped coming to the pueblo altogether, a visitor had traded Nicholas the glasses for one of his grandpa's hand-made pots at the community flea market. The glasses had an impressive on-board collection of music and old movies. The CBs replaced the glasses ages ago, since the glasses couldn't even connect to the System. Even if they were able to, the interface would be two-dimensional. Nicholas didn't want to connect. He listened to music alone, without the System's distracting images, and he liked it that way.

He unlaced a pair of polished black shoes and slipped them off, eyeing the scuffed leather before tossing them into the dirt with disgust. He yanked out a pair off-white python cowboy boots, slipped them on, and wiggled his toes. The skin on the sides was worn down to the unpatterned leather. Reaching into the side pocket of his pack, he hooked his index finger around a thin strand, and slid out a CB. He twirled it around his finger and flung it out into the desert. He zipped up his white down jacket and heaved the pack to his shoulder. With his thumbs tucked into the straps, he selected a song from his glasses: "Mountain Time," by Joe Bonamassa, live at the Beacon Theater in New York. One of my favorites. He jumped off the top of the platform, sliding to a stop across the gravelly dirt. He looked back up at the height of the platform with surprise, and said, "A little light on my feet," shaking his flaming head at the sky. Little did he know, how right he was.

147

"Don't start talking to yourself," he said, strolling down the centerline of the road. "People might think you're crazy or something. We wouldn't want that."

Bonamassa's music blared across the landscape. Nicholas was oblivious to the racket he was making. Sharing the dry wind with a soulful guitar lead, weeds and sagebrush forced their way up through veins of scattered cracks across the highway. The telephone and electric poles on the side of the road sagged left and right, their wires long since disconnected and broken. He walked for a mile, until reaching a grove of leafless trees at the edge of town. Doors opened and slammed with gusts of the wind. His heart stopped when he saw an old woman with wide eyes sitting on the porch of a rundown adobe near the road. Her thin blue dress fluttered with the wind. She sat near an open doorway leading into darkness. She raised her hand in a gentle high-five. No smile, probably beside herself with shock from the musical spectacle. He returned the wave, closed his eyes, and continued down the road, muting his music.

The road went up and curved to the right. He hung his head when he saw the high school. It had been a beautiful modern adobe once, light brown and red. The front of the building had been burnt and caved in. The rest of the structure was there but the insides were a mangle of twisted metal and half charred wood. "Well, I guess that's that," he said.

Three figures approached ahead. Like him, they had jeans and snake boots. Unlike him, they were all armed. The tall one in the middle wore a dusty black felt cowboy hat. He shouldered a Browning BLR lever action riffle with a scope. The other two had ponytails and long barrel pump shot guns. Nicholas pulled the handkerchief from his face.

The cowboy-hat guy said, "What the hell you want around here … what … dressed like a chicken and all?" A long scar jagged diagonally across his acne-pitted face.

"What business is it of yours … what … playing like cowboys and Indians and all?" Nicholas said.

The guy in the cowboy hat, Ruddy was his name, chuckled. "Guess you washed out of school." Ruddy was Nicholas's cousin. "What's with the white down jacket? That'd look better on my sister."

"What's with the cowboy hat, *Chief?*" Nicholas said with a smirk.

"He thinks he's the sheriff or something," Joe Armijo said, to the right of Ruddy. Joe wore a black down jacket over a denim shirt with black jeans and light tan lace-up work boots.

The other guy, Jesus Fragua, laughed. He rested his shotgun against his hunting jacket and patted the gun. "We're just out scouting for birds, foxes or whatever we catch moving. No game out here today, though. Somebody making a racket, sounded like a stereo or something. Scared everything off. You hear anything?"

"Nope," Nicholas said. "Quiet as a ghost town, save you three spooks."

"Things didn't work out for you at the bomb-factory high school, I guess," Ruddy said.

"Didn't," Nicholas said, searching the ground. "They're all sleepwalkers up there."

"I tried to tell you, ke-ya," Ruddy said.

"You're the turtle," Nicholas said.

"Yeah!" Joe said. "Nicholas beat Ruddy two years in a row

149

at the ten thousand meter." He chuckled at Ruddy. "You're the ke-ya, cowboy."

"Naw, I beat him at the hundred meter race," Ruddy said.

Jesus slapped Ruddy playfully across the chest with the back of his hand. "That was two years before, *son*. Nicholas beat you and everybody else in every race the next year. He won the Jemez Mountain 50-Miler the same year. You didn't even place … *ke-ya!*"

A long silence followed.

"I've been taking him water and food up there every three days or so," Ruddy said.

Nicholas turned eastward, squinting at a speck at the top of the mesa. It was his grandfather Chei's house."

Jesus slapped Ruddy again. "We've all been doing that, *son,* not only you."

Ruddy nodded. "I won't lie to, ya, Nicholas. He ain't doing well. The doctors won't even see him now. Said he was too sick. That's why I wrote ya."

"That's why *we* wrote," Jesus said. "You can't write!"

Ruddy said, "Chei tried to tell us not to. But we knew better. We knew you'd want to know."

Nicholas nodded at the ground. "You were right about that one." He sighed. "Where's Skinner?"

Ruddy pointed with the barrel of his rifle up towards the mountains. "Last we heard, he's up at the cabin toward the head of Ponderosa Valley, near the lookout."

"He won't let no one near the place," Jesus said. "So be careful if you're going up there."

"He didn't come around to see Chei?" Nicholas said.

They all shook their heads.

"You know how he is," Joe said.

"Yeah, I know," Nicholas said. He stared at Chei's house in the distance.

"I'd race ya up there," Ruddy said, "but I still need to bag some dinner."

"You couldn't bag your cousin," Jesus said laughing, "Lord, though, you've tried."

"Cut it out, Jesus," Ruddy said.

"Keep an eye out for mountain lions," Ruddy said.

Nicholas saluted and took off running.

Nicholas steadily jogged toward the top of the mesa. He kept his backpack tight against his chest, curling thumbs under the shoulder straps, the only sounds gravel and rocks underfoot, and his steady breathing. The neck of his guitar waved behind his flaming head. The pathway zigzagged back and forth up the face of the bluff. He quickened and his mind settled, running one with the landscape.

Reaching the top of the mesa, the mid-morning sun in his face, he breathed heavily but with control. He swallowed hard and stared at Chei's house. The windows were all open. White linen curtains blew softly in and out with the gentle wind. The adobe walls were cracked. He went to the porch and stopped at the entrance. The faded blue door had been taken off its hinges and tossed in the desert scrub in front. The dirt driveway was long since lost to nature. Footpaths led to and from the dwelling.

A tired voice came from inside the house. "You must be outta shape, boy! I can hear you breathing out there, boy." A long silence. "You gonna just stand there or come in?"

Through the front door, he took off his pack and set it on the buckled wood floor. He went to the kitchen. Chei sat in a large wooden rocking chair. His grey hair was tied back in a thick ponytail, bound at the back with a silver cuff. He had been barrel-chested, about five-foot-five inches, with strong arms and sturdy legs. He had weighed over two hundred twenty pounds the last time Nicholas had seen him, six months before. Since then, he'd wasted away to just a hundred pounds.

Chei stared at Nicholas with an open mouth.

"I haven't changed that much, have I?" Nicholas said.

"I can see you've got the fire," Chei said. He rubbed his eyes. "I just wish I could see it better for myself. Must be a sign my time is near."

Nicholas could sometimes be clueless. "You're gonna be fine," Nicholas said.

"Don't give me that," Chei said with a wheezing chest. "Don't kid yourself or me. Better to face the next life head on. Heck, after what I've been through, I welcome it."

Empty plastic gallon bottles were strewn around the floor, three full water jugs on the kitchen counter. Nicholas grabbed one and poured a glass for Chei.

"You drink it," Chei said. "From the sound of your huffing and puffing, you need it more than me."

Nicholas knew better than to argue with the man who'd raised him. He chugged the water and pulled up a footstool. He opened his mouth to say something. When he looked into the gaunt face of his dying grandfather, he cried.

Through deep coughing, Chei said, "Now, stop it! It's my time, that's all. It's my time. I don't want you crying about it again, you hear?"

Nicholas wiped his cheeks.

"I guess Ruddy told you?" Chei said.

"Yeah."

"I'll have to have a talk with those boys. They shouldn't have gotten you out of school."

Nicholas dropped his head. "It's just as well. You were right. They're all sleepwalkers in the Prefecture. They're sleepwalkers everywhere."

"Ever since you got those glasses and picked up that guitar, you wanted to know more about what's out there. But things aren't what they used be. People used to come here. As soon as they took on the Yokes, they stopped coming. Then most of our own went. Never saw any of them again. I thought I'd never see you again either, Nicholas."

"Everyone's got the Yokes there," Nicholas said. "They've got ahold of everyone. Can't do anything without them. Can't do homework, buy anything, eat anything, read anything – can't do nothing. I tried to use them. I put them on when I needed to do homework, but took them off as soon as I was done. I felt like they were doing something to me. I couldn't focus on anything anymore. I couldn't play the guitar even. I talked to myself sometimes. Everyone else wears them all the time. Heck, even sitting right next to someone, they'll talk to each other through the Yokes. If you do jumping jacks in the middle of a crowded room, no one will notice you."

Chei leaned forward and placed a shaky hand on Nicholas's shoulder and squeezed gently. "I'm proud of you, Nicholas. I'll admit, I was worried when you wanted to go. But you had to go see it, experience it, for yourself. Many have left Jemez and never come back. You're the only one who ever did." He leaned back and let out a sigh.

"They're still expecting me back, Chei. It seems they want me to pay back my education by working after school. I wouldn't have been issued a bus pass if Ruddy and the guys hadn't written to me." Nicholas hung his head. "I'm sorry for the things I said before I left."

"There's no need, Nicholas, there's no need. I'm just glad to see you before …"

"You're not going anywhere!"

"Don't kid yourself. The cancer's spread everywhere. I was supposed to be gone by last week. As bad as it is, I wish I was, except I wouldn't have seen you."

"What can I do for you, Chei?"

Chei turned to the window. "There's one thing, Nicholas."

"Anything."

"When I go, right away, burn this house down to the ground with my body in it. You hear me? Right to the ground. And quick. Don't try to salvage anything. Just burn everything. I don't want my spirit to be stranded around here. You hear me? I want to be sure to move on from this world."

Nicholas shrugged like it was nothing. "Sure, sure, I'll do it, burn it right to the ground. Right away. I swear."

Chei eased back in his chair. "I believe you. I know you will. You always do what you say. You're true to your word, even when you've got nothing good to say."

Nicholas hung his head and kicked an empty water jug on the floor.

"Aw, just spit it out, Nicholas," Chei said.

"Who are my parents?"

"The white woman taught our people the interconnectedness of everything. She turned into a white buffalo and left. Now she's returned. I found you on the mesa, when you were an infant, a white bison licking your face. You were just crying and crying. You had white hair before it turned black. You're the white buffalo, Nicholas. You're here to protect and unify us."

With an air of disbelief, he went to the kitchen sink, and tried the facet. "Is Skinner my Dad? I guess you're never going to tell me. I guess you don't have to."

Chei held his gaze at Nicholas. Tears welled in his eyes. "What I say is true, Nicholas, it's true. I know you don't believe me, but it's true. You'll see."

Nicholas went to Chei and leaned in to hug him. "I need a rest," Nicholas said. "Then I'll make us something to eat."

"Water and deer jerky is all I got. Compliments of Ruddy."

Nicholas nodded. He went to the worn couch in the front room and plopped down on his back, forcing a puff of stuffing from the sides of the green cushions. Crossing his arms, he faded into sleep with the cool dry morning breeze flowing over his face from the open door and windows.

He jolted awake. "How long have I been asleep?" he said under his breath.

He went into the kitchen and opened a cabinet. "Where did you say the jerky was?"

When he turned, Chei was slumped in his chair.

Nicholas rushed to him. He was dead. Nicholas closed

his eyes. "Go in peace. I believe you, if that's what you want. It's true."

A white aura swelled from the flame over his head and grew around Nicholas with a low hum. He went to the front room. Visible through the open window, from the east, rising in the sky with the mid-morning sun, something as big as a mountain, dark and menacing, approached. He opened his backpack and strapped on his electric guitar, a white Fender Stratocaster with a maple fret board. He put on his glasses with earplugs and ran a wire into the back of the guitar. With a silver pick, he struck the strings, blazing into the soulful notes of "Little Wing" by Stevie Ray Vaughn. The notes came deep and slow at first; the sound faint and flat, without amplification. As he played, his thick fingers crawled across the guitar neck with pull-offs and hammer-ons. The sound grew louder and fuller with reckless abandonment. The space around him waved with each riff like ripples in a pond.

His head rolled back and tears came down his checks. The deep sounds from his guitar grew warm at first and then turned hot. With each riff, the wood floor under his snake boots smoked. A sliver of wood ignited like a match. A wash of white on blue fire flowed from under his heels like a bucket of ignited gasoline thrown across the floor. The entire room blazed, the flames licking up the sides of the walls. White-hot fire poured out of every window in the house and engulfed the roof. Untouched by the fire, he played on in the living-room-turned-crucible, the house falling down into burning coals around him. For miles around, a bonfire could be seen on top of the mesa.

If anyone was awake in Jemez, though, they were watching the Sundog approach.

Chapter 26

REVEALING THE TRUTH IS IMPOSSIBLE IN A LIE WITHIN A WEB OF lies. Right and wrong are the same. You can't distinguish between the two when someone else holds all the keys to insight. Freedom and choice become illusions. That's fundamental to the System. Lulling you into believing you're making a choice. Once you believe that, you embrace prison, even learn to love it. How do you know you're not incarcerated now? When you put your feet on the cold floor tomorrow morning, ask yourself, *What would I do today given the choice?* Probably not sit behind a desk, stand behind a counter, stock shelves, talk on the phone, nor any manner of manual labor. You can't stop checking messages, skimming webpages, or shopping on-line. You can't say "no" to them, can you? You're in a prison and you don't know it. Like Irene.

Irene scrolled through the list of "true" and "false" questions. She tapped her holographic answers hanging mid-air over her desk and scrolled to the next question. The question:

"Who suggested the subject of the novel, *Dead Souls* to Nikolai Gogol?"

The choices:

"a) Gogol himself

b) Leo Tolstoy;

c) Alexander Pushkin

d) None of the above"

She pointed to "c". "Alexander Pushkin," and turned green. The next multiple-choice screen scrolled up. She finished the ten questions. "100%" appeared in mid-air.

A transparent image of Ms. Croucher, our homeroom and literature teacher, in silky white with grey-blonde hair in a bun, appeared at the front of the classroom. With a perky voice and bright eyes, she told everyone to read *Heart of a Dog* by Mikhail Bulgakov.

Ms. Croucher faded. Irene and the rest of the class skimmed a summary of the novel. The real Ms. Croucher, the one of flesh and blood, sat behind a tin desk at the front of the room, wiggling her bony fingers through the air, oblivious to the re-play of her voice and image, recorded years ago.

She smelled of musty clothes and tired perfume; a shadow of her recorded self, her eyes depressed and distracted.

We heard the school bell ring through our ear buds.

"Have a good day," Ms. Croucher said, hunched over her desk. A perky projection of Ms. Croucher appeared next to the seated Mrs. Croucher, and said, "Have a good day!" singing the word "day."

The students ignored both Ms. Crouchers.

Irene pushed herself up from the brushed metal school desk

and took her cane, its aluminum shaft supported by four short stubby tubes with black rubber knobs that squeaked across the floor. Her hips swayed like oblong wagon wheels about to come unhinged. Students flowed around her, talking over, but not with, each other.

When Irene reached the door to the hallway, a voice in her ear said, "Main hallway. Turn right." She skulked across the floor watching *Seven Samurai*, transparent, in-motion images overlaying her view.

A voice in her ear said, "Alert! Stop and hold."

Simon Thorp stepped in her way as her eyes followed the movie action.

"How'd you do on the quiz, Irene?" Simon said.

"Quiz?" Irene looked right and left until she saw him. "Oh, hi, Simon."

"Yeah, quiz. On Gogol. I only got one out of five." His blond hair was buzzed on the sides, sort of retro 1980s. He had a crush on Irene, even after her legs got sick. She still wouldn't give him the time of day.

As Simon stood in front of Irene, the ghostly images of samurai were slicing blades through his neck.

"I pretty much guess "c" any time I don't know the answer on a multiple choice," Simon said. "I figure I'll make at least twenty-five percent right over time."

A black-and-white samurai held a *katana* sword high over his head, screamed, "AAAAAAAAAAAAAAAAAAAAAAAhhhhh!," and charged through Simon.

Irene smiled. "That's a failing average," she said, her tone condescending.

"Yeah, yeah, you're probably right. I just figured it'd

be worse if I guessed randomly." He tapped his foot for some acknowledgement.

"I've got to go," she said. "My bus is leaving."

"Yeah ... yeah, me, too." He turned and left.

On the bus, Irene cycled through endless System views. With each flick of her finger, her surroundings changed: she sat at the edge of the Grand Canyon, watching the sunset; she stood on the sidelines of a kendo match; a manga artist demonstrated ink nibs; Inframan, in a red leather outfit and bug-eyed red helmet, shot blades out of his black gloves at Princess Dragon Mom, a blond Asian dragoness with a wicked temper. Irene divided her view into six curved stage slices of a pie from the side; on her left, she'd added a live concert (previously recorded) of Pearl Jam, the sound muted; and a documentary on samurai *bushido*. A news ticker at the bottom of her view announced an earthquake in California. She enlarged one of the stages and said, "Search, effects of earthquake. A row of videos came up; there was one about volcanoes. She said, "Search, super volcanoes." A list of calderas in North America came up. One was in California. She searched for "Yosemite". A result choice included "beach vacations". Before long she was watching a video about surfing culture in Hawaii. From her perspective, a surfer caught a tube down the center aisle of the bus.

Getting off the bus, several kids walked ahead of her along the narrow roadway. She twisted her back, dragging her legs up the street. Her cane scraped across the pavement with each crooked stride; the rubber knobs had rubbed down to the aluminum. She tripped at the curb walkway leading to our house. She caught herself with both hands, but her left knee slammed to the ground. She bit her lip and pressed herself back up. At the side of the house, she keyed in the twelve-digit security passkey. The door unlocked and opened with a beep.

Other than the glowing salt lamps on the table of Buddhas, the large wood-floored *dojo* was dark. La-La had put a Buddhist altar on the long narrow table. The air was smoky with incense. Three sets of dusty kendo protector suits sat against the wall with several bamboo swords lined up nearby in a rack. A small kendo shrine hung from the wall at the back. There was also an empty stand where Papa's *katana* and *wakizashi* swords once hung.

Irene struggled up the stairs from the *dojo* to the kitchen, made it to the second floor in a sweat, and into her room, tossing her bag onto her unmade bed. Sketches of forgotten anime characters covered her desk, which was strewn with dry ink pens. She plopped into the desk chair and faced the wall of posters, blinded by the changing System views. Manipulating the screens, her hands waved like a zombie trying to dogpaddle. As far as I was concerned, that wasn't far from the truth. I'd seen enough.

I slid the samurai blade under her CB loop at the back of her neck and pulled. The CB fell to the floor. Its green light faded and died. The voice in her ear said, "Check connection."

Irene's eyes batted like sand had been thrown in her face. She spun around at me and said, "What the *hell* are you doing?"

"I'm doing you a favor," I said. I held the *wakizashi* blade in my right hand, the sheath in my left.

She leaned over her knees, grunting after the CB, "I didn't see you at school today."

"I was sitting next to you all day."

She reached for the CB and hesitated.

"I came home with you, on the bus, as usual," I said. "Where were you, Irene?"

She snagged the CB, examined it, and dropped it as she slumped in her chair. "Just leave me alone."

"Let's go to the *dojo*."

"For what?"

"kendo, of course."

She snapped her head at me, her mouth contorted with pain. "Look at me!" Tears spattered over her trembling lips. She slapped the backs of her thin legs with feeble hands. "I said, look at my legs! They're crocked! I can barely walk! And you want me to do kendo?"

A tear rolled down my cheek. "I *see* you. I *see* someone who's given up. I *see* my sister, Irene. She's drowning. Her head is just below the surface. It's not too late, though. I'll take her hand. I'll help … just a little. But she has to help herself. If she doesn't start swimming, if she doesn't do something, anything, soon, she's going to drown."

I held the tip of the sword an inch from her nose.

"This was on our front steps today," I said. "Someone mailed it, addressed to us. You stepped right past it. You didn't even see it. You're not seeing a lot of things these days. Now *see* this!"

I twisted the blade to Irene. It was Papa's sword. Across the blade's side, in black marker, was written in Papa's hand, "I will see you again in mountains."

Chapter 27

PAPA LAY ON HIS BACK ON THE CONCRETE SLAB IN HIS CELL. IT was January and freezing cold. He'd been at Freedom Colony for a year. Months had passed since Coralee had met him in the factory hallway. He'd been doing his job, on schedule, without distraction, since then. He'd eaten his food, taken his showers, used the toilet, and taken his three-hour naps between eight-hour work shifts, and, all the while, blabbering on with phantom conversations, constantly pelted with numbing images of a life back home which no longer existed.

Every morning he was woken by a voice in his ear and told to go the factory fifteen minutes before the other workers arrived. Pallets would be waiting for him, leftovers from the day before, to be prepared for shipping before the work shift. He normally took the elevator alone to the first floor, and made his way from Apartment Block 8 down the causeway toward the factory. He would pass the administrative building on the way. It had the appearance of an apartment building, except for an "Administration" sign over the entrance. He often saw Coralee in the afternoons, standing at the end of the sidewalk leading from the causeway to the building, watching the masses of Employees flow from the factory back to their apartments. She'd smile, crossing her arms, like she was proud of them. Every so often (and it was rare) she saw someone take open notice of her. That someone would spend more time in Processing. If they were there more than once, they might not come back.

On this particular day, he got up and did his usual routine: picking up in the middle of a conversation, taking a dump, brushing his teeth, showering, and grabbing a fresh jumpsuit from a pile by the elevators. When he pressed the elevator button, though, nothing happened. He stood there for a minute, waiting; a voice told him to take the stairs. On the way, he tripped head over heels. Gathering himself, he stood, and kept going.

Underneath his jumpsuit, his shin was bleeding. He didn't acknowledge it. Just outside the exit from the apartment block stairwell on the sidewalk, the voice said, "Go down the stairs." He halted in mid-stride. He stopped talking and squinted. He looked left and right. The voice said, "Go down the stairs." He grasped at his neck. The CB was gone.

Rubbing his hands, he ran to the stairwell, climbed two flights up where he found the CB. He picked it up and made his way back to the sidewalk. As he went down the causeway, he turned his head to the administration building.

There was not a cloud in the sky, and the air was breezy and below freezing. He shivered, stopped, and gaped at the administration building.

"*Irene*," he said, his voice cracking. "*Edith*."

On impulse, he dropped the CB in the gravel off the causeway, and fast-walked up the sidewalk to the entrance of Administration. As he went into the stairwell and climbed, the voice in his ear said, "Go to the factory."

He ran up the stairs, out of breath by the time he reached Level 4. At Level 8 he peeked out the open stairwell. Maroon carpet led down a hallway of open doors. A nuked Employee shambled by. He slid in behind her, following closely down the hall. Nameplates hung outside the rooms. "Mr. Rusty" was one. He followed the Employee through a door at the end of the hallway. Coralee's name adorned the entrance.

"Go to the factory," the voice said.

He stepped to the left as they entered. The Employee continued to an expansive wooden desk with thin wooden legs. She placed a tray holding a steaming cup of tea on the credenza behind the desk and turned to leave. Papa must have been horrified to see Coralee sitting at the desk.

"Thank you so much, dear," she said sweetly to the Employee.

The Employee, Sarah Roberts, turned to leave the room, her glazed eyes fixed ahead. She didn't notice Papa. Once she was parallel with him at the doorway, Coralee said, "Hey, you! Hold it!"

"Go to the factory."

Coralee seemed to be talking right at him. He was standing right in front of her on the other side of the room as she spoke. Coralee worked her fingers like she was kneading bread dough in space over her desk.

Sarah stopped.

"Come back here and take this tray," Coralee said. "You didn't bring the lemon scone."

"Go to the factory."

Papa stepped behind Sarah as she turned to Coralee. As Sarah took the tray from the credenza, Papa stepped behind Coralee. Sarah turned and shuffled out of the room. With his back to Coralee, he stared at the wall. His *katana* and *wakizashi* swords hung there under soft amber light.

"Go to the factory."

Coralee hummed and grunted at something to herself. Papa carefully took the *katana* sword. Holding it to his left side, his thumb on the guard, he turned and faced Coralee's back. She was leaned over her desk. He unsheathed the sword silently. Rage gripped his face as he readied the blade high over his head to strike. Papa's swelling black pupils bore into the papery skin of the back of her pulsing neck.

"Go to the factory."

His eyes narrowed. He sheathed the blade.

Papa could see down the hallway from behind Coralee. Sarah was coming back from the far end of the hall. He turned, took the shorter blade from the display, and ran both swords up his sleeves.

As Sarah returned to the desk, Papa stepped out of her way. She placed a cup of tea and a separate saucer with a scone on the credenza. Papa shadowed her opposite side from Coralee and then stepped in front of her on the way out of Coralee's office.

At the entrance, Coralee said, "Hold it, you!"

Papa and Sarah stopped.

"I just wanted to say just how much I appreciate you, Sarah. I hope you know."

Silence.

Papa heard in his ear: "Go to the factory. Employee. Go to the factory. Employee. Go to the factory."

"Go on, now, shoo!" Coralee said.

Papa walked ahead of Sarah down the hall. He darted to the side as they reached the stairwell.

"Employee. Go to the factory. Employee. Go to the factory. Employee. Go to the factory."

He'd worked up a thick sweat by the time he reached the first floor. Once outside to the sidewalk, he slowed down to his usual zombified pace. The sweat frosted. As he approached the causeway he could see the CB was where he'd left it. When voices approached behind him, he took to walking in small circles around the CB.

"There he is," Mr. Rusty said.

Papa kept circling.

Mr. Rusty approached and grabbed Papa roughly by the chin. He forced Papa's face left and right, and pried open his mouth. He pulled down Papa's lower eyelid, and then pushed open his upper lid with his thumbs. Cheek to cheek with Papa, Mr. Rusty glared into his eye.

"Yep, his lenses are still in," Mr. Rusty said.

Mr. Rusty pulled on Papa's earlobe.

"He's got his buds in, too."

"What's wrong with 'em?" one of the guards said.

Mr. Rusty spotted the CB. He picked it up, examined it, and clipped it around Papa's neck. He stepped back, and said, "Whew! You stink!" He swiped a finger across Papa's forehead and down his cheek. "Yeah, you're sweating like a pig!"

Papa proceeded down the causeway as usual.

"A lot of sweat, just walking around in little circles out here," one of the guards said. "I mean … it's freezing out here."

Mr. Rusty shrugged. "This happens from time to time. Some of the older ones, ones who've been hooked into the System the longest, become a little antsy if they're unhooked suddenly. Their hearts start pumping, fast. Some have strokes." He started back to Administration. The other guards followed. Near the entrance, Mr. Rusty turned and watched Papa skulking toward the factory in the distance.

Once Papa made it to the factory floor, he retrieved a pallet jack as usual, loaded a pallet of CBs, and pulled it into the maze of corridors. Following the voice, he pushed open a sliding door into a storage room.

At the back of the room, near the sliding cargo doors, there were small carts with shipping supplies. He stopped at one of the carts, drew out the swords, and laid them across the floor side-by-side. Snatching a box-cutter from the cart, he sliced open the plastic wrapping around the pallet of boxes, and lined three loose CB boxes on the floor. He grabbed a role of shipping tape and taped the boxes together. He sliced through the top of the boxes crudely and grabbed the short blade. He held it pensively.

"Employee. Proceed."

He grabbed a black marker, yanked out the blade, and wrote, "I will see you again in mountains." He snapped the blade back into its sheath, and forced it into the gash in the boxes.

"Employee. Proceed."

He tapped the boxes closed and addressed it, "Irene & Edith Song," with our home address in Oklahoma City.

Papa tossed the box on top of the pallet, returned the shipping

168

supplies, and pushed the pallet next to a long row of other pallets.

He pulled the pallet jack back to the Factory floor for another load. Mr. Rusty was waiting.

"Stop, Employee," Mr. Rusty said.

Papa stopped. Mr. Rusty unzipped the front of Papa's jumpsuit and yanked it down to his ankles. With his hands behind his back, Mr. Rusty circled Papa, examining his nakedness up and down. "Why so slow today, Employee?"

No reply.

"You don't look sick to me." Mr. Rusty stepped closer, nose-to-nose with Papa. "I scanned your file on the way over here. One more distraction and your employment is terminated. I like to think everyone gets a break, though. Besides, I'm not in the mood for another firing today. And then there's the cleanup."

Mr. Rusty stepped back. "Pull up your jumpsuit, zip it up, and go back to work."

Papa complied.

The marked CB boxes containing the short blade were still sitting on top of the pallet of CBs where he'd left it. The *katana* blade was there, too, lying next to the boxes. He'd probably left it there by accident. Good thing, otherwise Mr. Rusty surely would have terminated Papa.

Facing the address down, Papa set the three boxes containing the short blade on top of the pallet, and taped the plastic wrap in place. Papa slipped the long sword into his sleeve.

Weeks later, the *wakizashi* blade was delivered to our door by regular mail.

Chapter 28

SHORTLY AFTER KILLING HIS PARENTS AND SLAUGHTERING A FEW strangers on the roadside, Jeremy hummed a tune, strolling down the grassy median of Miller Avenue. He had the bright look of someone on a shopping spree in a gun store after winning the lottery. A large passenger bus approached from the two-lane street on his left. Another hummed at him over his shoulder. Looking back and forth at them, he said, "Drive into each other."

The buses passed him, whipping his hair wildly around his face.

He gritted his teeth. "Crap!" he said. People who crave power are never satisfied. He still didn't know the full scope of his abilities, which hadn't come with an instruction manual, but as it turned out, he had limits, like the rest of us supers. The buses were automated. He had no control over the inanimate, just user access.

The super-huge UFO floated from the ocean, moving eastward. Its rim cut through the sky over Mill Valley. Jeremy kept to the median, eyeing the floating inverted mountain with guarded curiosity. Once reaching the intersection of Camino Alto, he stopped in the shade under a clump of redwoods and watched the traffic. Mostly buses and a few municipal vehicles, dump trucks, street cleaners, and windowless personnel carriers. As the light turned yellow, he sprinted to the middle of the intersection and stopped, facing the arched entrance to Tamalpais High School, home of the Red Tailed Hawks.

Even knowing what I know now, I hoped he'd get run over. But traffic stopped anyway. Traffic swelled on either side of the intersection, public transportation passengers busily carrying out the day's CB affairs, unaware of the traffic jam. Most people out and about were completely oblivious to their surroundings, defenseless against unperceived threats. Steps ran from the arched entrance of the school up a hill to a two-story yellow administration building with a clock tower. Faded classroom buildings sprawled around the hillside.

He skulked at the school until he noticed a large military transport jet flying at the edge of the UFO overhead. He said, "Right there," and then pointed to the clock tower. "Crash into that spot!" Given his abilities, with the power to create great joy and harmony and the world around him, it was sad the way he opted for horrifying destruction at every opportunity.

The transport jerked off course and dropped into a nose drive. A high-pitched whine zeroed in toward him. The plane was bigger than he'd realized. The piloted gunship with high-caliber weapons and lasers mounted on its sides came in, out of control, over Miller Street. It plowed diagonally across the overgrown football field. The fuselage slid sideways past the end zone and burst into black clouds and flames. The fireball and wreckage roared across the baseball

172

field toward the school entrance. Jeremy stood in its way. He turned and ran.

A large flaming jet engine tore into the redwoods as he dove past them and into the concrete ditch. The wreckage stopped at the archway of the school, except for a tire that smashed through a side window of the administration building.

Wet and muddy, he walked back to the center of the intersection, surveying the wreckage. "This'll wait," he said.

With much of the traffic cleared, another bus was coming. Jeremy went to the bus stop in front of the school and pressed the virtual call button hovering over the curb. Too busy on the System, people in the bus didn't even notice the crash scene. They certainly had no idea that a devil had joined them for their last ride. The door closed and the bus went onward down Miller Avenue. The sign at the front of the bus read: "San Francisco." The final destination for the bus riders.

Chapter 29

AFTER LEAVING HIS DAUGHTER'S FUNERAL, MARTIN TOOK AN automated government bus to the front entrance of the campus of the Central Intelligence Agency just outside of Washington, D.C. Within a forty-foot thick concrete wall surrounding the sprawling CIA grounds, a twenty-foot black wrought-iron fence, topped with coils of razor wire, was wrapped around the new Headquarters Building, made from white marble in the shape of a massive, stair-stepped pyramid. Funny how the government's HQ of spying looked like Freedom Colony. But it was no accident.

Employees flowed from the bus and were funneled into a short Plexiglas tube, scanned for weapons, devices, digital information and anything else of interest. At the end, an expansive row of individual booths awaited Martin, where he inserted his CB in a crystal socket. A faint green laser ran up and down his face, and he pushed through a revolving door, greeted by a beefy gauntlet of soldiers in exoskeleton suits wearing helmets with black visors, clutching short assault rifles to their chests.

"What's up with this?" he said under his breath. He had never seen such a goon squad on CIA-controlled soil. Especially not Marines. Only Paramilitary Operatives in the Special Operations Division had jurisdiction over security threats there.

A female voice in his ear said, "Martin Lorien, Deputy Director of the Director of the Central Intelligence Agency. Good afternoon." Also hearing his identification, one of the soldiers stepped into his path.

Martin raised his eyebrows at the soldiers. "Everything okay?" he said.

"Martin Lorien," the soldier said. His face muscles bulged, pressing overgrown cheeks against the underside of his dark visor.

"That's me. Why are you here?"

The soldier said, "Proceed to the Headquarters Auditorium for a National Announcement."

Martin raised his eyebrows. "What *announcement* might that be?"

"You'll find out at the auditorium."

"Sure, right after I go to my office." Martin started around the soldier.

Two more soldiers stepped in his way.

"All senior personnel are to go directly to the auditorium," the soldier said.

"I will go to my office first," Martin said pointing at the headquarters entrance behind the soldier.

"You'll proceed to the auditorium," the soldier said.

"Do you know who I am, soldier?"

"You are Martin Lorien, a Deputy Director of the Central Intelligence Agency."

Martin glared at the soldiers. "I don't see any rank on you, soldier."

No response.

"What's the matter? Just a private? If that's so, you've got no authority over me, Private. And Marines have no jurisdiction here. Now step out of my way."

The soldier flexed his back. He took a step forward, bumping into Martin. "I'm under orders to take you to the auditorium by *any* means necessary." ·

Martin stared into the soldier's dark visor, finding detached eyes there. The kind that look but do not see. Knowing that the soldier had been conditioned to mindlessly carry out any order, impervious to any reasonable discussion, Martin turned and followed the sidewalk to the North.

After the path doglegged down the east side of the building past rows of parked shipping trucks, someone called his name in a hushed voice. Rachel Bluewater, the CIA Director, waved to him from a narrow space between two shipping trucks. He darted to her, keeping his head low. They shuffled through rows of vehicles and huddled behind a garbage dumpster.

"What the hell is going on?" Martin said. "They wouldn't even let me in the building."

"It's Freight!" Bluewater said. She had on a long silk and wool windowpane skirt and white oxford shirt with the sleeves rolled up to her elbows. Her dark brown hair was pulled back in a messy bun. She blew a few strands out of her face. "He's going to announce to the nation the president's dead. Freight's in charge … for now."

"He can't do that! We don't know where the president is."

"We don't know where the vice president's plane is either. His plane supposedly went missing on its way to Mount Weather. But it doesn't matter. As long as the president's missing, Freight's running things. And there's no one to ask questions."

Martin put his hand against the side of one of the dumpster and hung his head. "Except us, if it's not too late." By that point, he probably felt a little like Papa upon his arrival at Freedom Colony, shocked with realization that he'd found himself in a prison.

"Which explains why these Neanderthals are here," she said, fixing her bun. "After today's announcement, you can bet there'll be no questions. Heck, most won't even remember what's happened."

A soldier took a heavy step from the other side of the dumpster. He smiled and tipped his helmet. "Director ... *Deputy*," he said. "I'm sorry to interrupt. But you'll miss the announcement if you don't *keep moving*." A threat, not a courtesy announcement.

Known as "the Bubble," the ceiling of the Headquarters Auditorium's igloo-shaped structure arched overhead in a dome covered on the inside with large plaster disks enhancing the sound. Originally designed in the 1950s, it had been renovated and rewired multiple times.

A bald woman in a grey suit checked each Employee at the door, two soldiers backing her up with merciless stares. Two more soldiers were stationed at the top and bottom of each center and outer aisle. The woman shined a green black light over into Bluewater's eyes and both ears. She grabbed Bluewater's CB and held it to the end of the light, which beeped and said, "Rachel Bluewater, Director, Central Intelligence Agency." Stone-faced, the woman said, "Thank you, Madam Director. There's a seat for you at the front of the room."

Bluewater made her way down one of the center aisles while Martin was also checked in. "Where are your lenses?" the woman said to Martin.

He took off his plastic-framed glasses and twirled them between his thumb and index finger. "I'm one of the lucky ones -- can't wear contacts." He handed her the glasses. "They're paired to my CB."

She took the lenses and passed the light over them, followed by a beep. Stretching her thin lips over polished white teeth, she smiled. "Be sure to keep them on," she said, and handed the glasses back to Martin. "There's a seat for you in the media booth here at the back."

"Whatever *you* say," Martin said.

Chapter 30

WHILE MARTIN WAS HUDDLING WITH THE CIA DIRECTOR BESIDE the dumpster just before the announcement, Tabitha wrestled with a spaghetti of wires under the workbench in her container. By nature, catastrophes are unexpected. However the one about to be wrought by her was indubitably positive, if still painful for those still under the System's thumb.

"You can put the space saucer on this thing?" Lenny said, squinting close at the dark face of an ancient flat screen television.

"I can put my *video* on it," Tabitha said. "I can put *us* on it." She snaked an electric cord down back of the bench and plugged it in. Her right stump pushed the wires around.

Korea stood just inside the container entrance crossing her arms, looking a little disappointed that Lenny had returned, interrupting her rare one-on-one time with her daughter. "Okay, Tabitha," she said. "Let's get to the smokehouse now that we have the video. Let's look at it later. That thing out there …"

Not hearing Korea, Lenny nodded at the shelves of blank

screens. "But the only moving pictures you ever shown me were of other people somewhere else."

"Movies, Lenny, they're called movies. This will be a movie, too, *our* movie. You're going to be in the movies."

"Well, didn't I film it?" Korea said, sounding perturbed for not getting credit.

"Girl, I don't believe that!" Lenny said.

"You just wait and see!" said Tabitha. Clutching a knot of wires, she crawled out from under the bench. Examining the wire ends, she said, "These ain't the ones I need."

She went to the far end of the container to a tall stack of electronic devices several feet thick. She pulled out a DVD player, jostling the electronics.

"Be careful, girl," Lenny said.

Korea threw up her hands and walked out.

Tabitha yanked a wire with multi-colored prongs from the back of the DVD player. "This is it! This is what I'm looking for!"

She hurried to the bench and fingered three wires into color-coded sockets, pressing down on the base of the large flat screen with her stump as she plugged the wires from the video camera into sockets below the front of the screen.

"Okay, then, let's see if it all works."

"I have no doubt," Lenny said.

Tabitha pushed a button at the bottom of the screen and flipped a switch on the side of the recorder. The screen faded to a wall of blue. As the recorder hummed to life, the blue screen revealed white lettering: "Play," "Pause," "Stop," "Rec," "Rev," and "FF"; symbols pulsed beneath each.

"It's a mystery to me," Tabitha said. She examined the video recorder. "This first button matches the one on the screen." She pushed it.

The screen came to life with static dissolving to a jumpy video of Tabitha.

"Hey, that's you!" Lenny said.

"Hey Mom, Look!" Tabitha said, turning. But Korea was gone. She sighed, "Mom's going to go crazy when she sees this!"

The video zoomed back. Behind Tabitha, the Grand Teton Mountain range rolled majestically across the screen. A large UFO hung over head like a reflection of the mountain beneath it.

Lenny leaned on the workbench. The CB box she'd found that day fell, knocking a wire across the floor.

"Oh, my God!" Tabitha said.

Lenny held his hands up. "Sorry, I'm sure it's not broken. There's more of those things at the dump."

Tabitha grabbed his arm. "You're a genius!" Tabitha said.

"Well, if you say so."

She fetched the wire, unraveled it, and plugged it into the end into the television. "See! Look at this, Lenny. We can hook up the CB. Maybe we can show the video with others."

"But those things never worked."

"They will now."

Chapter 31

I CAN'T READ MINDS. NOT AS FAR AS I KNOW. EVEN SO, WHEN I look back in on my polygraph test, I'm pretty sure Martin suspected I wasn't telling him everything. Even with the ability to know the answer to any question asked, intuition is sometimes more reliable. One thing's for sure, mind reading or no—polygraphers don't like you asking any questions. They think it's a form of deception. An instant fail, if you ask too many. In fact, it just a control thing.

"You were saying before there was a big bang and you and Irene were thrown to the floor," Martin said.

"Yes," I said.

"Tell me what happened next. Step by step."

Eager to finish the questions and get home, I nodded. "Sure, sure. La-La was yelling something from the back of the house. I groaned. At first I thought she'd heard the bang in our room. I looked out my window and saw her waving for us to come out. I thought maybe something was on fire. I told Irene, slipped on some jeans and met them outside. La-La and Irene were frozen like pillars in the back next to a koi pond."

Martin groaned. "Ponds are *illegal*."

I shrugged. "Tell Papa that. Anyway, there was a huge halo around the mid-morning sun. Instead of one sun, though, there were three. At first, I didn't know what I was seeing. I figured it was like a rainbow or something. Beautiful and everything, but I was tired. As I turned to go back inside, I saw the look on Irene's face. Pale fear. La-La had been rambling something in Chinese but her voice trailed off. I turned. There were things in the sky coming from the extra suns. And they were getting big. I'm sure you remember. Did you see them when they first came?"

Yes.

"What did you think they were?" Martin said.

"You mean the UFOs?" I said.

He ran his fingers through the air again. "Please just answer the question."

"I froze and watched. I thought my eyes were playing tricks on me. I waited for my eyes to clear up. I thought the vision would fade. Didn't happen. The more I watched, the clearer I could see them. Almost all the UFOs went off in different directions. But one of them —a big UFO —came towards us."

"The UFOs," I said, chuckling under my breath. "I saw a UFO! … Look at that UFO! … I knew what I was seeing. Still, saying it out loud makes me laugh. The whole idea still sounds silly, even after seeing it with my own eyes. When I was looking right at it I couldn't believe it.

"One came right down over Oklahoma City. Big as an anvil thunderhead. Bigger than a mountain! It was *too* big, really. You know, when you see movies or hear stories about UFOs, they're usually the size of a small disk or ship or whatever, crashed in a field. A couple of skinny guys with bug-eyes get out. They kidnap someone or hook up with a friendless kid. A UFO is something that fits in a government jet hanger, like at Area 51. Not something as big as a city, up there floating around, saying 'Hey, here I am —a *big* spaceship—you can't miss me *now. In ... your ... face! And now that we're here, we're just going to hang out and chill ... in ... your ... face! We ain't doin' nothing. We're just gonna watch you watchin' us!*"

"Why do you call them 'spaceships'?" Martin said.

"I don't know. That's just what people assumed. The UFOs, Sundogs, or whatever, must be a ship from outer space. I didn't know what they were and I still don't. What do you think they are?"

"What happened next?" Martin said.

"The thing just kept getting bigger and bigger as it came closer. It must have been going super-fast, considering how big it was. It was almost as large as Oklahoma City, if not larger.

"We just stood outside like a bunch of dummies, watching the thing for I don't know how long. Something in the back of my mind said, *Hey, your arms are numb!* I woke up to how cold it was. I only had on a pair of jeans and that Blondie T-shirt. I went inside to put on a jacket. I looked out the kitchen window to double-check I'd really seen it. And it was still there. La-La and Irene came in behind me as I turned on the flat screen in the living room.

"Irene surfed through the few news and social sites that could still be accessed from the screen. Some sites mentioned the Sundogs, but only in viral videos of talking dogs, dancing babies, and wedding bloopers. You'd think there'd be *millions* of UFO videos.

187

There weren't. Thousands, maybe, but only a few were reported. Other videos were posted on social feeds. But you know what the CBs showed."

"Nothing," Martin said with a grin. His face turned pale and his poker face returned, probably mad at himself that he'd answered one of my questions.

"Nothing! Right? The few that mentioned the UFOs described the same thing we were seeing over Oklahoma City. But when I heard what they were saying, it sounded nutty. There were UFOs over San Francisco, Santa Fe, Colorado Springs. One up in Wyoming somewhere. Also a few in Japan, some in and around China, and a few in Europe and some in South America. Argentina, I think.

"The reports about UFOs described the same thing we had here in Oklahoma City. Views of mountain ranges, cities and county sides -- all of them with clear blue skies or clouds, sometimes with people pointing overhead. No UFOs! I looked at the thing out the window and I wondered if I was imagining it.

"Did you think you were going crazy?" Martin said.

"Well, I tested it myself. I stepped outside again, and pointed the CB to the UFO to make a video. I recorded a few seconds, came back inside played it through the flat screen. Nothing but a lonely white cloud meandering across a blue sky."

"I went back outside, and took slow, careful steps, one after the other, doing walking meditation on the gravel pathway, thinking carefully about each step. I spun around at the sky again, thinking I could force myself to wake up from a delusion with a dose of mindfulness. The UFO was still there. I scrutinized it for a few more minutes. Not my imagination. I could see it. It had to be there. For real. So, no, I wasn't going crazy.

"I hurried back inside and plopped on the sofa with La-La and Irene. La-La sat with crossed arms on a footstool watching Irene channel surf. Most of the news sites didn't mention the UFOs. One referred to a UFO 'hoax'. A few reported a mirage over San Francisco, and then put up some videos of clear skies over the Golden Gate Bridge. Other reports concluded that people had mistaken Sundogs for UFOs, which is what people started calling them. End of story.

"I told Irene what I thought. She was wondering, too, whether our eyes were playing tricks on us.

"La-La seemed to have the gist of what we were saying. She pointed to the sky out the window and said, 'No mind.' Not sure if she was making a statement or asking a question.

"As if reading each other's thoughts, Irene and I jumped up and went outside again. La-La shuffled after us. We just stood there for several minutes, craning our necks at the thing. 'I'm not imagining that,' Irene said.

"'No way,' I said.

"'No mind,' La-La said.

"What makes you think you weren't imagining it?" Martin said.

"If we were imagining it then what blew away your goon squad?"

Martin wiggled his fingers through the air. No response. But I thought I saw a smirk.

"What did you do next, Edith?" Martin said. He sounded sarcastic.

"We were getting scared. That huge thing, just hanging there, as big as the city, made us feel like anything could happen. *Anything*.

I don't know what La-La or Irene were thinking, but the more I stared at the Sundog over Oklahoma City, the more my imagination went wild.

"What if the thing landed and the doors opened up? I thought, sure, nice aliens might step out and tell us the secrets to the universe, or a bunch of monsters might come out, eat us all alive, and move into our houses."

"How do you know that didn't happen?" Martin said.

I didn't like where he was going, so I just ignored him. "I think La-La could feel our fear. She insisted we all go to the *dojo* to meditate. La-La used it for a Chan room when she moved in. She had arranged the altar on a long table with a Shakyamuni Buddha in the middle, and two Bodhisattvas, Guan Yin and Manjusri, on either side. Her statue of Manjusri had a large flaming sword in his right hand. A large incense pot sat at the front of the altar. We lit three sticks of incense and took turns praying in front of each Bodhisattva and the Buddha, putting them into the pot. She prayed for a long time in front of Manjusri.

"What did your grandmother pray for?"

"I don't know, she usually mumbled fast in Chinese, although I could hear our names, and Papa's and Mama's. Then, La-La wanted us to meditate for about fifteen minutes."

"What was that about -- meditation?" Martin said.

"Well, usually, we just sat down on our meditation cushions, crossed our legs, cleared our heads, and counted each breath, one though ten, over and over to focus our mind."

"Are you counting your breath now?"

I started to say "no," but I had to think about it. I'd been practicing meditation for so long, I counted my breath all the time, naturally, whatever I was doing. I said, "Well, maybe a little, but not consciously. Mama taught us to meditate like that when we were kids, before she died. So it's part of me."

Martin ground his teeth and twisted the air with tense fingers. "Go on."

"At first, I didn't even want to sit. All I could think about was those UFOs and all my questions and fears. But then I just wanted to forget about them, too. I wanted to just focus my mind and see if the UFOs were still there when we were done."

"Were they still there afterwards?"

"As clear as day."

"Did the Sundog ever communicate with you?"

I laughed. "I guess not."

"What do you mean, you 'guess'?"

"I don't know. I guess in a way it was saying, *'Hey! Look at me, I'm here!'* All I know is I could see it."

"Do you know if anyone else could see it?"

"I went to the front window to get a better look at the thing. Even though it blacked out most of the eastern sky, no one was out there in their front yards looking up. The street was eerily quiet, empty except for one person. Mrs. Caprock stood alone in the middle of the street wearing a trench coat over her nightgown. She had on snow boots and a wool hat, and she was swaying back and forth like a ghost. I yelled at Irene to come outside to help her."

"Who was Mrs. Caprock?"

"Our neighbor. She lived alone and we sort of kept an eye on her, helped her around the house after her husband left."

"What happened to Mr. Caprock?" Martin said.

He was transferred to the Freedom Colony, Western Kansas.

Trying to ignore my inner voice, I said, "Buddy was his name. I just heard he died, a heart attack or something."

"Did you go to the funeral?"

"Papa said there hadn't been a funeral or anything. Apparently all of their family were out of town and couldn't travel to the city. There was just a small memorial later; that was it."

"Did Mrs. Caprock ever tell you what happened to her husband?"

"No. We just understood Buddy was gone; he'd died. Anyway, once we got outside, Irene hugged Mrs. Caprock, who nearly fell over.

"'Are you okay, Mrs. Caprock?' Irene said.

"We were standing just under the outer rim of the UFO, which was blocking the sun. Wiping away her tears, Mrs. Caprock kept looking at the UFO, then back at Irene, holding her forearm to block the sun.

"'There's no shadow,' Mrs. Caprock said.

"I couldn't believe it. The UFO blocked the mid-morning sun, but it cast no shadow. The ground was in direct sunlight. I held out my arms. I could see sunlight on my hands, and my own shadow, for that matter. I closed my eyes and lifted my chin. I could even feel warmth from the sun on my face. When I opened my eyes, thought, I still couldn't see the sun. I could see the UFO—an inverted heap of charcoal pancakes fit for a giant. Still, it was like the Sundog wasn't there.

"I looked back and forth from the UFO to the shadowless ground several times," I said.

"Mrs. Caprock was shivering, so we took her to our house to warm her up. La-La was still flipping through new channels, most of which had gone back to reporting viral videos and crime stories. The screen buzzed, 'Emergency announcement in two minutes!' We flipped through the channels, finding the message blaring everywhere with a count-down ticker.

"When the time ran out, a serious guy in a military uniform, with narrow eyes and grey hair, appeared and said the reports of UFOs were a hoax. He said the United States was under a cyber-attack. Separate planes carrying the president and vice president of the United States, and a bunch of other important people, had crashed, killing everyone on board. He said the UFOs seen by some in the sky were actually holographic images projected by our hacked CBs to cause fear and panic. But we shouldn't panic, he said. The UFOs weren't real. That's why they didn't show up on CB videos. We could verify the hoax by the fact the UFOs didn't cast a shadow. According to him, the government was fighting back. Then he wanted us all to sing the national anthem. Of all the stupid things! An over-dub of voices started singing and morphed into high-pitched hums. Strobe lights alternated in different colors. That's when everything went crazy.

"I started feeling sick and dizzy. The emergency announcement broke off and was replaced by a grainy video of a strawberry-blonde little girl with a ponytail and a Red Sox cap in front of a backdrop of mountains. At first I thought it was a joke. This little girl was pointing behind her and waving her arms back and forth. She was so happy, like she was about to come unglued. She said something like, 'Hello everyone. My name is Tabitha. I live in Lizard Creek, Wyoming. This is my home.' She smiled gleefully as she made rabbit ears with her fingers and jumped them up and down across the screen, like it was show-and-tell at school. I wondered whether the little girl actually knew her image was being projected to every CB on planet Earth. Of course, no one cared much about that little girl. Everyone did care that her video clearly showed a UFO floating over the mountains just behind her. The video zoomed in and out from the UFO, covering every visible inch of the thing. It was just like the one over our house.

"Then the video broke off. I fell to my hands and knees and puked my guts out like I'd just been let out of an out-of-control circus ride. I kept heaving until nothing came out. When I finally stopped, sitting on my hands and knees, I saw that Irene and Mrs. Caprock had had the same gross response. And trust me -- it was *gross*. The whole floor around us was covered with puke."

"Why do you say the video was projected to everyone on Earth?"

It's the truth.

I was a little peeved he didn't care to talk about all the puking. "Well, it seemed like everyone in our neighborhood saw it at least. That's when we heard the growing roar."

"Roar?"

"Yeah, at first it sounded like a few voices outside. But it turned into a riot. Wiping puke off my face, I got up and went back outside. Irene, Mrs. Caprock, and La-La followed. Up and down the street, people were running out of their houses. Covered in vomit, they looked like they were escaping burning buildings without any smoke or fire. Some were literally running around in circles in their front yard, just screaming."

"What were they yelling about?"

"Once we got out into the street, we could hear them yelling things like, 'Turn it back on, turn it back on, turn it back on!' or a combination of, 'What happened?,' 'Where is it?' or 'Come back!' There was this one guy down the street, a lawyer, holding his head with both hands, shouting, 'Hey now! Just hold it!' over and over, like he was trying to stop someone from slowly driving a knife into his chest.

"People flooded into the streets. Most of them ran around yelling like chickens with their heads cut off. Some of them looked up, seeing the UFO for the first time. As the crowds grew, more people were saying things like, 'Hey, what the hell is that thing?' still trying to get their CB to work, trying to take pictures. Others shouted, 'Is that real?' 'What is it?' and so on.

"A loud boom cut through the shouting from overhead. I almost expected to see lasers or something coming from the UFO, burning up people and things. Instead there were several white streaks of smoke making a beeline towards the UFO, which just moved out of the way. I couldn't believe how fast it was—unnatural. Almost like watching a film with sections snipped out to artificially speed things up. Something that big just isn't supposed to do that. And there was no sound either, other than the roar from the missiles, or whatever they were. It seemed clear the government actually *did* believe the UFOs were real. I mean, they were shooting at the things."

"During the whole time you were outside, did the Sundog do anything to Irene?" Martin said.

"Like what?"

"Did it try to communicate with her?"

I shrugged. "Nothing that I noticed."

"You didn't see anything unusual?"

"Other than a gargantuan UFO, a mid-air missile strike, and a puke-drenched mob yelling in middle of the street?"

Martin shifted in his seat. "Okay, bad question. What happened next?"

"Armored vehicles entered the front gate of the Prefecture. One drove right down the middle of our street through the crowd. A soldier in body armor surveyed the masses from a large mounted turret on top. As it came closer, we could hear a loud speaker blaring, 'Return to your homes. The System will be restored shortly.'"

"Everyone turned toward their houses as the armored vehicle passed. We were making our way back to the house when the earthquake hit."

Chapter 32

Shortly after Tabitha's breakout video and the earthquakes, Martin was staring himself down in the mirror of the CIA men's bathroom. He held his wet face over the sink and leaned on both hands, probably wondering where things had gone wrong. All of the toilets behind him were filled with heaving spy guys.

Martin splashed water over his face. Gazing into the reflection of his own dark pupils, he said, "Is this real?"

A man in grey trousers next to him loosened his tie and said, "That's exactly how I feel." He splashed water over his hair and dabbed his scalp with a wad of paper towels. "That was some System glitch there. I felt like my brain was about to come out of my head."

"Is that what it was, a 'glitch'?" Martin said.

The guy looked sideways at Martin with a doubtful expression.

Martin eyed the other guy's CB lying next to the sink. "If I were you, I wouldn't put that on for a while."

A voice in his ear said, "Go to the Headquarters Auditorium."

They smiled at each other in the mirror.

"I ain't going anywhere SAL," the guy said, referring to the nickname CIA operators had given to the System voice.

A female voice—human this time—broke in over an intercom speaker system. "Cancel that," she said. It was Bluewater. "Return to your workstations and wait for orders." Her voice cracked off and broke back in. " … And take off your CBs and lenses! Leave in your earbuds until further notice. I'm sure you'll know the difference between me and a computer."

"Sometimes I wonder," the guy said.

"I know what you mean," said Martin, "Just don't tell her."

On the way to his office, Bluewater's voice chimed in his earbuds, "Meet me in the bubble on Sublevel 4."

Off the elevator, the foyer wasn't much bigger than a walk-in closet. A tired brunette sat behind a thick glass window. Two heavily armed paramilitary men in suits, wearing bulletproof vests and helmets, crowded her back.

"Go to the auditorium," the SAL voice in his ear said.

"Hello, Mr. Lorien," the woman said. "Please insert your CB and I'll buzz you through."

Producing a CB from his pocket, he stuck it into a socket in the wall. A siren went off.

"Don't worry. You're cleared, even though it's telling these two guys to detain you." She hesitated. "Oh, and you must be special. It's also telling them to terminate your employment with extreme prejudice."

The door buzzed open.

"I'm glad you're on our side," Martin said, probably wondering whether she knew one 'side' from the another.

The white hallway beyond the door stretched for over fifty yards to his left and right. He went right. Every so often, someone exited a door, shifted their eyes nervously, hurried down to another door, pressed some digits into a keypad, and looked around again, entering. Such paranoid little minions ignored Martin, seeing and hearing only what they were told.

He turned left at a T, walked another twenty-five yards to a crossroads of the hallways, and turned right. Seven doors down, he pushed through an entrance to a janitor's room. Bottles of cleaning solution, rags, and sponges lined metal shelves around the wall. Three metal sinks were bolted down in the middle. Two paramilitary types with bulletproof vests gripped short assault weapons, guarding a door at the other side of the room.

"Bluewater?"

The blond waved Martin forward.

The other one, a redhead, pointed to a metal box on the side of a sink filled with water. "Put your CB, earbuds, glasses, and any electronic devices you've got in the box," he said.

Martin tossed everything in. The redhead patted him down and searched his ears, nose, and mouth. The blond guy closed the box and dropped it into a sink.

"Stand against the wall with your face toward us," the blond said. Martin held his hands over his head as the redhead shined a beam of blue light over Martin from head to toe, told him to turn, and repeated the process. "Clear," the flashlight said.

"You can go in now," the blond said.

Martin opened the door, revealing Bluewater in a small

closet with a metal drain in the middle. Wet mops hung from the wall, giving off a pungent smell. She stepped out of the way for him to close the door.

"People will start talking if we keep meeting this way," Martin said.

"At least people will be talking to each other," Bluewater said.

"What the hell happened in the auditorium?"

"Do you remember Project Animal Farm?"

Martin shook his head and paused, half-forgotten memories seeping back. "Oh, yeah. It was a Psy-Ops program used to keep the Colonies under control, years ago after the mass migrations from the flooded coasts. The riots got out of control. It was introduced via the CBs. Kept everyone distracted, pacified, even satisfied."

Bluewater nodded. "You remember more than I figured. But tell me this, do you remember where you were this morning?"

"Sure, I was at the Pentagon with you and Secretary Freight."

"Well, no. You weren't. Not exactly. Don't you remember?"

Martin shook his head at the floor. "At home I guess."

"Martin, for God's sake, you were at your daughter's funeral! You attended the meeting at the Pentagon from there."

He squeezed his eyes with his thumb and index finger.

"Do you remember her name?" Bluewater said.

His lips quivered and contorted. He cried without tears. He finally said, "Brandy?" Tears came as he held a hand over his face. "Brandy, Brandy, Brandy. Forgive me. I can't believe I forgot you. Forgive me."

"Martin, this is happening to *everyone, everywhere*. At

least – here in the United States—as far as we know. You may not remember everything … I'm not sure I do yet … but Project Animal Farm was a Department of Defense project. At first, it was supposed to only be used in the colonies. But then the economy tanked, food shortages came, and rioting spread. People lost their jobs and houses en masse. The unrest in the colonies moved to the prefectures. The prior administrations, and Congress, got scared. Animal Farm was applied to the prefectures and anyone using a CB. Social unrest turned to widespread bliss. The economy picked up. There was a new source of cheap labor and it came with a bonus—complete cooperation. The CBs already presented a System view that overlaid everything—the public already trusted it, wanted it, needed to have the things they wanted—entertainment, shopping, blogging, whatever—so they were more susceptible to its controls. Long ago, it was said, 'The medium is the message.' *How true.* And the message is control."

"Who created Animal Farm?"

"You did, Martin."

The blood drained out of his face. He put his hand against the wall. "If there's anything else you have to tell me that's going to shatter my world, please just tell me now."

"There are things I've forgotten, too, Martin. There's probably going to be more to come. But I saw this coming for some time." Bluewater rubbed her forehead. "It was little things at first. I noticed I was forgetting names, dates, appointments—things I should remember."

"That's typical."

"Yes, but then I began to forget people who had left the agency, who had gone to a Colony, the policies of the last administration, projects I'd worked on a few months back, et cetera, et cetera. The things I'd forgotten were cherry-picked out of my mind."

"How did you know?"

"By chance. I had an old tape recorder in my office. It was a gift from an old colleague, a spy gear relic, hidden in an antique rotary telephone. I was playing with it one day, and just for kicks, started keeping a journal once a week—just a summary—of what'd I'd done. I'd review it at the end of each month. After a couple of months, I forgot about the tapes. Several months passed. I came across the tapes by accident and listened to them for kicks. I couldn't believe my ears. It was like I was listening to a stranger. The tape was analog, so it couldn't be manipulated by the digital system. That's when I knew, for sure, my memories had been changed or erased. Which brings me to what happened today."

"The *tapes*," Martin said with a weighty tone. "*Tabitha*."

Bluewater nodded. "That's right," she said, "*Tabitha*. Her video (if she was acting alone) was analog, like my tape, physically recorded, not digital. You wouldn't think a simple analog video could disrupt a global system. Whatever she did, she may have the key to undoing Animal Farm. No offense, Martin, but your little project was just *too* good."

"The question for me, though, is how did my 'little project' wind up in the hands of the Defense Department?"

"As best as I can piece together, Defense just won out with the last administration. Freight was still the Secretary. He argued Animal Farm should be under the primary guidance of Defense since its primary purpose was national defense. Not only was it used to pacify the dissatisfied masses, but also to program a new kind of soldier, completely fearless and obedient. After Defense got

202

control of Animal Farm it used it to gain political advantage. One indiscretion gone unchecked led to a complete lack of restraint."

"Which leads me back to my question about other surprises. Are these UFOs even real? Are the president, vice president, and the others actually dead? Is Freight the president now?"

"Those are the things we're going to figure out. Tabitha, it seems, is the key. The System has crashed. There are a lot of people waking up, now, and they're seeing UFOs. There're areas across the United States completely without System access. Defense is racing to reconnect them, to put things back the way they were."

"And I guess we're racing to Lizard Creek."

"You got it. And you can bet Freight is on his way there, too."

"And what of Animal Farm?"

"That's where you come in, Martin."

Chapter 33

Trying to unplug from the System is like struggling to kick any other habit. You don't fully understand the problem you have until you've given it up for a bit. And so denial keeps you from stopping. That's why intervention from others may be needed but are not the full solution. You still have to see the truth yourself and want to have it.

Sunlight flickered off the *wakizashi* blade in Irene's eyes.

"Papa?" she said. She cupped her eyes in the palms of her hands and sobbed. "I can't believe it. I forgot him. I can't believe it."

"I wondered whether you were forgetting *me*," I said.

"I live with you."

"And yet you don't *see* me. Irene, You don't notice a lot of people and things. Can you even tell me whether anyone is living in this house with us?"

"It's just you and me."

"La-La lives here, too. I thought you were just becoming

withdrawn, upset about Papa dying. After you picked up the CB again, you hardly noticed La-La or me. She'd cook us dinner and you'd just come down, take your food, and go back to your room, like a zombie. You didn't even see us. You'd even talk to yourself, over us, like we weren't there. You never unplugged your CB, not even at night."

"No, I take it off at night."

"No. No, you don't. I've peeked in at you plenty of times."

The CB I'd cut from her neck still lay on the floor. She leaned over and picked it up. "I need it to do things. I can't do homework without it. What else am I supposed to do for fun?"

"When was the last time you dictated a story or drew a picture?"

She gave me a blank look.

"Before Papa died," I said. "It was before you started using the CB."

She flipped the CB in her fingers. I wondered if it was too late, if I could get through to her, even with proof of that Papa was alive.

She snapped the CB end up on her desk and held out her open hand. I handed her the samurai blade. She grabbed the handle with her left hand and rested the blade on the palm of her right.

"It's Papa's handwriting," I said.

"Yes, but when did he write it?"

"It had to be after he left! It wasn't there before. I remember!"

"He could have written it on the on the morning of the bus accident. Maybe someone just found it, thought about keeping it for a while, then felt bad and mailed it back to us. They didn't send a note because they wanted to be anonymous."

"Look at the package it came in." I held up the three boxes. "CB packages. And look at the address label. That's Papa's handwriting, too."

"It could have been written by anyone."

"You know it's his!" I flung my arms in the air. I felt like I was still dealing with the System, not my sister. "Oh, well, if you don't believe Papa sent us this, then give me back the blade."

Irene pulled away as I reached for it.

"Oh, so you want it now?" I said.

Silence.

"Irene, the only way you're going to understand is to come with me to school tomorrow." I snatched the CB from her desk. "Without your CB."

It wasn't fifteen minutes before Irene came to my room asking for her CB. I told her "no," of course. First, she claimed she needed to check messages. I mocked her. "Who's trying to get in touch with you, the President of the United States?" I said. "It can wait." Then she wanted to do her homework. I reminded her it could be done from her flat screen. When she knocked on my door a third time, I just told her to go to bed.

Irene struggled into the kitchen, lost and tired, her eyes searching for System images that were no longer there. La-La turned from the stove. She smiled to Irene and said, "Morning," singing the word. It was one of the few words she knew.

"Morning," Irene said.

La-La turned and gave her a big smile. Irene hadn't said anything to La-La for some time.

Irene sat on the opposite side of the table and rested her cane next to her as she sat down. "You have my CB?" she said.

"I have it, here," I patted the front pocket of my jeans.

"I'll have to have it back once we go to school … to do my assignments."

"I'll give it back to you when I say."

La-La brought a bowl of porridge, with chunks of sausage, corn, and bok choy. She slid it in front of Irene with a glowing smile. She gestured to Irene's neck and said. "Good, good." I wondered where La-La was getting the food. They didn't sell those kinds of things at the nearest food station.

Irene nodded and clenched her left fist as she slurped the hot porridge with her right.

The bus picked us up at the end of our street. Irene went for the handicapped seat at the front. I touched her arm. "Let's sit at the back of the bus. There's something I want you to see."

The bus hummed away from the bus stop as we made our way to the back. My sneakers tacked on the sticky floor with each step. The headrests of the orange seats were black with oily buildup. Some were slashed and marked with graffiti. We could see down the center aisle from the two seats at the back.

Irene grimaced. "This is filthy."

"You never noticed before, did you? The CBs blanket everything—this bus, the school, home, and everything you see, everything you do, everywhere you go, even your dreams. It makes everything look like paradise. Without the CB, you see things as they really are. With them, the System shows you what it wants you to see. Watch this."

I got up from the back seat and walked halfway down the

aisle toward several kids and people on their way to work. All of them were waving their fingers in the air like groping blind mice. I turned and smiled at Irene, flapping my arms like a chicken, sticking out my tongue. Leaning against one of the seats with my arm, I scratched my butt in the face of a woman dressed in medical scrubs and a coat. No one noticed. An automated voice said, "Please remain seated while the bus is in motion." I shrugged and went back to Irene.

"You practically have to punch someone in the face for them to notice you," I said.

"And this is how I've been?"

I nodded. "Worse. Wait until we get to school."

Ms. Croucher shambled into the room as the bell rang. The other students were already in their seats, silently playing with their CBs.

The day's assignment appeared over everyone's desk. Ms. Croucher's cheery holographic face delivered a pre-recorded lesson, telling us to read part of a paragraph from *The Master and Margarita* by Mikhail Bulgakov. Signaling Irene to leave her CB on her desk, I led her to the front of the room.

The students read their screens. I whispered for Irene to follow me out of the room. She hobbled through the talking image of Ms. Croucher, while the real one sat slumped at her desk.

"She didn't even see us," Irene said in the hall.

"Ms. Croucher doesn't see anything that's not on the System. Most people don't. Sometimes students do, maybe because they're younger. We have about forty-five minutes before we have to come back. Ms. Croucher and the rest of the class will see a projected image of us sitting at our desks as long as the CBs are there."

"Don't we have to finish the assignment before the end of class?"

"If we don't finish our assignment in class … and we won't … we'll just finish it before school tomorrow. It's the same every time. Trust me. I usually do the work from my flat screen back home so I don't have use the CB at school."

I led Irene down the hall toward the double-door exit. Each classroom was the same. A tired teacher hunched over his or her desk, students playing with empty space.

"Why didn't you wake me up before? Why did you let me go on like them?"

"I tried! You just don't remember. After Papa died, and especially after you got sick, you just withdrew more and more into the System. For a while, I just gave up. Then Papa's sword arrived."

Just outside the back exit of the school several cement park benches lined the side of the building. Simon Thorp, Aariti Sharma, Margaret Mathers, and Benjamin Zielinski were there already.

"Whoa! Look who's here!" Simon said. He stood up from the table, putting his hands on his hips, blushing at Irene, who combed her fingers through her matted hair, suddenly more conscious of her appearance.

"If it ain't the Queen of Kendo," Aariti said. "Does this mean you're ready to do some kendo?"

"Not any time soon," Irene said.

"That never stopped the sensei from San Francisco," Aariti said. "He walked with a heavy limp. Remember, he came here for the national competition?"

"The nationals were held here?" Irene said.

"She'd remember if it had something to do with her *winning* the nationals," I said.

"You've lost some weight, Ben," Irene said.

Margaret rolled her eyes at me with a knowing look.

Ben's curly dark hair shook with nervous energy as he nodded and pulled at the front of his blue and white striped shirt. "A couple of pounds," he said. "Sometimes I think I should go back to the CB, though. It seemed to help me stop snacking all the time."

"That's like saying you want to do drugs just to lose some weight," I said.

Aariti looked around, mouthing the words, *Who are you talking to?*

"Ben, why don't you try kendo?" Irene said.

Ben blushed and pulled at the front of his shirt.

"He did it before you pooped out on us," Simon said. "But he'll come back if we all come," Simon said.

"You're not welcome," I said to Simon. The smiling face that he turned to me held soulless eyes that sent a chill up my back. I flicked out my contact lenses, and dug the earbuds from my eyes. "Ugh. That's about all of that I can take."

"What are you talking about?" said Irene.

"Take your lenses and earbuds," I said. "Just do it," I interrupted, "trust me."

Following my instructions, Simon and Ben disappeared. "What happened to them?" Irene said.

"Who?" Margaret said, smirking into a pocket mirror. "Oh, you mean lover boy and wimpy kid."

"They're motivators—not real—the System's way of keeping you hooked up," said Aariti.

I held out my hand, showing Irene my CB. "Even when you leave your CB behind, your contact lenses and earbuds will connect with any CB. Unplugging from the System is an illusion itself if you don't sever it completely. Otherwise, you'll never know for sure what is real and what isn't."

Irene gave me a deadpan stare. "How do you know we're not still plugged in now?" she said.

"Practicing kendo is one way," I said. "It's too nuanced and subjective for the System to duplicate. In the System you can practice basic moves, but when sparring with others in *keiko*, it disconnects."

Margaret said, "I can't say I miss kendo. All that yelling in Japanese. I can yell in English just fine." She puckered her fresh lipstick and snapped the mirror shut with a wry grin.

"I haven't seen that color," I said, stretching my neck toward Margaret. "Is it Violet Steel?"

"Is this all you guys have been doing?" Irene said. "Playing hooky and dress-up?"

"There's watching you get a crush on a non-person while basking in self-pity," Margaret said.

My heart jumped into my throat as Principal Smith walked around the corner with crossed arms. "What do you kids think you're doing?" he said.

"Can you just unplug him?" Irene said.

Under my breath, I said, "It doesn't work on real people … unfortunately."

Smith held up our CBs by their clasps. "Put these on and get back to class!"

Irene stood and hobbled over to Mr. Smith. She politely took her CB and slipped it around her neck. "We're sorry Mr. Smith. It won't happen again."

The next day, Irene went to class with Papa's samurai blade taped around the center staff of her cane, pointing upward like a beacon, and yet still invisible to most. From then on, instead of slipping out the back door of school, we just unplugged from the System and pulled our desks into a circle at the back of the room. No one noticed.

Chapter 34

Maybe it's a good thing I can't read minds. It's scary to think about perceiving Jeremy's thoughts. Maybe they'd work their way under my skin, slowly turn me into him, like he did to other people.

By the time he reached the Golden Gate Bridge, everyone who had been on the bus was either dead or bleeding out. I'd give all the details, but trust me, they're better left unsaid.

He pushed the emergency stop button half way across the bridge, got out, strolled to the railing, and looked up at the UFO, centered over the bridge. He smiled at it, probably questioning its purpose, while at the same time, admiring it for the incredible powers it seemed to have brought him. The bus closed its doors and hummed into the city with a load of death, as if everything was right with the world.

He turned to the west, looking over the railing toward the churning ocean below, as if contemplating a jump. His coming victims should be so lucky. He turned with a grin and watched traffic pass. After a few minutes, he spotted a semi truck carrying a tanker of gas, entering the bridge from Marin County heading to the city. Seeing the face of the driver, Jeremy muttered, "Drive your truck head-on into that bus."

The truck veered from its lane and hit the bus. The truck driver was killed instantly. A few in the bus were also killed, many others badly injured. Traffic clogged the roadway from both directions. Jeremy spied a motorcycle cop. Glee spread over his face. If only he could have understood happiness, the carnage to follow might never have happened.

As the policeman took off his helmet, Jeremy said, "Shoot the tanker."

The policeman drew his semi-automatic pistol and unloaded his clip at the tanker. Only a couple of bullets pierced the metal shell; the rest made dents and ricocheted. Gasoline sprang out of the two holes and pooled on the ground.

To the policeman, Jeremy said, "Light a cigarette!"

The policeman searched his pockets for something that wasn't there. The entire bridge was jammed with traffic. Jeremy surveyed all faces as he could see and muttered, "Light a cigarette." Everyone Jeremy could see on the bridge rifled through their pockets and bags. Jeremy noticed a single puff of smoke toward the San Francisco side of the bridge. A blond guy, dressed in a charcoal suit, leaned against the railing, taking a long drag on a cigarette. Punishable by a penalty of ten days community service, smoking had become the folly of the rich and careless. For this guy, it was his last sin.

"Run to that gas truck over there as fast as you can … with your lighter," Jeremy said.

The suit guy took off in a sprint. He passed Jeremy, huffing

216

and puffing, and made it to the tanker in a sweat.

"Now roll around in the gas," Jeremy said. The suit guy obeyed. "Stand up and light your lighter." The suit burst into a torch, and the guy seemed to come back to awareness, screaming. The policeman also burned up in agony since he'd been standing in the expanding pool of gasoline by that time. The flames engulfed the tanker; after a few seconds, it belched open with a violent explosion. A fireball gushed down the rows of traffic, igniting every person and thing in its way. A blast hit Jeremy, too. Those standing around him were blown to the ground. Outlining Jeremy was a flaming bird of prey with an elongated beak, a sharp rack of antlers and expansive wings with claw-like hands at the ends. People ran around him howling on fire.

Getting to his feet, Jeremy laughed at the macabre spectacle he'd created. He said, "Jump off the bridge." Like a flood of burning flies, everyone in sight flew off the bridge, spiraling into the water in streams of smoke.

That's when the earthquake hit the Bay Area.

Chapter 35

As the sun dipped below the Teton mountains, the sliver of sky encircling the rim around the UFO over Lizard Creek turned dark blue. Twilight phased into night.

A low-flying X-24 scramjet hugged the valley floor, racing north. An automated voice said, "Ten minutes." Six exoskeleton soldiers checked their weapons.

Colonel Gaddis' image appeared on the soldiers' view. "The girl and her family are the primary objections. Other radicals are expendable. Secure any video equipment and attachments." His face faded.

The scramjet raced from the river valley and stayed low over Jackson Lake, kicking up a wake of water spinning from its four rotor blades.

The pilot said, "Colonel Gaddis."

Gaddis' face scrolled back over his cockpit dash.

"The Sundog at twelve o'clock, directly over Lizard Creek," the pilot said.

"Proceed as planned," Gaddis said.

The craft darted over the top of Donoho Point—an island in the lake off the western shores—and bore down on Lizard Creek, swirling water into a blizzard of dirt as it buzzed the small village of shipping containers.

Cargo doors sprang open from the hovercraft. Four of the soldiers leaned out manning mini-guns. Hearing the roar from the sky, residents of Lizard Creek rushed outside, probably thinking the UFO had awoken with something to say. The hovercraft swept over them, video-searching their faces for Tabitha's biometrics.

The village had been hit with an earthquake a few hours before. Most had survived unscathed. There were a few scratches, broken bones, and busted noses. They were shaken up after being tossed around like bee bees in their boxcar containers. A few of the containers were lying on their sides.

There was no way Tabitha was going to hide in her container when the second most interesting visitor to Lizard Creek flew around making a racket, which is what the swarms of helicopters and their crews were counting on. Tabitha's face was spotted just outside the opening to her container, picked up by face recognition.

Her father Esau ran towards her, trying to yell something over the hovercraft's roar.

The helicopter swung over Esau. One of the soldiers said, "That must be the dad. Stun him."

An electric pulse hit Esau in the chest and he collapsed to the ground. Lenny came up from behind Tabitha and pulled her inside the container.

Colonel Gaddis' voice chimed in. "Forget about the parents. Get the girl!"

Four soldiers rappelled out of the helicopter. Before their boots hit the ground, they twisted counterclockwise, as if they were being drawn outward by the blades of a ceiling fan. The helicopter spun with them and whirled out of control over the lake. A low hum followed and transparent tubes snaked from the UFO, connecting with the helicopter as it burst into gravel-sized pieces over the water.

Silence returned to Lizard Creek.

Chapter 36

Sitting at his desk the day after the earthquakes, Martin rubbed a gold locket between his thumb and forefinger. The chain dangled in the air, twirling in rhythmic circles. Out his office window in the CIA Headquarters, over the trees and the swollen, grey waters of the Potomac River, across Maryland in the distance, the mid-morning sun cast long shadows.

A voice in his ear said, "Colonel Harold Gaddis."

Martin slid the locket into his left front shirt pocket. He touched the corner of his desk, which lit up into a square alpha-numeric touch screen. He pressed a blinking spot at the bottom right.

Colonel Gaddis appeared on the screen. "You look like I feel," Gaddis said.

"Long day."

"Long … Day," Gaddis said. "You guys and gals finish wiping up after yourselves?" He referred to the collective vomit joined by billions the day before.

"The same as you, I guess," Martin said.

"I've got a question for you folks over there at Langley," Gaddis said.

"Fire away," Martin said.

Gaddis chucked. "Fire I shall. We sent a task force up to Lizard Creek to find that Tabitha girl."

Stone-faced, Martin nodded.

"We've lost contact," Gaddis said.

"And?"

"And … you know anything about it?"

"It's your mission. How would I know?"

Gaddis bared his teeth. "Do you recall a project called 'Animal Farm'?"

"Sounds familiar."

"You were the Project Head."

"It must have slipped my mind, like a few other things."

"You'll have to refresh your memory.."

"Says who?"

"Secretary Freight."

"Seems to me I was supposed to just forget about that whole thing."

"We can help with that."

Martin ignored the threat.

Gaddis said the earthquakes had hit hardest out west. They were particularly devastating in Oklahoma, New Mexico, Northern California, and Wyoming. The System controlling CBs, located deep underground at Los Alamos, New Mexico, run by the world's largest and most powerful network of super computers, had been knocked off-line. North America was cut off. If left to their own thinking, without Animal Farm, people would begin to remember things forgotten. The public would want answers to things they'd learned to ignore. Society would come apart. Free thinking leads to chaos.

The process of waking up would be painful and slow. At first, most would deny the reality confronting them, demanding a return of the CB world. Over time, they would have no choice but see the world around them as it really was, a process, which could be sped up by an event commanding attention. Mountain-sized UFOs floating about in the clear blue sky fit into that category. Before long, people would be asking, "Hey, who's running things around here, anyway?" or "Where's my wife?" Everything would go wild quick.

Gaddis thought like most products of authoritarian government. He believed that critical thinking, undertaken in private, is an inherent threat to national security. Anyone wanting to read, write, shop, travel, or communicate with others in private were assumed to be a threat and had to be controlled or eliminated. Most were cast into the Wild, where people had the freedom of privacy, sure, and also had the right to starve in anonymity. Others, deemed to have qualities the System could use, were sent to one of the thousands of colonies.

Gaddis, and his masters, were desperately fearful of the collapse of the System, to them a cataclysmic occurrence that would unhinge the colonies, and turn the prefectures into the Wild. Los Alamos had managed to get part of the System running again. But things weren't working the way they were supposed to and there was little to no content available to keep people preoccupied. Something had to be done to set things back right, in System terms.

"You're going to Los Alamos to fix the System," Gaddis said.

"Things are a little chaotic here."

"They're chaotic everywhere, and it's going to get worse. You may or may not be aware that just about everything in the San Francisco area is a black hole."

"The System is down everywhere."

"That's not what I mean. There's no communication in or out. None. No one knows what's happening in Northern California. It's a priority problem."

"The whereabouts of the president is more important isn't it?"

"We've got people on it. Right now, we need you to maintain order and bring the System back up to speed."

"I'll have to clear it with Bluewater."

"She answers to Defense now, and so do you."

Martin's face turned red.

"We're sending over a SCRAM-copter to your office now," Gaddis said. "It should be there in fifteen minutes. Meet it at the helipad. You'll be in Los Alamos within the hour."

Chapter 37

THE CABIN, A RAMSHACKLE CONSTRUCTION OF SCRAP WOOD CAKED together with dry sod, clung to the upper side of a dry ravine in the mountains. Tall cedar trees with skeletal limbs leaned their withered claws over the cabin, protecting it from the sun.

Nicholas knocked on the rickety screen door. Cool air flowed out from the darkness beyond. No sound. Nicholas turned, feeling as though he was being watched. No one was there, at least, not behind him. Something had followed him, though. The Sundog hovered directly overhead. He could see out over the hills and mesas of Ponderosa Valley, which poured into the Jemez Pueblo far below. Miles beyond, blue sky peeked past the Sundog rim.

Into the cabin he said, "Skinner! You in there? It's me. Nicholas."

Something heavy clanged inside, followed by rustling and heavy footsteps.

"I guess you burnt down the place like he wanted," said a faceless voice from within.

Nicholas took off his glasses and hooked them to the collar behind his neck. "You gonna come out here or just hide in there like a scared granny?"

"Ain't you cocky, now!"

Skinner Tosa walked out of the shadows behind the screen holding a large assault rifle across his chest. His long black hair, streaked with grey, was tied back in a ponytail with twine. He carried himself with a boldness that said, *Shake your hand or break your face—no difference to me.* The sleeves of a maroon and navy blue checked flannel shirt were rolled up to his elbows past ripped forearms. His shirttails hung loosely over worn blue jeans. Creases ran from the edges of his cheeks to the edges of his mouth.

"Are you going to invite me in, or do I have to stand out here all day long?" Nicholas said.

Steely grey eyes regarded Nicholas. Skinner blinked with the indifference of an alley cat, ignoring the question. He kicked the door open against Nicholas. A grin sprang across his face and said, "I'd crossed you off for dead, son."

"I came back when I heard about Chei," Nicholas said.

Skinner pushed him back and pointed the barrel of his rifle to the sky. "You brought a stray back with you."

Nicholas raised his eyebrows at the UFO, centered directly over the cabin.

"I didn't bring it," Nicholas said.

"I saw it mid-morning when Chei's cabin burned. Do you know what a Sundog is?"

Nicholas shook his head.

"I remember hearing about them in school once," Skinner said.

228

"You went to school?"

"I've tried to forget. Sundogs are like rainbows or something. Happen when it's cold in the morning, like at the North Pole or something. A mirage of two smaller suns appears in a halo on either side of the morning sun. That's what happened this morning. Several of these things came out of the two smaller suns. This one," Skinner said pointing with his rifle, "came here. The rest went off in different directions."

Skinner grabbed Nicholas' shoulder and spun him around to feel the guitar through the soft case. "Still got the Strat, I see, but where's the amp? I know Chei don't have one."

"Amp?"

"I could hear you playing "Little Wing" from miles away, son! This whole cabin was shaking."

Nicholas shrugged.

Skinner regarded Nicholas through slit eyelids. "Well, I'm half glad you see it, too."

"Of course I see it. I ain't crazy."

"Yeah, well something don't figure. Did you notice it don't cast a shadow?" Skinner stepped around Nicholas and held his hand out into direct sunlight, casting a shadow over the dirt. "See what I mean? That there UFO stretches for miles. I can't even see the sun and my hand still casts a shadow. It's like it's not there."

"Let's go inside?" Nicholas said. "That thing makes me nervous."

"Why do you think I was holed up inside? fOne way or another, we're gonna have company -- little green men or G-men— take your pick."

Pale faced, Nicholas turned toward the UFO.

229

Skinner slapped him on the back. "Follow me."

Skinner led Nicolas through the kitchen to the bedroom. He drew out a flathead screwdriver from his back pocket and pried up a section of the floor, revealing a large round manhole cover raised half a foot off the dirt. A hole as big as a fist had been cut through the top.

"A manhole?" Nicholas said.

"A manhole. In the desert! Weird ain't it? I found this out here after you left. Damnedest thing I ever saw. It was locked tight. I got curious, so I pulled a blowtorch up. Just got weirder after I cut it open."

"And the cabin?"

"It was here already. Been locked up and deserted for some time ... until I took it over."

Skinner laid the gun on the floor and pulled at the top of the manhole with both hands.

"Cool toy, by the way," Nicolas said, referring to the rifle, outfitted with two barrels stacked on top of each other, an optical scope over and a laser flashlight under.

"My new girlfriend. Listens to everything I say and don't talk back."

The manhole swung open.

"Where did you find it?" Nicholas said.

"You'll see." Skinner pointed into the open manhole. "After you."

A metal rung ladder led down into darkness.

"Don't worry," Skinner said. "It's safe."

Holding his pack with his left hand in front of his chest, Nicholas shimmied down. After a full hundred feet his boots hit gravel. He jumped onto the rocky floor and waited. He couldn't see anything until Skinner followed with the flashlight at the end of his rifle.

"Ever seen anything like that?" Skinner said, shining his flashlight at the wall, a chipped and uneven surface that looked like black glass.

Nicholas reached for the wall.

"Careful, it'll cut you," said Skinner.

Nicholas kicked around at the gravel, mostly black shards from the wall. "What is all this?"

"Your guess is as good as mine." Skinner circled the gun's light and pointed to his left and right, revealing an expansive black tunnel. "About fifty yards or so down that way there's a locked gate. I've been down to the other side in a ravine. The gate's covered with about ten feet of rock and dirt."

"A secret passageway?"

"Secret, yes. But passageway? Not sure, at least not for people."

"Where does this lead?" Nicholas said, pointing in the other direction.

"You'll see." Skinner walked ahead. Nicholas followed. "I'm guessing this is an emergency spillover, if something goes wrong."

"Goes wrong? With what?"

"Whatever they've got up at Los Alamos. It's a bomb factory. Remember?"

"That's over sixty miles away!"

"About twenty-five miles as the crow flies."

"Still a long way."

"Shouldn't be a problem for you."

Skinner's light hit something ahead. "There it is," he said, pointing. The light revealed dozens of plastic milk cartons of water, stacks of canned food, and a few cardboard boxes.

"You're full of surprises," Nicholas said. He went to the stash and pulled out a small package marked, "MRE."

"Meals Ready to Eat. They're all meatballs and BBQ sauce. Take as many as you can, just in case," Skinner said.

"Where'd you get these?"

Skinner talked over his shoulder as he packed a backpack. "You'll see. I must admit, I didn't think I'd be taking these back up there."

"Let's stay here, then, see what the thing up there does."

Skinner heaved the backpack to his shoulders and buckled a harness around his hips. "Not an option, son. Like I said, someone or something's going to wonder why that thing came to my cabin. Bet you anything it's dead center over you even now."

"Then I'll go on foot up top. You stay here."

"No can do. My gut tells me something will check this place out sooner or later. Whether you stay or go, I'm moving on. I'm thinking the best place to hide is right up there under the bomb factory. Maybe they'll figure it's what the UFOs are interested in, not a scrawny Indian boy from the pueblo."

They walked up the tunnel for several miles before coming to a gate. Heavy metal bars, two inches thick, ran across the length of the tunnel.

"It took me a day to cut through," said Skinner, pointing at two sections where the bars had been melted away. He took off his backpack and pushed it through the opening. From the other side, he said, "There's no latches on these bars. They weren't meant to open.

232

No, this tunnel ain't for people. It's an exhaust of some kind."

Nicholas looked through the bars, past Skinner, into the darkness behind him. "Makes you wonder if something could come rushing down."

"Yeah, but what the heck, right?"

They went on and stopped at a pile of empty MRE packages. "Rest stop," Skinner said.

Nicholas winced as he pried his pack off his shoulders and eased it down against the curved wall. He arched his back and ran his fingers through his long hair. "I could use a nap."

"We won't stop long. Just a few minutes."

Nicholas plopped down on the gravel and leaned against the cool black wall. "I need at least thirty minutes."

"If we stop, the UFO stops, son. If someone's watching that thing … someone who knows this tunnel is down here … they may come check it out sooner than later. If we keep moving, they may just assume the UFO was following the tunnel to Los Alamos. Remember: no one's supposed to be down here."

Nicholas rolled his head toward Skinner. From the limited light, he could barely see the outline of Skinner's head. "You keep calling me 'son'. Are you my father?"

The gun light flashed across Skinner's worn snub-nosed boots. An uncomfortable silence passed. "Didn't Chei tell you?" Skinner said. "You're the white buffalo, born from the white lady." He snatched his pack and stomped up the tunnel.

Nicholas unzipped his pack and slung the Strat around his shoulder. He took a swig from his water bottle, tossed it in his pack, and heaved it across both shoulders. He could see Skinner's light several yards ahead. Nicholas thumbed a pick from the strings, and belted into the guitar lead, "River Paradise," by Stevie Ray Vaughan.

Blue light swelled from behind the surface of the glassy black tunnel walls. As Nicholas noodled his fingers over the fret board, the light ebbed and flowed in churning waves as if pulsing from inside a transparent aquarium. With each riff, the strings amplified the warm sound, rolling with the light.

"Cut that out!" Skinner said.

Nicholas stopped. The tunnel fell dark, save for Skinner's gun light.

Chapter 38

As I'VE SAID BEFORE, POLYGRAPHERS OFTEN USE THE SAME PLOY. They start nice. Gain your trust. Spend time talking about you. Ask easy questions about your name, address, favorite food, and so on. Move on to your friends and family. Talk about where you grew up, went to school, telling you all along, *You're doing so well*, and, *This won't take much longer*. They give you a false sense of security, make you think there's nothing to worry about. And then just when you thought the test was nearly over, whammo! *You're a damn liar!* There's no denying it. The machine says so. *And we thought we had an understanding here,* they'll say. *We thought you were going to tell us the truth!* You're taken off guard. A knot swells in your gut and throat. *Is there something you haven't told us? What is it you've been lying about?*

The thing is, they don't know from sic'em whether you've been telling the truth. And it doesn't matter what they know. They just want you to *believe* the machine knows. It gives them the opportunity to squeeze you like a wet rag for any information you've been holding back. You're so scared that they can see into you, knowing what you didn't tell them, that you'll offer it up like a present. Little did you know, the machine didn't tell them anything about your veracity. They don't know whether you told the truth or not. But they do now. Thanks to you. Sucker!

"Have you ever been in an earthquake?" Martin said.

"I've felt a few before. You know, it's Oklahoma. Little earthquakes happen every so often. I remember one morning, while having cereal before school, the floor just jerked about a few inches, which was scary because we had a concrete foundation. There was another time, just before Papa left, when we were practicing kendo, and the windows just shook. I thought for a minute they would pop out of their frames. But this time was different.

"After the patrol cars came, telling everyone to go back home, I turned to Irene, holding up the rear. The whole street started waving like someone was spreading a bed sheet, kinda peaceful at first … until the first wave reached us. There was no time to react. It threw Irene into the air. She landed right on my chest, knocking the air out of me. I was so scared, I couldn't breathe anyway.

"I have no idea how long it lasted. It seemed like minutes but was probably seconds. When it ended, La-La got to her feet and checked on Irene. She was still gasping, like she had asthma or something. Irene nodded. She was okay. I grabbed her hand. She was bleeding a little from the top of her head and lip. She didn't have any broken bones; just startled.

"We were okay. The rest of the Prefecture—not so much. Every house on our block had some damage. About six places around us had completely collapsed. Then the screaming started.

Jenny and John Blakely lived a couple houses down on

the other side of the street. Mrs. Blakely was out front screaming, literally pulling her hair out. I'd never heard a person make sounds like that before. I hope I never do again.

When the worldwide vomit hit, and people came outside yelling about the blacked-out System, Jenny and John had come outside. But their daughter Aimee had stayed in the house. The second floor of their house just pancaked on the whole bottom floor. It was weird because the top floor looked untouched. Aimee was underneath it all. Their gas lines busted and then the fire started. We rushed down there to see what we could do. It was hopeless. I held Jenny back from the house while John hurried around the flames calling, "Aimee!" People stared at the burning house from their front lawns. No one came near to help. Some tested their CBs, trying to take a picture or call Emergency Services, as if that was helpful. It got hot fast, pushing us back to the street. Jenny bellowed on her knees. John held her. And that was just the beginning of the losses for our Prefecture.

"The fire from the Blakely house spread to the two houses beside it. One of them burned down with the family inside. They were still too shocked from the System failure to help themselves. Neighbors watched stoically as the house turned into a pile of cinders. We could see rising smoke from several other houses on the block to the west of us. We could hear screams for help from all over. Some of the voices close, others far away. Fire trucks never showed up.

"Irene asked the Blakeleys to come to our house. But Jenny didn't want to leave the spot where her daughter had just died.

"Our house was basically intact. La-La was shaken up, but fine. The red brick walls supporting the front of our house had been destroyed, exposing the insulation. Several of the windows were broken and the front door was jammed shut. Many of the kitchen dishes were shattered and strewn around. Every piece of furniture had been moved or turned over.

"After taking inventory of the damage, La-La had me clean up the kitchen and gave Irene the living room. La-La went the Chan room, chanting, "Amituofo," as she worked. The statues were still standing on the altar, although it had been moved half-way across the room. In a way it seemed silly to be straightening up our house while several other houses in the neighborhood were burning. Maybe people were still trapped. I think La-La wanted to just keep us all distracted. A way to keep everyone calm. Besides, three girls like us weren't going to put out any fires or save lives. "

"Edith, I think this is a good point to run through some more questions," Martin said. "After that, we'll talk about your sister a little."

He sounded pretty bored. "Yeah, I was wondering if you were ever going to get to her. I mean, that's what I figured you wanted to know about anyway. Her and the UFO."

"That's part of it," he said. "Now, sit back and relax." He fiddled his finger through the air in front of him, and then read off a series of questions, including many of the same ones he'd asked before. "Have you truthfully answered all of my questions?" he said.

"Yes."

"What happened to your Papa?" he said.

The same answer came to my mind. *He went to the Freedom Colony, Western Nebraska*. I said, "He died in a bus crash," this time more relaxed and evenly.

"Why did the Sundogs come?"

"I don't know."

"What are the Sundogs?"

"I don't know."

"Are you in communication with the Sundogs?"

"No."

"Is Irene in communication with the Sundogs?"

"I don't think so, no."

"Are the Sundogs real?"

"Who knows?"

"Just answer the questions honestly."

"I guess they are. I can see them."

"Are beings inside the Sundogs?"

"I don't know."

"What happened to Mr. Caprock?"

An answer came to my mind: *He went to Freedom Colony, Western Kansas.* I told Martin he had died because that's what I was told by his own wife.

"What do I have in the left front pocket of my shirt?"

The answer came to mind again: *A gold locket with a photograph of your daughter, Brandy.* I said, "I don't know."

"Who is the current President of the United States?"

Sophia Martinez.

I thought a public announcement had told us some guy named Fright (or was it Freight), was now president. But Sophia Martinez came to mind instead. I couldn't remember either way, so I hesitated and finally said, "Sophia Martinez."

Martin went through the same questions three times. For several minutes, he twisted thin air in different directions.

My hip hurt again, shooting pain down my leg, making it

harder to remain patient. Several minutes passed with no sound, just Martin's annoying silence. All I could think about was going home, getting out of that room that was closing in on me.

While thinking about my plight, I didn't even notice Martin glaring at me. I could feel my heart race for a moment. I said, "What?"

"Edith, I thought we had an *understanding*," he said, drawing out the last word. "Did you not *understand* what I told you before?" I nodded, unsure what he was referring to. "Don't you *believe* I can tell whether you're lying? Don't you *know* that?"

I shrank in my chair. "I'm telling you *everything* I know. I'm telling the truth."

"Well I don't think you are, Edith. I don't think you're being honest with me at all. I don't think you're being *straightforward*. I don't think you *really* want to go home. At first, I thought you did. I thought you wanted to walk out of here with your grandmother and go home. I thought you wanted to put this all behind you."

"I do, I do, I do! I want to go home. I want to do whatever it takes. What is it? What do you want from me?"

"I want you to be honest with me, Edith. When I ask you a question, no matter how unimportant it may seem to you, you've got to tell me everything, and I mean *everything*!" He was not the same mild-mannered person who walked into the room. Before, he was casual and easy going, the sort of person who could bring out a pair of Prada high heels to try on at a salon, serving mimosas and kissing your butt. (That's how I always imagined it anyway.) Then he became a cop who'd just arrested me for shoplifting those heels.

"I've told you everything," I said.

"Edith, not all answers you've given me are true, are they!"

"I think they're all true."

"Edith, just think, of all the questions I've been asking you, don't you feel unsure about some of them?"

I thought for a minute, reviewing the questions in my mind and blurted out the thing weighing most heavily on my mind. "Berlin is *not* my favorite band!" My face dropped in my hands like I'd just admitted to murder. "It's Lady Gaga! I'm sorry, I'm *so* sorry ... I know, you'd think it was the Misfits, Metallica, the Stooges, Iron Maiden, or even the Velvet Underground, the Clash, the Police, the Cure, Ministry, the Ramones, Split Endz, Squeeze or something like that for God's sake! But it's Lady Ga ... Ga ... , okay! Ga! Ga! It's Lady Gaga!"

I lifted my face from sweaty palms, expecting him to be relieved. I was. Happy that I'd come clean. He wasn't. His fists were clenched on the table. His jaw muscles ground his teeth as his cold blue eyes bore into my soul.

"Edith ... I *really* don't give a *damn*. I don't care about metallica maiden or squeezed ends or whatever. And I ... can ... positively ... guarantee ... you ... that ... I ... do ... not ... care ... about ... Lady .... Gaga." He spat each word, his mouth twisting each syllable with forced lips. "What *does* concern me ... *Edith* ... is that you just admitted to lying to me ... twice ... once when I asked about your favorite band and again when I asked you whether all of your answers were truthful. So you *lied* again even when you had the chance to correct your answers."

Martin took off his glasses and placed them on the table, setting them down with the care of a soldier placing a land mine. He rubbed his red eyes with one long stroke, using his thumb and forefinger. "Edith, I'm worried for you. I'm worried you are not taking this seriously. I'm worried how your grandmother will react if she learns you will not be going home today. I'm worried you will be spending a lot more time here. And I'm worried whether you will stand up to what *they* have in store for you if that happens. You need to come clean about a few things, Edith. I need an immediate and unequivocal answer to these questions. If you cannot answer them clearly and without equivocation, then I'll just wrap this up and leave you here. Leave you to -- *them*! Are you ready to cooperate?"

Tears streaming down my face, I nodded eagerly.

"Will you answer all of my questions truthfully and without qualification?"

"Yes."

"Have you truthfully answered every question other than the two we've discussed?"

"No."

"Good. Now tell me immediately, which questions you didn't answer truthfully."

I hesitated, maybe only a fraction of a section, but it seemed like an eternity in my mind, which raced through the calculated lies I'd told. For the first time, I felt I knew—for sure -- Papa wasn't dead, and I knew where he was. I didn't know why. I didn't have to confirm it. I just *knew that I knew* without any doubt. I also knew where Mr. Caprock had gone.

"I think I know what *actually* happened to my Papa."

Sometimes, no matter how practiced an actor, no matter how hard a person tries to put on a poker face, even when there is apparently no change in expression, there is something, maybe a vibe, an odor, or pheromone, *something*, that says 'I'm surprised!'

Somehow I could tell my answer was *not* what Martin was expecting, even though his angry face was unmoved.

"What do you think happened to him?"

"I think he went to Freedom Colony, somewhere in Western Kansas?"

"You don't think he's dead?"

"I think maybe not."

"Why do you believe that?"

"I don't know." I regretted saying anything about my ideas about Freedom Colony, whatever it was. My mind raced about the samurai sword we received in the mail. What if he was alive and he'd sent it? Then maybe talking about the sword could get him in trouble.

"Well, did someone say that to you?"

"No."

"Did your grandmother or sister tell you that?"

"No."

"Then why do you think it? What do you think Freedom Colony is?"

"I don't know, I think I heard it somewhere but I'm not sure where. You know, as I sit here, maybe my mind just made it up because I want to tell you something. All I can say is ... since I believe that's where Papa went, it makes me feel unsure of my answer to your question. Maybe I'm just imagining things because deep down I just want to believe Papa is still alive, even though he's gone forever."

Martin bore into me with pensive eyes, like something I said resonated with him. "Are there any other answers you are *unsure* about?"

"For some reason I believe Mr. Caprock may have also gone to Freedom Colony, whatever it is."

"Didn't you tell me he's dead?"

"Yes, that's what I thought."

"Did Mrs. Caprock tell you her husband went to a place called Freedom Colony?"

"No, no one told me, like no one told me about Papa. *I'm trying to be perfectly honest with you here*. I don't know where I got the idea but somehow it's just what I think and it makes me uncertain about the answer I gave you, so I want to be *straightforward*, as you say. Maybe I dreamed it and my mind just made up a happy place for them to go. Freedom Colony sounds nice."

Martin stifled a chuckle and then shot a regretful look at the floor. "Is there anything else you lied about?" he said.

I didn't think I'd really lied about anything, as he said, but I let it go. "I stole some nail polish from Margaret Mathers in third grade."

"Oh, give me a break! Forget that!" He put his glasses back on and flipped his fingers. "My graphs, Edith! I see your perspiration, and brain waves show you were *lying* when you talked about the Sundogs! I can see you know why they're here, what they are, and who's driving them! Why do you think that is? What is it you're not telling me about the Sundogs?"

My mind raced over everything I knew about the Sundogs with the urgency of a hoarder who'd lost one of her thirty-three pairs of snowmen salt and pepper shakers. The information had to be in there somewhere! Maybe I knew more about the Sundogs than I would even admit to myself. All of the images my mind had captured of the Sundog over Oklahoma City ran through my mind: everything

La-La and Irene had said about them, the video of Montana Tabitha, Jenny Blakely screaming her daughter's name, "Aim .... ee, Aim ..... ee, Aaaaaaim.....eeeee!" as the Sundog hovered overhead, doing nothing as usual. I questioned everything I'd told Martin, everything I knew about the Sundogs, until I wondered if I even knew my own name -- Edith.

With bewildered eyes, I said, "I don't know, I really don't know. I don't know what they are? All I know is what I've seen. There's more than I've told you so far, of course, more about Irene."

"Yes, yes, we're coming to that. But think carefully. Is there anything about the Sundogs you haven't told me so far?"

"No, I mean, I don't know." I was actually feeling stupid for not being able to remember something I didn't know.

"Just tell me what you think, whether you know or not, tell me what you think they are. Why you think they're here?"

I wiped sweat off my forehead and rubbed it on the orange legs of my jumpsuit. I said, "I've had a lot of theories. I thought they must be spaceships from another planet, outer space, or whatever; they're filled with little aliens, examining us like a bunch of bugs, laughing. That scares me because it makes me think they might just wipe us out like a boy blowing up an anthill with a cherry bomb. And I've wondered whether they're something like a cosmic virus, something here from another dimension, to suck the life out of us and then take all the resources of the earth. Or they could be part of an immunity system of the earth and the sun, something reacting to the infestation of humanity, something sent to fight us off. I mean, since the oceans have risen twenty feet world-wide, and the falling temperatures in American and Europe, the immigration problem, disease, crime, you name it, maybe something decided to put an end to the mess we've made. But the bottom line—I don't know what they are or why they're here. I wish I did. If I knew, I'd tell you!"

"Why do you believe the oceans have risen and global temperatures have fallen, and everything you said?" His concerned expression seemed genuine.

"It's all true, isn't it?"

Yes.

Martin's face reset to an inscrutable stare.

"Most people don't know it," I said, "or they've forgotten it all, thanks to the System everyone is so wrapped up in. But I still remember things from when I was little."

Martin's attitude lightened. "Well, those are some pretty bleak pictures. Regarding the Sundogs, why not conclude they're full of friendly aliens who just haven't opened up their doors yet? Once they do, they're going to tell us how to solve all those problems you mentioned, and then we'll all live happily ever after. There'll be peace on earth with plenty of Kumbaya to go around." Martin chuckled, happy with himself.

"Maybe they're not there at all," I said. "Maybe they're just clouds and soon, they'll just fade away in the sky like smoke. Maybe this whole thing is a hoax caused by mass hysteria—a System glitch."

"Funny you should say that, Edith. Maybe that's it. Maybe the whole thing was *your* imagination."

"Do you believe the Tabitha video was a hoax?" I said. "Where were you when everyone else was puking?"

In the CIA Headquarters Auditorium.

"At your headquarters?" I said.

246

Martin's smile disappeared. He twisted something on his view. The window screen came to life with the video of Tabitha Sparks. As far as I knew then, it was still the only video of a Sundog. I watched the jumpy video, thinking again how real they looked, thinking about the other things I saw them do with my own eyes. "You tell me, Edith. Is the video a hoax?"

"I don't think it's a hoax, at least, not now. I mean -- hello -- you know what happened with Irene. But, at first, there were a lot of questions, a lot of doubt. The big question everyone was asking: 'Why can a twelve-year-old girl capture a UFO with an antique video recorder, but more advanced digital videos cannot?'"

I stopped, holding up my arm with the clips on my fingers, and waved them at Martin. "Come to think about it, you guys probably have poor Tabitha locked up somewhere underground, hooked to a machine like this, dontcha?"

No.

Any warmth in Martin's demeanor turned back to stone. He twisted his thumb at the window screen of the Sundog, and said, "Go on."

"Some believe the Tabitha video was just a hoax. Something about old analog technologies being easier to fake. News feeds suggested lenticular clouds often appear near mountains, which supposedly meant the Tabitha video was really just a cloud."

"That's a big word," he said. "Lenticular."

"I don't know why I remember it. Irene and I joked about it. Anyway, I don't care what people say. Tabitha's video of the UFO was exactly the same as the one we saw floating over Oklahoma City on the first day. There're no mountains in Oak-City. And the surface of the UFO was smooth, like it had a hard surface, not smoky like a cloud. Tabitha's UFO was the same shape as the one over our house. It seemed unlikely to me … that a girl hundreds of miles away could make a hoax using an image of a Sundog exactly like the one over my house. I guess we all know now her video was real."

"Can you give me any objective proof that the reported UFOs were real?"

I slapped my open hands on the leather recliner. "When you guys tried to take Irene it blew up your soldier boys. There's some *objective* proof. Duh!"

Chapter 39

On his way to ground level Martin met Bluewater in the water closet. She clutched her hips. "You can do this, Martin," she said.

Martin leaned against damp mops on hooks against the wall. "I don't even remember how Animal Farm worked," he said.

"You're not going to help them *fix* it! Just delay the System from coming back online as long as possible. At least until we figure out what's going on, until we find out what happened to the president."

"I don't think I can. Even as I stand here, I still don't remember anything about it." He sighed. "And with everything that's happened, I don't feel like there's much to fight for. What's the point?"

Bluewater frowned. "If you don't delay them as much as possible, if the System starts up again, you may not even remember your own name. Just figure out a way to kill it."

Martin's shook off a chill and straightened his back. "Aye,

Aye, Madam!" with mock conviction. Martin reached for the door knob. "Since you're asking me for miracles, find that Tabitha girl ASAP. If you figure out how she managed to interrupt the System -- it could be the key."

"Already working on that. You just hold up your end. We'll be in touch."

The engines of an X-24 scramjet roared on the CIA headquarters helipad. Clad in a black jumpsuit and visored helmet, the co-pilot waited aside the hovercraft with a second helmet in his hand. He exchanged Martin's soft leather briefcase for the helmet. Martin strapped it on and climbed into the craft, taking an empty seat behind the cockpit. A black pressure suit stitched to the form-fitting seat, cupped him into a reclining position. His helmet clipped into the headrest. The co-pilot snapped together a five-point harness at the center of his chest. The pressure suit inflated, immobilizing Martin's legs and feet. The co-pilot checked the suit, knocked on Martin's helmet, stowed the briefcase, and climbed into cockpit.

The quad-rotors, snugged into the disc-like wings which fanned out from the front and back, revved to a piercing whine. The craft leapt off the ground, hesitated mid-air, dropped a few feet, and blasted into the starlit night sky, arching over the Appalachian Mountains to the west. At the speed of sound, the rotors switched off and folded into the hull. As the sky cracked again with a bang, hitting another speed barrier, the scramjets under and over the craft ignited, racing at nine thousand one hundred miles per hour.

Chapter 40

PRESIDENT MARTINEZ BLINKED AS THOUGH A HANDFUL OF SAND had been thrown in her face. Chunky vomit spread across the table and dripped down her lap, pooling on the white linoleum floor. She yelled out and wrung her hands, then wiped her lips with the sleeve of her neon purple jumpsuit. She pushed back from the table. Vomit ran from her lap to her bare ankles. She went to a kitchen sink, and pulled out the drawers, finding a cotton rag with red stripes. Wiping her mouth and face first as best she could, she cleaned off all the puke from her suit.

Regaining a limited sense of wit, she arched her neck around with the urgency of a caged cat. A false window revealed a polished steel wall next to a breakfast table. A metal cot and stripped mattress waited on the other side of the room. Track lighting ran over the bed. She peered into the bathroom with wide eyes. Catching sight of her face on the steel mirror, she touched her cheek and rubbed the back of her head. Her long locks had been lopped off as if with a chainsaw, her makeup smeared around her face.

She spun around. Walking up to the vault door, she yanked off her CB and plugged the bottom end into a socket next to an alphanumeric keypad. Nothing happened. She hammered the keypad with both fists, yelling, "Hey! Hello? What the *hell's* going on here? As President of the United States, I *ORDER* you to let me out! Now!"

From a conference chair, Colonel Gaddis watched President Martinez throw a tantrum in her cell. His view broke with random static. A grainy image of General Bishop, head of the Marines, appeared on a screen next to the scene of Martinez.

"We've got problems here," Bishop said. "How much longer before the System is back up?"

"We've got people working on it now," Gaddis said. "It won't be long."

"I hope Freight knows what he's doing," Bishop said. "Where is he, anyway? I've been trying to reach him at the Pentagon. Either no one knows where he is or no one's saying."

"He's around, I'm sure. And we have our orders. Proceed as planned."

"You'd better restart the System, for your sake and mine. The public is starting to come around. If you don't, I don't know how long I can keep Martinez under control this way."

On the Martinez screen, she was upturning the bed and kicking over chairs.

"You don't have any choice. It's a matter of national security. Don't you remember what she wanted to do after the emergency was declared? Shut the System down. Can you image what would happen with everything that's going on? It'd be mass anarchy!"

"I'm starting to wonder," Bishop said. "A lot of people are. Aren't you? To tell you the truth, I don't remember why I'm doing any of this."

"There's nothing to wonder about. Just follow your orders. Once the System is back up, we'll be back on track."

Chapter 41

FUNNY HOW THE SYSTEM TARGETED CHILDHOOD MEMORIES AS IF they were the most threatening. They didn't contribute to efficiency, so they had to go. But they made us who we are. Without them, there's nothing to motivate us, no point of reference for future decisions, no touchstone for good or bad. By design, the CB world slowly ate away at the very foundation of our identity. If too much time passes, allowing the System to do its work, when you wake up from its nightmare, the question is, *What is your purpose with no sense of self?*

Irene sank into her bed, her knees pulled to her chest, heels on the side rail. As though trying to dry the ink, she waved an old photograph in her right hand; in the other, a cutout picture of a stark granite mountain.

In the photo, Papa grinned at the camera, hugging Irene and me in front of our house. Irene had a fresh bandage on her left check. All of us had several scratches and bruises. Papa had some dried blood on his forehead form a scalp wound which wouldn't stop bleeding.

We were fifteen then. He was happy. Gleeful even. There was something more in that smile – fear left over from a close call.

Looking over Irene's shoulder, I said, "I remember that day. Mrs. Blakely took the picture."

"How could you forget?" Irene said. "See our faces. Those huge smiles. We were just happy to be alive."

"I wish I could forget it. It was the scariest thing that ever happened to me … to us …. up to that time."

But she hadn't forgotten. A good sign.

The picture was taken the day an F-5 tornado tore through Oklahoma City. When a large tornado comes, there are three main rules: get out of the way; go underground; or hunker in an interior room, like a closet, bathtub, or under a stairwell, and hope you survive it. Hiding in a vehicle, mobile home, or under an overpass is suicide. Escaping to a ditch or creek isn't much better. Flash floods sweep people away. And then there's the grapefruit-size hail. Get hit in the head with those a few times and it's lights out.

We knew it was coming. There was plenty of live news. The tornado first touched down in some pastures south of El Reno. A thin white funnel cloud snaked down in a narrow loop from the wall cloud and turned black when it hit the dirt. Electricity from power lines exploded like fireworks. The roof of a slaughterhouse was ripped off and a few homes in a rural Prefecture were hit, knocking down brick walls. No deaths, though. Not yet.

The tornado picked up strength and turned into an F-1 as it came into Yukon with hurricane wind speeds from a hundred and seventeen to a hundred and eighty miles per hour. A crowded grocery store was slammed. Superficial wounds mostly. About fifty homes east of there had similar damage. Normally, people can easily survive a tornado that big in a house or sturdy building. One poor guy was killed in his backyard by flying debris when he tried to save his cocker spaniel.

Leaving Yukon, the tornado continued to rip up farmland and structures. It lost strength as it passed south of Lake Hefner, southwest from our home. We watched on the flat screen in the living room. The storm moved eastward. All the reporting meteorologists had trajectories with it going due east, likely petering out before hitting central Oklahoma City, comfortably south of our house.

Papa let out a sigh of relief. As I started back to my room, the storm took a sharp left turn and headed north along of the eastern shore of Lake Hefner. The tornado fed off the lake, spewing a wall of water to its east. A ball of debris—rubble and twisted metal and power poles—spun off west into the Lake. It followed Hefner Parkway north, grew to an F-5 two miles wide, and headed toward the dead center of our neighborhood. We had less than fifteen minutes to find shelter.

The middle school four blocks away had the nearest storm shelter. We all had a small bag packed, ready to go. Out of our front door we saw the pitch-black southern sky. The street was eerily quiet. No wind. With everything deserted, it was like we'd just come out of one of those fake houses in a nuclear testing sight just before a thermonuclear bomb was dropped, sirens howling.

Papa didn't have to say anything. We just ran as fast as we could. After a block, we could hear the approaching roar of the tornado. I was too scared to look back. The wind picked up and sucked toward the storm. My throat swelled.

We ran harder down the middle of the street. As we reached a four-lane road, we could see the roof of the school in the distance. I was losing my breath. Papa ripped off my backpack and threw it with a grunt to the side. Irene tossed hers off, too. She and Papa grabbed my hands on either side and pulled me as we raced ahead.

A block away, the roar of the storm grew. It sounded like a freight train. I looked over my shoulder and I wished I hadn't. A huge wall of poles, rooftops, and trees churned toward us. Buses and trucks streaked through the air like missiles.

Once we reached the sidewalk of the school leading to the front entrance, there were several other families and random people with us. The debris ball of the tornado was a block away. When we reached the doors, an entire roof of a house exploded into splinters when it slammed into the brick wall of the school about twenty feet to our right. A police car hit nose first into the sidewalk on our left. Papa yanked on the large metal doors. They didn't budge. He banged on them, yelling, "Open! Open! OOOOOH … pehhhnn!"

Ms. Croucher pushed from inside as Papa yanked frantically. The high pressure from the storm had sucked the doors closed. Wind rushed through the door as the tornado closed in. We sprinted through the large linoleum hallway. From behind us, a long board shot through the narrow windows of the doors and buried itself into the metal casing of a locker at the other end of the hall, missing my face by inches.

The hall turned, descended in a downward slope, and turned again, becoming a long basement-level hallway, lined with handrails and classroom doors. The space was crammed–parents with toddlers, pets, middle-aged women with large handbags,

258

elderly people clinging to walkers next to their doting daughters, school staff wringing their hands and telling everyone to stay down close to the walls. People were banging on the windowless doors to the locked classrooms, which were already jammed full.

The F-5 tornado hit the school dead on. I thought the roar was going to vibrate my brains into gel. Papa pulled us into the crowd as far as we could make it before the building tore away over our heads. He pushed Irene and me to the wall. I fell over a man clutching three crumpled paper sacks. He must have been too scared to feel my knee jammed in his back. I rolled over and Irene plopped onto my stomach. Papa sprawled over us both. The ceiling was gone. I could see a raging chaos of blackness racing overhead. Since we were just below the surface, we were protected from the direct blast of the winds. But that didn't last.

What had been designed as a storm shelter turned into a wind tunnel. Three-hundred-plus miles-per-hour winds rushed in at us. A tangle of wreckage—busted two-by-fours, tires, desks and couches, twisted street signs, and sheet metal—slammed into the curve at the end of the hall. If the hallway had been straight, the debris would have rushed straight though, killing *everyone*, right then and there. Those in the middle of the hallway with nothing to hold onto were immediately swept out and up into the churning tornado to their deaths. The rest of us cried out in horror as we clung to the handrail begging for our lives.

The railing was designed to hold the weight of winter jackets of four-year-olds, not a frantic mob. A long section of handrail broke loose from the wall. Dozens flew down the hallway and up into chaos.

Our handrail ripped away. I'll never forget the sound of Papa's screams. "No, No, No! Not my darlings! No ... *Not ... my ... darlings!*"

I never felt such terror—to hear *Papa* sound like that! I'd forgotten he'd ever called us that. With that display of raw unguarded emotion, in my heart I knew we were all about to die. I could feel the wind force its fingers under me. It lifted the man under me off the ground, sending Papa, Irene, and me tumbling through the hallway. Grasping handfuls of air, I found the leg of a guy who'd latched onto a remaining section of hand railing. To my left, Papa was clinging to a metal door-handle with his left hand. In his right, he had Irene's forearm. A bloody gash ran across her right cheek to her ear. The wind gained strength.

The skin rippling across Irene's cheeks, she screamed, "Papa!" her tone raw, naked fear. She knew she was about to die.

Screaming through the wind, Papa said, "I will never let go! I ... will ... NEVER let go! I will ... *NEVER* ... LET ... GO!"

Irene screamed.

As suddenly as it'd come, the wind stopped. The tornado passed and the roaring sound of the train raged away, killing many more in its wake.

With Irene's forearm still in his clutches, Papa found me nearby, holding onto the handrail. He pulled us to his chest in a large bear hug. I could hear him crying, over and over, "I love you! I love you! I love you! I'll never let go."

The storm had missed our house. Homes two blocks away had been swept off their foundation. That's why we were smiling in the photo. We'd dodged a bullet, sure, but we could have avoided it altogether if we'd just stayed at home.

Papa said we needed to live in the moment more, appreciating all we have. After that, he planned for us to go camping at Yosemite National Park. Irene had always wanted to go. I have to admit, I was excited, too, although I wasn't really into camping. Irene had printed a copy of the photograph of us in front of our unscathed house, and cut and pasted a picture of Yosemite's Half Dome into the background. We never made it to Yosemite.

As Irene sat there on the bed, years later, she looked up at me, waving the Half Dome cutout in her hand. She flipped it over. On the back, in Papa's handwriting, it read, "I will see you again in mountains." Tears streamed down her cheek.

Irene handed the cutout to me and said, "He must have written this before he left."

"Before the bus crash?"

"I don't think there was a bus crash, Edith. Papa is *alive*. He's the only one could have known this message was there. He's the only one who could have written it on the sword."

"So where is he then?"

"I don't know, but when I find out, I'll do anything to get him back.

Chapter 42

From the Golden Gate Bridge, eastward across San Francisco Bay, Jeremy watched the wave come over the landscape of Sausalito to Oakland, the land appearing like the ground had turned to liquid.

The foundations of the two bridge towers supporting the suspensions turned to mashed potatoes, bending the Golden Gate inward like chopsticks. The span flung people, dead and alive, into the water with busses, trucks, and police cruisers.

The center of the roadway snapped. The towering support on the north side, which was already burning, broke into two large chunks, the tallest part falling headlong into the white-capped waters, the lower piece slouching up against the Marin County coastline. The southern tower and a long span of roadway on the San Francisco side wriggled with the repeated earthquake shudders.

Jeremy clung to the pavement on his stomach near the railing. He sprang to his hands and feet. Keeping low, he crawled several feet before leaping up twenty-five feet to the side of the tower. He stuck there like a spider.

A massive suspension cable snapped, leaning the remaining tower toward the bay waters. The span ripped away from the road. He crawled up the sheer side of the falling tower, picking up speed on all fours, faster than he had ever gone on two feet on solid ground. Once the bridge had bent more than thirty degrees, he leapt to his feet and ran upward, pickåing up speed.

As he approached the tip of the tower, at fifty degrees, it split in half, catapulting him into the air. He arched his back, reached upward, and ascended toward the center of the UFO.

Chapter 43

A KNOCK AT THE DOOR.

"Just a minute," Tabitha said, her voice shaky. She snatched a canvas tarp and grunted as she threw it over something in the corner. She switched off a lamp and went to her workbench. She snatched a flat-head screwdriver and tapped its handle on the table, faking work sounds. "Almost ready."

"Can I come in yet?" Esau said.

She sighed and whispered, "*Dad*." She wiped her brow with her right hand, scratching her forehead. *Her right hand!* She twisted her prosthetic back and forth under a workbench light. From the stump of her forearm, an anatomically correct and fully functional right hand had been attached. She held out her left hand next to the new one, mirroring the touching of her index fingers of both hands from her pinkies to her thumbs. Other than the metallic appearance, the false hand moved as naturally as her real one, but with the noise and hum of a robotic appendage. She closed her eyes. Her mechanical hand fell to thousands of metal dice across the workbench.

She rubbed the end of her left stub and unlocked the door. "You can come in now, Dad."

Esau opened one of the swinging doors of the container and came in from the night.

"Working on something?" he said.

"Yeah," Tabitha said.

He smiled warmly and opened his arms. Tabitha hugged him. He sat on a stool and pointed to the pile of metal and plastic parts. "New project?"

"Something like that," she said, pushing the parts together into a pile on the rough surface of the workbench. She hopped up to a stool.

"We've got two new visitors in camp."

"Like the ones from the sky?"

"Soldiers."

Tabitha nodded. "How do you know they're soldiers?"

Esau slid a heavy hand over the top of his head. "I know something about them, Tabby. I've never told you this before, but before you were born, before I met your mother, even before we moved to Lizard Creek, I was a soldier ... once."

Tabitha's eyes swelled. "I thought we always lived here."

"*You* have always lived here, Tabby. I lived in a different place, a different world, before you came along. What seems like a lifetime ago, I was a member of a special group of soldiers. Called Rangers. They were so special, in fact, the army signed us up as a test group of super soldiers."

"Wow, you were a *super* soldier."

"That's what I thought. But it wasn't so super after all. The army wanted to plug us into these metal robots. It all sounded exciting. Of course, we didn't really have a choice. We were taken to an underground base somewhere in California, had us put under so we couldn't even see where we'd been taken. They made us *super*, all right. Stripped our minds, reprogrammed through and through. After months of treatment and training, we went outside again—at night—on training missions.

"During one of the missions, my hovercraft, like the ones you just saw, crashed somewhere out in the desert. By then, I'd practically forgotten who I was. I survived the crash and woke up, remembering some of myself. The trauma must have done it. I don't know. I was awake enough to know I wanted out. I crawled out of my *super* suit and limped into the wilderness. They must have assumed I'd burned up or maybe just didn't care to track down damaged goods. Either way, no one found me.

"A clan of Bedouins picked me up before I could die from dehydration or sunstroke. They took me east to Arizona and tried to sell me. When I broke free, I eventually made it north to Utah, where I heard rumors about a camp south of Yellowstone. I came here and met your mother, Korea. Then you came along."

"Why haven't you ever told me before??"

He sighed. "I wanted to forget my past, Tabby. The person I was, the fighter, the soldier, the *killer*—that's not me." He held out his hands. "This Esau ... the one you know ... is me, the real me, before I ever became a soldier."

"Is Esau your real name?"

"It's my real name now." He cut her off. "Don't ask. I don't want you to know, in case anyone asks."

"Who's going to ask?"

He pointed to the ceiling. "Those people from the sky would

ask. They were here for you, Tabby. I was one of them once. I know what they can do and I know they may do you harm."

Tabitha's eyes looked like they were going to pop out.

"You posted a video to the System, didn't you?" he said.

"How do you know?"

"I know about such things from my past life. And ... our visitors told me."

"I didn't ask anyone to come here."

"Not on purpose, you didn't. But there's a woman and a man in the camp asking for you by name," Esau said. "They want to talk with you. They say they're not with those from the sky. They came by some pretty serious-looking off-road vehicles. They say there's a revolution going on and they believe you have the key. We haven't told them you're here, but they know, just the same. You know what they're talking about, Tabby?"

Tabitha blushed. She nodded. "I think, maybe."

Esau scanned around the room. "What?"

Tabitha rested her stub on the workbench and closed her eyes. Esau's eyes widened as the parts vibrated, spread out evenly across the workbench, narrowed in a straight line, and fell in on top of each other, forming a long tube. The end slid to the rounded stub of Tabitha's forearm. As the pieces fell into place, tightening in on each other as though pieced together by invisible hands, Tabitha opened her eyes and held her prosthetic out at Esau, wiggling her fingers. Tears streamed down her face. She said, "Look, Dad. My hand!"

Esau's eyes watered. "Tabby, I can't believe it. I can't believe it." He caressed the back of her prosthetic.

"I can actually *feel* that, Dad."

"We can't tell this to anyone, not even Lenny. They'll want to take you away."

"When I said 'maybe,' this is not what I meant."

Tabitha flipped a switch. A light bulb hanging at the far end of the container blinked into life. "You've shared your secret, Dad. Here's one of mine."

She flipped back the tarp from the corner. Made in the same way as her prosthetic, an anatomically correct duplicate of Tabitha stood in the corner. It turned to Esau and smiled. "Esau, please meet Tabitha," Tabitha said.

Chapter 44

SKINNER SHUFFLED HIS BOOTS THROUGH GRAVEL MADE OF BLACK glass. "Take a look," he said.

They'd reached a fork in the tunnel. To the right, Skinner's gun light pointed into another tunnel. A few feet past the turn a large round metal wall blocked the way—no door handle, no window, no keyhole. Just a flat metal barrier with a round crease about six feet in diameter.

Skinner patted the wall. "If anyone or anything was meant to pass through there, it's from the other side," he said.

Nicholas kicked the wall with the heel of his right boot. "Feels thick." He touched scorch marks around the crease.

"I tried to weld through it some time ago," Skinner said, "but I gave up."

Nicholas shrugged. "Wouldn't be the first time."

"Let's keep moving." Skinner stepped back into the tunnel, the gun light as his feet.

Nicholas came along, shifting the weight of his pack. "You know, I was thinking … " he said.

"I hope it's not contagious."

" … If this UFO's still following me, and it's still directly above me right now, then someone who knows this tunnel is here is eventually going to figure out the UFO is following this tunnel and come down to check on things."

The tunnel lit up with intensity of ten thousand suns.

A voice from a bullhorn blared. "Stop right there!"

Nicholas froze, his dark skin ashen in the super-bright lights. Skinner stopped, shifting his weight back and forth. "Who goes there?" he said, with a casual attitude, out of place under the circumstances.

"Put down your weapons!"

Skinner smiled and cocked his head. "Who goes there?" he said.

"Drop your weapons! This is your last warning."

Skinner grinned.

The earthquake hit. The lights went out except the one on Skinner's rifle. Nicholas watched it spin through the air in slow motion. Images of heavily armored soldiers, Skinner's smiling face, Nicholas' wide eyes, the curved black glassy walls of the tunnel caving in on itself, falling rocks, flashed in the darkness.

Gunfire erupted. Something grabbed Skinner under his arms and pulled him to the metal wall. The ground and walls jerked in every direction. Shudders continued for several minutes. When it stopped, Skinner lay on his back in blackness, coughing violently.

"Nicholas?" Skinner said.

No answer.

"Nick?"

No answer.

Skinner yelled. "Son!"

"I *knew* you were my Dad," Nicholas said.

"You little chindi!" Skinner said.

"This little devil just saved your life, Dad."

Skinner grabbed Nicholas' hand and drew it to his chest. It was sticky wet.

"Dad?"

Skinner coughed up blood. "In the chest. That's it. There's just no way."

Nicholas dropped Skinner's hand. Rustling in his pack, he tuned the guitar and played *Rivera Paradise*, his fingers glowing blue. An incandescent color pulsed from the strings, filling the cramped area between the metal door and a rocky cave-in. The blue and burning white light washed over Skinner's wound. The bleeding stopped, the hole closed, and fresh skin formed over the gash.

Everything went pitch dark again when Nicholas stopped playing.

Skinner sat up and rubbed his thumb over his chest. "You sure you ain't a devil?" Skinner said.

"Stand back," Nicholas said. "I think I might be able to make it through this door."

"Give me a minute. I was dead just a second ago."

Skinner crawled across the ground and found the curved wall. He followed it away from the door until he met the rubble from the cave-in. "The tunnel's collapsed," he said.

"Just stay behind me."

Nicholas unleashed a barrage of metal riffs from Pantera's

Mouth For War, note for note. Blasts of hot white and red beams shot from the headstock, pounding with each pick attack. The wall went from dark orange, red, to white hot in the middle. Kneeling behind Nicholas, Skinner covered his face. A molten hole burned through the four-foot-thick wall.

Nicholas stopped. Drops of melted steel, filling the niche with dim light, cooled and froze in place around a crude hole.

"Metal doesn't get the respect it deserves," Nicholas said.

Over Nicholas' shoulder at the gaping hole, Skinner said, "I'm just glad you didn't take up the clarinet."

Chapter 45

IT WAS SHIPPING DAY. PAPA PULLED THE PALLET JACK INTO THE storage room as usual. One of the bay doors at the far end of the room stood wide open. A single forklift busily loaded pallets of CBs into a truck. Several other trucks had been loaded and had departed on their routes. A guy leaned against a supply cart, smoking a cigarette; Reggie, the same guy who'd busted Papa before.

Reggie pushed his ball cap up and said, "Look here … if it isn't the *live one* from before."

The fella driving the forklift, Jim, leaned out. "Sure enough, Reggie. Now are you going to help me load this truck or do I have the live one do it myself?"

"Only one of us can drive it," Reggie said. "Besides, I do all the driving outside this place."

Papa passed Reggie and placed the pallet at the end of the row. On Papa's way back, Reggie punched him in the cheek. Papa's head rocked sideways and he nearly fell. He kept moving, though, without catching Reggie's eye or offering any reaction.

Reggie turned to the back of the truck. "Yeah, this one's *Rehabilitated*. And good! Reggie felt a tap on his right shoulder. When he wheeled around, the point of a *katana* sword snipped his nose. Reggie dropped his cigarette as Jim drove the forklift out of the truck.

Holding the sword in his right hand, Papa held out his other hand for Jim to stop. To Jim he said, "If Reggie does what I say … if Reggie hands me his CB … I won't have to take off his head."

Reggie's neck shrunk into his shoulders.

Jim leaned forward on the steering wheel. "I think Reggie is going to do anything you say, mister." Jim sounded like he was enjoying the situation.

Reggie slipped off his CB and placed it in Papa's hand.

"Now you," Papa said, pointing to Jim.

Jim reached for his CB. Papa said, "By the clasp. Don't touch the CB itself." Jim did as he was told and tossed the CB to Papa's feet.

"Now both of you … take out your lenses and earbuds," Papa said.

Reggie and Jim complied.

"Now, you, in the truck," Papa said. "Park the forklift in the truck and come back out here with the keys."

Papa held the blade against Reggie's neck as Jim followed the instructions. Jim walked out of the back of the truck, whistling.

Papa tapped Reggie on the shoulder. "You two go into the back of the truck." Papa's voice was smooth and resolute. His calm, deep tone suggested he might be capable of anything.

Reggie gazed into the dark confines of the half-loaded truck, probably wondering if it was the end of the road. "What are you going to do to me?"

"Nothing … if you do as I say," Papa said.

Papa walked behind Reggie with the sword pointed as his back. Jim stood off to the side of the truck. Jim shrugged, holding his hands out to his sides, as if to say, *I'm just along for the ride.*

Once Reggie was inside the back of the truck, Papa said, "Now take off your clothes and toss them out here."

Reggie whined. "Aw, you gotta be kidding me!"

Papa patted the blade in his left hand.

"I don't think he's kidding," Jim said.

The voice in Papa's ear said, "Proceed."

Reggie's jumpsuit and cap flew out and landed on the ramp, piece by piece. Papa laid the sword next to his left foot and undressed, putting on the clothes. Jim was about twenty feet away, staring at the sword.

Stepping into the pantlegs, Papa said, "Jim … I can have the sword back in my hands and at your throat before you're halfway here." He zipped up the suit, two-times too big for him. He pulled on the white cap – the only thing that fit.

Papa picked up the sword and held it at his left side. He threw his green suit into the back of the truck. "Put this on for size," he said to Reggie. "It'll keep you warm. Besides, you'll probably be wearing one before long."

The voice said, "Proceed."

Once Reggie zipped up the green jumpsuit, Papa pointed. "Go to the seat of the forklift." Then he pointed to Jim. "Grab a roll of tape and wrap his hands around the steering wheel. Then wrap his

277

ankles together, tape them to the pedals, and tape his mouth closed, too. I don't want him making any noise."

Once Jim had followed the instructions, he took the keys out of the forklift, closed the back of the truck, and locked it. "Now what?"

"Reggie is the driver of the truck?" Papa said.

Jim nodded.

"Go to the driver's side."

After Jim slid the ramp under the truck, he closed the bay door with an automatic switch. He and Papa exited the building through a side door opening to a narrow metal stairway leading to a large blacktop area around the truck. On a busy shipping day, the space was full of loading trucks. The other trucks had already been loaded and had left. Jim walked toward the driver's side door of the semi's cab and opened it. He grabbed a handle to pull himself up, but Papa said, "Stop." Jim froze, glancing behind him. Papa was too far away for Jim to kick him.

"Step back down here," Papa said. "Slowly."

Jim looked back into the open cab of the truck.

The voice said, "Proceed."

"Step back down here, now, or I'll rip you open."

"Who'll drive the truck?" Jim said. He didn't move.

"I'm driving this truck with or without you," Papa said. "I'd just as soon kill you both right here and now, which would make it easier for me. If I'm caught, that's it for me, anyway. So I've got nothing to lose. May as well take as many down with me as possible. Maybe you want to be the first? Or maybe you want to do the right thing ... and *get down from the side of the cab right now?*"

Jim eyed the sword again. He inched down off the cab and

stood off to the side. Papa climbed into the driver's side of the cab and found a compact semi-automatic 9-millimeter handgun holstered into the side of Reggie's seat. Papa snapped it out and pointed it at Jim.

The voice said, "Proceed."

"Is this what you were looking for?" Papa said.

Jim shrugged.

Papa searched the rest of the cab. He found a switchblade in the glove box on Jim's side.

"Come around from the other side and get in," Papa said.

Jim opened the door and climbed in the passenger seat. He clicked on his seatbelt and pointed to the center console between the passenger and driver's seats. "You missed something."

Papa found the small hidden compartment and pulled out a .38 revolver.

"You didn't want to save it for later?" Papa said.

"I hate guns," Jim said.

Papa reached for an ignition key and found none.

"It starts with Reggie's CB," Jim said.

Papa inserted the end of the CB into a socket on the dash. The diesel engine chugged and then roared to life. Papa released the brake and put the automatic transmission in drive.

"Have you driven one of these things?" Jim said.

"I drove a smaller truck for a short while when I was in college ... a long time ago."

The voice said, "Stop and hold."

Papa drove down a blacktop road to a twenty-foot chain-link fence topped with coiled razor wire. There was a guard checkpoint in the distance.

"You can obviously do as you wish," Jim said, "but I don't see how you're going to pass this checkpoint. You don't look anything like Reggie."

The voice said, "Ready for inspection."

"Naw, I'm the spitting image of Reggie." Papa cupped the 9-millimeter in his left hand, pointing it at Jim sideways. "If I hear a peep out of you …."

Jim held up his hands playfully. "I'm the least of your concerns. I just want to see if you pull this off."

Papa drove the truck to the next checkpoint. The cab of the truck was at the same level as a small booth where a guard sat wearing a helmet and dark visor. Papa gripped the pistol tightly with his left hand and casually rested his right forearm on top of the steering wheel. He smiled into the guard's face.

"CBs," the guard said, messing with empty space. The guard's nametag read: "Nevel Jones."

Papa held out Reggie's CB to the guard who swiped a wand over it just under Papa's chin. A computer voice from inside the guard booth said, "Reggie Duane."

The guard faced Papa and nodded. He said, "Next." Papa held out Jim's CB to the guard. He gripped the pistol and smiled sideways at Jim. The guard scanned Jim's CB. The voice said, "Jim Croft." Jim reached over Papa to take his CB back. Papa and Jim were nose to nose. Papa pressed the pistol against Jim's gut. Jim eased back into this seat and slipped the CB over his neck. The guard eyed Jim and Papa again, and said, "Speed it up, you two. You're the last truck out of shipping … *again*. If you keep this up your next visit will be a one-way trip."

The security fence rolled back. Papa said, "Will do," and pulled away.

"What the hell?" Jim said. "Nevel looked right at you!"

"He only sees what the CB allows him to see. The CB told him I was Reggie. He'd never question it. You should ask yourself what you're overlooking. By the way ... give me back the CB."

Jim took off the CB and tossed it on the dash. Papa drove ahead as the security gate at the next row of razor wire fences opened near a sign reading, "Minefield."

"What is this place?" Jim said.

"It's a slave camp."

"Naw - it's a prison. You convicts just make CBs here."

"Criminals? Is that what they tell you? I came here believing I could work off some debts and save my family from being evicted into the Wild." Papa pointed to the pyramids in the distance. "Who do you think lives in those buildings?"

"Convicts."

"Those are cells where the thousands of so-called *Employees* live. You know something stinks about this place. People here aren't criminals. They're slaves. And most of them don't even know it."

Jim chuckled. "I guess everyone in prison thinks they're innocent."

"Don't you have a family member or friend who's died or disappeared recently?"

Jim rubbed his eyes. "Maybe. Not sure. Seems so long ago."

"Don't put your CB on for a few days. Take out those earbuds and contacts. You'll be surprised what you remember."

The next security gate opened as Papa's truck approached.

281

The fences lining the roadway on the other side were marked, "High voltage." They approached the polished metal gate of the outer concrete wall of Freedom Colony.

Jim rubbed his temples. "I think I was married before and got a divorce. Nikki was her name. After the divorce, I never saw her again."

"Are you sure you had a divorce?"

"Crud," Jim said, holding his forehead with both hands.

"You remember now?"

"I don't think you're going to like me very much."

As the gate at the exterior wall came back, several armored vehicles blocked the exit. "Sorry," Jim said. "I triggered the alarm when I touched the CB back at the first security checkpoint.

Chapter 46

Given pressure and time, you'll eventually tell a polygrapher everything. Whether you want to or not. He'll accuse you, condemn you, degrade you, wear you out. In the end, you'll want to tell him everything, confess to anything, just to get it all over with. Unless a small voice in the back of your head reminds you that the whole thing's a sham.

Martin's eyes were swollen and his cheeks drooped. Without any *real* windows, I didn't know whether it was day or night. I figured it hadn't even been twenty-four hours since I'd been kidnapped with Irene from our classroom. For all I knew, it was three in the morning, and it didn't matter, since we were over three thousand feet below the surface in a place called "29 Palms," whatever it was.

It's a DUMBS.

Well *that* tells me *everything*, I thought. My sore hip was bothering me again. Martin let me take a restroom break. With him just feet away, and me behind the sliding door, I realized just how flimsy the construction of the room was. I could hear Martin strolling around out there to stretch his legs. He could easily break in if I tried anything funny. And I was probably being watched by video as I sat on the one-piece metal toilet with no lid, performing the number two I'd put off as long as possible. There comes a time when modesty gives way to the call of nature. If anybody wanted to watch then they should see all the glory. *I still won't be taking a shower*, I told myself, hoping I would be leaving soon.

My orange jumpsuit down around my ankles, I leaned over the round stainless steel drain cover bolted to the floor. The metal pipe beyond disappeared into blackness, smelling more like a well-oiled engine than a bathroom. The faintest hum and clicking came; hardly audible, but it was there. Something mechanical at the end of the pipe; the first sound I'd heard outside that room since I'd arrived. Like a seed grows into an oak tree, the idea swelled into the notion that I could leave, with or without permission. I also felt despair, facing the fact for the first time that was on my own. I couldn't count on Papa, La-La, Irene, or anyone. *I couldn't help them unless I helped myself.*

I finished my business and checked myself in the mirror. I looked worse than when I first woke up in this place, whatever it was.

It's a DUMBS.

I shook the thought out my head, lightly whipping my platinum bangs over my darkened eye sockets, smirking slightly and thinking, *It certainly is – dumb!*

I zipped up my jumpsuit and returned to the chair. Martin hooked me back up to the polygraph machine with the care of a doctor handling a burn victim. He pulled on the tubes around my chest, asking if it was too tight. His hands were strong but moved with a sort of forced sensitivity, like he was secretly afraid of me. He checked the clips on my fingers again, and returned to his seat. He patted the locket in his front shirt pocket.

"Before we resume the questions and answers," Martin said, "Let me refresh your memory." He twisted an invisible vault dial in mid-air and the window screen came to life with a familiar scene: a wide-angle view of the street in front of my house, the perspective from overhead like some of those old-time war videos taken from a heavily armed helicopter somewhere in the Middle East, miles away from its targets, as it mowed down so-called enemy combatants with unforgiving gun turrets. Unlike those bloodbaths, his video was high definition. I presumed they got video from the perspective of a micro-drone hovercraft or something like that. I could see the front of our house to the left and the heavy metal wall entrance two blocks down the street. The entrance rolled back, revealing the grille of a large military vehicle. Although the video had no sound, I could remember the deep rumbling from the heavily armed vehicles parading into our Prefecture. All in all, there were six of them, painted white with the words, "Meadow Oaks," the last carrying Prefect Sheriff Garth Tillman and a couple of his deputies.

Watching the video of the convoy coming to a halt in front of our house, still damaged from the earthquake, I remembered what had happened, and dreaded what was about to happen. I gripped the leather arms of my chair as I watched dozens of soldiers in exoskeleton body armor and helmets with blacked-out visors pour out of the vehicles, brandishing short black machine guns.

By this time in the video, two days after the UFO showed up, we had known there was a small army just outside our front door. La-La, Irene, and I had gone downstairs and huddled on the couch as the soldiers took up positions outside our front door. Another group went around to the back. Part of me wanted to yell, *Tell the guys around back to knock, we're not going anywhere.* We would have come out the side door from the Chan room, where the garage used to be. La-La apparently wanted us to wait, making them either knock or let themselves in. After all, we didn't know how they'd react with all those weapons if we just came outside. One of the soldiers knocked on our faded red door. Irene was yelling that the door didn't open. It had been jammed shut since the earthquake. I guess the leader thought her yelling didn't sound friendly so he kicked in the door--doing us a favor, really--and the soldiers bolted into the house.

From the angle of this video I was watching with Martin, we couldn't see what was happening inside the house. Of course, I'd seen it with my own eyes. As the soldiers rushed inside from the front, Irene had said, "Good morning, what can we do for you?" I couldn't believe my ears. She forced out the words as if saying, "Do you mind if you stop for a minute to chat?" to an oncoming freight train.

Ignoring Irene, the soldiers pushed us off the couch and forced us face down to the floor with their knees in our backs. The guy on me cracked two of my ribs. They identified Irene and peeled her off the floor. The way La-La screamed scared me. "Eye … reen!" she wailed, drawing out each syllable with a Chinese accent as though the emphasis summoned a greater power to bring an end to the terror of having her crippled granddaughter ripped away. I screamed, too. I was kicked in the face while I was still on the floor, which nearly knocked me out. I could still see the waffle-stomper soles as they connected with my forehead and nose. I felt more angry than I'd ever felt, despite the pain involved. The guy who kicked me picked up Irene's cane and went out the front door hooting, as if they were the good guys.

Those were the parts I dreaded. The next part--not so much. On the video, two soldiers dragged Irene by her arms through the front door and outside. The soldier who had just kicked me marched in front of them, twirling Irene's short-sword. La-La and I had been forced up from the floor and were being led out the front door. The soldiers pulling Irene approached the back of an armored vehicle, open and ready to devour its prey.

The rest of the soldiers relaxed. Prefect Tillman and his deputies loitered around with crossed arms, beaming satisfaction as they decocked their weapons. The group from the back came strolling around the side, proud of a job well done.

Without any warning, a crooked bolt of thick blue lightning shot down from above and connected with Irene's sword. Though the video was silent, I could still hear the abrupt wail from the guy holding it. His whole body turned white hot until he was burned out of existence. Glowing blue, the sword dropped to the ground and rolled across the ground, scorching the earth. The soldiers dragging Irene had just enough time to let go of her before they were picked up and catapulted out of the video into the Wild. The two soldiers with La-La and me let go and ran for the armored vehicles. The rest threw down their weapons and hustled down the street toward the metal gate. Prefect Tillman was yelling something and waving his arms. With a low hum, beams of something like tubes of snaking water hit the armored vehicles, which imploded inward as if they'd been hit by a torpedo underwater, bursting apart in a hot blue eruption of dice-sized pieces. The leftover nuggets of the vehicles belched out of their center in a plume of hot air. The pieces of the broken vehicles separated into little parts and bounced across the street. The video cut off.

Martin turned from the window screen, leering at me with a mix of satisfaction and disgust. "I knew some of those soldiers," he said. "Good people."

"Your friend, the parade master there, kicked me in the face. Did you know him, too?"

No.

"Yes, he had daughters, Chris and Monica—*twins*."

"Really?"

No.

"How does it make you feel, being responsible for making two girls fatherless?"

"Well, I never wanted anyone to die."

"Is that so? If you had just turned yourselves in you'd be back home and *everything* could have been avoided."

I didn't argue with him. I just wanted to finish up, tell him everything, and go back home. Sure, I felt bad for those who'd died and felt worse when I saw the video, even if I had been kicked in the face. But the guilt Martin was laying on my shoulders had no weight because I knew, somehow, he was lying to me. He wanted me to feel responsible. I didn't, though. I'd still play along with him and answer all of his questions if it got me home.

Chapter 47

THE X-24 DROPPED OUT OF MACH 1 SOUTH OF THE RIO GRANDE Gorge Bridge and dove into the canyon, snaking its way southward through the cliffs and bluffs lining the river until it reached the small fingers of mesas running westward up toward Los Alamos National Laboratory. As the hovercraft banked right and left, following the dry river in the night, Martin could see the dark mass of the Sundog overhead masking the starry sky.

The hovercraft followed a valley on the southern side of the sprawling Laboratory. The valley opened into a flat area surrounded by low-lying piñon trees. The aircraft landed in a deserted parking lot west of a boxy two-story building made of two long rectangular structures parallel to one another and connected by an enclosed concourse.

The straps around Martin's legs, arms, and torso slackened, and the lining within the form-fitting seat deflated with a hiss. The co-pilot manhandled Martin as soon as the pressurized door swung open from the aerodynamic fuselage, prying him out of the chair. Martin pushed back the co-pilot.

"I got it, I got it," Martin said.

"You may feel dizzy for a few minutes," the co-pilot said, holding Martin's forearm.

Martin pushed him back. "I said I got it."

The co-pilot shrugged and said, "Then stand clear!" and returned to his seat.

Martin stumbled to one knee, forced himself up, and limped away, dragging a lame left leg which had fallen asleep. The torrent blew him to both knees as the hovercraft lifted from the sunbaked blacktop. The jet engines ignited, and he covered his ears and kneeled to the ground. When the sound subsided, he sat back on his hind legs. Weeds and dried scrub poked through spider-veined cracks across the lot. The white parking lines had worn away long ago. Turning north he could see the glow from the TA-3, one of the larger cluster of buildings making up Los Alamos' isolated technical areas scattered across the mesas.

In awe, he lifted his gaze to the Sundog overhead, which was covering the mountains and valleys around Los Alamos and beyond. It was the first time he'd seen one up close. Its undercarriage to the west nearly scraped the mountaintops at the rim of the dormant super volcano. He got up, put his fists on his hips and yelled up at the UFO. "Well, here I am!" His voice faded in the wind, hissing through the pines. "So, what do you want?"

A glass door with peeling sun-shield tint opened from the rectangle building. A faded sign at the head of a sidewalk, connecting the parking lot to the building, read, "TA-16: Weapons Engineering Tritium Facility." A chunky late-middle-aged woman, her shoulder-length dark and greying hair in a ponytail, fast-walked toward him with an agility of an athlete who'd been in better shape. Her unbuttoned khaki vest covered with zippered pockets and clasps rippled in the wind. Wearing a pair of dusty hiking shoes, chambray shirt sleeves rolled up to her elbows, and weathered jeans, she pushed a narrow pair of black-plastic-rimmed glasses up her purpled-veined nose and straightened a loose rectangular silver and turquoise bolo tie with Mimbres step patterns.

"Doctor Lorien, Doctor Lorien, Doctor Lorien," the woman said. She rubbed the tops of her hands in circles. "I'm so glad, so glad, you're here."

Doctor Lorien. He didn't say so, but he didn't remember he had a doctorate in anything. He answered the woman with a blank stare.

"Don't you remember me?" She cocked her head to one side and put the backs of her hands at her waist. "It's Judith." She took off her glasses, shifting her face side to side. "I know I've aged a little, I've put on a little weight ... just a little ... but don't tell me I look *that* different."

He smiled warmly. "Of course ... Judith."

"You don't remember me at all," she said. "You're breaking my heart." She smiled knowingly and turned her back on him, walking toward the building as he watched her go.

She waved for him to come along. "Don't worry, Martin ... don't worry. It'll come back to you. Trust me."

Martin followed her inside where she led him down a long hallway of buckling linoleum, beige wallpaper peeling away from crumbling walls. "Excuse the appearance," she said. "The earthquake wreaked havoc on everything around here. Still, the older buildings,

291

like this one, fared better than the others. Back in the late twentieth century, this area disguised development and storage of weapons-grade tritium. It was actually one of the first insertion sites."

"One of the insertion sites, yes," Martin said, having no idea what she was talking about.

"We don't use this entrance much anymore, and even then, this was a back entrance for a long time. We had to open it back up after the main entrance collapsed during the earthquake. We're still in emergency mode here. There've been several cave-ins."

Martin nodded.

From a vest pocket, she produced a ring of laser-cut keys on a chain and smiled. "You don't remember the Teardrop, do you?"

He maintained a stone face.

"It'll all come back to you," she said, hurrying around a left corner. Stopping at a metal door, she inserted a long key and twisted three times until a mechanical voice said, "Identify." She unclipped a cardkey with her photo from the snap-buttoned pocket flap of her shirt and pushed it into a narrow slot in the door. "Judith Barlow," the door said. "Clear."

After three thuds, the door cracked open a few centimeters. Judith yanked on a metal handle. The door hinges whined open. "This place has been here since the Cold War. Can you believe it?"

"Yes, actually," Martin said.

Judith dropped the key ring into her front vest pocket with an air of finality. "You'd better remember yourself soon, Martin. This stoic-spy-guy-attitude you're giving off is starting to bore me."

"Well, I wouldn't want to bore you."

"Dry smart-ass humor is a start," she said over her shoulder, passing through the door. She turned right, leading down a sloping hallway with a smooth concrete floor under antique fluorescent lighting that had burnt out long ago. She flipped out a penlight. They followed the hallway for several yards, dropping more than fifty feet. The walls fell away to a sloped concrete slab. The narrow pathway ran down the middle, as if a meteor had skidded up to a concrete wall, and the wall rose up to a reinforced ceiling supported by rows of I-beams.

Judith went to a black metal niche bolted into the side of the wall next to a huge round brushed-metal vault door. A blank keypad was bolted to the bottom inside the niche. She stuck her head inside. White light blared over her face. A female voice said, "Judith Barlow. Identify." Alphanumeric characters lit up on the keypad. She made several keystrokes, and said, "Judith Barlow."

The door said, "Clear," then hummed and clicked, followed by three thuds. The door eased open. When it was wide enough for them, she went through and waved for him to follow. Twenty feet into a wide tunnel, the concrete ended, revealing a black glassy tube. He reached out to touch the surface.

"Be careful, it's sharp," she said.

He pulled his hand back, rubbing his index finger and thumb together.

"This was one of the first insertion points," Judith said.

"So you said."

"Boy, you don't remember anything, do you?"

"It's coming back to me slowly."

She gave him a doubtful nod. "Let's hope so."

They found a light-rail train sitting in darkness. Like an amusement ride, its top was exposed, and had sections with golf-cart type seats facing backwards and forwards. Judith got into a seat with a control panel at the front and turned a key. Halogen lights shined down the long black tunnel sloping downward and fading into blackness.

Martin took a seat next to her like a rodeo cowboy climbing on a mad bull for the first time. "Don't worry, I couldn't crash this thing if I wanted," she said, pushing the control lever forward. He was probably more worried about the destination than the ride. The train hummed and edged forward. The concrete path soon fell away, exposing dual tracks running over a bed of black glassy shards. The temperature dropped quickly.

"The Subterrene was first developed and tested in this tunnel," she said, raising her voice over the wind and hum. "This is something of a museum ... that is ... if you have a Q-clearance or above."

"I have a clearance."

"Yeah, as far as I know, there's no limit to your clearance. You're sort of a celebrity around here. But don't let it go to your head."

"I won't."

"I swear ... you'd better lighten up soon!"

The tunnel continued downward for several hundreds of yards before its diameter doubled and the passageway forked. The rails to the right continued roughly the same height of the first tunnel. The larger tunnel went to the left. She stopped the train at the fork and pointed into the smaller tunnel to the right.

"That's where we're headed, but we'll take a short detour first. I want to show you something." The rails led down the larger tunnel for another thirty yards and then ended at a low concrete barrier. They got out and walked into the train's lights, which blared into a domed cavern over a hundred feet tall. A ten-story steel support structure of I-beams had been built in six vertical segments. Boreholes evenly pockmarked the surface overhead, as well as the bowl below, looking as though construction of a geodesic dome had been abandoned.

"This is where we found it," Judith said.

"Just assume I don't know anything about anything."

Judith's eyelids fell lazily halfway shut, suppressing a playful smile. "Boy, they wiped your brain *clean*, didn't they?"

"To hear *them* tell it, *I* wiped it."

"And you don't remember any of this?" She sounded unconvinced.

He shook his head.

"Do you remember our daughter?"

His eyes widened, then narrowed. "Do you remember her name?"

"Brandy."

Silence.

"How is she?"

"Dead."

Judith cupped her hand over her mouth. She grabbed his left shoulder. "Oh, Martin, I'm so sorry, I'm so sorry! I didn't know."

"I was attending her funeral when the Sundogs showed up, I know that much."

She mouthed, "Sorry."

"I guess this means we don't have a history," he said.

She let her arm drop heavily to her side and turned to the cavern. "I'll let you figure that one out for yourself." She pointed

295

her finger to a spot in the middle of the steel girders. "That's where they found it."

"It?"

"Right. You don't know *anything*. It—the Teardrop."

He raised his eyebrows.

She pointed behind them and continued: "As I said, the Subterrene tunneled this out. Quite an amazing thing, actually. It's essentially a long mechanical earthworm. Remote controlled and nuclear powered, it was developed here at Los Alamos, naturally, since this place is the birthplace of the atomic bomb and has a history of breakthroughs in laser technologies. The head of the Subterrene is essentially a mass of high-energy lasers, which melts anything—and I mean anything – that's in front of it. Once it's put into the ground, it burns through earth and rock, leaving a glassy black tube behind, with little to no debris, which means there are no leftovers to haul out, a considerable time and money saver. It also makes it easier to conceal. If we had to take all the dirt and rock out, someone would ask questions. And with the molten tube the Subterrene makes, the tunnel doesn't need to be reinforced. There's little to no infrastructure to be built, depending on its use."

"How fast does it dig?"

"Seven miles a day."

"Then, when was this place made?" Martin sounded shocked.

"The ground on this tunnel was first broken in the late 1980s."

Martin gazed into the void of the tunnel. "Over a hundred years ago? At that rate, there could be thousands and thousands of miles of these tunnels by now. How many miles are there and where do they lead?"

"I was hoping you could tell me that, spy boy."

He turned and walked to the edge of hollowed out dome. He spotted a narrow pathway of crude and cracked concrete leading down the side with a metal handrail. "And the Teardrop—what was it?"

"We still don't know. We do know a few things about how it reacts. But we're getting ahead of ourselves. After they put the Subterrene to work back in the 1980s, everything was going fine at first. You saw the tunnel. It didn't even go a mile before it just stopped, which was a huge problem, since it didn't go in reverse. After the thing cooled off, it was partly disassembled from behind, put back together and restarted. It appeared to be working fine but just wouldn't go any further. They finally dug in around the sides, which was no easy task, since it was sitting in the middle of a huge patch of melted granite. The digging went around the sides and to the front until they found it."

"The Teardrop?"

"The Teardrop. At first, there was just a little bit of blackness exposed through the granite. The odd thing was … aside from what had already happened … whatever was buried in the rock … it didn't register on any scanner. It showed up as part of the granite encasing it.

"The granite around it was jackhammered away, exposing the black object. It looked like a perfectly formed water droplet--a huge round inflatable exercise ball on the bottom side, with a cone tapering into an infinitely sharp point at its top. Other than its looks, they called it the Teardrop in part because of all the trouble it had caused.

297

"It just got weirder and weirder after that. Once the Teardrop was about ninety percent excavated, load lifters were brought in to move it out of the way. But nothing would budge it. Someone finally noticed the thing didn't even reflect light. Consider any black object. Black will always have a shine to it, no matter the surface. But this thing seemed to completely absorb light like a black hole.

"In the effort to move the thing, they used lasers and diamond-tipped jackhammers on it. Nothing could even scratch it. They excavated under and around the Teardrop. Once completely freed from the granite, the thing just fell softly and directly to the ground, bouncing a few times like a party balloon, the top ever pointing upward. Once it came to a rest on the ground, it became unmovable again. Weird, huh?"

Martin nodded and gestured to the dome. "Obviously something moved it."

"More like someone, the poor sap. When the Teardrop fell, the lead scientist, Doctor David Blithe, a metallurgist of all things, lost his patience and grabbed the tip of it without gloves. Grasping the tapered top, he just froze. His face went blank and stayed blank. He just stood there with a thousand mile stare. A colleague yelled at him to take his hand off the thing. He obeyed. At the time, it didn't occur to anyone, but that little detail was critical. Sometimes, if you put too many super smart people in one place, they're collective IQs seem to cancel out common sense.

"Dr. Blithe didn't wake up from his trance. As you might imagine, he was immediately taken to the Los Alamos Lab medical facilities, which has a great deal of experience in treating heedless scientists hurt working on secret and dangerous projects. Sometimes I'm amazed no one here accidently blew up northern New Mexico, what with all the risky experiments that have gone on up here.

"Anyway, as Dr. Blithe was being treated, the Teardrop remained unmovable. Testing on the Teardrop and treatment of Dr. Blithe continued. While Dr. Blithe was basically comatose, his body was still functional. Like a vegetable, he didn't acknowledge anyone with a smile or conversation. However, he responded to any verbal instruction. If his wife said, 'Open your mouth,' when trying to feed him, he opened his mouth. He followed any cue from anyone. He walked around the room, did jumping jacks, stood on one foot, used the toilet, anything like that, as long as someone told him to do it. He'd even jump off a cliff, probably, but no one ever suggested it to him. But if left alone, without instruction, he did nothing. After a year of this, his wife signed off on his living will, designating him as deceased. For all intents and purposes, he was. His wife and family attended his memorial. Of course, he wasn't there. The government took Blithe back into the tunnel one last time, just to see – to make sure—that touching the Teardrop wouldn't snap him back out of his trance-like state. Someone told him to touch the Teardrop and he followed the instructions. He didn't come out of his trance, but when he touched the damn thing, it moved like a balloon, bouncing across the tunnel floor.

"Dr. Blithe could pick up the thing and carry it around. This obviously solved the problem of moving it, which was relocated for more testing and study. The Subterrene continued with its mission. It created this underground complex. The Teardrop stayed here for a while, until another one was found by the Subterrene."

"Where was it?"

"Out in California, underground … Anyway, so, there you have it."

"What do you mean?"

"This is why you're here."

"No, no, no," he said, shaking his head with a smirk. "I'm not here to gawk over a black crystal ball found in the dirt. I'm just here to help reboot the System."

"You *still* don't remember? The Teardrop *is* the System, hon."

Chapter 48

NICHOLAS FRETTED *FOR THE LOVE OF GOD* BY STEVE VAI. Dancing light blue and green waves of colors pulsed and danced at the sides of the black glassy tube, illuminating the way forward.

Behind him, Skinner ruffled through his pant and shirt pockets. "You got a match?"

"Nope."

"Well, can't you make some sparks with that guitar of yours?"

"I don't want to blow off your fingers."

Skinner shuffled out to the side in the gravel. "Here, I'll put it down on the ground. Try to light the end."

"You want to smoke? *Now*?"

"I almost died. I especially need to smoke. *Now*!"

Skinner tossed the Pall Mall Blue to the ground. "Just light either end. It don't matter."

"You smoke Pall Mall lights? Isn't that a contradiction in terms?"

"They don't mess with my allergies."

Nicholas kept strumming with a scowl.

"Just light the damn thing!" Skinner said.

Nicholas aimed and segued to an aggressive vibrato on the lower E string on high neck. A light burst out of his headstock. The cigarette sparked into a wisp of smoke.

Skinner leaned over the rising vapor and breathed in deeply. "Well, I guess it was worth at least one heavy drag." He stood and lost his balance, feeling dizzy. "Say, that was pretty concentrated stuff." He slid another cigarette out of his shirt pocket. "Do it again."

Nicholas kept strumming and walked away. Skinner snatched the cigarette and caught up. He smiled at Nicholas' back as he buttoned the cigarette pack into his front shirt pocket.

"Maybe we should go back," Nicholas said.

"Naw. We've come this far."

"They were waiting for us back there because the UFO, or whatever it is, must still be centered directly over us."

"So?"

"So, they're going to see the thing moving off in a different direction, following another one of their tunnels."

"And if we go back you can bet we'll find an angry pack of G.I. Joes waiting for us. Heck, they're probably already coming up the tunnel from the cabin."

After several more miles they took a break with an MRE and a nap. Pushing on for less than a mile, they found a niche on the right side of the tunnel with a steel ladder inside running up and down through a narrow tube, sealed off by hinged metal covers above and below.

Skinner squatted, ran his hand over a hexagonal keyhole, and felt the thick hinge. "Probably an emergency exit."

Nicholas tapped his boot on the floor's manhole. "I wonder where it goes?"

Skinner faced the blackness of the tunnel. "I say we stay on this level for now."

"Why not just go up and out?"

"We don't know it will lead out. And if we're up top, we'll be exposed, easier to catch. Besides, I found food and water on this level before. Maybe we'll find it again ahead."

Nicholas shrugged, and kept strumming and walking. After almost a hundred yards they stopped at a spot where the tunnel had collapsed.

"Maybe you can burn us through," Skinner said.

"And maybe the rest of this tunnel will collapse on us if I try."

They backtracked to the niche.

"Up or down?" Nicholas said.

"You're the one with the licks. Dealer's choice."

Nicholas pointed his headstock at the floor. Skinner grabbed his forearm.

"You know, if we bust the lock it may trigger an alarm."

"The alarm's been tripped already. Besides, the power's out."

"When you melted through the last sealed wall, I didn't hear any alarms."

"Maybe it was a silent alarm."

"Maybe. Maybe not. Just saying, try to burn a hole through without busting the lock."

Nicholas shrugged. "I'll give it a try." He shredded out some licks from Van Halen's *Eruption*. A thin orange beam snaked out of the end of his headstock, billowing out like a thin plastic tube filled with gusts of air. It bored into the top of the metal cover and widened.

As the beam swelled, nearing the locking mechanism, Skinner lightly touched Nicholas's forearm. "I think it's about right," Skinner said.

Nicholas held out a straight arm before Skinner could check out the hole, and burned a passage through the hole over their heads. "Just in case we need to get out later."

Skinner shimmied through the hole and started down the ladder. Nicholas took off his pack. He held it over his head as he followed. After nearly six hundred feet down, Nicholas stopped. "This is crazy, I'm going back up. I can barely hold this pack anymore."

"Quit your whining. I hear something just below. We're almost there."

"I can't hear anything but your panting."

They went down another four hundred feet until Skinner tapped his boots on something metal. "Uh, oh," he said.

"'Uh, oh' doesn't sound good," Nicholas said.

"I think we've reached the bottom."

"Which is good."

"Not good. I think I'm standing on another manhole cover, and it's locked."

"Great!"

"Try to burn through it again."

"You're in the way and my headstock is pointed up." Nicholas shared a few vulgarities and said, "I'm going back up."

"Wait, wait, wait. Let me climb up past you and you come down here. Maybe if you just strum a little, or something, it will pop the thing open."

"And then again, maybe with you in front of the headstock, it will just blast you a new manhole."

"Well, that'd make one more opinion around here, anyway. Let's give it a shot."

Skinner climbed upward, wedging himself behind Nicholas, who forced all the air out of his lungs to let Skinner pass. Catching his breath, Nicholas eased downward and stood on top of the metal cover, tapping his snakeskin boot. "Now what?"

"You tell me, son. You're the one with the super powers."

Nicholas tapped his foot, thinking. A deep vibration ran up the metal rungs. Nicholas kept tapping, the vibration grew deeper. He hummed the opening riffs to *Cochise* by Audioslave. He tapped slower and harder. The vibration steadily grew, ebbing and flowing with his taps. The metal hatch softened, its surface turning into a gritty mix of graphite fibers. He continued to tap, sinking into the mix like quicksand. Nicholas fell through the hatch, the remnants crumbling.

Skinner climbed down the metal rungs, kicking his way through the edges of the pulverized hatch. He dusted off his jeans in the faint green light of another tunnel. "Where the hell are you?"

Nicholas shook his hair as he got to his feet. He checked his guitar, slung it around his shoulder, ready to play, and heaved his pack to his back with both arms. "Right here, Pop."

"Pop, now, is it?"

"I'll stick with Skinner if you want."

305

Skinner rubbed his jaw. He held his hand out in the green light. "At least we can see."

They were in a smaller tunnel, ten feet in diameter, the floor lined with a grey cushy walkway, the sort used to make a running track. The tunnel curved to the left and right, the green light reflecting off the familiar glassy black surface. Skinner started down the left pathway. Nicholas shrugged and followed, flipping a guitar pick in his right hand. After several yards, they noticed a brushed steel vault door in the side of the tunnel.

Skinner peeked into a small round window. "Can't see anything."

"Should I try to open it up?"

"Naw, let's not push our luck. Let's see what's up ahead."

They passed several other vault doors, staggered on either side of the tunnel, until they came to an intersecting tunnel twenty feet in diameter with a track down the middle.

"This green glow is giving me the creeps," Nicholas said. "I can't tell where it's coming from."

Skinner peeked around the corner. "Weeny."

"Knucklehead."

Skinner smiled over his shoulder and pointed to the other side. "Looks like this smaller tunnel goes on over there." Before Nicholas could say anything, Skinner hurried crouching across the tracks. Nicholas shrugged and ambled along behind him.

The tunnel came to an expansive domed cavern as big as a football field. The floor of the room sloped downward with the relative depth of a spoon, while the walls banked up, arching over with the headroom of a stadium. Above and below, curved metal girders spread like a web. Thousands of ladybug knobs lined the brushed-steel spaces between the beams that converged at the center of the room at four sharp metallic prongs, like an engagement ring setting. Instead of a sparkling diamond, the unholy blackness of the Teardrop perched on top. From the ceiling, a copper chimney flared down, hovering just over the tip of the Teardrop. A turbine, rising from the floor, aimed at the chimney opening, the Teardrop held between the two.

Skinner took a couple of steps into the room. "What the hell?"

Nicholas stared at the Teardrop like he was hypnotized.

Skinner slapped the back of his hand against Nicholas' forehead. "Wake up!"

Nicholas blinked, and rubbed his eyes.

"What is it?" Skinner said.

Nicholas leered at the Teardrop. "I don't know, I don't know … it's like … it's like … I *know* this thing."

"You've seen it before?"

"Not exactly. More like … felt it before. I can't explain exactly."

Nicholas made for the Teardrop, striding with fearless curiosity. For the first time, Skinner looked worried. He checked around to see if anyone had seen them and followed. "Hold up there, son. Hold up."

"I just want to check it out."

They stopped at the Teardrop's base. Skinner reached up to touch it.

Nicholas knocked his hand away. "Don't!"

Skinner winced. "Damn! Do that again and I'll whack you upside the head!"

"Just don't touch it."

"Why not?"

"It's just a feeling. Trust me. Don't touch it, no matter what!"

Like an impulsive child putting his hand into a fire pit to see what would happen, Nicholas shot out his palm onto the side of the Teardrop. A ball of blue light exploded, knocking Nicholas and Skinner back in a wave of energy, the color dissipating in powdery sparks. Skinner landed on his chest. His face skidded across the metal floor and crashed into one of large metal ladybug knobs. He rolled over on his back, holding his cheek and nose. Blood dripped down his jaw. "What the hell are you doing, boy? I think you broke it." Pressing his fingers against his nose, trying to stop the blood, he turned every which way.

"Nicholas?" Skinner said. "Nicholas!"

"Up here."

Nicholas swung back and forth through the air as if skateboarding on an invisible half-pipe. He pivoted at the top of each turn, sliding back down through the air on the soles of his boots, rising again to the top and coming back down again. The Teardrop bounced around the room like a ping pong ball.

"Check this out!" Nicholas said. He pushed with his right foot and raced around the outer rim of the dome. He sped low to the floor and appeared to skid to a halt. He stepped out of thin air to the ground and held out his hands. "Not bad, eh?"

"Yeah, you never cease to amaze me." Skinner sounded unimpressed. "So, tell me, Scooter, how are you going to put your new plaything back?"

The Teardrop bounced near Skinner and away again.

Nicholas jumped up, kicking from his left leg once, and chased after the Teardrop. He caught up with it several times but each time he reached out for it, it slipped away. It was too big to hug. There were no handles to grab onto. He tried to snatch it by the pointed top. He could barely grasp it, but when he tried to squeeze tighter, it slipped out, like there was a layer of electricity surrounding it. Nicholas returned to the floor near Skinner. He put his pack down. With his guitar around his shoulder, following the Teardrop's trajectory through the air with his headstock, he thumbed out a pick, readying an attack on the strings.

Standing out to the front and left of Nicholas, Skinner held out his hand. "If you're going to do what I think you're going to do, I think you should be careful with your choice of riffs."

Nicholas smirked and nodded.

"Like, spare us *Creeping Death* by Metallica." Skinner touched his nose. "I don't think I'd survive."

"Right," Nicholas said. He relaxed his shoulders and closed his eyes. He caressed the strings of the frets with the tips of his fingers. With the smooth groove of a sincere lover, he eased into a strum. Skinner smiled right away, stretching his neck and shoulders with the soothing beat. Bouncing off the wall from a random trajectory, the Teardrop slowed and curved away from the wall. Nicholas kept strumming, swaying with the rhythm. It circled around to the center of the room. Just as it came to a rest in its four-pronged setting, Nicholas and Skinner echoed the chorus of *Come Together* by the Beatles.

As Nicholas opened his eyes and smiled proudly at Skinner, the soft green light in the domed room snapped to a rude ultraviolet light, blaring down on them. There were two other tunnels on the far

309

end of the room, directly opposite from the tunnel where they had entered. They could hear voices echoing from one of the tunnels.

Nicholas took off his backpack and tossed it to Skinner. Then he turned his back, curling his arms out like stirrups for Skinner to climb on.

"There's a first time for everything," Skinner said, as he jumped on Nicholas' hips.

With Skinner on his back, Nicholas shot through the air toward the tunnel where they'd entered, sliding out the exit just at the moment the voices at the other end of the dome entered.

"Voilà," Judith said, holding out both hands like a proud schoolgirl.

Martin stopped at the edge where the floor ramped down into the Teardrop chamber. "Can we go down there?"

"For sure. Follow me."

Judith skipped down the metal slope and hopped over the guides crisscrossing the floor.

Martin kept his eyes on the Teardrop as they neared it. Although she tried to act nonchalant, Judith kept quiet, respecting the solemnity of the Teardrop's inner sanctum.

She stopped a few paces from it. "Don't touch it, of course," she said.

"Not after the story you told," he said. "Why is it on pins?"

"Keeps it higher--less interference from other frequencies." She held out her hand. "I brought you down here to give you a visual history. Makes it easier to explain … and I thought it might jar your memory.

"For several decades after this thing was found, every kind of test was performed, as you might imagine. The Subterrene tunneled the majority of this place out. The rest of this dome was excavated over time and the inner structure built.

"The Teardrop didn't stay here all the time at first, back when Dr. Blithe was still alive. He moved the Teardrop to and from other underground testing spots as needed. Many of the tests were violent and radical, which is why we're so far down. This thing was hit with every laser, drill, hammer, several conventional weapons … It was even blasted with a small nuclear weapon. Nothing even came close to putting a dent in it. The scariest thing is it seems to be infinitely smooth. Even with an electron microscope, the Teardrop does not have any indentions or markings. And it's perfectly round at its bottom and symmetrical to its tip.

"Before Dr. Blithe died, a critical feature of the Teardrop was discovered. While he and the Teardrop were being transported to this dome, coming back from another test, he started singing."

"Singing?" Martin sounded doubtful.

"Singing?" Judith nodded.

"And?"

"Well, it was more like sing-talking. He was sitting on one of the train segments, his hand on the Teardrop, and in a monotone voice, he sang *Purple Rain.*

Martin rolled his eyes. "He sang *Purple Rain*? By Prince?"

"You know your post-modern music, dude." Judith shrugged. "There's no inherent meaning to the song, as far as we know. Turned out one of the technicians riding with him was listening to that PoMM music through a cassette tape player with headphones. They were popular then. A retro thing, you know. Enthusiasts thought music sounded better in its original analogue format. An old-is-new thing. Whether true or not is beside the point; it was strictly forbidden to bring any outside media or data into high security area like this. They cut the guy a little slack and reassigned him to a non-secure area. After all, it was a major breakthrough."

"What, the Teardrop likes PoMM from the 1980's?"

"No … it's not a Prince fan, as far as we know. It simply interacts with and changes analogue signals."

"Not digital."

"Nope, and it's still a mystery as to why. The leading theory is that digital signals have a finite number of values, meaning their range of signals is limited. The resolution of an analogue signal, on the other hand, is essentially limitless. Some tone-purists believed analogue sounded better. The problem is, the signal degrades, giving rise to so-called background or white noise. Digital signals--all kinds, not just those from music--while more limited, don't degrade and are more predictable. That's why the entire technical world has been based on a digital system since the late twentieth century."

"Music equipment isn't the only thing that makes analogue signals," Martin said. "Mechanical things also send them out."

"You're smarter than you look. The Teardrop was likely hit with some analogue signals when subjected to testing. And so, why didn't Dr. Blithe make some noises then? As it turned out, it only reacts when it's in motion, and only Dr. Blithe could put it into motion."

"Could he also take it out of motion?"

"Yes, if he touched it again, it reset like concrete--completely immoveable. It was one of the problems with the testing performed in the early days, done when it was immoveable. *And thank goodness.* I can't imagine what would have happened if a nuclear bomb had been directed at it while moveable. We still probably don't know its true function, but it seems to act like an amplifier. It amplifies and makes perfect the essence of any analogue signal thrown at it. Since music was the first signal discovered, testing continued with Dr. Blithe as the ultimate guinea pig. Black-op military types were standing in line to test various theories on the Teardrop, but those tests were dangerous, and probably would have killed Dr. Blithe. Since he was still useful, partnered as a testing subject with the Teardrop, psychological testing was the main focus. During the last couple of decades of his life, great strides in psychoanalytical science were made, including new understandings of the workings of the brain. Awareness could be directed."

"You're talking about mind control," Martin said flatly.

"*Your* specialty. Despite new knowledge gained from the Teardrop and Dr. Blithe, the applications were still limited. Close to the end of his life, when his body showed signs of natural ailments, he was instructed to put the Teardrop in motion, after which it was guided into the four-pronged setting you see here."

"How long has it been there?"

"About sixty years or so. Scientific advances in the understanding of the Teardrop have pretty much ceased. Other government departments, some with various harebrained theories, were given their crack at it, as long as no one physically touched it. The main concern wasn't so much whether it would fry someone else's brain, but maybe just freeze up, never to become moveable again, since its human partner, Dr. Blithe, was dead and no one else wanted to touch it."

"Well, this is all fascinating," Martin said, "but I'm here to restart the System. What's this got to do with that."

"I hoped bringing you down here would jolt your memory. I don't know … put it into overdrive or something." Waving her left arm at the Teardrop, she said, "As I said, this is the System core."

"I thought you said it was dormant for sixty years."

"No, I said scientific advances pretty much ceased, at least until you came along For your post-doctoral work with all that background in psychiatry and digital programming, all that understanding of physiology and coding, and that doctoral thesis—only you would name it *Animal Farm*. You proved it was theoretically possible for subjects to be programmed into following suggestive instructions and even into accepting unfavorable circumstances. But your theory was still imperfect. Your subjects didn't fully accept the program they were presented with, even when they did so willingly. What you didn't know, until you came here, was that your program was flawed because you were relying on digital systems, and you didn't have the Teardrop."

Martin raised his eyebrows at the thing, closed them tightly, and pried them open.

"You still don't remember?"

"Nope."

"You didn't apply to come here. You were invited. A lot of money was thrown at you. You accepted, of course, not knowing why they wanted you. After obtaining the necessary clearances, you quickly developed the theory that, if converted to an analogue signal, then repurposed into a digital signal, Animal Farm would function like clockwork. In essence, the digital format is a series of ones and zeros. In other words, it's a bunch of true and false statements. But that's not how the mind works. The mind works in nuance. There's always something that's ambivalent, something that cannot be translated into a perfect "yes" or "no," like the white noise of analogue signal. You're the one who came up with the idea of translating the raw Animal Farm program into analogue, sending it in a flood of signals at the Teardrop, here in this chamber, then repurposing and translating it back into digital. The result was revolutionary. Subjects accepted Animal Farm without any question, even eagerly. Animal Farm grew like a virus."

Martin's face flushed at the Teardrop with hate. "You're telling me ... this thing, whatever it is ... is in my head."

"I'm telling you it's in *everyone's* head."

"And we still don't know what it is?"

"That's right."

Blood rushed across his face as he cocked his head to the side. They stared each other for several moments.

"Since everything on the System is processed through the Teardrop, everything is subject to manipulation. Nothing can be verified."

Judith nodded. Her jovial attitude had evaporated.

"So how do we know that what we think we know is actually the truth?"

"That's the question, Martin. Can't *you* answer it?"

Martin's eyes bored into Judith. Seconds passed. "Seems to me the real question is ... *Why the hell should we turn it back on?*"

Judith smiled. "You see, we *do* think alike, you and me. It's like you're reading my mind."

"You say this thing is still in motion?"

"Yes."

"For how long?"

"Sixty-ish years."

"In the same position the whole time."

"Yes."

"Has it been sitting at an angle the whole time?"

Judith jerked her head around. The spike atop the Teardrop was angled to the side.

Martin walked to the other side of the Teardrop. He knelt to the ground. He wiped his hand across the brushed steel behind one of the girders. When he brought his fingers up, they were covered with streaks of blood. "Is this yours? Because I know it ain't mine."

Chapter 49

K<small>NUCKLES WRAPPED ON METAL</small>.

"Come in," Chairman Beth said. She sat at the end of a long cedar table. The Council Chamber in the center of Lizard Creek was housed in three metal containers set side by side, their inner walls cut out to enlarge the space.

Beth leaned on her right elbow, resting it on the back of a wooden chair, her curly red hair with its white streak pulled into a tight bun. The sleeves of her chambray shirt were rolled up to her elbows. She tapped her toes, surveying the room over a freckled nose.

The pair sitting at the opposite side of the table wore form-fitting navy blue jumpsuits with metal sockets on their forearms, legs and torso, front and back. Black polymer zippers, undone just below their collarbones, ran down the front.

The bald woman had dark eyebrows, thick and sculpted elegantly over her large blue eyes. Her expression was a bit jaded, and she smiled softly as if at a private joke. Her eyes and lips had mascara and gloss. She had strong cheeks and full lips. Her cover-girl face sharply contrasted with her military outfit and athletic physique. Narrow at the waist, her form-fitting attire left little doubt her chest, shoulders, and thighs had been sculpted and refined with more attention than her eyeliner. Several buckles and polymer clips covered her shoulders and thighs.

Her partner, a blond guy with the same haircut but no mascara, ran his right index fingernail under the nails on his left hand. Like the brunette, he had spent time in the gym. Neither of them looked bulky. Their bodies had the hard lean structure of rock climbers. On the left side of their chest each visitor wore an oval navy blue patch with a black spear sewn into it.

Beth gave the woman a blatant up-and-down look. Lenny, sitting near the guy in the jumpsuit, flexed his thin bicep and shrugged with resignation.

Esau stepped in, sizing up at the two new arrivals. His knowing eyes were set on their faces, moving from one to the other, an expression of contempt on his face. The female visitor returned his gaze with interest. Beth nodded at Esau. Looking outside, he said, "Come in. It's okay, I'm here." With her chin tucked, Tabitha followed him into the room. She stood just behind his right hip, latching onto his waist.

The bald woman's eyes widened. Her partner pushed his butt to the back of his chair with a smirk. Despite the airs of disinterest put on, they were keenly alert.

Beth gestured to two chairs at the head of the table, near the exit, opposite her seat.

"We'll stand for now," Esau said. He glanced to his left at the door left ajar which allowed a quick exit. "I just want to hear what they have to say."

Beth waved her left hand over the empty table and smiled to the visitors. "You're up."

The woman smiled at Esau and said, "You look lost." Her voice was confident, smooth, with a hint of Slavic accent.

"You shouldn't talk," Esau said.

The blond guy snorted, a soft chuckle.

The woman's eyes shifted to Tabitha with a warm motherly glow. "You must be Tabitha."

Esau's eyes scrutinized their uniforms, studying the patches on their shoulders. "Where are your CBs?" he said.

The woman shrugged.

"Name and rank?" Esau said.

"I'm Oxana," she said. "This is my partner, Tim."

"You're Paramilitary Operatives in the Special Operations Division of the CIA," Esau said.

Oxana's eyes glistened. Tim's smile withered.

"Well, obviously, that's exactly it," Esau said. "I think you'd better explain yourselves. Why did you try to take her?"

"You mean those from the helicopter?" Oxana said.

"Who else?" Esau said.

"Wasn't us. But they are why we're here. We're here to protect you from them."

"Now, why don't I believe that?"

"I don't blame you," she said. "I'd be thinking the same thing. All I can do is lay it all out on the table." She unzipped her jumpsuit a little more. Running her fingers across the edge of the table. "You've obviously noticed the visitor in the sky."

319

Beth chuckled heartily. "No, we didn't notice something as big as a mountain floating up there."

Oxana shifted her eyes to Tabitha. "Tabitha here noticed it. She took some videos … and shared them with the rest of us. By the way … nice videos, Tabitha."

Tabitha squeaked out a "Thanks," still holding onto the back of Esau's waist belt. "My mom also helped." Esau tapped her shoulder with his right hand.

"You picked up her video post on the System," Esau said. "So what? I'm sure there must be millions."

"What are you talking about, Esau?" Beth said. "The *System?*"

Keeping her eyes on Esau, Oxana said, "Your carpenter's been keeping secrets from you, Madam." She tapped her knuckles on the table. "If you think this table is made well, you should see what he can do on the battlefield."

Beth slammed he palm on the table. "Enough pycho-games! Tell us why you're here and what you want, or get out!"

Raising his eyebrows to Oxana, Esau said, "We're waiting …"

"You're wrong, Esau, about the video, that is," Oxana said. "Worldwide, there's more than one of those UFOs, around twenty or so. Many have seen them. *But no one has been able to capture one on video or even take so much as a photograph of them. No one, except for Tabitha here.*"

"Right on, girl!" Lenny said.

Tabitha smiled back at him and then scowled at Oxana when she saw her watching.

"I don't believe you," Esau said.

"Believe me or not, it's the truth. And there's more."

Esau nodded for her to continue.

"When I said Tabitha shared her video with the rest of us, I meant *all of us* ... the entire world."

"Everyone saw my video?" Tabitha said smiling.

"Everyone, everywhere, Tabitha. Every child, mother, and father. Every schoolteacher, grocery clerk, waiter, doctor, lawyer. Every government employee, at every level, in every country in the world. Everyone--at least, everyone who was connected to the System."

"The president saw it?"

Sadness swept over Oxana's eyes. "She should have seen it. We're not sure, which is part of why we're here." Her eyes shifted to Esau. "You asked about the CBs. Worn and used by just about everyone, they permeate every facet of life. People see life through the lens of the CB. With a line tapped directly into everyone's mind, governments and corporations have been using them to control public opinion, affect buying habits, even control population growth and reduce the spread of disease by discouraging physical contact. But the level of control was still limited. Although the powers of suggestion, focused through the CBs, were powerful, there was still a finite level of control, tempered as a strong suggestion, rather than a command. In the last couple of decades, the U.S. government, and many others, raced to maximize the level of control. It was all secret, of course, the testing projects beginning with the military." She slighted her head toward Esau. "With your background, you *know* what I'm saying is true."

Esau instinctively reached his hand for Tabitha, either to

protect her or, remembering the horrors he had escaped, for his own reassurance.

Oxana continued: "The testing was brutal on many of the subjects. Some died. Sure, you could be angry at the government, blame it for wickedness. Maybe it's wrong, it should be stopped. But remember it was a new arms race. Every government in the world was looking for a way to control minds through the CB system, which was growing and expanding at the social level like a virus. If a government figured out a way to totally control the mind first, then other governments would have to find a way to prevent it. To do that, they'd have to be able to control minds, too. The alternative was to just shut down the CBs, which wasn't a real option.

"A few years ago, the level of control had increased exponentially, but it wasn't instantaneous. As it turned out, the mind still had to be reprogrammed, the neural connections rewired. After a few years, the level of control seemed to be unlimited, which presented a new problem. Everyone, including every government official, even the president, was hooked up to the System through the CBs. As the control took hold, before completely reprogramming the collective minds, some—the president for one—asked the bigger question: *Who's really in control here?*"

"Are you making all this up?" Lenny said.

"I was thinking the same thing," Beth said, shaking her head. "I mean, this story you're telling is the kind of story we *want* to believe ... But you know, it just sounds like fantasy."

"The parts about testing on soldiers are true," Esau said, "I don't know about the rest of it."

Oxana went on: "The president became concerned the level of control was so great that the government could actually lose sight of who or what was running things, maybe even subtly take over the functions of government. To combat this threat, the president secretly repurposed part of the mission of the Special Operations Group within the Special Activities Division of the CIA. We are Paramilitary Operations Officers. Our mission includes defending against a hostile takeover of the government with the control of CBs or any other means."

"Yeah, you and your partner—One Bullet Bob here—are a real big deal," Esau said. "But you still haven't explained your interest in Tabitha."

"After the Sundogs arrived, the president declared a national emergency. Martial Law was declared, not that many noticed, since martial Law of the mind had already been in effect. Then the president, vice president, and those in line for succession, disappeared."

"What, like a magic trick?" Beth said, with a smile.

"They reportedly died in plane crashes caused by the Sundogs," Oxana said. "We actually believe they're alive, at least for now, and that the Sundogs are an excuse for a coup."

"So who's in in control, who's running the government?" Esau said.

"Richard Freight, Secretary of Defense, is in control," Oxana said.

"And you answer to him?" Beth said.

"We answer only to President Martinez."

"And if she's dead?" Esau said.

"Then we still carry out her orders."

"Which are?" Esau said.

"Protect against the worst case scenario. Prevent the System from taking control of the government."

Crossing his arms, Esau chuckled. "That battle should have been fought long ago, before the CBs were even introduced, before this new level of control was used. How do you know the System hasn't already taken over? How do you know you're not already under the control of the System, or you're not on a mission for the System?" Oxana opened her mouth to say something. Esau held out his hand. "You know … you still haven't told us what a twelve-year-old girl has to do with any of this."

"As I was saying, we believe a coup is underway. However, when the System's final solution was about to be implemented, it crashed. Instead of complete control over everyone with a CB, everyone was unhooked. Minds which were accustomed to being controlled were abruptly left to think and act on their own. The sudden freedom was actually upsetting for most. People didn't know how to think on their own without responding to external stimulus. The immediate reaction was similar to that of a heroin addict undergoing violent withdrawals."

"They puked?" Esau said.

"Everyone puked everywhere at the same time, literally," Oxana said.

"Gross," Lenny said.

"Cool," Tabitha said.

Oxana smiled at her. "Kinda funny, isn't it?"

Esau pushed Tabitha back behind him, glaring at Oxana. "You haven't told us why any of us should care about any of this," he said. "The government didn't care about us, or anyone else living out here in the Wild, for years and years. Millions were forgotten, left behind by all your so-called progress. Now you're telling us your little world has come crashing in. So your playthings don't

324

work anymore. Well, boo hoo! Take a few pills for your tummy ache, go back home where you came from, have a nap, and leave us alone."

Ignoring Esau's outburst, Oxana said, "You know what's even cooler?" to Tabitha, still peeking around Esau's waist.

Tabitha shook her head shyly.

"You're the one who made everyone puke," Oxana said.

"I don't see what's so cool about that," Lenny said.

"It seems Tabitha's the one who crashed the System."

Esau went pale.

Noticing Esau's subtle change in demeanor, Tim stared at Esau, giving him a knowing nod. "So you can imagine the level of interest there is in Lizard Creek."

"The men who arrived in the helicopter—that was nothing," Oxana said. "Next time there will be more men, more helicopters, more of everything, and soon."

"Wait a minute," Beth said. "I know Tabitha is smart, but you can't tell me she crashed your big System or whatever ..."

Oxana shrugged. "I know. But it's true. She somehow figured out a way to take a video of the Sundog and posted it on the System, whereas no one else could. She may not understand how it happened. But whatever she did crashed everything. Which is why many others will come here –to figure out how she did it. That's why we're here, I don't mind telling you. Only, unlike your other visitors, we want to reproduce what she did to destroy the System. That's why she should be protected. It's our highest priority."

"This is all a little heady," Beth said.

"So you're not with those sky people?" Lenny said.

"We're here to protect her from them," Oxana said.

"Seems to me we don't need you," Esau said. "We have a UFO on our side."

"For now," Oxana said. "What makes you think it's taking sides? Maybe it just wants to observe Tabitha for a while without any interference."

"Maybe it wants to protect her," Beth said. "I notice you didn't bring any weapons. Worried the UFO will protect Tabitha from threats?"

"Just being cautious."

"You're not so cautious," Tabitha said.

Tim flinched.

"Are you armed?" Esau said coolly to Oxana.

"Search me," Oxana said.

Tabitha stepped out from behind Esau. Her eyes scanned Oxana's jumpsuit. Oxana flinched when her front pocket snapped open. A long poly-carbon card slipped out on its own and somersaulted, end over end, down her arm to the table. Her belt buckle snapped off, slid down her leg and joined the card. What appeared to be an empty holster for cuffs unclipped from her waist and connected with the other things on the table. Several other hard plastic items came out of her pockets and boots. The pieces assembled themselves into a crude semi-automatic handgun.

"I guess you're not so careful, after all," Esau said.

Oxana's sober eyes studied the handgun and shifted to Tabitha. "Neat trick. Maybe you can show me how you did that?"

Tabitha said, "Maybe." She brushed her fingers over her eyebrows. "And maybe you can show me how to paint my face."

Oxana smiled. "That I can do."

Chapter 50

DESPERATE TIMES CALL FOR DESPERATE MEASURES. OR SO THEY once said before losing their minds. A purpose remembered is a life saved. And so it began, the resurrection of man's meaning. But not without a fight.

Mr. Rusty pushed Papa out of the armored vehicle, rolling him across the cobblestone causeway. Cold gusts of air flapped Papa's over-sized white jumpsuit. Coralee stood over him with her hands on her hips, blocking the sun.

"You are never leaving here," she said. "Haven't you figured that out yet?"

Mr. Rusty handed the *katana* sword to her. "This is all he had," he said.

Four guards surrounded Papa. The chain link gate clanged shut in the distance.

Coralee thumbed open the sword from its scabbard. The blade gleamed in her eye. "Where's the short blade?"

Mr. Rusty shrugged.

"There's no two ways about it," she said to Papa. "You're going to tell me."

Papa's eyes floated off to something in the distance. Rusty kicked him in the nose. "Tell us now," he said. "We'll make it quicker for you."

Papa spat a wad of blood onto Mr. Rusty's boot.

"Take him to his Exit Interview," Mr. Rusty said.

The guards hooked Papa by the arms and legs and carried him down the causeway. On time with the shift change, a crowd of Employees streamed up the causeway from the Factory. Coralee shouldered the *katana* blade and marched behind Papa.

A cracking sound split the sky as a wave swelled under Employees on the causeway. When the groundswell reached Papa, the guards and Coralee were thrown backwards in somersaults. Papa tried to steady himself on all fours as more waves came, along with loud pops. Apartment Block 2 gave way, pancaking on top of itself. Apartment Block 7 followed. The exterior walls of the Processing building twisted but held. After several minutes, the shaking stopped.

Hundreds of Employees, scattered across the causeway all the way down to the Factory, got to their hands. A large bald man stood with his arms out as if he were walking a high-wire. He gaped at the collapsed apartment block, looked around, and blinked at his fingers. Turning to Papa, he said, "Where am I?"

Chapter 51

Irene woke before dawn. She snagged the CB from the nightstand and hesitated with the loop just above her head. She huffed and cupped it in her left hand. "Habit," she said, rolling it across the lifeline in her palm. She snapped it end up on the edge of the nightstand.

Pushing herself up and sliding her thin legs to the floor, she held her hands out in front of her face. She pumped her hands into loose fists, then extended her fingers, over and over several times, until dropping them with an exhausted sigh.

Grabbing the cane handle, she pointed her left elbow to the ceiling and pushed herself to her feet. She took a few shaky steps and plopped into a swivel chair at her desk. Dressed in a pair of panties and red halter-top with a retro yellow Wonder Woman logo across the front, she spun around with her cane to her chest. As she slowed, she unsheathed the *wakizashi* blade, which had been knotted to the cane, and pointed it to the sky. Coming to a stop, she lowered the blade to her face, and mouthed the words, "I will see you again in mountains."

She sheathed the blade into its scabbard and examined the wall over her desk. Long before Papa left, before she got sick, she'd pasted posters of her favorite movies there. Classic *Star Wars* and *The Matrix* movie posters were centered, side-by-side. An *Inframan* poster was tilted off at an angle to the left and the *Seven Samurai*, with Japanese titles, was pasted to the right. A large parchment of high-quality paper was centered at the top, displaying a pen-and ink hand-drawn image of Wonder Woman, twisting her arms in action, her lasso flipping to one side, blocking bullets with her wrist cuffs.

Irene grinned, flung open a small drawer, and slipped out a piece of drawing paper. She fetched a G-pen, a nib, and an ink well. She whetted the nib and drew an arching line.

The prominent edges of the samurai crescent-moon-bearing helmet came first. A bell-shaped protector flared out around the neck and shoulders. Sharp eyes pierced over a small nose and mouth. Black hair flowed back from underneath the helmet. Mail followed her figure like scales, running from under her jaw, over her neck and breasts. Curled protectors rippled down her shoulder. The medallion of a butterfly emblazoned across her midsection. Armor snugged over her thighs, ending just below the knees. Long vertical shin guards wrapped around her calves. Traditional samurai sandals clad her feet and toes. The drawn character wielded a long *katana* blade, ready for battle.

Irene dropped her pen. She sat back in her chair, crossing her arms. "Samurai girl?" She smirked. "Too obvious … cheesy." She cocked her head. "The Monarch." She nodded. "*The Monarch!*" She wrote the words at the bottom of the drawing in graffiti lettering.

She pushed herself up from the desk with both arms and shuffled to her closet with her cane.

After several moments of struggling in sweat, wearing her faded blue uniform, she stepped out of her closet. Swooning in the mirror, she sighed, her weight shifted to her left foot, right shoulder drooping. Her long black hair was a mess. She grabbed a brush from the dresser and combed her hair back into a thick handful, binding it into a bun. Snapping the brush back with finality, she grabbed her cane, and made her way into the hallway.

Aariti, Margaret, and I were lined and waiting in the dojo, dressed for practice. After we bowed in, I figured she'd go slow. I didn't know she'd move like molasses. It took us an hour just to practice thirty body strikes. For an hour and a half, in the ready position with swords drawn, we did nothing but foot work, sliding our feet back and forth across the wood floor in slow motion. We stayed focused, of course, but I must admit, going slow made me want to just yell and run circles around Irene.

Over the following months, Irene led each class in the traditional way, only in slow motion: strikes to the mid-section; strikes to the hands; strikes to the head; then foot work. During each class, at least an hour and a half long, we'd practice a basic technique. No idle chatter during class. Irene didn't allow it. The only talk was counting in Japanese, the instructions of each technique to be practiced, and the yells of each student, all of which were hollered as loud, and with as much spirit, as possible.

After a few months of that kind of practice, Margaret finally said, "Are we going to do anything besides play red-light-green-light?" Margaret's question, and her frank attitude, were out of place. Still, it had to be said.

With calm eyes and a twisted face, Irene ordered us to suit up in full protectors and get ready for fighting practice. Game on!

Although Papa wasn't there, I felt like things were returning to normal, especially with Irene's spirit back in the *dojo*. A week later, the Sundogs showed up and things went crazy again.

Chapter 52

JEREMY SAT ON A WOOD BENCH, CUPPING HIS FACE LIKE A BOWLING ball. After two days of running amok with depraved debauchery in San Francisco, he was losing steam.

He peeked through his fingers at the polished wood floor of the observation tower of the pyramidal de Young Museum in Golden Gate Park. One of the large panels of glass which spanned the floor to the ceiling provided a panoramic northern view of San Francisco. A stream of smoke rose over the hills. On the other side, the ruins of the Golden Gate Bridge smoldered. The eastern sky burned orange with the coming sun. Fallen from hillsides across the bay, houses and buildings lay submerged under the murky waters. Farther south, in the center of the San Francisco Prefecture, the Transamerica Pyramid Center was the only skyscraper left standing. Buildings over twenty stories tall had toppled, turning downtown into assorted piles of burning debris. The top half of the Sutro Tower, a three-pronged radio tower, had been snapped away, leaving the remaining stickman structure disjointed and twisted. The city was eerily quiet and still.

There were no screaming, sirens, or rescue crews. The streets were empty except for crushed remains of burning buildings.

On his feet, Jeremy arched his back and rolled his shoulder. From the de Young tower, he overlooked a plaza, filled with crowds of men, women, and children, young and old, standing motionless. They watched the tower with an outward expression of expectation. Some were well dressed, sporting torn business suits and gowns, others were in khakis, shorts, or light sweaters; hikers and bikers, waiters and laundrymen, truck drivers in ball caps.

A woman in a sequined ballroom dress had lost her hand. Blood ran from her wrist, pouring over her patent leather high heels. She collapsed, bleeding to death unnoticed. One man in jeans and bowling shoes balanced on one leg, the bone from a compound break piercing through the other pant leg. A teen girl in a fast-food uniform had a metal rod sticking out of her chest. Blood spattered out of her mouth as she wheezed, fell onto her knees, then onto her back with one final cough, suffocating in her own blood, while the crowd watched the tower.

Peering down at the masses from the window, Jeremy scratched his right ear. The thousands in the plaza, and those massing in Golden Gate Park and beyond, simultaneously, in perfect unison, scratched their right ears. He rubbed his nose. They all rubbed their noses. They rubbed bony flesh. He cocked his head to the left side and hopped on one foot. The masses did, too. Everyone smiled placidly, but in their minds they all believed they were living a horror of fire and pain projected to them by the darkest side of Jeremy's malicious imagination.

He approached the glass pane and kicked it once with his right foot, shattering the glass and the entire panorama around him outward as if a bomb had exploded from the top of the tower. Arching his neck upward and pumping his fists, he mimicked the spreading wings of a bird of prey. A primal elk screech blared out of his mouth, imbued with the low gurgling growl of an alligator. The screech swelled as he flexed his arms to his side, the sound vibrating through the structure of the tower, thudding through the ground of the plaza and beyond through the city. He stepped off the ledge, spreading his arms over his head, flapping transparent wings. As his feet hit the sidewalk below, a single jolt shook the ground. He stretched out his arms, and the image of a red and black scaled bird, with taloned hands and the forearms of a dragon pulsed through the vapor around him. Standing at twenty feet, he'd grown considerably. He'd also sprouted some new virtual attachments: black bony antlers hung on either side of the crown of his head. Greyish claws jutted from the ends of leathery wings.

A cloudy black bubble formed around him with a hum and burst, the darkness dissipating like the static of a tube television before he could blink. He flexed his claws, shrugged, and stepped forward, surveying the crowd. "This will do!" he said, giving a double-take overhead. The Sundog, which had been centered directly overhead, had drifted to the east.

Startled, he bounded up to the tower's peak, crouched on the ledge like a monkey, and catapulted himself into the sky. Reaching his hands out, vapors of humidity outlined him, a bird of prey, arms and legs segmented into joints of metal, sheathed in feathered black and red mail. With the rack of an elk, an elongated beak of an eagle, and the teeth of an alligator, he raced upward, bat-like wings thudding with each swing. A huge tail, scaled in heavy metal, snaked out behind him. Although the human Jeremy remained, floating through the morning sky, the demonic mirage of a flying beast ghosted around him. He darted low over the ruins of San Francisco, through the air out over the cold waters of the bay to the north of Treasure Island before shooting to the top of the suspension tower of the eastern span of the Bay Bridge.

The Sundog kept moving eastward, veering to the south. He closed his eyes, listening to the wind howl as he explored areas of knowledge previously unknown to him. In addition to the power to control just about anyone within eyesight, he could know all information fed to and shared from anyone connected to the System, which was the next best thing to reading minds. And by intercepting the System feed, he could control people connected to it, make them follow every command with few limitations.

His ability to control people meant he could also see and know everything a person had experienced through the System, which meant he could know just about everything they'd ever known. Since he could order people to tell him everything they knew, his knowledge was limited only by the collective knowledge of those connected to the System. And so he could effectively tap into the System as a whole, knowing everything it knew, unless the connection was severed.

He did a double-take at the suspension cables behind him. Like birds on a high-line electrical wire, hundreds of people were perched like hawks with placid eyes.

To a young man in a business suit clinging nearby, Jeremy said, "Hey, you! Do you have the time?" The man looked at his watch. He came to his senses, seeing where he was, and screamed, falling head over heels from the cable. Jeremy watched with a grin. Before the man hit the water, Jeremy said, "Okay, stop and come back up here." The man's descent slowed and he darted back up and lit on the cable where he'd been before, maintaining the same blank look.

Suddenly, the others in Jeremy's hanging zombified group sang *Come Together*.

Bemused, Jeremy raised his eyebrows. "Okay, so you're Beatles fans," he said. And without warning, he hunched over the side the bridge and puked his guts out. Wiping his mouth, he noticed his CB was glowing again. He looked back at those clinging to the cables. His limited perspective of the world had returned, with little information and only two-dimensional views.

Gathering himself, he said, "You have a point," to the people on the bridge.

"Say, 'Yes, sir!'", he said.

They said, "Yes, Sir!"

He pointed to the suit guy he'd almost killed. "You! Why did you say those lyrics?"

The suit guy said, "We were told to say it."

"By who?"

"Freight."

Jeremy laughed. "Pardon?"

"Freight."

"Well, you're not making any sense," Jeremy said. "Let's try this." His eyes widening, Jeremy could see the suit guy's System view. It was completely black. He scanned the CBs of everyone within his sight. They were black, too. He spotted the mountain horizon to the east, and found the most distant person within his view. Through that person, and their System connection, he saw someone just beyond the horizon: a truck driver in a white jumpsuit was toying with something through his CB connection. Coursing the System via the trucker, Jeremy searched for anyone talking about the "Sundogs" or "UFOs." Pockets of people, here and there, were looking up at the sky, marveling about the Sundog.

He scoured through System views of users to the south, where he found a heavy concentration of talk about Sundogs around China Lake, a naval air field near Death Valley. He tried to force his way into the System network there. Something pushed back. He tried harder. Something pushed back so hard it snapped his mind out of the System. Angry, he frowned at the Sundog, moving farther east.

"China Lake will wait," he said.

He gazed over the north peninsula of San Francisco to Marin County and Sausalito, then over to Oakland, and as far south across the Bay as he could see.

"Come to me, right now!" he said.

Hazy dark towers streamed into the sky from the cities and hillsides around the Bay. People drew together like a swarm of angry wasps, coagulating into a mass over the rough grey waters of the bay, blacking out the sunrise.

"Let's go," he said,

Chapter 53

CORALEE LAY ON HER BACK, LOOKING UP AT THE BLUE SKY. A FAT Employee stood over her, blocking out the sun. "Hello? Where am I?" he said.

She pushed herself up on one elbow. Her jaw jutted out with the appalled anger of a grandmother who'd just had her purse snatched. *How dare you!* her face said.

The man put out his hand to help her up. She rolled over on her knees and got to her feet, still clutching the *katana* sword. Five other men and one woman pressed toward her, barraging her with questions:

"What is this place?"

"Who are you?"

"Where's my son?"

"What's going on?"

"How did I get here?"

"What happened?"

"Where'd it go, where'd it go, where'd it go?"

She gawked at the collapsed pyramids and surveyed the damaged administrative building. Her wrist snapped and she turned her head just in time to catch a glimpse of Papa's back disappearing in the crowd, having snagged the sword out of her hands.

Her eyes swelled in horror. With the conviction of a battle cry. She screamed, "Lock Down!" The words blared through the causeway, hanging over the Employees, and then fading into to high-plains sky.

Mr. Rusty and two guards made a path through the Employees with Coralee and the other guards in their wake. They pushed people back on their heels and bulldozed over a few who were too dazed to move out of the way.

Keeping his head low, Papa snaked his way down the causeway, the *katana* blade sheathed at his left hip with his left thumb over the guard. As he turned down the short pathway to Apartment Block 8, he gave a sudden glance behind and halted.

"Buddy?" Papa said.

Buddy Caprock limped toward him. "Rory?" Buddy said. "Is that you?"

Papa patted Buddy's shoulder and grinned. "I can't tell you how wonderful it is to see you!"

Buddy held his head like he'd just stepped off a rollercoaster. "Where am I?"

Over Buddy's shoulder, Papa could see Coralee and her crew enter the front doors of Administration. He turned to his apartment block, resting thoughtful eyes on it for a moment, and scanned down the causeway to the intact factory building.

The masses of Employees on the causeway pulsed with confusion, scurrying every which way. Some of them milled around aimlessly for something, not quite sure what. Others returned to the nearest apartment block, trying to get in, not noticing it had collapsed.

Papa jumped on top of a five-foot concrete wall lining the causeway. "Listen up! Listen up! Listen up!" Papa said. He yelled through cupped hands up and down the causeway. "There's been an earthquake! Return to the factory!" He pointed back down the causeway. "It may be the only safe structure. Come with me. I'll explain everything!"

Chapter 54

DETAILS, DETAILS, DETAILS. FOCUS TOO MUCH ON THE BIG ONES AND you're bound to overlook the more important small ones. Sometimes it's the small things that are quite literally screaming at you, but you're too distracted to recognize them. For me, it practically took a slap in the face, but I slowly realized that I could know things, if I just asked. Just another small detail, but oh so important.

Martin's eyes jerked back and forth, leaning back in his chair, his chin low and his hands loosely at his sides. He could have been asleep as far as I could tell. I jumped when he said, "Let's talk about what you were doing immediately after the earthquake. Did you notice anything unusual about the Sundog?"

"Well, I don't know what you mean by 'unusual.' I supposed the strangest thing was it just hovered like a cloud while everyone went on about our business, cleaning up and surviving."

"So the Sundog didn't do anything the first day to communicate with you, Irene?"

"I can't say it's ever communicated with us. I don't think we felt any different from anyone else, just trying to cope."

"What were you doing for food and water?"

"The first morning after the UFOs and earthquake, La-La went around the house trying all the faucets, light switches. Power and water were off. Our CBs still had some charge left but no connectivity, no way to communicate.

"The first night, we didn't eat anything. We were still in shock. Hunger hit the next morning. We still had Papa's old charcoal cooker pushed up against the back of the house. It was an ugly thing. Papa hadn't even covered it, so it was rusted from exposure."

"Charcoal cookers are *illegal*," Martin said.

"Arrest him," I said, feeling happy with my snappy response. But a sudden jolt of sadness followed. My throat swelled. Before I could cry, I went on talking as though I could just mow through my feelings by sheer will power. I ignored a thin tear rolling down my cheek and continued: "La-La rolled the cooker to the back patio. It was full of spider webs and crickets."

"Did your Papa ever see it like that?" asked Martin.

No.

"No, of course not. He was gone." As I said "gone," I could hear it my tone. Just *gone*, not dead. "Irene and I put on our coats and hats and scraped it down with steel brushes as best we could.

"We normally had at least twenty-five gallons of purified water in the house, delivered twice a month with the rest of the food. The earthquake happened the day before the next delivery, so we only had about five gallons left.

"La-La prepared what little meat and vegetables we had. Once that was cooked in the hot pot, we'd be able to drink the leftover broth, though it'd be good for only a day. Anyway, if we didn't eat-empty the fridge, it'd go bad in no time.

"La-La got the coals going. Once the water boiled in two pots on the grill, she put fish and squid balls in the pot with the remaining sliced beef. Irene and I chopped the bok choy, dried mushrooms, carrots, and corn cob, lining them up on the oval platter. It all went into the pots with rice and noodles, along with the last two eggs.

"Where did she get that kind of fancy food? The black market?"

"I never asked, and I guess I didn't want to know. Anyway, having the caldron of meat churning on our back patio was like sending up a neighborhood flare for dinnertime. As soon as La-La put in the meat, Mary Rodriguez, the neighbor behind our house, came outside, circling around the broken fence separating our yards. Bundled up in a heavy Babushka scarf and parka, she kept saying, 'Smells good, smells *very* good!' After about five or six more comments, La-La held up a couple of bowls with fish balls and corn, and called to Mary. La-La kept all the sliced beef for Irene and me.

"Before the hotpots were even done, we'd heard shouts from the street. 'Something smells good,' they said. I felt relieved when La-La brought the pots in to the kitchen stove. She ladled out the vegetables first, separating them into three large bowls, then added some broth and divided the meat.

"At the kitchen table, with the steam rising from the two pots, slurps and busy chopsticks were the only sounds. Aside from the UFO blocking out the sky, sunlight shone through the window, hitting the tile floor, dusty from us tracking in back and forth. In the silence of the muted afternoon light, it was feeling like the first morning after Papa left. Just as the thought came to my mind, Irene leaned back in her chair. '*Where ... is ... Papa?*' she said, tapping her foot on the tile floor with each word.

"Asking it out loud was like repeating it hundreds of times. La-La toyed with the jade Buddha around her neck, tears welling up in her eyes. "Papa, help us! Come back, Papa!" she said.

"It was like another earthquake had hit. We already suspected Papa was alive but there were still nagging doubts. *Was the sword just a sick joke? What if he really was dead?* Her apparent confession confirmed our dreams and fears. I still felt like maybe she was just trying to make us feel better for the moment, giving us false hope.

"Irene grabbed her cane and went to the doorway overlooking the *dojo*. A faint orange glow silhouetted her figure from the salt rock lights on the altar. I could almost see the ghostly images of Papa, when we were six years old. We had nipped at his legs as he tried to do his kendo workouts, playing with us patiently. Before long we were practicing with him. He made small *shinais* for us. There we were again, two little girls swinging bamboo swords with deadly cuteness, proud to be doing something important with their Papa, bigger than life.

"Even with all the strength she'd regained, Irene was weak, tottering at the top of the steps over the *dojo*. A tremor ran through her legs and arms. She arched her neck toward the ceiling. "Papa! Papa! Papa!" she said.

"Whether true or not, I think we both *felt* Papa was alive. With the earthquake and all … it made us miss him, and need him even more. And it made me hesitant: if he really was gone, then our fantasies were just setting us up for more heartache."

"So it was your grandmother who told about Freedom Colony?" Martin said.

"So Papa's still alive at a place called Freedom Colony?" I said.

Yes.

Martin looked perturbed, maybe more at himself than me. "Just answer the question," he said.

"La-La never mentioned it."

"Then where did you first hear it?"

"I don't know, or at least, I'm not sure. Maybe I just made it up, desperately wanting to know where he was."

Martin looked unconvinced.

Chapter 55

A PLUME OF SMOKE BLEW OFF THE ROOF OF A WATER TREATMENT facility on the side of a bluff at the southern edge of Los Alamos National Laboratory grounds.

Once airborne, Nicholas got his bearings. Skinner clawed into his back. Nicholas picked rapid-fire arpeggios from hell on his guitar. The eastern sky bled orange from the approaching sunrise under the rim of the UFO. A splashing layer of blue and white flooded out of the end of the guitar's headstock, washing a transparent pathway through the air. He kicked the left heel of his boot out, surfing in a wide arch with each turn, looping up and around the rim of a giant half-pipe of ripples left behind by his sliding boots.

Skinner pointed. "Bandelier!"

Nicholas surfed low over the ground, skidding to a stop across the dusty ground. Skinner jumped off, hunkered down, and scurried across an open space ringed by low-lying rock walls, forming a hoop like a circle of empty boxcars. He jumped down into a round kiva, four feet deep, offset inside the hoop.

Nicholas slung his guitar to his back, hopped into the kiva, and settled cross-legged against the sunken inner wall in the morning shade. "What are you so worried about?" he said. "I got you out, didn't I?"

Skinner pointed at the Sundog. "The UFO's moving. See it?"

Nicholas tossed a few pebbles at the tips of his boots before glancing up. "It followed me to your cabin, remember?"

"It's not following anymore."

Nicholas watched it move. "What the hell?"

"Maybe it has something to do with that football down there."

"Who knows?"

Skinner relaxed and put his back against the crumbling wall, regarding the Sundog. "You think it's why you can do things?"

Nicholas shook his head. "Maybe I could before and just didn't know. Maybe this is all a dream. After all, it's like I always *imagined*."

Skinner peeked up over the rim of the kiva, scanning the ruins, then up to the Sundog. "You know … this pueblo kinda looks like the UFO." He pointed up. "There … little rectangular segments fanning out from the bottom … like a top."

Nicholas frowned. "Naw. The UFO's perfectly round. This pueblo isn't. I've always thought this kiva was more off-center like the Cerro la Jara lava dome in the Valles Caldera over there."

"Well, I don't know what you're talking about, but you should know. You're the one who won the Jemez 50-Miler foot race through the Caldera … where the UFO is headed."

Chapter 56

Tabitha blushed in the compact mirror at her painted face. She held the tips of her trembling fingers over her checks.

"I'm pretty," she said.

"*Downtown*, young lady," Oxana said, pressing her lips. She held out a lip balm. "This is for you."

"I can keep it?"

A yellow bubble swelled around Tabitha and popped, dissipating the lamp light.

"Did you see that?" Oxana said.

Tabitha twisted the balm and smeared it over her lips. "See what?"

With red eyes, Oxana checked over her shoulder at the open container door. "Maybe I'm just getting tired."

Hinting at the coming sunrise, a sliver of sky was turning light blue at the distant edge of the Sundog outside. With all of the excitement from the soldiers from the sky, following the catastrophic earthquake, the camp stayed awake through the night. Esau was out there in the dark, watching them.

Oxana held Tabitha's shoulders. "Tabitha, I'm afraid we're running out of time."

"What do you mean?"

"If your protector up there goes away, some very bad people will come here. And they're not going to talk about face-painting. They're going to have a lot of questions, and unlike Tim, and me, they'll do anything to you, and to your parents and friends, to get the information they want."

"Mean things?"

"Mean things ... things too mean to talk about." She took Tabitha's hands. "Tabitha, we're friends aren't we?"

Tabitha nodded eagerly.

"I need you to tell me how you recorded the video ... how you got it on the System."

Tabitha shrugged. "It's nothing. With the video camera Lenny and me found a long time ago."

"Was it hand held, part of a CB, or what?"

"There it is." She pointed to a shoulder-held camera as big as a large tool box on the far end of the workbench.

Oxana went to the camera. She tapped the eject button. "Goodness. VHS! I only heard about these. It's huge."

"Takes great video, though," Tabitha said. "Want to see the UFO?"

Oxana turned with a grin. "I've seen it. Everyone has. The thing is, we need to know how you got your video on the System."

"I know," Tabitha said, rummaging through a small pile of devices. She held out a CB.

Oxana examined it. "It's an old one, sure enough. I think it's the *first* version of it. But I still don't understand how you got video from the camera to the System? Your camera is analogue. Even this old CB is digital."

Tabitha shrugged one shoulder, tilting her head. "Yeah, well, I don't know what you mean— 'analogue' or 'digital' and all — I only know that when I hooked this video camera to the CB, the video didn't want to go in. There was something blocking it. So I unblocked it."

Oxana's face turned to white. She said, "You mean you just willed the video into the CB like you made the gun?"

"Sort of. I can't describe it. It was like something in the CB ... everything about it ... didn't fit. So I just made it fit. Then the video went right in. Easy as peas." Tabitha smiled.

Oxana held her hands over her mouth muffling her words, "Oh my God!"

Rolling thunder stirred in the distance.

Esau barged in, clenching his fists with a dark face. "What the hell are you doing?"

"That's not thunder," Oxana said with a hard voice, "and those aren't ours."

Tim sprang into the container. "The Sundog is moving. And they're coming!"

Darkness fell over Oxana's face. "They're coming for her! She's more important than you know!"

"She's my daughter! She's more important than life!"

"We've got enough room for her and the parents," Tim said.

"I'm not going anywhere without Lenny," Tabitha said.

Lenny stepped into the container. "You go without me, girl! I'll be fine."

"Is there anyone else listening in out there?" Oxana said. "They may as well come in now."

Korea and Chairwoman Beth stepped in. Beth shrugged.

Lenny continued. "I'll be all right, girl. But you've got to go, little one. This place was always too small for you. Just don't forget about me when you're famous."

"She's already famous," Oxana said. "And there's enough room for you, too, Lenny."

Vibration of the approaching hovercraft hummed through the floor.

"We've got to move! Now!" Tim said.

Esau patted Lenny on the shoulder. "Go with us," he said. "You're family."

Jackson Lake fed the Snake River, which ran eastward out of Lizard Creek, then twisted back south. Oxana and Tim led Tabitha, her parents, and Lenny down the southern bank along a line of pine trees. A loud snap was followed by a high whine of a spinning reel. Thin camouflage nets pulled off a pair of large off-road vehicles. The Assault All-Terrain Vehicles, or "AARVs," looked more like lidded cooking pots with legs than military transports. The grey hulls were slightly oblong and round on top and bottom. Two extendable propellers, incased in hollow discs, angled to a flat nob on top. Tinted windshields curved over the cockpits. Twin gun turrets pocked out of the noses below. Under the propellers, gun barrels were bound together like a handful of straws, pointing forward. Six low-profile all-terrain wheels–a polymer hub with knobbed tread—extended from the hulls on collapsible metal legs. The intake for the propulsion system humped out on either side of the tops of the hulls. Short tails extended backward – the handles of the pots – forming an "X" tail of an arrow.

A red oval line crazed across both hulls as clam-shelled doors opened. Tim climbed into one of the cockpits.

Oxana pointed to Korea and Lenny. "You two go with Tim," she said. "Esau and Tabitha are with me."

Esau kissed Korea and squeezed her.

"You take care of her," Korea said.

"We'll be right with you," Oxana said over his shoulder.

Korea knelt and held Tabitha's tear-streaked face. "We're all together."

Lenny patted Tabitha on her head. "No worries, Tabby."

Tim yelled. "We're running out of time!"

Tabitha soft-punched Lenny in the gut. "Just keep your head down."

As a low whine rose from the AARV, Oxana checked Tabitha's and Esau's buckles and swung visors over their heads. The insides inflated, forming a tight cushion around their heads.

Oxana hopped in the pilot's seat and said, "Hold on! You're in for a ride."

A helmet automatically swung over her head. "All clear?" she said.

"Kick it!" said Tim over the radio.

The assault hovercraft battalion swept over the top of Signal Mountain. The tight formation of a dozen Xa-13s buzzed into Lizard Creek. The co-pilot of the leading craft surveyed the landscape on his System view inside a blacked-out visor. "Target acquired," he said. Tabitha's shipping container was highlighted on views of all the flight crews.

Two Xa-13s flanked the shipping container. Six Talos soldiers rappelled out of the sides of each: four landed on top of the container and two on either side of the entrance.

The lead Talos said, "Nobody's home."

One of the other hovercrafts broke in. "Picking up VHF and OTH signatures to the east."

Oxana banked hard northward low over Pacific Creek, flanking the Grand Teton Mountains, Tim hugging her tail.

"Where are you going?" Tim said over the radio. "Riverton is southeast."

"We can't outrun them. There's too much open space on a straight shot."

The AARVs raced over the north ridge of Gravel Mountain and drew up over Enos Lake. The still body of water was surrounded by rocky outcroppings and sparse pines. As the AARV hung low, the water erupted in a cascade of explosions.

The ARRVs disappeared, black smoke rising over turbulent waters.

A pair of Xa-13 hovercrafts floated above the fading ripples.

"I think we got them," one of the pilots said.

"I don't see any debris," the other said.

Toward the southern end of the lake, the AARVs shot out of the water and jetted toward the north fork of the Buffalo River. They headed eastward into the deep valley between the rocky mountains of the Grand Teton wilderness. Four Xa-13s swung in behind the AARVs as Oxana led them low over the rocky surface of the north face of Soda Mountain. Tim flew close to her side.

"We can't outrun them," radioed Tim.

"Tell me something I don't know!" Oxana said.

"Three more—twelve o'clock!"

"Dive!" Oxana said. "There's no time!"

Rising over the jagged edge of Soda Mountain, the hovercraft fired. Oxana flipped a switch. Her AARV fell out of the sky. Three missiles thundered past her cockpit and curled back. Tim's AARV was also falling. As Oxana's AARV dropped past the jagged edge of the mountain's north face, the missiles acquired Tim's vehicle and slammed into its hull with crushing booms.

Tabitha screamed, "No!" as she watched the AARV carrying her mother and Lenny peel open in a fiery blossom. She kicked and screamed, trying to unbuckle herself. "Mom, Mom, Mom!"

Esau yelled at her. "Tabitha! Stop! Tabitha!"

She stopped kicking but kept screaming, watching the rocks below rushing up at them. The AARV jolted like it had been snatched by the hand of a giant. Six off-road wheels attached to multi-jointed arms had extended from the side of the AARV. Oxana drove down the side of the mountain at one hundred and twenty miles per hour. Approaching the high-altitude tree line, she reactivated the propellers and brought the AARV back under control in flight just below the pine tops.

They reached the bottom of a small basin between the mountains. Without clearing the tops of the high mountains, the only way out was due north into the east-west riverbed of the Buffalo River. Four more hovercraft pressed into the basin and unleashed incendiary bombs, turning the whole area into a crucible. Three of the Xa-13s waited at the north end. Oxana wove through the blinding flames. The right rear wheel caught on a passing branch and tore off.

"Not good," Oxana said.

Tabitha was still crying. "Dad!" she said.

"Tabitha," he said, trying to sound strong. But no more words came.

Oxana saw an opening. Revving the trans-drive internal engines to maximum, she pushed eastward up and out of the basin, passing between two Xa-13s. As the AARV topped the southern peak of Soda Mountain, a missile glanced off its back and exploded. They hadn't received a direct hit but it bent the short tail boom into an L. Carried forward by inertia, they spun out of control into a deep crevice on the southern face of the Mountain.

"We're in trouble," Oxana said. "They hit our tail. We're going down."

Four hovercraft drew in over the crevice like sharks ready for a feeding frenzy.

"Where's the explosion?" one of the pilots said.

Moments passed. Nothing. Two more Xa-13s joined the watch party. Still nothing.

One of the Xa-13s called out. "Got her!" The pilot's visor-screen identified the AARV, due south, flying low across the Nowlin Meadows.

At full power, the Xa-13s came down the side of the mountain in pursuit. One of the Xa-13 co-pilots zoomed his System view in on the AARV. Aside from the missing wheel, it appeared functional. "I could have sworn we just put that tail out of commission."

"Say again," her pilot said.

"Target acquired."

"Once you have a clear shot … fire at will."

The Xa-13 closed in on the AARV just past Simpson Peak down a long valley of towering trees leading towards Upper Brooks Lake. As the first Xa-13 came over the tree lines, the waters were still churning and swelling.

"She's submerged again," the co-pilot said.

"She can't stay down forever," one of the pilots said.

As the hovercraft took up positions around the lake, one of them took a direct hit on its hull from a missile, bursting apart in fireless chaos. At the same time, a second hovercraft took a hit to its side. It spun out of control and crashed into the water. As the other hovercraft took evasive action, a missile skimmed its nose, exploding moments later in mid-air. Four more hovercraft crested the trees around the lake.

The AARV jumped out of a small niche in the trees and headed southward, staying low along the valley. Oxana pushed the throttle to the max. The Xa-13s acquired the AARV in their sights and pursued.

"Tabitha, girl?" Oxana said through her helmet communicator. "You still with me?"

"Tabitha!" Esau said.

"Yes," Tabitha said. Her voice filled with grief.

"Good work back there!" Oxana said.

"Mama … Lenny!" Tabitha said.

"I'm going to make them pay," Oxana said, "but I need some more help, girl." After the AARV had been hit over Soda Mountain, Tabitha had repaired it by willpower. "If you have any other tricks, now's the time to share them."

Heavy machine gun fire ripped through the tops of the trees near the AARV.

"Can you make this hunk of junk fly faster?" Esau said.

"I don't think so, Dad. I can't make something out of nothing," Tabitha said. "I need more material."

"I can help with that," Oxana said.

A group of hovercraft chased the AARV to the northern edge of Brooks Lake. The others blocked the western, eastern and southern shores. There were ten hovercraft in all. The AARV dove into the waters and disappeared.

The hovercrafts spread out.

"Stay alert," the lead pilot said.

As soon as he'd spoken, the AARV lunged up from the water, its wheels extended, latched onto one of the hovercraft like a claw, and splashed back into the murky blackness.

"What the hell?" one of the pilots said.

Two hovercraft circled around the rippling waters. The bodies of the pilot and co-pilot floated to the surface with scattered debris.

"I'm picking up the six Talos soldiers at the bottom. They're still alive."

The pilot of the lead Xa-13 surveyed the scene. The grey Pinnacle Buttes loomed from the west. Six other hovercraft held tight around the edges of the lake.

At the southern end of Lake Brooks, something came out of the water between two hovercraft, hitting them with two missiles. The tail section of one of the Xa-13s ripped off on impact, and the remainder spun out of control into the water. The other hovercraft peeled apart in layers of flames.

The strange craft took off to the south, disappearing low over the treetops in the forests and meadows beyond.

"After them!" the commander said.

"What about the Talos?"

"Leave them. We're running out of time."

The Xa-13s pursued, the jagged mountains giving way to rolling valleys and pasture land. A thin green belt of vegetation on either side of the river led into the stark badlands past the ghost town of Dubois.

"Tell me what that thing is," the commander said to his co-pilot. "It's faster…"

"There's no match on the System but it's been down," the co-pilot said. "Maybe it's just a glitch."

"It don't matter," the lead pilot said. "It's toast, anyway."

The six remaining hovercraft flanked out on either side as they bobbed low over the hills and crevices of the landscape of arid red mountains and buttes horizontally chiseled with layers of light tan veins.

Oxana gave the craft full power, hugging low over the Painted Hills. A wall of white water shot up from the river below as she approached the slanted red cliffs.

"Tabitha?" Oxana said.

"Yes."

"Ever seen the first manned space craft?"

"No."

An image of the Vostok 1 rocket, with its flaring rocket engines blasting off, came up on the screen in Tabitha's helmet. "Okay," Tabitha said.

Then another image came up. "A guy named Yuri Gagarin rode it into space."

"It doesn't have wings or anything."

Oxana smiled. "You're reading my mind, girl."

As the lead pilot and the six other hovercraft shot around the cliffs, Oxana hovered at an angle, giving Tabitha a clear view. The propellers of the Xa-13 broke off from the tops, flipping away behind them. As the hovercraft dropped out of the sky, their exteriors peeled away, debris falling in on itself. Seven balls of crude metal slugs fell out of the debris and slammed into the side of the cliffs.

"Is that what Gagarin's capsule looked like?" Tabitha said.

"Exactly," Oxana said.

Chapter 57

THE LIGHTS IN THE TEARDROP'S CHAMBER FLASHED DEEP RED.

"What's that?" Martin said.

"Something's happened," Judith said.

Voices echoed from an entrance at the far side of the chamber.

"Sounds like Charlie," Judith said.

"Nice guy?"

"He's an ass. By the way ... you were supposed to come to TA-3 and enter through the CMR Building."

"And why didn't I?"

"I wanted to talk to you first."

"Martin!" a man said, approaching them with two armed exoskeleton soldiers. He was thin with pale skin and narrow plastic rimmed glasses. He brushed his fingers through his stringy brown hair, the other hand toying with the CB around his neck.

"That's me," Martin said.

"It's been a long time."

Martin smiled and nodded politely.

"You don't remember me?"

"Not yet."

"Charlie Conrad," he said, crossing his arms. "We worked on Animal Farm together, back in the day." Charlie wore a white short-sleeved button-down shirt with a turquoise bolo tie and a grey vest with pockets.

"Sure, back in the day," Martin said.

"You were the project leader, Martin," Judith said. "Charlie was an administrator with me."

"Thanks for reminding us, Judith," Charlie said. "I'm the project leader on Teardrop now."

"You sure are," Judith said.

"Since you know that, Judith," Charlie said, "please explain why you disobeyed my explicit instructions, namely, to bring Martin to the entrance at Building 29?"

The two soldiers shifted their weight behind Charlie, looking distracted from being unplugged from the System.

"Oh, sure," Judith said. "As you know, for over a hundred years Building 29 has contained plutonium and uranium processing and storage facilities. After a disaster, like an earthquake, the building is automatically quarantined. The other two entrances are damaged. So I met him at the old entrance, where hazardous activities were shut down ages ago."

"It doesn't explain anything. Those storage vaults are outdated and empty. I overrode the quarantine."

"Yes, I know, but you didn't have authority to do that. No one does until the vaults have been checked out by Hazmat."

Charlie clenched his fists.

Shouting echoed from the connecting tunnel.

"Doctor Conrad," one of the soldiers said, her voice husky. "There's been an incident. We need to go back to our squad."

Charlie nodded. The soldiers thudded out of the chamber.

"So, they think you can fix it?" Charlie said.

"I'm skeptical, too," Martin said, sizing up the Teardrop.

Three exoskeleton soldiers re-entered the chamber. To Charlie, the lead said, "Sir, there's been a breach."

"Explain," Charlie said.

"The emergency escape at the back of Tunnel 2 has been bored open with something."

"Weld it shut."

"We can't. The hatches, everything, are gone. The hole has been ripped open, *wider*. It's like something twice the size of the hole was forced through it from top to bottom."

Charlie looked at the soldier with big eyes.

The soldier tipped his head to one side, listing. "Sir, the Sundog ... it's moving off to the west."

"Away from the lab?" Judith said.

The soldier nodded.

To Martin, Judith said, "The Sundog followed one of the old tunnels up to the lab."

Yeah, in fact, it stopped right over this chamber," Charlie said, "just as you arrived, Martin, then it moved on."

"It stopped right over the Teardrop?" Martin said.

"It's obviously the source of the breach," Charlie said to the soldier. "Just seal the hole up as best as possible for now. My orders are to keep working until our job is done, no matter what."

The soldier nodded and tromped out of the chamber.

Charlie's critical eyes fell over Martin. "It's time for you to be reacquainted with yourself."

Bolted to the floor in the middle of the round room, a red leather chair waited for Martin as he passed through a vault door into a room shaped like a ball, its walls covered with brushed steel all around. He put on a pair of wrap-around goggles and eased back in the chair.

A low hum filled the room. Through his goggles, the ceiling morphed into a vision of expansive rolling green hills under an azure sky. The sound of shuffling reeds flowed in the breeze. Nearby, an image of a man arose out of the grass, walking toward him. As the figure neared, Martin could see the man was himself.

"Hi, Martin," the projected Martin said, running his fingers through his hair.

Sitting in his chair, the real Martin reached to run his fingers through his hair, and bumped his index fingers against the top rim of the goggles.

"If you're watching this," the projection, Not-Martin, said from the grassy reeds, "you don't remember me. You probably don't remember anything of yourself. But trust me … Trust yourself … It was all for your own good." The projection chuckled.

"For whose own good?" Martin said under his breath.

The Martin projected on the grassy hill reviewed everything Judith had told him back in the tunnel. The System was a digital world transposed over the real world. Its main purpose was systematizing the human condition, making every aspect of a person's life—mind and body more efficient.

Frederick Winslow Taylor had been Martin's guiding inspiration. Taylor had invented the idea during the Industrial

Revolution. He streamlined the life of factory workers by breaking each task of an assembly line down into discrete, measurable steps timed with a stopwatch, enforcing efficiency and profitability. Subjective thought and human reasoning had no role in the quest for maximum efficiency.

Although people of the twentieth and twenty-first centuries hardly knew it, being preoccupied with ideological battles like communism versus capitalism, Taylorism imbued every aspect of production in the modern world, eventually adopted as the central philosophy by the early creators of the Internet. Taylorism endured more than any other philosophy. As these early pioneers of the so-called Internet learned, any average user could be trained to interact like an obedient factory worker. And users willingly, even eagerly, obeyed their instructions. Search engines and their endless links, videos, chats, shopping carts, photos, and data kept the mind constantly distracted with small tasks, preventing users from engaging in unconscious thought. By design, this meant things like critical reasoning and creative thought diminished, and were even rooted out. According to Taylorism, subjective thoughts of the worker are the enemy because they cannot be measured or systematized; they're necessarily inefficient, in the mind of a machine, therefore, subject to termination.

As the use of the Internet grew, so did the mass population's efficiency as processors of the early Internet's glut of information. What the average person did not know, or refused to acknowledge, was that the neurological synapses of their brains were being rewired. Minds began to interpret text only as a method of linking to other data, instead of as a primary method of conveying ideas for the sake of comprehension and reflection, subject to one's own judgment.

Internet companies noticed that the more the public used the Internet in a constant state of interruption and distraction, the more their collective memories were impaired. People accepted the conventional wisdom on any subject. Investigative journalism, a relic of history, was replaced by whatever trended on limited websites. Even if raw news was actually reported, public opinion was manipulated by false projections of the common public consensus. Instead of digesting a story and making critical decisions, users accepted the prevailing interpretation of the news, particularly if most sources reflected that interpretation, true or not.

Governments also noticed this trend. They understood a dangerous tool had come under the control of companies with no loyalty to their countries. Taking the lead to recapture a growing power over its populace, the U.S. government passed the Digital Freedom Act. The stated goal was to keep the online world safe for citizens. Its real purpose was to pry control over the mind out from the hands of industry, placing it squarely in the hands of the state. The first step was to centralize the Internet with the creation of the System. The purpose of the System was to control society by maximizing efficiency in all things.

By the time the first generation of the System came online at Los Alamos, the first CB's were released. Instead of viewing the Internet through static computers or handheld devices, the System was viewed through prescription contact lenses which worked in tandem with an oblong crystal worn around the neck – the CB.

Like the CBs used by truckers in the 1970's, CB meant Citizen's Band. People loved the retro name. But it was no simple radio. Everything a person saw and heard was the System; every wall, floor, doorknob, person, park, window, building, animal, tree, cloud, sidewalk, everything, was overlaid with the perspective of the System. In turn, every action – brushing teeth, opening and closing doors, walking on the sidewalk, dressing, working, making love, arguing, talking, listening, everything, could be measured and made more efficient. Every mind in the world which used the System became subject to Taylorism's systemization for maximum efficiency. It has been said that man's universal purpose has been a search for meaning, and once found, living out that meaning. The System universalized life's meaning into mindless efficiency, another name for slavery.

Unaware of their new purpose, users of the old Internet and first versions of the System lost a little memory. Because of constant disruptions and distractions, long-term memories slipped away en masse. The brain discards that which it does not use. People relied on data stored on the System as their source of long-term memory, and such data were subject to tinkering. For children raised from birth on the System, their brains hardly developed any ability for long-term memory. Although the effect of the System on brains of the public at large was dramatic and powerful, it was not absolute. Unlike a computer, the brain is creative, a quality born out of a subjective thinking process, which is heretical to Taylorism.

Creativity simply does not compute in digital terms. In its basic form, the System was limited to a series of 1s and 0s, yes's and no's. The mind is infinitely more complex. There were untold areas of the mind a digitized System could not reach. By turning the flow of all information of the System into a single sound, then passing it through the chamber over the Teardrop, the essence of the System was given the same depth as analogue sound while maintaining its digital quality. Once directed back into the System, its controls could reach the creative depths of the mind. Memories could be wiped clean like a slate and filled with any information and ideas acceptable to the state and its partners. Efficiency became the absolute purpose of all at the expense of freedom.

Not everyone accepted the new virtual world. Owning a CB, and accepting its view of the world, became synonymous with success and status. Some refused to use the CB. They soon found themselves without a job or a house, cast out into the Wild, where crime and starvation prevailed, due in part to the mass migration trying to escape the rising of sea levels from the coastal areas hit by hurricanes as often as severe rain storms and tornadoes.

Despite the growing population in the Wild, the number of manufacturing workers dwindled. There weren't enough people to keep up with the consumer demand of System users. The control over the mind lent itself to the resurrection of de facto slavery across North America. Mental slavery had already been accomplished, but this added form of physical slavery was not based on any discrimination of race, color, creed, or persuasion. Unlike the bondage of the past, the slaves of the late twenty-first century embraced it. If a person were to find themselves in financial difficulty, they still couldn't declare bankruptcy. They were assigned to any of a number of colonies – slave camps — across America. Once there, their view of reality radically changed. Facilitated by the System, their conscious minds (what little was left of them) embraced a false projection of the daily routine they had known before coming to the slave camp. Their unconscious minds worked with Tayloristic efficiency, building widgets, maintaining power plants, growing genetically altered crops, and other such labor for the public good. Each view of reality remained predictable, constantly reinforced by the System.

As the projected Martin closed his lecture, he said, "With the System, society works efficiently. But there is a danger. If human long-term memory is a thing of the past, then how can we ever be sure we remember who's actually in control? Whatever you do, just remember ...."

Martin's goggles went dark. He yanked them off and threw them across the floor. Judith was standing at the entrance.

Martin sat up from the chair and winced. He held his lower back and said, "How long have I been sitting here?"

"Several hours."

"I can't believe it. What time is it?"

"Mid-morning. While you were being distracted, they took the opportunity to try to pry into your head and figure out what you know. No such luck, especially with the System down. Now that you've seen your own video, does any of it ring a bell?"

"I didn't know I was such a jerk, if that's what you mean."

The vault door hummed and opened behind Judith. Charlie stepped in.

"Hi, Charlie, we were just talking about you," Judith said.

Charlie shifted his eyes between them. Speaking to Martin, he said, "Well, can you fix it?"

Martin sat up and straightened his shirt. "Absolutely."

"Are you sure?" Charlie said, sounding unconvinced. "I've watched your video several times. There's no technical data."

"It must have triggered something in my memory," Martin said.

"What do you remember?"

"Enough to repair the System," Martin said, stretching his interlaced fingers. "No problem. It'll be a snap."

"Oh, *well then*, what a relief," Charlie said. His sarcasm was palpable. "Then by all means, go directly to the Control Room 2. Everything's waiting for you."

As Martin strutted up the steps and out of the room, he patted Charlie on the shoulder. "Don't worry, Charlie, I've got everything in hand."

Judith followed Martin out and down the tunnel. Charlie's eyes bored holes into their backs.

Once out of earshot, Judith said, "Are you kidding me?"

"Don't ever kid a kidder."

"Fine, well, anyway, you've got a call, kidder."

"Where?"

"In the women's restroom."

"Oh, of course."

Martin followed Judith to a larger intersection tunnel cutting across another smaller tunnel. Judith pointed Martin to the right. "This connects back to the tunnel we just left in a huge arch. Everything's connected down here."

After passing a couple of vault doors, she led him through a doorway like another vault, but which, once pressed, swung open on hinges. "The women's restroom," she said.

They stepped into a dark room. The door swung shut.

Martin lost his balance on narrow metal steps. He leaned on Judith for balance.

"Easy, there," she said.

"Lights?"

"We'd better keep them off. Power usage is logged."

As his eyes adjusted, Martin could see a faint glow toward the other side of the round room.

"There's an old smart phone on the toilet seat. I'll wait outside to keep an eye out."

Martin went toward the light. Opening the stall door, he found an old-style smart phone, the lit screen projecting a blank wall.

Martin picked up the phone and said, "Hello?"

"Identify," a female voice said from the phone.

"Come again."

"What is your ASSN?"

The voice was asking for the private password given to every senior CIA employee, used for only secret projects. He wasn't about to divulge that to an unknown voice over an unsecured communication.

"This is Martin Lorien. I'm short on time, sleep, and patience. So, cut out the nonsense and just tell me what you have to tell me."

A bald woman with a beautiful face appeared on the screen. "Your biometrics from the video are confirmed. That's enough."

"Who are you?" Martin said.

"I'm Rachel's friend."

"What's your message?"

"I have someone to introduce you to."

The bald woman moved out of the screen. The angle of the video dropped to the freckled face of a girl with a pony tail. "Hi," she said.

Martin dropped the phone to his side and raised it back to his face as he stretched his neck. "Look here, little girl, I don't know what this is about, but I think you should put your mom back on the phone."

"My mom's dead," she said.

The voice of the bald woman said, "Tell him your name."

Hesitating, she said, "Tabitha. Tabitha Sparks."

Martin's face flushed red and white.

Tabitha nodded to a voice off screen. She said, "Oxana wants me to help you."

"*Oxana* is her name?" Martin said. "I'll have to make her acquaintance sometime."

"That can be arranged," Oxana said off screen. "Tabitha, tell him what you told me about your video, everything."

Tabitha told Martin how she'd forced the video onto the System. After she was done, Martin was speechless.

"Well," Oxana said.

"I've heard a lot of tall tales lately," Martin said.

"Show him what you showed me before," Oxana said.

Tabitha held up her arm. Martin watched the screen as several pieces of metal and plastic formed over her stump into a hand.

"Could be digitally enhanced," Martin said.

"What about this?" Tabitha said.

The smart phone in Martin's hand burst into thousands of small pieces, cascaded down his forearm, and formed a mechanical spider, which crawled hip his upper arm to his shoulder, pressing the screen shot of Tabitha's face to his.

Martin stifled a yell. The spider backed down to his bicep. As he picked it off his arm, it turned back into a smartphone, Tabitha still smiling on the screen.

"Okay, you've got my attention," he said.

Chapter 58

Papa stood on top of a table in the middle of the factory. He held the sword over his head as he paced back and forth, yelling, with his right hand cupped around his mouth.

"Listen up!" Papa said to the thousands gathering to him. "You are at a slave camp in Kansas. Some of you have been here for years. You thought you were home with your family and friends. No! You've been working in this factory!"

Most had blank faces and tired eyes.

A husky man at the front held up his CB. "It's not working," he said.

A woman with her hands on her hips to the left said, "What … are … you … talking … about?"

A tall skinny man said, "Are they going to turn the power back on soon?"

Farther behind her, Richard Chen, who'd arrived at Freedom Colony with Papa, said, "Let's get out of here!"

Papa smiled and nodded.

A voice yelled from the crowd. "I don't understand. I was just at home, having dinner with my wife, Kitty. She wants me to take out the trash … now."

"What's your name?" Papa said.

The man held up his hand. "Stanley Westerly."

A woman's voice shrieked from the crowd off to Papa's right. "Stanley! Stanley! Stanley!" His wife pushed through the crowd toward him. Stanley hugged her, crying, "Kitty, Kitty, Kitty," over and over.

The crowd erupted in a chaotic roar of voices yelling random names. Several more found their loved ones. Most did not.

"We've got to leave, now," Papa yelled, "while we still can!"

"Where will we go?" a voice from the crowd said. "I'm from Cincinnati and I don't even know which direction it is."

"Yeah, I'm from Chicago!" a woman said.

Sarah Roberts pushed through the crowd towards Papa. "I don't care if we go into the Wild," she said. "I'm leaving!"

Chapter 59

MARTIN CURLED HIS FINGERS OVER THE DESK AND TWISTED. "Edith, I just have a few more subjects I'd like to cover with you before my final questions. Tell me when you first knew the Sundog was following Irene."

"I think it was more suspicion than knowing. Late afternoon, on the day after the Sundogs came, a sense of fear had fallen over the Prefecture. The night before, we'd heard gunshots and teams of hovercraft. For the first time in my life I didn't know what was happening in the world beyond our own street. That morning a deputy walking the neighborhood left a flier on our door. It said martial law had been declared and everyone was ordered to stay in their homes until further notice. Violators could be arrested. Looters *would* be shot on sight.

"At sunset, two soldiers knocked on our door. They just pushed past La-La when she greeted them at the side entrance, came right through the *dojo* into the kitchen. They were armed with short machine guns over their chests, pistols holstered at their belts. The leader, a redheaded guy with freckles. The woman, a brunette, had an attractive face with a chin and cheeks chiseled by steroids, which explained her large thighs, forearms, and biceps. While the redhead was talking, she moved her black-gloved hands in front of her chest, like her CB was working, at least partially.

"They introduced themselves as 'Bob' and 'Ricky,' probably made-up names. Bob was trying to quiz La-La about everything, wanting to know how many lived here, our names, ages, dates of birth, CB numbers, and even our blood types and eye colors. Irene answered the questions as best as she could for La-La while Ricky fiddled with the System. Ricky snapped her fingers in the air and nodded at Bob with an air of finality. He pulled out a sheet of QR-code stickers, asking to see each of our CBs. When we produced them, Ricky connected each to a small metal box, and slicked on one of the stickers. According to Bob, first thing in the morning we could take our CBs to Seasonal Leaf Market at the intersection of Memorial and May on the southwestern border of our Prefecture, where we could have a gallon of water and five protein bars for each sticker. Each CB owner had to be there *in person* to get the goods.

"Irene asked if there were any exceptions for the injured or physically challenged. The market was three miles away, after all. The deputies shook their heads at Irene's cane without a hint of pity. Without another word, they marched out. Just the way they walked, their heels pounding through the dojo, made me resent them.

"We were all silent for a few moments. 'If there's water and food to be had up there,' Irene said, 'then we'd better get it. We can't afford to pass it up. It'll take us at least an hour to walk up to the store, maybe more. They said it'll be open at eight o'clock in the morning. So to make sure we get our share, we should be there at least two hours before. If we're going to arrive by six o'clock, we need to start by three o'clock.' In other words, we had to leave earlier to accommodate Irene.

"Irene hung her head and limped down the hall as though she had already been defeated by the journey to come. I went to the doorway from the kitchen over the *dojo* and put my hands at my hips, shaking my head, listening to Irene making her way up the stairs to her room.

Studying the long shadows drawing across the *dojo* floor, I said, "Papa where are you?"

La-La squeezed my shoulder.

Chapter 60

THOUSANDS OF EMPLOYEES FIDDLED WITH THEIR CBs.

"I don't have any reception," a man said, close to Papa.

"I've got to reach my son," a woman said.

"Folks! Don't you understand? When those CBs come back on, you'll think you're back home, but you'll still be stuck here!"

"I don't think you're going to convince everyone," Buddy said. "They'll either listen or not."

"If you want to get out of here, now's the time!" Papa said, calling over the crowd. "I know a way."

"Let's go!" Sarah said. "Anyone who wants to leave will follow!"

Papa hooked his CB from his neck, spun it around like a sling shot, and released it into the crowd. "Cut this off if you want freedom!"

Several hundred tossed away their CBs.

"After you!" Richard Chen said.

Papa waved his arm. "Follow me!" With the sword in his

left hand, he ran down the work table and jumped off the end, into the parting crowds of green jumpsuits. Some followed him. Others kept playing with their CBs, taking the same steps to reboot them, over and over.

Papa wound through the maze of hallways, Buddy several paces behind, trying to keep up. "You can do it, Buddy!" Papa said.

Hundreds followed Papa into the shipping room. He waited for Buddy near the cargo doors as ex-Employees pressed in.

Papa climbed atop one of the wrapped pallets of CBs.

"Once we open this shipping bay, a road goes through two checkpoints to the final wall, and then to the outside."

"What then?" Mr. Chen said.

Before Papa could answer, there was another question. "What if the checkpoints have armed guards?"

"I don't know," Papa said. "I *do* know I have two daughters at home. Their names – Irene and Edith. They think I'm dead! They don't know where I am! They don't know what's happened to me! And I am willing to do anything—and I mean anything—within my power, short of killing innocent people, to get back to them! I am willing to confront whatever's beyond these doors to find my family! What are you willing to do?"

Papa jumped down and threw open the loading bay door. Without looking back, he flung himself into the sunlight.

Buddy turned to the hundreds of stone faces. He clenched his fists and yelled at the ceiling, "Aaaaaaaaaarg!" and jumped after Papa.

The first security gate was unmanned but locked. A thick bullet-proof glass window had been shuttered at the security booth.

The booth was flanked by twenty-foot chain link fences with layers of coiled razor wire at the tops. The poles at each end of the gate were made of thick I-beams bolted into concrete slabs.

From a sprint, Papa jumped up onto the center of the gate and climbed. More than halfway up, he yanked frantically back and forth on the gate. Several other people followed. The rest of the ex-Employees rushed the gate, pushing until one of the poles buckled. Keeping up the pressure, they broke the fence and rushed ahead, Papa leading the way.

As green jumpsuits flooded the narrow roadway toward the next checkpoint, the road exploded in their midst. Dirt and debris arched up and out like a fountain, spewing people on fire. Another explosion erupted nearby. Heavy machine gun fire tore into them from three separate gun nests atop the slender pyramids lining the perimeter of the Colony.

Still running like a madman down the road, and nearly to the next checkpoint, Papa stole a look over his shoulder at the horrific scene. Buddy huffed to keep up. The next explosion was meant for Papa. Instead, it hit the gate and the guard station.

Papa's face flushed with anger as he unsheathed the sword and yelled, "Don't stop! Run for your lives! *Run!*"

People screamed through the smoldering checkpoint. From loudspeakers atop the gun nests, a familiar voice echoed across the perimeter.

"Halt!" Coralee said. "Halt or all of you will be terminated. Emergency power has been restored. The minefield under your feet is reactivated. Start back to the factory, now!"

Papa turned and yelled, "It's a lie!" and ran ahead.

In the years that Freedom Colony had been open for business, there had been a handful of escape attempts. The facility had been built to handle a full-blown riot if necessary, but nothing even close had ever happened. Not even a sit-in or hunger strike. The System had been more effective than barbed wire or machine gun nests. The guards were accustomed to passive Employees who didn't resist. So when the final gate opened, Mr. Rusty and his crew were ill equipped to deal with a full-on prison revolt. He'd called in all eight armored personnel carriers, facing the oncoming flood of enraged Employees at the exit of Freedom Colony. Mr. Rusty stood proudly in front, as though the mere sight of him and his big toys were enough to stop an angry mutiny. He was very wrong.

Papa raced at Mr. Rusty with his sword over his head, letting out a primal yell in a tone suggesting something worse than impalement was about to happen. The gravity of the situation dawned on Mr. Rusty too late; he just turned and ran in the opposite direction, taking off into a wheat field. The remaining guards were overrun by the Employees, some of them beaten unconscious, others stealing off after Mr. Rusty. Even though they were armed, not a single shot was fired.

The arsenal nests unleashed a storm of gunfire at the armored vehicles. But Mr. Rusty had parked the armored carriers, open and running, so close to the exit they were shielded from a direct hit by the exterior walls of Freedom Colony. There were too many people to fit in the carriers. As explosions slammed the wall, Papa had the carriers pulled into a line, giving the escapees cover on the opposite side, as the caravan eased out of range.

After a hundred yards, they stopped to yank out all of the tracking GPS devices. The group decided the carriers would go in eight opposite directions, one heading south. Those who couldn't fit inside clung to the top. As for Papa's carrier, it was unanimously agreed it would go directly to Oklahoma City, the home of their savior.

Chapter 61

MARTIN SCANNED THE SYSTEM WITH ERRATIC EYES AS I RECOUNTED our trek to the market.

"La-La woke us up at two-thirty. When my feet touched the cold wood floor the backs of my ears curled with regret. I cradled my head over my knees. Groaning like a zombie, I struggled into faded black jeans, and noodled my arms into a black-and-white-striped Sex Pistol T-shirt, the words 'God Save the Queen' and a defaced photo of Queen Elizabeth across the front.

"In the bathroom, I snaked fingers through my jet-black hair—permed straight—and puckered my lips in the mirror, saying 'Good morning ....' Before I got to 'beautiful' my heart stopped. My natural color was dark brown. Days before the UFO came, I'd re-colored everything. My roots should have been showing again, which didn't surprise me. I *was* surprised to see my roots were platinum white, even lighter than my suicide bangs and pigtail fringes."

Shifting his weight, Martin said, "So your roots turned white around the day the Sundogs arrived. Do you think the Sundog did it?"

"I don't know. As far as I could tell, it never paid me no mind. I mean, Irene and I aren't even identical twins."

"Would it make a difference to the Sundog if you were identical?"

"I don't know," I said. "I don't even know why I said it. I don't know what connection is, or whether there is a connection. I only know what I've seen."

"Go on," Martin said.

"La-La called after us from downstairs. I grabbed my favorite black Converse All Stars and bright red socks, put on my white down jacket with red seams and hurried down to the kitchen. La-La kept pointing at my feet and head, shaking her head, repeating, "No. Cold." So Irene lent me her trail shoes with pink and white soles and a light sky blue wool hat with a Hello Kitty licking a lollipop.

"'Don't you have anything else?' I said to Irene, holding out the hat like a dead rat.

"Irene shook her head with a smirk. 'Nope,' she said.

"She was lying. I knew it. She knew it. She just wasn't going to let me wear her favorite clothes. Reminding myself it was seven miles to the market and back, I caved to comfort over fashion in a world of anarchy. Still, I turned the Hello Kitty hat inside out and pulled it down over my ears.

"Irene had on Papa's black-and-white-checkered fleece-lined hunting hat, the flaps hanging down over her ears. Papa wore it in bitter weather to cook black market steaks.

I held out a bottle of water to Irene. "You don't have to go, Irene. The water may be back on tomorrow."

"And maybe it won't," Irene said, sliding the bottle into her jacket.

"We checked our CBs and followed La-La out the side door. She had bundled herself up in one of Mama's light brown business overcoats. Outside the door, she snagged the handle of an empty metal basket with two wheels and squeaked down the dark walkway to the faded blacktop street.

"At first we were oblivious to the Sundog hovering directly over our house. That is to say, to the extent something that big could be directly over anything. Passing the burnt rubble of the Blakely's house, La-La pointed to the rising moon, half eclipsed by the UFO's outer edge.

"With Irene, it was slow going. We kept to the side of the street as others moved past us. Once we turned west at the southwest gate on Memorial Road, the moon was completely eclipsed by the Sundog. But moonlight shone through, like the sun did, basking over the river of glowing CBs coursing through the streets. *So much for getting an early start,* I thought.

"Graffiti caked a faded concrete wall, three feet thick and fifteen feet high, running parallel with Memorial on our left. There was another two-lane blacktop on the other side of the wall, flanked by an elevated highway.

"A smaller ten-foot brick wall separated our side of Memorial from the neighborhoods on our right. It had come apart and crumbled in several places during the earthquake, exposing houses, burned, collapsed, looted, or all of the above. We passed the Marston house. I had never met them, but they were notorious preppers. I'd heard they'd saved up a year's worth of food and water, and some illegal guns and ammunition. Apparently everyone else knew it too; with their back yard exposed by a broken wall, all the house windows were shattered and their furniture, clothes, and belongings were strewn around, some of it dragged out into the street. I hoped the Marstons had abandoned the place, not wanting to think they were still inside, dead. I squeezed Irene's arm, then pulled away, embarrassed.

"Fraidy cat," she said.

"You're the one with the Hello Kitty hat," I said.

"That you're wearing."

"Inside out."

"You're a pussycat inside, and you know it, no matter how much you try to hide it," Irene said.

"I bumped my hips to hers, almost knocking her over. She'd regained a lot of strength since staring kendo again. But her limp still dogged her.

"La-La was pulling the metal cart from behind. She focused intently on her feet, taking pains to keep Irene's slow pace, probably counting her steps in meditation.

"The crowd grew as we proceeded westward. I watched people: a young couple with a swaddled infant in a stroller; two middle-aged women arm-in-arm, walking briskly ahead purposefully; a group of five young men in their early twenties bunched together and talking in hushed voices like they were up to no good; an old woman in a wheelchair pushed by a balding man, probably her bachelor son.

"I fantasized seeing Papa's floppy blond hair in the crowd. In my mind's eye, he'd see us, come rushing over, and hug us. He was back and everything was going to be okay. He was taking us to a better place he'd prepared. *Stop torturing yourself!* I thought.

"Sometimes I think Irene reads minds. Interrupting my

doubt, she said, 'Papa's alive.'

"'Maybe it's just a fantasy,' I said. 'Maybe someone is just playing with us. Maybe Papa wrote the message on the sword and someone just returned it to us anonymously. If he's alive, where is he now?'"

"'In mountains,' she said.'"

"What mountains?" Martin said.

"Well, it was just a figure of speech. You remember the sword. 'I will see you again in mountains.' I understood what she meant. Papa was going to come back and take us camping at Half Dome in Yosemite. It was just a false hope. That's all. I wanted to tell her she was fooling herself. But I didn't want to shatter her fantasy. Anyway, I doubted whether she could complete the seven-mile walk. As we chatted, her breathing had become labored."

"'Irene, are you sure you want to do this?' I said to her, holding out my hand. 'Give me your CB. I'll walk you back to the corner, you can make it to the house from there, and I'll catch up with La-La. We'll try to talk them into giving us your share of water and food. Even without it, we'll probably be fine, the water and electricity will come back on soon, everything will be back to normal.'

"She gave me this incredulous look as she skulked along the street. I reminded myself she was stubborn, so I just shut up.

"After our first mile we came to another Prefecture gate at the intersection of Memorial and Western Avenue, a four-lane road running north and south. Two large generators hummed in the center of the street, surrounded by chicken wire, powering four towers of halogen lights, flooding the area brighter than day. The concrete wall on the east side of the metal gate had fallen, leaving a huge gap fenced off with two layers of chain-link stacked on top of each other. A doublewide metal-framed door was set into the wall on the west side of the gate in front of a bulletproof kiosk where a Prefect Deputy usually sat. The metal shutters of the kiosk had been locked down behind the thick glass and the door was blocked with three metal beams.

"A crowd of ramshackle Wildlings clung to the other side of the chain-link fence, many of them pressing their faces desperately against the wire, pleading to six soldiers with black visors, their grimacing mouths twitching with hatred. A pair of deputies in helmets and flack vests hung back near the abandoned kiosk. I'd never seen a deputy outfitted like a soldier. They were out of place, looking uncomfortable in the extra body armor.

"As we crossed through the lights, we could better see the people gathering on the other side of the fence. Some of them were couples, wearing wool caps, jeans, and hiking shoes. Others were families with crying toddlers or younger children. There was a teenaged boy wearing our school uniform. Many were yelling out addresses, some even holding worn identification papers, begging for the soldiers on our side of the fence to confirm their identities. Some looked like vagabonds, echoing the cries of other desperates with families, making all the pleas from the other side of the fence sound contrived.

"A middle-aged man from India stood near the kiosk, shouting something urgent at one of the soldiers. He was over six feet tall and overweight, his lower chin jiggling as he spoke. He waved his arms, holding papers in his hand. The sides of his camel hair overcoat flared with each gesture. I recognized him: Aariti Sharma's father. Then I saw her at the gate, pressing her face against the fence near the barred door. Mascara was smeared down her cheeks, joining with blood from a broken nose, dripping off her chin.

As we neared the other side of the intersection, closer to the kiosk, we could hear Mr. Sharma pleading with the soldier, who blandly told Mr. Sharma his daughter couldn't come back in since the System was down; no one's identity could be confirmed. None of it made any sense. The soldiers' CBs seemed to be working.

"'Do you think I'm lying?' yelled Mr. Sharma. 'Do I look like a liar? Look at her!' he said, pointing his outstretched arms and open palms to his daughter. 'We're from India! She's Indian! She looks just like me! She's my daughter! You don't need a CB to know these things! Look at this photo! It's us, the three of us—me, my wife, and Aariti — together in Delhi. Am I a liar? Am I?'

"Unmoved, the soldier just stared through Mr. Sharma.

"Without a word, Irene turned toward the kiosk.

"La-La took Irene by her lower arm, hissing something in Chinese. Irene shrugged her off. Before we could stop her, Irene stood in front of the two deputies, pointing her finger at Aariti."

"'She is my classmate, Aariti!' Irene said. She mechanically moved the point of her index finger to Mr. Sharma. 'That's Aariti's dad! They all live in this Prefecture. I've been to their house!' Her finger then pointed to the barred door. 'Now, for God's sake, come to your senses and do the right thing!'

"Behind Irene, Mr. Sharma was quietly nodding his head. His eyes shot back and forth from the deputies to Aariti. The soldier had half turned to the deputies, grievously shaking his head with a grin.

"One of the deputies, short, and overweight, with three days of stubble on his double chin, said to his partner, 'This is baloney,

Tyrone! I'm letting the girl in. Back me up if anyone else tries to come past.'

"Tyrone followed the chubby deputy to the door without a word. The soldier yelled, 'Stop right there! We have jurisdiction here! Stop! I order you to stop!' But Chubby and Tyrone had already removed the bars from the door before any of the other soldiers could stop him."

"Chubby turned to the soldier. 'This is our Prefecture, jarhead! I don't care about your jurisdiction.' He turned and pointed to Aariti through the fence. 'Girl, you come over here to this entrance, before it's too late!' Aariti pressed through the crowd along the fence toward the entrance. Chubby unlocked one of the double-wide metal doors and swung it back, exposing a battered gate on the other side. Several men were pressed against the fence. Chubby leveled his machine gun at them. 'Clear a way for the girl or I will clear it the easy way!' he fired a warning over their heads, and then brought it back down in their faces. They moved back, letting Aariti squeeze past to the gate. As she reached it, Chubby opened the lock while Tyrone gave him cover, snapped the gate open as Aariti squeezed in, then re-sealed the double-wide doors.

"The soldier snagged Aariti by the arm as she ran toward her dad. 'You really shouldn't have done that,' he said, leering at Chubby. He lifted his visor, drew out a black semi-automatic pistol and held it to Aariti's head. In my heart of hearts, I knew he would shoot her right there in front of Mr. Sharma. Then the rattling sound of fast hammers tapping on sheet metal erupted behind us. As I turned, I saw a bloody man falling from the fence back into the screaming crowd on the other side. We could hear the wailing of a woman. All I could think of was Mrs. Blakely yelling, "Aim … eee!" The soldiers shot three other men climbing the chain-link fence. Wildlings fell and disappeared. In the chaos, Aariti ran to her dad. They hunkered down and shuffled out of the flood lights. La-La pulled us away by the elbows.

"The eastern sky turned faintly blue as we left the Western Gate behind us. The windows of the food distribution station on the northwest corner were shattered and the place had been looted. The shelves had all been stripped bare, leaving nothing but broken bottles and trash around the floors. Three dead bodies lay around the entrance, one of them stuck halfway into the shattered door on his face, a pool of blood around his head. Another one was on his back, balanced on a window frame, his head hanging upside down facing us with a gaping mouth. Two soldiers stood over the third one, a woman on her side with a broken bag of rice clutched in her hand. I remembered the flyer that had been posted on our door: 'Looters will be shot.' The soldiers posed, as if proud they'd lived up to their promise.

"The crowd moved ahead indifferently. La-La pushed us from the back, almost knocking Irene to the ground. This time we hurried to leave the ugly scene behind. Others had kept their heads down and eyes forward, shuffling past without even glancing at the dead. People's response to such horrors reminded me of the way they were ignoring the Sundogs directly overhead—after a while those things just weren't there anymore. I faintly wondered about what other inconvenient truths we were ignoring.

"The glaring light at the western intersection faded as the burnt orange sunrise grew, revealing the Sundog overhead, hovering there lower to the ground than before. No one was talking about it or taking notice of it, but it was there, its presence pressing down over the homelessness, sickness, hunger, death, loneliness, and desperation, without a care. It was like a big toy top with multiple layers of dark charcoal pancakes layered one on top of the other, each growing larger from bottom to top. The base tapered out like a vintage zoom camera lens pointed at the earth, its circumference hanging directly over us for roughly a quarter of a mile. It appeared flat. I couldn't tell if it actually had a surface or was an opening to a bottomless pit. The notion gave me the creepy feeling we could be sucked upward into an unforgiving realm of black eternity.

"The crowd thickened as we arrived at the intersection of Memorial and Pennsylvania Avenue, a mile away from the market. The Penn entrance was the largest in our Prefecture. Running north-south, it had been locked and braced shut with metal beams. A crack three feet wide snaked across the pavement. Most people jumped the distance. But with Irene, we waited our turn to cross a makeshift bridge of scrap boards.

More soldiers skulked in the toll booths and on each corner, surveying the crowd. Others milled onto Memorial from the north off Penn, heading west toward the market. Irene veered to a concrete retaining wall on the side of Penn and took a seat. She laid her cane across her thigh and wriggled her ankles. I could see she was in pain by the pulsing purple veins at her temple. La-La and I joined Irene and took turns sipping from the water bottle.

"Irene called out to the pair of soldiers standing a few feet away. 'Hey, when do you think they'll have the water back on?'

"The shorter of the two turned. We could barely see his eyes through his visor. I wondered if he'd even heard us."

"'Hey, how much farther to the market?' Irene said.

"The taller one whirled around, his machine gun pointed at

our feet. 'Hey, kid,' he said. 'Get a move on if you want any water!' He turned away and chuckled something to his partner under his breath.

"La-La waved her hand at Irene to keep her quiet. We helped Irene to the pavement before she could say anything else.

"We went less than a quarter of a mile before the crowd stopped moving. We pushed past people before a wide-eyed man in a beard and a 'Mexican-American War Veteran' ball cap grabbed me by the arm just above the elbow and snapped, 'No cutting!' As he jerked me back, I spun around and ran sideways into a Hispanic woman holding an infant, then rammed my shin across the metal feet of an empty wheelchair being pushed by a red-haired woman bundled up in a paisley scarf. I tore the palms of my gloves open on the faded blacktop as I fell and rolled across the ground. People skipped over me indifferently. La-La was there, holding out both her hands to keep me from being trampled, saying 'Okay, okay, okay, okay.' I looked up at the Sundog as La-La took my hand.

"'Watch where you're going, Edith,' Irene said loudly. I think she just wanted those around us to think we were sorry.

"I drew close to Irene. 'The UFO is directly over us,' I said.

"'Yeah, it's big,' Irene said.

"'It was right over us at Western, too.' I pointed up at the Sundog lens. Irene yanked my arm down.

"'Don't point!' she hissed. 'Ignore it like everyone else!'

"The line moved about as fast as Irene walked. Once we got closer to the market parking lot, I could see two huge grey tent tops. Crowds flowed into them from the north and west.

"The market was on the southwestern boundary of the Prefecture. The elbow of the twenty-foot wall had completely collapsed, leaving about thirty yards exposed which had been fenced off like the Western Gate. Masses coursed in waves on the other side. About a hundred soldiers and a handful of deputies were stationed around the fence. A few were stationed on top of large tanks behind the turrets of machine guns. Others hunkered behind sandbags. Those on the other side of the fence were more desperate than angry. They watched as people on our side came out with bottles of water and food, and hurried away down the road as fast as they could.

"As our line flowed into a tent, we met several pale-skinned men and women, all of them with shaved heads and light blue jumpsuits. They directed lines of people to metal fences neck high. Irene asked one of the women a question. Cold and mute, she swung out a karate chop hand into the air, directing us to our new line. La-La waved her hand in front of the woman's glazed eyes, shrugged, and sighed, yanking her metal cart along.

"The gates clanked against each other at the joints as we snaked through the corral, until we came to a short, fat woman sitting on a tall metal stool behind a podium, her feet dangling from the stool.

"'CBs,' she said.

"Irene held out an open hand at La-La and me. Irene took La-La's and passed their CBs to the woman. 'These belong to me and my grandmother,' she said. Irene nodded her head for me to hurry. 'This is my sister Edith.'

"I stared at Irene, my eyes bulging, as I searched every pocket. I had it when I left the house, I knew for sure, but it was gone; it probably fell out of my coat pocket or even stolen, when I'd been pushed around by the bearded war veteran.

"Reading my mind, Irene said, 'On the way up here my sister was attacked by a homeless man. He stole her CB. Do we still get our three portions?'

"The fat lady paid no attention. With quick pudgy hands, she put the CBs one at a time into a socket on top of a black box on her podium. The box made a whining sound which cycled from a low hum to a high pitch, followed by a click and snap. She handed the CBs back to Irene, and leaned over the podium, glaring at me. The whites of her eyes were speckled, her chubby cheeks spidered with tiny red veins.

"'You two don't look anything alike,' she said. 'She has green eyes, you have blue.'

"Leaning heavily on her cane, Irene snatched off my cap, and said, 'Look again, look at her eyebrows, cheeks, and noses. We're exactly the same!'

"But the fat lady wasn't looking at my nose. A hard scowl fell over her face, turning to Irene. 'She's got blonde roots, sweetie! There's no way, *no way*, she's your sister.'

"Irene gawked at my head as the lady swiveled around and yelled behind her. 'Greggy, son! We've got another *fish-out-of-water* over here.'"

"Greggy wasn't the fat lady's son. He was a six-foot-eight-inch soldier who'd been loitering behind a towering stack of water jugs on a wood pallet. Greggy moseyed around to the podium, munching on a protein bar in his left hand, and holding his machine gun with his finger on the trigger in his right. 'Where is he, Tilda?' Greggy said."

"'He's a she,' Tilda said, thumbing at me. 'Blondie here.'

"Before we realized the seriousness of the situation, Greggy snagged me by the neck as Tilda said, 'If she doesn't have a CB, she'll have to go!'"

"'Go!? Go where!?' Irene said.

"'The Wild,' Tilda said, pointing to the mob on the other side of the fence.

"Greggy yanked me away by the neck and headed toward the gate about forty yards away. Although I couldn't breathe, I tried to dig away Greggy's banana fingers. La-La's screams faded. Just as I was about to pass out, Greggy let go. My face in the dirt, gasping and rubbing my neck to catch my breath, I pulled Greggy's hand away. It took me a moment before realizing I held Greggy's hand like we were about to arm wrestle, except there wasn't anything attached to it past his forearm. I tossed the severed arm aside and propped myself back on my knees. Nearby, Irene held the *wakizashi* blade out in her right hand like a torch, her left hand hooking her cane at her side like a samurai warrior. She stood over Greggy with fury in her eyes, a look so unfamiliar it scared me.

"While Greggy was screaming for his mama, holding the stump where his arm had been, the mob outside pushed over the fence. A riot flooded into the Prefecture like a tsunami of black debris, heading for the pallets of water and protein bars. Several of the soldiers fired off bursts from their automatic machine guns directly up at the Sundog. A loudspeaker blared, 'Stop! Stop! Stop! Go back, or you … will … be … shot! Go back, or you … will … be … shot! This is your final warning! Stop!'

"People rushed forward. Then … the strangest thing happened. The guy on the speaker sang *Come Together* by the Beatles.

"Even stranger — Greggy, still clutching his bloody stump,

also sang along. Just about everyone on our side of the fence, the soldier and the lines waiting for their rations—everyone—was singing the tune. However, what followed was anything but pensive, echo-driven guitar riffing.

"I understand why the mob pressing in from the Wild didn't stop. They were starving, after all, and somewhere in the back of their frenzied minds, especially after hearing the soldiers singing, they probably thought there was no way they'd be shot. Even as I sat there on my knees, watching those poor souls surge, many of them families, I, too, believed those soldiers would pity them. I was wrong.

"A roar of machine guns opened fire. People dominoed to the ground in crumpled piles of blood, their screams suppressed by the sound of the arsenal. A man fell to his knees, a hand to his abdomen as another high-caliber bullet took off his extended arm above the elbow, followed by another to his neck, silencing his agony. A mother with dark hair in a ponytail and sheep's skin coat, hand-in-hand with her pre-teen daughters, whirled around when the gunfire erupted. She fled back to the fence as they hunkered low to the ground, almost crawling. Bullets ripped open their backs as they reached the wall. A group of five young men in football jackets, carrying crude two-by-fours and faces of determination, were cut to shreds in mists of red. Bodies fell to the ground in a wave, as though there were an invisible tripwire, bowed forward in an arching wedge which caught the surging crowd unaware, many of them holding hands. The show of solidarity commanded no mercy.

"Mesmerized by the horror before me, still on my knees, I raised an eyebrow at the UFO. It hovered there, in all of its dark hugeness, a monolith of indifference. Irene interrupted my daze, slapping my face side to side. Her mouth moved but I heard only silence. La-La was there, too, grabbing my right arm, forcing me up to my feet. As the gunfire continued, we hurried away, ducking into the narrow aisles formed by the pallets of water and power bars. We emerged near the thick line leading back to Tilda's tent. Huddled to the ground, we followed it backwards and turned north onto the first neighborhood street. We were met by a ramshackle barricade of furniture and refrigerators manned by a bunch of guys with clubs probably wishing they had guns.

A barrel-chested man in a black parka and 89er baseball hat held out his hand like a wizard casting a spell. 'Halt!' He said. There's no foot traffic through here.'

"Irene held her hand up like a surrender and led us forward. 'Mister, they're shooting people up at the market." She told them what had happened. Irene kept pressing toward the bearded man, who shifted his weight with uncertainty.

"'We've had a lot of break-ins," the bearded man said. "Many have been hurt pretty badly by looters.'"

"'We've been hurt, too,' Irene said, pointing to me. I wiped a patch of blood off my forehead. I'd bled all over my Sex Pistols shirt—kinda cool except for the pain.

'We don't want any trouble,' I said. 'We just live a couple of miles east from here on Cimarron Street.'

"The bearded man waved us in, giving us directions. After we made it through the neighborhood, we followed Penn Avenue northward with a larger crowd, and wound our way through 150th Street and Western, until we found the eastern entrance to our neighborhood, where we met another barricade manned by John Blakely and a bunch of other frazzled looking guys. Irene told them what had happened at the market.

"Mr. Blakely shook his head. 'What is the world coming to?' he said.

"'I don't know,' Irene said. But it's going to get worse.' She looked at the UFO.

"After everything that had happened, I was surprised to find our house as we'd left it. As Irene unlocked the side door, I looked up again. The UFO was still there, low overhead and maddeningly silent.

"'Don't you think it's following us?' I said.

"'No question about it,' Irene said.

Chapter 62

Martin exited the women's restroom with Judith cupping his elbow.

"What'd you do with the smartphone?" she said, whispering.

"I flushed it."

"Great. They sewers are strained once a month."

"It won't matter by then." Fingering a pair of glasses in his pocket, he pushed a new pair – courtesy of Tabitha via parts from the smartphone – up the bridge of his nose. The girl had become Martin's fly on the wall everywhere he went.

Judith shrugged as they turned the corner. Charlie and a soldier were waiting for them.

"Doctor Lorien. Dr. Stout," the soldier said.

"What's with all the 'doctors'?" Judith said.

"Both of you, please step to the side and place your hands on the wall," the soldier said.

"Is there a problem?" Martin said, sounding bemused.

"Just do as he says," Charlie said.

Martin placed his hands to the wall softly, like it might push over. Startled, Judith also complied. The soldier frisked Martin first. He found the pair of glasses and a locket in his front pants pocket. The soldier clicked the locket open, revealing a photo of Martin's daughter Brandy playing in a sandbox. The soldier clicked it shut and handed the items to Charlie. Judith had a Case pocket knife and a bag of mushed M&Ms.

"What were you two talking about in the restroom?" Charlie said.

"Who says we were talking?" Judith said.

"We could hear you in the women's restroom," Charlie said.

Martin heard Tabitha's silent voice in his ear say, "I messed with their hidden video cameras in the girl's room. They couldn't hear anything we said."

"What's the matter," Martin said, "having technical difficulties?"

Charlie squeezed his fists. "What were you two doing in the restroom together?"

Judith dropped her arms and slid one around Martin's waist. "I know there's a policy against fraternization among employees," she said, "but we're old friends and everything, and with the world coming to an end, well, it seemed like a good time to …. reconnect."

Charlie's red face went blank and still, as if he couldn't or didn't want to process the information.

Martin took his hands off the wall. "Sure, we were in the restroom together, making noises, and we weren't *talking* about anything," he said. "It's just been a while since we've seen each other."

"That's strictly forbidden. No employee ..."

Martin cut him off. "You know what Charlie? You got us! You caught us red handed! Now what are you going to do about it? Arrest us? Or do you want me to fix the System?" He offered his upturned wrists for cuffing.

The soldier smirked, dropped the glasses and locket into Martin's front pocket, and strolled down the tunnel into darkness. "Go ahead," the soldier said over his shoulder, "Cuff 'em, Chuck."

Martin swiveled back and forth on a stool in front of a wide panel of computer controls overlooking the Teardrop chamber from the window of Control Room 2. Several flat screens lined the control board under the window. "Very old school," Martin said.

"You should know," Charlie said, "you designed it."

Judith took a seat beside Martin.

Charlie leaned over Martin. He inserted a key on the control panel. A square plastic cover flipped open, exposing a pink button.

"Pink?" Martin said.

"You tell me," Charlie said. He hit the button with the palm of his hand. The Teardrop chamber hummed. An electric red outline of an alphanumeric keyboard came to life on the desktop under his fingers. The flat screens glowed dimly black. At the upper left-hand corner of each screen, a white cursor blinked.

Martin typed a row of random keystrokes and pressed "Enter." He pushed up on the arm rests of his chair to better see the Teardrop through the control window.

"Nothing," Martin said.

"You said you could fix it," Charlie said. "You've got *everything in hand*, right? So fix it."

Martin smiled and pressed "Esc." The cursor on the screen reset to the top left of a blank screen. He typed a basic algorithm, defining the initial operating instructions for the System. Charlie leaned in, nodding and humming in agreement. Then Martin's algorithm became more complex and lengthy.

Charlie pointed. "What's that supposed to mean?"

"Hey!" Martin said. "You're breaking my concentration." Martin typed fast for over thirty minutes. Pressing "Enter" with a snap of finality, he nodded.

The humming from the Teardrop chamber stuttered and choked.

Suddenly, Martin, Judith, and Charlie all sang *Come Together*.

When they stopped, a view had returned to Charlie's and Judith's contact lenses. Martin could see it, too, with Tabitha's lenses, but his view was different, something like watching the System by flat screen.

Charlie rubbed his eyes. "What the hell was that?"

"We were all singing the Beatles!" Judith said.

Martin shrugged. "Maybe I liked the Beatles."

"Maybe?" Charlie said.

"I don't remember everything yet," Martin said. "But I do, in fact, like the Beatles. It seems reasonable to assume I programed it that way, so when the System is rebooted I would know it was working." It was all a lie, except for liking the Beatles.

Charlie waved his hands aimlessly through the air. The sight of him was reminiscent of a blind person feeling his way through a room. "I only see a basic structure. There's no functionality. What did you do?""

"I re-booted the System," Martin said. "That's what you wanted, right? It's fixed. Easy as one, two, three."

"But it's not working! What was that algorithm?" Charlie said. "It wasn't in your memory banks."

Martin tapped his forehead. "Sure, it's ... right up here," he said. "Just waiting to be pried out." He'd actually typed in something Oxana had dictated to him. He got up and stretched his arms.

"Wait a minute," Charlie said. "It's still not working!"

"The System is operational." Martin tapped his glasses. He touched a few links but nothing happened. "The System will take days to completely reboot. Until then, it won't be working properly ... if you know what I mean."

"No, I don't," Charlie said. "Explain."

"The operating system—Animal Farm—must be re-paired *directly* with every person; so, *every* CB will have to be reconnected to the System—manually—before they will *work* properly."

"You mean before CBs can interface users?" Judith said.

"That's putting it politely," Martin said.

"What do you mean, every CB?" Charlie said.

"Every single CB, otherwise, they won't work, at least, not the way you want them to ...."

"You're talking about billions," Charlie said.

"More than ten billion worldwide."

"How are we supposed to manually reconnect every CB to the System?" Charlie said.

"You just reload the operating system. It's easy, but it has to be uploaded manually, otherwise the CBs with the old operating system still won't work. People will be able to just scan through the System, asking their own questions and so on, instead of just responding to the stimuli fed to them."

Martin cut Charlie off before he could ask another question. "Charlie, I'm tired and hungry. I'm going to eat something, take a shower, and sleep before I answer any more questions, or do anything else for that matter."

"I'll take you," Judith said.

Martin gave Charlie a lazy salute and followed Judith out of the control room.

Chapter 63

TAKE THIS JOB AND SHOVE IT! THAT'S WHAT I LIKE TO THINK PAPA and the ex-Employees thought as they raced away from Freedom Colony in an armored personnel carrier.

The digital readout of the personnel carrier showed three hundred fifty miles to go before empty, enough to make it to Oklahoma City, barring any mishaps.

Twenty-three people went with Papa's carrier, some inside, some hanging on top. He, Buddy, and Nikki were the only three from the Oklahoma City metro area. Doug Masterson and two others were from Dallas. Sarah, Richard Chen, and some others were both from Houston. There were a few others from small places in between. Jesse Davidson was from Enid, north of the city, the first stop on the way south.

Papa drove east from Freedom Colony, turning south a mile-section before US-281, following crumbling blacktops, overgrown with weeds, the road disappearing at times in the prairie grass.

After crossing the Kansas-Oklahoma border, Papa came to

more than one washed-out bridge. He'd double back a mile or two until he found another road through, slowing the pace.

Nearing Enid, the carrier was down to a quarter of a tank. Not enough to make it to Oklahoma City. Jesse knew of an abandoned farm a couple of miles north of Enid. After some searching, they found it, and parked the carrier in an abandoned metal hay barn.

Jesse wanted to go home to see his wife. But before any of them could go anywhere, a few things had to be hashed out.

On the dirt floor, they huddled in a circle to face the stark reality that they were all wanted. Anyone looking for them knew that their former homes—if they were still there—were the likeliest place they would show up. And they were out of food, water, and gas.

Jesse was adamant he could find water and gas near town. So he went out on foot just after sunset. If he got caught, he'd tell them the others were long gone and he didn't know where. But if he didn't make it back by dawn, they should assume the worst and move on.

That night was the toughest. It was first time in years that most of them had slept without the System. There were a lot of nightmares, yelling out in darkness. Papa couldn't sleep at all; a good thing, too. He stopped several from sleepwalking out of the barn into the wilderness. When he slapped them awake, they thought they'd been heading to the factory.

At dawn, Jesse returned on a three-wheeled bicycle, pulling a cart loaded with five-gallon gas cans, shrink-wrapped bottled water, bags of frozen vegetables, a stack of brown coveralls, and a flat of chicken-broth cans.

He stopped inside the barn with a grin.

Everyone swarmed at the back of the cart, tore into the

packages of water, and handed out bottles. Nikki examined an unopened bottle and peppered Jesse with questions.

Sounding relaxed, Jesse had completely ignored the plan and had just gone home anyway. He found his house, but there was no way he'd ever lived there. He remembered his house, a basic ranch style, red brick structure, in a Prefecture of cookie-cutter homes. The house he found last night had been abandoned years ago, long before he'd arrived at Freedom Colony.

Still dressed in his green jumpsuit, he'd walked through the hulled out structure. He knew every room, every doorway, even the color and type of shag carpet. There was a single framed photograph of downtown Enid from the early twentieth century. His wife had purchased it at a flea market, or so he'd believed. With all the things he remembered, there was no question he had *never* lived there. He was no older than twenty-three, he was sure. He had married his wife fresh out of college when they were both twenty-one. But the house had been vacant for over ten years.

After telling his story, everyone was so dumbfounded no one cared to ask him where he'd snagged the supplies. They all wondered what they would find when they returned to the place they called home, whether all of their memories about life outside Freedom Colony were imagined, implanted by the System.

Papa downed a bottle of water, threw it into the dirt, and went to the entrance of the barn, taking in the expansive view of the shimmering grass, stretching as far as he could see. He turned. "This doesn't make a bit of difference to me," he said. "I *know* where my home is. I *know* I have two daughters – Irene and Edith. And I *know* they need me."

"I felt the same way," Jesse said. "As I stand here, even now,

I can hardly believe it, but it's true. I have no home. If I ever did, I've forgotten it. Do I have family and friends out there somewhere, in a bigger city somewhere far off, who know me better than I know myself, who miss me or need me? I don't know. Maybe it was all just a dream, implanted by the System."

"I don't know about y'all," Nikki said, "but I'll never be satisfied unless I see it for myself. I *know* I've got family and friends in the City. I've got to believe that. Without it, I'm nothing. I'm going there, no matter what. If I find nothing, and my life's been nothing but an illusion, then at least I'll have some answers!"

"Maybe we're just programed like this so if we ever break out of the Colony, they'll know where to find us," Richard said.

"Then they would have followed Jesse back to us," Sarah said.

Papa regarded Jesse with suspicion. "I'd think they'd be here by now," he said.

"Maybe they're on their way!" Richard said.

The group argued about what to do next. Papa went to the cart behind the tricycle, and without a smidgen of modesty, stripped nude and pulled on a pair of coveralls.

As he buttoned the snaps above his chest, he said, "This is just a gut feeling, but I think we should get out of here."

"I'll go with each and every single one of you," Jesse said, "to help you find home. But the first one who actually finds their home as they remembered it has to take me in until I get back on my feet. I have nowhere else to go."

"I'll take you in," Papa said, "but even if I find my home as it was, and find my daughters, I'm taking them back to the Wild."

"Are you kidding me?" Richard said.

414

"Think about it," Papa said. "What other choice do you have? If you stay at your old home you'll probably just be arrested and dragged back to Freedom Colony. You can either go back to Coralee—oh, she'll be waiting with open arms—or take your chances and start a new life."

"I'm wondering if leaving Freedom Colony was such a good idea," Jesse said.

"I know you're joking," Papa said.

"You know, the thing is," Jesse said, "there's nothing going on out here in the Wild, at least not around Enid."

"What do you mean?" Richard said. "This isn't the Wild. We're just ..."

Jesse cut Richard off. "No, no," Jesse said, shaking his head. "I could see the outer wall of the Enid Prefecture two blocks away from my house—at least what I'd thought was my house. I went right up to the wall, followed it several blocks in each direction. I was so out of it. I think I almost wanted to be caught. I'd always been told you'd get ambushed if you ventured out. I thought there were Wildlings lying in wait for us to just step one foot out. Wrong again. Yeah, this is the Wild, and there's nothing and no one out here."

Sarah chimed in: "You're saying the walls of the Prefectures are keeping people in, not keeping people out."

Just then, the distant rumble of a diesel engine reached the barn. They all stepped toward the carrier.

Papa peeked out. "It's coming from town," he said.

"Probably checking to see if I've returned home," Jesse said.

"Did you disturb anything?" Richard said.

415

"Not at my house," Jesse said.

"Then where did you find the bike and supplies?" Papa said.

"I found the bike in my old deserted neighborhood," Jesse said. "Then I looted a military base, a mile outside the Prefecture, on its own, without no fence, nothing, as far as security. There was a small storage room with a walk-in freezer out back."

"Seems a little too easy," Nikki said.

Papa grabbed a bottle of water and examined at it. He cupped his hand over his forehead. "You know what I think?" he said.

That was pretty much the last thing Papa remembered for several hours. He woke up lying on the floor of the armored personnel carrier.

"I think he's coming around," Sarah said.

Richard stepped over Papa, knelt down, and slapped his face around a few times until Papa said, "Stop!"

Papa pushed himself up on his elbows. "What the hell!"

"The short of it," Nikki said, "Jesse went off and got himself caught. His whole story was a bunch of nonsense. His house was inside the Prefecture just where he thought it was, and so was his family. They'd forgotten him, but like a lot of people, they were waking back up from the System, remembering things. Soldiers were waiting for him, too. They held his family hostage, told him he could return (probably a lie), if he delivered a bunch of supplies and a story to us."

Buddy helped Papa up to a seat in the carrier. Papa turned to Nikki, Richard, Sarah, and Buddy. "This is it?" Papa said.

"Everyone else passed out about the same time you did," Buddy said, "everyone who drank the water, anyway."

416

"As soon as you fell we could see trucks coming in the distance," Sarah said.

"There was no time to get everyone into the carrier. Heck, most were riding on top," Richard said.

"Jesse just hung his head as we grabbed you and as much of the gas as we could, and busted through the back of the barn to the north," Buddy said. "We followed a dry creek below the grass-line west for several miles."

"And they didn't catch us?" Papa said.

"Boy, they tried," Nikki said.

Richard slapped her on the shoulder. "This girl can drive like a maniac," he said.

"Whatever's in this thing is faster than greased lightning," Nikki said. "I'll bet they regret giving Jesse any gas."

Papa rubbed his head. "Where are we now?"

"Sitting in a ravine a mile to the north of our Prefecture," Buddy said. His face gleamed. "We're home!"

Papa rubbed his head again. "Holy smoke!"

"Looks like there's more going on around the Oklahoma City Metro than in Enid," Buddy said.

"What?" Papa said.

"A crowd is trying to make it into your Prefecture," Richard said. "This morning, around dawn, in our overalls, Buddy and I got out and walked within view of it."

"We came across a couple of guys—they looked like regular old farmers if you ask me—walking to the Prefecture," Buddy said.

"There's a rumor the government's handing out food and water and anything left over will be passed out to others in the Wild,"

Richard said. "There are a lot of people heading to the southwest corner."

"Maybe it's our chance to get in from the other side," Papa said. "I can't thank y'all enough. I know you want to get on home the same as we do." He slapped Buddy on the back. "It's time we let you go."

"Hold on," Nikki said. "We've been talking," nodding to Buddy, "and the rest of us aren't going back home so quick. We already know they'll be waiting on us. I'm not willing to take that chance for a boyfriend and my mother in a nursing home, God bless her. Sarah's divorced with no kids and Richard's single, so there's no immediate family waiting for them."

"Makes sense, but I can't expect you to wait for me."

"We're willing to take a chance on you," Nikki said. "We owe you that much."

"I'm going in to find Rose," Buddy said. "Then I'm coming back and we're going into the Wild."

"I'll go back in a few months … maybe … to check on family," Nikki said. "But not now."

"Where will we go?" Papa said.

"Where were you going to go with your family?" Richard said.

Papa hung his head. "I always told my daughters I'd take them camping in the mountains. So, I'd go up toward Colorado until I found a place to camp at the base of a mountain, next to a river, where I could fish and hunt."

"Sounds like as good a plan as any," Sarah said.

Papa and Buddy set out mid-morning. They found a section of wall on the Prefecture's north side which had collapsed from the

418

earthquake. Two rows of barbed wire had been strung across the hole, leaving gaps and no guards.

They climbed into the backyard of a single-story ranch-style house, and unlocked a side gate to a deserted neighborhood street. They walked for miles before making it to our block. When he saw the damage, Papa rushed into our house about the same time Irene was slicing off Greggy's arm with wicked samurai precision.

Mrs. Caprock—Rose—was home, though, sipping coffee as though she'd been expecting Buddy. Her coffee cup, made with her last drop of water, was still steaming on her kitchen table when he came in and shouted her name. She just about had a heart attack, breaking her mug. Still in her nightgown, she ran to him in the foyer and hugged him. He helped her pack a bag and they said their goodbyes to the only home they could remember.

Papa left a note for us face up on the kitchen table, telling us he was alive and coming back for us. He signed his name, writing, "I will see you again in mountains." When he went to check on Buddy and Rose across the street, they were ready to go. About that time, the water came back on. Papa filled four plastic jugs and returned them to the personnel carrier. It was growing late, so Papa waited out the night outside the Prefecture without sleeping.

When he came back, we'd gone to school. La-La was home, beside herself with joy to see him. "School, school, school!" she'd told him.

With the *katana* blade and a change of clothes, he took off on foot for the school, nearly three miles away. As he neared the front entrance, he watched with surprise as the UFO moved away, disappearing to the north. He craned his head sideways, as if fighting back an ice cream headache.

Cupping the end of the *katana* into his armpit, he marched down a long two-lane driveway toward the school. Halfway there, ten armored personnel carriers sped past him and parked in a circle at the entrance. Soldiers poured out of the carriers and into the school. As he neared, they came back out carrying Irene and me, our arms and legs cuffed and black hoods over our heads.

At that moment he heard my voice scream in his head, "Help me Papa!" When he'd seen us like that, his own kids, helpless, being manhandled by soldiers, and with me calling out to him, he'd had enough. As they threw us in separate carriers, Papa attacked the soldiers.

Looking back, seeing him then, no matter how many times I conjure it, it brings tears to my eyes. Desperate rage—it's about the only way to describe it. I've heard of parents doing crazy things to protect their kids. A father who jumped into a river after his four-year-old daughter went over a waterfall when there was no way he'd save her; he just couldn't live with the idea of watching her fall to her death alone. That's what Papa must have been feeling. That's what he did for us at that moment. And, I suppose, that's what wrenched my heart. He'd been willing to risk it all but all that time we'd done nothing for him, as far as I knew. We'd never let that happen again.

His sword flashed, and sparks flew from the arms, head, and sides of the soldiers, who struggled to subdue the Tasmanian devil who'd unleashed his wrath on them. During the melee, Papa managed to yell our names. I didn't know until later, when I discovered I could know things, that I'd actually heard him from inside the carrier. I'd thought it was imagined. And it makes me cry every time I look back on it.

Papa's onslaught was quelled. One of the soldiers stunned

him with a baton. After he was sedated, Buddy and the others were caught, and returned to Freedom Colony for rehabilitation. Since Papa was considered permanently disabled, he was slated for termination.

Chapter 64

JEREMY STOOD AT THE PEAK OF MAMMOTH MOUNTAIN WATCHING the orange sun rise. Even in June, the peak was covered with snow.

The lens of the Sundog stopped over the center of the Long Valley Caldera. At twenty miles long and eleven miles wide, the basin of the super volcano was filled with pine trees. White-tailed deer grazed through the scrub brush of rolling desert hills. Creeks, fed by mineral hot springs, snaked along scattered meadows, hugging the bases of mountains and pouring into rippling lakes.

Dark clouds rolled through the sky over the mountain, and under the Sundog, from the northwest. They boiled and thickened. Jeremy smiled as they arrived. They weren't clouds but masses of flying people. With the grace of a falling black sheet, they parted and settled across the edges and peaks of the mountain rangers encircling the caldera.

Jeremy had followed the Sundog from the San Francisco Bay Area. On the way, he kept searching the System for talk about the UFOs, or "Sundogs," as many were calling them. After Irene and I had been abducted to 29 Palms, there was a lot more virtual chatter about Sundogs leading down to a Marine base to the south. That's when he learned about us. He listened to what some were saying: we were dangerous, we might have special powers, and so on. But he still couldn't put his mind into 29 Palms. He also found out about Papa and how important he was to us.

"I'll have to meet this *Papa*," Jeremy said as a plume of gasses shot out of the ground at the center of the caldera under the lens of the Sundog.

Without any further warning, a pillar of magma blasted out of the ground at the Sundog. From Jeremy's perspective, the spreading lava overhead followed the undersurface of the Sundog, turning the sky into a sea of fire. Upon reaching the edges, beyond the peaks of the surrounding mountains, the fiery flow curled around the Sundog's rim, drawing over the top and collecting into cylinder into the sky toward the sun.

Chapter 65

As I've said, a polygraph isn't really a test per se. It's more like a mental procedure, a false situation created by those administering it to squeeze information out of you with time and pressure. You must believe that the polygraph machine can tell whether you are lying. And if you do, the questions, and the ratcheted accusation against you, coupled with your desperate desire to just get it over with, squeeze the confessions out of you. Most people just tell the truth. In the end, when scolded for breaking their promise and not cooperating, they throw up their arms and confess about stealing something from a sibling, cheating on a third grade spelling test, or fudging an expense or two on their taxes. And so the polygrapher and his masters learn that subject has nothing to hide. Every so often though, someone confesses something significant. A false resume, second wife, drug use, burglaries, all sorts of things. But as far as I know, I'm the only person who admitted having super powers.

I shifted in the recliner, my butt really hurting. Martin was getting to the end of his questions.

"The water was back on when we returned home," I said. "We threw our coats and things on the kitchen table and went to bed. The next morning, the soldiers came. How did you know it was following Irene?"

Directional lasers.

"So Irene's movements were matched with the path of Irene's CB?" I said.

Yes.

Martin frowned at me.

"The water was kept off on purpose, wasn't it?"

Yes.

"So people would come to the Market and other places to reconnect their CBs, making it easier to track who the Sundog was following?" I said.

Yes.

Martin flipped a hand in the air like he was conducting an invisible symphony.

He sighed. "Edith, I think we're just about done. I only have a few more questions and you can go. Sit back and relax."

He asked the questions about my identity and musical tastes, whether I'd ever lied to him, and whether I believed this machine showed him whether I was lying or not.

"Who told you your father went to a place called 'Freedom Colony'?" he said.

"No one."

"Have you seen your father since the Sundogs came?"

"No."

"Has he been back home?"

Yes.

My heart skipped. "No."

"Has he been in communication with you since the Sundogs came?"

Yes.

Again, the voice. I didn't know where the answers were coming from. I didn't know whether Martin was just playing games with me, somehow implanting answers into my head to see if I told him 'the truth.' So, that time, I just told him what I was hearing from the inner voice. "Yes, I think so," I said.

"How?"

"He sent us his sword."

"Any message?"

"Yes. On the sword, he wrote, 'I will see you again in mountains.'"

"What does it mean to you?"

"Maybe Half Dome at Yosemite."

"Have you ever been there with him?"

"No."

"Did he want you to meet him there?"

"No."

"Does the note mean anything else?"

"Just means he's alive."

"Where's the sword now."

"Irene has it. Maybe you have it now."

"Do you think your Dad's still alive?"

A tear welled at my left eye. "Yes ... maybe ... I don't know."

"Who first mentioned the phrase, 'Freedom Colony' to you?"

"I don't know."

"Why did the Sundogs come?" Martin sounded impatient.

"I don't know."

"What are the Sundogs?"

"I don't know."

"Are you in communication with the Sundogs?"

"No."

"Is Irene in communication with the Sundogs?"

"I have no reason to think so."

"Are the Sundogs real?"

"I don't know."

"Are sentient beings inside the Sundogs?"

"I don't know."

"What do I have in the left front pocket of my shirt?"

A gold locket with a photograph of your four-year-old daughter Brandy. I felt it was dangerous to tell him I knew the answer. I said, "I don't know."

"Who is the current President of the United States?"

"Sophia Martinez," I said.

"Where is President Sophia Martinez now?"

USNORTHCOM under Peterson Air Force Base in Colorado Springs, Colorado.

I shrugged. "She lives at Peterson Air Force base in Colorado Springs, I guess. Go figure."

Martin's focus on the space before him intensified as he twisted the air.

Except for the last question, we went through the questions three more times. Martin sat there for at least ten minutes, his fingers massaging invisible dough. As I watched him out of the corner of my eye, I asked myself, *Is he really looking at the System?*

No.

What is he doing?

He's listening to the Secretary of Defense Freight and Tabitha.

Tabitha -- the video girl?

Yes.

What's she got to do with the Secretary of Defense?

Nothing.

What's the Secretary of Defense telling him?

It was a lot of information and I didn't like what I heard. Losing my temper, I leaned forward in my chair and said, "You're not going to let me go!"

Surprised for the first time, he said, "We had a deal, remember? You're not being truthful with me."

"What have I lied about?"

"The Sundogs! You know what they are! You know why they are here!"

"I told you, I don't know!" I said, pointing a finger at him.

"You're lying!" he said. "I know you're lying!"

"You don't know anything!" I said. "What I do know is this lie detector doesn't do anything!" I yanked off the wires from my head and shook them at him. "These wires don't tell you anything. You don't have the slightest idea of whether I'm telling you the truth or not! I'll tell you what I do know, *Martin* .... I know you're carrying a locket in your right front pocket, and in the locket is a photograph of your four-year-old daughter, *Brandy*! She was run over right in front of you when she ran out in the street. You blame yourself! She never would have died if you'd been holding her hand!

You were attending her funeral on the day the Sundogs first came, weren't you!" I had no rational way of knowing those things. But *I knew* because I'd asked.

Martin shot up out of his chair, his right hand in his shirt pocket. His eyes flickered to the vault door like a mouse considering whether he could safely make it to his hole before a cat pounces.

I leapt from my chair, my fingers, arms, and chest still attached to the wires. "You're sweating, Martin," I said. "Are you *lying* to me?" As I took a small step forward, a surge of electricity coursed through my body. My spine bowed backward. My arms curled to my chest, my clenched fists pressing into my neck under a rigid jaw, grinding my teeth. I fell to my knees, my heels curling to my back. *Stop*, I thought. Just as my hamstrings and lower back were about to snap, the electricity subsided. I forced open my eyes, everything colored a light green. Still in pain, I tore the wires from my chest and fingers, and unwrapped the blood pressure gauge from my arm. I rolled away from the chair and lay on my back, my head to the vault door as it chimed, "Secure," with knocks and clicks from its internal workings. Martin had left.

Chapter 66

WALKING WITH JUDITH, MARTIN FOLLOWED A TUNNEL TO A LIGHT rail train. Two heavily armed security guards waited at a security desk. One of the guards stood and faced them, her eyes dodging back and forth.

"Nothing," the guard said. "The System sees your face but it doesn't recognize you."

"The System?" Judith said.

"It's up and running," Martin said. "But most of the functions are still reloading. It should be operational soon."

The soldier checked their badges and nodded. "You two are good to go," she said. She held and open hand out to the light rail train behind them.

The doors hissed closed. Once seated, the small train hummed into a tunnel, moving upward into darkness.

"Why did you turn it back on?" Judith said.

"What do you mean?" Martin said.

Judith wiggled her fingers in front of her face. "Isn't

the System coming back up? There's something there but it's all blank."

"The general structure is coming back. But Animal Farm isn't coming back anytime soon, right Tabitha?"

A ghostly image of Tabitha emerged with a smile in the seat next to Judith.

"Good work, Tabitha," Martin said.

"It's nothing," Tabitha said.

"Why bring the Teardrop back on line at all?" Judith said exasperated. "Why not just leave the whole System down?"

"I never said the Teardrop was running," Martin said.

"Now the System stream stays digital after it passes over the Teardrop," Martin said.

"So what?" Judith said.

"So the System will never gain the depth analogue, remaining incapable of interacting with the subjective mind. Once the System is running again, it still won't be able to control as it did before," Martin said. He nodded at Tabitha. "Any sign of the President?"

"No sign yet. But maybe we'll have more information as the System finishes booting up."

"Keep looking," Martin said.

Chapter 67

A FEW HOURS AFTER THE UFO BLEW UP THE SOLDIERS IN OUR front yard, close to sunset, Irene and I knocked on Mrs. Caprock's door. No answer. She knocked harder. "Mrs. Caprock? Hello? Are you in there? It's Irene and Edith."

Heavy footsteps, then the door swung open. A heavy bald man stood there wearing a white pressed oxford shirt and grey vest with black wool pants. "Irene," he said with a grand smile. He beamed at me. "And this must be Edith." He talked to us like a long lost uncle who thought we'd just won the lottery.

We gawked at him like a couple of dorks.

"You're probably wondering who I am," he said. "I'm Mr. Gaddis, your new homeroom teacher."

Nothing registered on our faces. He glanced at the Sundog with a hint of fear.

"Where's Mrs. Caprock?" Irene said. Her tone was pointed and unfriendly.

I cocked my head. I could see past him into the living room

and kitchen beyond. All of Mrs. Caprock's things were still there, even two coffee cups on the kitchen table.

"She moved out," Mr. Gaddis said.

"In the middle of the night?" Irene said. "She was here just yesterday."

"I'm afraid so," Mr. Gaddis said with a smile. He glared at Irene.

"Where did you take her?" I said.

He leaned against the door with his right arm, his casual attitude unnerving. "I didn't do anything with her," he said. "I just moved in."

"Baloney," Irene said.

"I presume I'll see you two in school."

"School?" Irene said. "I doubt the school will be open, after the earthquake, and everything that's happened."

His grin was starting to make me angry. "Oh, it'll be open. And I expect you to be there bright and early."

"What, next week?" Irene said.

"Tomorrow, of course," Mr. Gaddis said.

Irene and I caught each other's eyes. We nodded at the Sundog directly overhead and dropped our eyes on Mr. Gaddis, followed by our chins. We said, *"Don't ... think ... so."*

Mr. Gaddis dropped the smile. "Irene," he said.

"Mr. Gaddis," she said.

"How's your grandmother—*Loo-Loo* or whatever you call her—doing?"

As our smiles melted, he looked over our shoulders. I couldn't help turning my head.

"I heard a nasty rumor that her visa was forged."

"That's not true!" Irene said.

Mr. Gaddis raised his chin to the Sundog. "No reaction there." He crossed his arms. "As for your friend Mrs. Caprock, I heard she was evicted for defaulting on her mortgage or something."

"Bring her back!" Irene said.

Mr. Gaddis held out his arms as though feeling for raindrops. "I'm still here," he said. The sarcasm in his voice made me want to kick him where it counts. His hands dropped and stepped closer. "Edith, I've heard you've been illegally downloading music and videos. Piracy's a five-year sentence and a one-million-dollar fine."

His point was clear. As far as we knew, the Sundog would protect Irene, *not necessarily her family and friends.*

In a chilling monotone, Irene said, "See you in class, Mr. Gaddis. We look forward to it."

As it turned out, the only thing Irene had to look forward to was a punch in the face.

Chapter 68

I CURLED INTO A BALL AND ROLLED TO MY FEET, STRETCHING MY arms toward the ceiling. The room was too quiet after what had just happened. The shouting. Nearly getting shocked to death. I shrugged at the false window and took a seat in Martin's chair, peering into his briefcase. Except for the half-eaten sushi, it was empty. The small box still sat on the tabletop. I snatched it, turned it over, and tossed it across the table.

Did that machine actually tell him whether I was lying? I thought.

No.

I threw the briefcase into the false window. One of the shutters fell off its hinges. The holograph buzzed to life, revealing a pristine view of a clear still pond surrounded by autumn trees, red and orange, with a full winter moon hanging overhead, reflecting off the water. With my thumb and index finger, I pinched out my contact lenses to mute the System view. But the autumn-pool-winter-moon remained. Without my prescription contacts, I shouldn't be able to see any System views, or so I thought. The view switched, revealing a close-up of Martin wiping his forehead with the back of his forearm. I must have really rattled him.

"Edith, I'm disappointed you chose not to cooperate. You still have a lot of explaining to do. You're clearly not telling me everything." His eyes were moving back and forth, reading from a script I couldn't see. And I realized, *he didn't know I could see him.*

Why can I see him without the contacts?

No answer.

"I'm going to return tomorrow, Edith," Martin said. "I expect complete cooperation from you. If you resist or throw another tantrum, your interview will be terminated. And I don't mean you'll be going home."

I thought about the small metal ladybugs lining the inner walls of my round cell. *I'll bet they shoot bullets and gas*, I thought. *Anything else?*

Flames.

"In the meantime," Martin said, "I suggest you lie down and rest."

The sound broke off but I could still see him on the screen. He wiped his forehead as he talked to someone off camera. His demeanor went from the calm, cool, and collected, to haggard exhaustion. He looked into the camera and saw my wicked smile. Before he could say anything, the video switched back to the autumn-pool-winter-moon.

Feeling tired, my shoulders slumped. I went to the futon and plopped onto the pillow, curling my knees to my stomach. Tears rolled across my checks and dripped from my right temple.

Can they see I'm crying now?

Yes.

I pulled a pillow over my face.

Can they see my face now?

No.

I mouthed the word, "Papa," under the pillow, thinking, *Papa, I miss you! I need you, Papa! Where are you?*

Freedom Colony.

What the hell is this? I thought. *What the hell is this voice in my head? Why do these answers keep coming to me? Who is talking to me?*

No answers.

Losing patience, I asked, *What the hell is Freedom Colony?*

A debtor labor camp.

What's that?

Where debtors pay off debts.

Papa was sent there to pay off debts?

Yes.

Did he have a choice?

No.

What if he'd refused to go?

Non-compliant debtors are sent to penal work camps.

That didn't sound good. *Why didn't he tell us where he was going?*

Drafted debtors are bound by confidentiality.

What if he had told us?

Debtors who breach confidentiality are sent to a penal work camp.

What is the nearest penal camp?

The Justice Colony.

Where is it?

McAlester, Oklahoma.

Well, I guess that explains what happened to Simon and Benjamin.

So Papa's still alive?

Yes.

I bawled harder. "Papa, Papa, Papa!" I screamed into the pillow. I didn't care if *they* could tell I was crying. I missed him more than ever. Fear and anger welled in me.

Did they ever plan to return us home?

No.

I wanted to claw Martin's eyes out. *Then how do I get out of here?*

The vault door is the exit.

It's locked, I thought.

How do I unlock the vault door?

Type in the passkey, insert the key and turn it.

I don't have the key. I cried some more. In frustration, I asked, Where's the key?

On the kitchen table.

I opened my eyes. With the pillow over the back of my head, I rolled over to my stomach. From under the pillow, I could see something on the table I'd not noticed before. It had the crude handle of a screwdriver, except the head was shaped like a key.

Is that the key to the vault door?

Yes.

What's the passkey?

Type: [ctrl] [alt] [delete] at the same time. When "ID:" appears on the screen, type: "Martin I. Lorien", and when "Pass:"

appears, type:

xqtOOwLuZCXefVY5H75cEzrkB2s6NjXJy3fJL5NZKzg=

The length of the passkey surprised me. I couldn't even remember the numbers for my own combination lock at school.

How do I know the passkey?

No answer.

Who is this? I thought, referring to the still small voice in my head.

No answer.

I asked for the passkey to the vault again. The answer seemed to be the same as before. It was so long I couldn't be sure.

Can I know anything I ask?

No answer.

Answer or no, it dawned on me that the answer was 'yes.' So I asked the most important questions first.

Who had a crush on me in high school?

Neil Davis and Rick Van Meter.

Great. Neil was the class goof. Nice guy, but just … just no way! I should have paid more attention to Rick, though. I wish I'd known then! But that wouldn't have changed anything, I guess. He was on the football team, out of my circle of New Wave geeks. We hardly ever even spoke.

Who stole my favorite white head phones at school?

Aariti Sharma.

Ungrateful witch!

Will I get married before I'm thirty?

No answer.

Am I … and Irene … adopted?

No.

Am I going crazy?

No answer. Well, if I was, I probably wouldn't say so, assuming I'm talking to myself.

After entertaining myself with my burning questions, I moved onto some of the bigger mysteries.

Who killed John F. Kennedy? Who built the Pyramids? Did Big Foot or the Lock Ness Monster exist? Why isn't there a current President of the United States? Who's running things? How was the universe created? When was it created? Was the universe created?

The answers to many of these questions unsettled my sense of reality and some of the answers I didn't even understand. Many of those questions had no answers, also including, *Has earth ever been visited by aliens from another planet? What are the Sundogs and where did they come from? Who created the universe? Who am I?*

Chapter 69

Blackness brightened into blinding white light.

Papa struggled against the straps. His CB glowed red.

He lay at an angle, strapped to a bench and completely nude. To his left Nikki and Richard, to his right, Sarah and Buddy struggled.

"I'm sorry … so sorry … it's come to this," a voice said from behind them. Coralee walked between Papa and Nikki. She leaned over Papa, shaking the sword in his face. "You can't say I didn't try with you," she said. "I really did, you know. I gave you every opportunity, overlooked a lot of things, just to give you a chance to make it."

Papa spit in her face. She straightened, letting the spittle drip from her nose to her lapel.

To Sarah, she said, "At least we had some good times, eh?"

"Where are we?!" Nikki said.

"Termination," Coralee said. "Don't worry, it's fast. After

a short exit Interview, you'll be *free*. We don't call this 'Freedom Colony' for nothing!"

"You mean we can just walk out of here then?" Buddy said.

Someone stifled a laugh behind them. Coralee gave a wicked smile.

"Let the others go," Papa said. "They were just following me."

"The others are already back to work," Coralee said, glancing at Buddy. "But your little crew *here* caused most of the trouble. We've already tried rehabilitation with you—*Papa*. But it's no use. You're all Permanently Disabled."

Coralee leaned over Papa and said, "Before we let you go, though, there's one more question I have: where's the other sword?"

A burst of air rushed out of her mouth as though she'd just been punched in the stomach. The lights dimmed as she balanced herself on Papa's shoulder. She pointed her nose to the ceiling with a deep breath like she'd risen from a deep ocean, and let out the air into Papa's face, her eyes peeling open solid black.

"Irene has it, you dimwit!" Coralee said, answering her own question. She blinked, regaining her focus. "Well, if it isn't *Mr. Papa*!" Coralee said. "Pleased to meet you." She eyed Papa from head to toe and laughed. "My, what a predicament you've gotten yourself into here. I can help you, though. And once we get to know each other better, I'd like to meet Irene and Edith, too! We've got so much to talk about!" Jeremy was the one asking for introductions, speaking through Coralee.

Chapter 70

I ASKED QUESTIONS. *WHERE AM I? HOW DOES THE VAULT OPEN? What is on the other side of it? What is the floor plan of this place? Where are the exits? Who is on patrol and what is their schedule?* The answers came as fast as I could think. Each answer led to another question.

After a while I got up and went to the restroom. When I was done, I passed the kitchen table and pocketed the key. I asked if anyone had seen me pick it up. *No.* I yawned and lay back on the bed facing the wall.

The lights in my room went off after a while because of the lack of motion. I closed my eyes, wide awake, and kept asking questions.

When the room was dark and still, I rolled to the side of the futon closest the wall and followed the edge of the room around to the vault. Pressing the keypad once, its buttons back-lit in red, then I typed in the characters as they came to mind:

xqtOOwLuZCXefVY5H75cEzrkB2s6NjXJy3fJL5NZKzg=

A female voice said, "Martin Lorien. Please verify secondary key."

Unexpected. *What is the secondary passkey?* I asked and typed the answer:

BzEXiUqCWzWIQC4VNE5yl

F6vuQXAhqurqUcIsHaBRA4=

"Insert key," the door said.

I pulled out the key, slid it into the long socket, and turned.

"Thank you," the vault door said.

"You're *welcome*," I said.

A hissing sound from the edge of the vault door ruffled my hair as the door eased open to a small anterior room with soft light. There was another vault door ten feet away. The keypad came to life as I touched it.

"Passkey," the vault said.

I asked and typed the answer:

jE9qTig81tq2WDTp4COYRf62beoYjrnTiYYj51BoV68=

A small holographic screen rose over the keyboard.

"Verify," the door said.

When Martin Lorien went through this passageway earlier, he'd placed his hand into the screen. Just as I was beginning to panic, I felt a rustle in my pocket. Instead of the key, I pulled out a screw driver with a prosthetic hand on the end. *This is crazy,* I thought. I shrugged and held it into the screen.

"Thank you, Martin Lorien," the door said. I dropped the hand back into my pocket, wondering what I might find the next time I reached down there.

The door hissed open. A long corridor filled with dim blue lights curved to the left. I ran until I met another vault door. Asking questions, I typed:

Master Administrator – 29 Palms.

The screen appeared: "Passkey."

I typed the answer:

1kHHIeb7rOsBTelqV4JtAXQEshFaDP4q4K5MIbjUpjY=.

Then the screen: "Confirm Passkey:"

I typed: *qe6nYBUeYVKwiO+9CrcpQ1LyKHJHo4qna8cLH B2/Ygk=*

The screen asked, "Site?"

I typed: *Talos.*

Then: "Level:"

I typed: *L6.*

"Door:"

I typed: *PodDoor5c.*

"Function:"

I typed: *Deactivate.*

The screen defaulted back to, "Door." Asking a few more questions, I repeated the same process several more times.

I asked whether anyone was in the corridor on the other side.

No one.

Were two guards still stationed at the security desk in the larger corridor ahead?

Yes.

I kept asking the same question until the answer was, *No.*

I pulled on the door. It opened to a large black tunnel, which curved to the right and left. Blue light filled the rough glassy surface of the tube.

A low hum echoed down the tube to my left. I sprinted

barefoot over a metal floor in the opposite direction, passing four other vault doors.

When I reached the end of the corridor, the black walls telescoped in thick metal segments inward to a reinforced polished metal door. I touched a clear glass square which illuminated red, revealing the numbers of a ten-key pad.

A female computer voice said, "Identify." Though the voice was silky, it sounded like a gong in the relatively crypt-like silence of the tunnel.

A voice echoed behind me said, "Hello?"

A blank holographic screen appeared in mid-air to the right of the key pad, wanting me to place my hand or face there.

Instead, I typed:

943058108393809274095556010123605304789034791638507893401010 1011

The key pad screen turned into a small alphanumeric screen. I could hear boots tapping behind me. I typed:

Talos – L6 – Door 6

Then:

Talos – L6 – Door 7

And:

tovwQct/zMPctEbbdZPYIl51faZqBL4trWOAJVuYDdM=

The door clicked, knocked, and hummed open, as green light spilled in from a larger tube corridor about twenty feet high.

A voice to my left said, "Well, that was quick, Phil."

Another thick metal door swung open from the opposite side of the corridor.

"Hello? ... Phil?" the other security guard, Lukas, said.

The two doors swung open until their edges nearly touched,

mere inches apart, in the middle of the large corridor. I sprinted to my right, away from Lukas. He could have seen me if he'd gotten on his knees to peek under doors, but he didn't.

Lukas activated his CB. "Phil? Come in," Lukas said.

I kept sprinting, following the curved tunnel, racing past rows of crates for over a hundred yards. When I reached the end of crates, a helmeted metal-clad soldier reached for me.

I fell to my knees and slid across the floor, cupping my arms over my head. I peeked up at the frozen army of exoskeletons. Nothing happened. I hopped to my feet, and waved over the visor of one of the soldiers. No reaction. I tapped on the helmet. The soldier twisted slightly at my touch, hanging by metal wires attached to a heavy metal rack on wheels. I lifted its visor. No one was home.

I slid my hands over the chest and arms. The body felt like metal snakeskin. When I squeezed it, the surface responded defensively like a python, cold but alive. I asked a few questions. The rest of the suit wasn't hollow – just the upper torso and head. *So who's supposed to wear this?* I got an answer I didn't understand at the time, and later, I hated it. A grey-on-black patch on the left chest read, "Talos." Some of the other suits were marked with "Talon" in white on the right arm. Consisting of a full-bodied exoskeleton made from the same snake-ish material of Talos, there was room for a complete humanoid. Talos was only designed for dismembered torsos.

Remembering the time, I ran faster. Up ahead, a large round vault door, nearly as wide and tall as the twenty-foot corridor behind, was swinging shut as per my instruction, just a little sooner than I'd figured. If it closed, there would be no way out for me unless I went back and reprogramed it again. The door mercilessly inched toward closure as I ran faster.

On the other side, a light rail train waited with its doors open, just as I had arranged. Two security guards manned the desk. Holding my breath, I made it for a train car. The doors closed behind me as I slid inside the train compartment and collapsed on the floor, gasping for breath.

Breathing easier, I peered over the round nose of the train. The tracks led downward and ahead for three miles to Level 7, where there were more cells, laboratories, weapons, and vaults. But I got no answer when I asked, *Who (or what) is down there?* As I stared, asking more questions, two people boarded two cars ahead of me. I lay on the floor and rolled to the feet of the seats. The train jerked backwards and pulled out of Level 6, heading up a long incline toward Talos 5, a half-mile away.

When the train arrived at Level 5 it followed a curved tunnel around to a security desk. The doors slid open.

I could hear talking.

"Hey, Mira ... Tony," a guard said. She sounded husky.

Tony and Mira mumbled something.

"See you later then," the guard said. Aside from her manliness, she sounded chipper, eager to talk.

A moment passed.

"Hey, Carey," the guard said.

"Yeah, hey, Wanda," Carey said. He cut her off before she could respond. "Got to do some more neural testing on the new specimens before Monday."

Carey stepped into my car. I almost peed my pants.

Wanda called after him. "Working tomorrow, then?"

Carey stopped. I could see his profile in the window of the train. With pale fingers, he combed his hair over a bald patch and straightened his gold-rimmed glasses. "Maybe. Not sure. Why?"

"Maybe we could play some chess," Wanda said. "You and me."

Carey hesitated, looking into my train car. For a moment, I thought he saw me. "Umm," he said.

God! I thought. *Guys!* Maybe it was the combination of stress and lack of sleep, but I nearly jumped up and yelled, *Just make up your mind, dude!*

"Uh, sure," Carey said. He stepped back from the train and the doors closed. I could hear him chatting with Wanda. After a few more moments, the doors opened again. This time he entered a car immediately opposite from Wanda's desk. The train began to inch forward and I could see Wanda's reflection. She'd been beautiful once, probably elegant, but her jaw and check bones had turned thick. She wore a Talon suit, the black visor lifted up. I cringed as I took in the reflection of her form, a body covered with the snake-like metallic skin. Whatever it was, it wasn't womanly. Unlike the stripped down Talon suits I'd seen, Wanda was fully armed with wicked handguns holstered over each breast. A large rifle was slung over her back. As the train pulled away, I could see the satisfied smile on her face. *Go get 'em, Wanda*, I thought.

The train picked up speed as it climbed toward Level 4, where it entered another glassy tube, circled around, and stopped in front of a security station. As all the doors opened, I peeked out and saw three people in lab coats entering two cars ahead of me. A Talon guard faced the train and another had his back to me, both making

451

small talk. The coats were going down to Talos 6. This was not my plan. I wanted to go up, not down.

So I crawled out of the train and rolled underneath. Ducking below the windows, I squeezed between the rounded train exterior and the wall. Halfway down the length of the train, across from the security station, the glass cut open the back of my jumpsuit, slicing into my shoulder blade. I nearly screamed.

Moving forward, I reached an intersecting tunnel just as the train started backward. If I didn't do something, in a few seconds I'd be exposed to the Talon guards. Feeling a whiff of air, I ran into the tunnel, which glowed purple from within. I pressed buttons at the first vault door I reached, and stepped inside a room lit in red.

"Who's there?" a voice said.

I crouched to the ground and held my breath.

"Is someone there?" The voice sounded weak.

I edged toward a Plexiglas coffin laying on a gurney and found a holographic screen on its side. "Robert 8," it said. Vital signs blipped on readouts below the name. I cupped my hands over the side and saw a human torso with a metal cap over his head. The space between his ears and the crown of his head was shorter than normal. Metallic sleeves cuffed the short stubs where his thighs and upper arms had been.

When Robert 8 twitched, I nearly jumped out of my skin and bumped into an IV on wheels.

"Who's there?" the voice said again. "I can hear you."

I peered over a row of the Plexiglas boxes.

"If anyone can hear me," the voice said, weeping, "Please help me."

I crawled down to the third box. The screen read, "Ken 6."

Inside, his head rocked back and forth. He still had his arms and legs but red plastic bands cinched his thighs and biceps, cutting off circulation. He wouldn't have his limbs for much longer.

"Somebody help me! I can't feel my hands and feet!"

Something rustled in my pocket. This time I pulled out a pair of wire cutters. I just stared at them, paralyzed by astonishment. *What the hell is going on here?* My neck shivered and I shrugged.

Cutting off the bands with a hushed voice, I said, "What's your name?"

He held still, his breath deep and heavy. "I'm Dillon. Who are you?"

After severing the last band I realized thick metal cuffs still held his wrists and ankles in place. I shook the cutters like maybe they'd turn into a hacksaw or whatever was needed. Nothing happened. I shot looks around the room, thinking I might find someone or something in one of the corners watching, amused with my quandary. Nothing. No one was there.

In a low voice, I spit out the first thing that came to my mind, like trying to kick start my stalled brain. "I'm Superunknown, Dillon."

He gasped. "Irene, is that you? *Irene!*"

My heart nearly stopped. Trying to recover *again*, I asked questions about this Dillon. *Does he know my sister, Irene? Where is she? Who is* he?

No answers. And the more I asked in vain the more I felt like falling down a rabbit hole. "Be careful you don't get lost, girl," I whispered to myself.

I just focus on talking again. "Remember, Dillon," I whispered through clenched teeth. 'Superunknown!' Say it!" I didn't even know what I meant. I just wanted to hear my own voice so I didn't go nuts.

"Superunknown," Dillon sobbed.

"Don't forget, Dillon."

"I won't ... *Superunknown.*" He struggled against the cuffs. "Don't leave me!"

I shoved the cutters in my pocket and patted my jumpsuit over them like trying to spring a jack-in-the-box. I pulled the cutters out again and hissed, feeling foolish for expecting to find anything other than the same cutters.

"I won't forget you, Dillon. I'll come back for you."

"Don't leave me!"

The longer I stalled the more likely I'd get caught. I sensed I had to keep going *alone.* "I can't take you with me now. But I promise ... I *swear* ... if I get out of here ... I'll come back for you, Dillon."

"Promise?"

"*Yes.* Just remember ... Superunknown."

I could still hear him repeating the word as I pressed the passkey. Exiting to the purple tunnel, he cried, "*Irene, where are you?*"

Chapter 71

MARTIN TOOK A BITE FROM THE MINI-BURGER. KETCHUP AND thin watery pickles pushed out the sides. He wiped a dab of yellow mustard from his chin. The white bun was soft, evenly toasted. The patty, five percent mystery meat, the rest was corn, false grill marks painted on with food coloring. Two more burgers waited on a metal cafeteria tray as he pushed the second half into his mouth, washing it down with a corn-syrup soda.

"Hungry?" Judith said.

Martin nodded. "These burgers just make me hungrier."

"Tell me about it," Judith said, patting her thighs. Running a short fingernail under her stubby index finger, she said, "You never told me what you and Bluewater talked about."

Martin took another bite, gazing over the top of the bun. Rachel Bluewater?"

Judith nodded.

"I never said I talked to her?"

"She was on the call before I passed it to you."

"If you say so." He took another bite.

"Then who were you talking to?"

He held up a finger, then gulped. "I never got a name."

"Well, what did she tell you?"

"She?"

"Oh, stop."

He took another bite, chewing as he said, "You know … there are still a lot of things I don't remember. How about you?" His eyes twinkled at her through his glasses.

Judith shrugged at the empty cafeteria hall. Rows of foldout metal tables on locked wheels lined the room. Off-white walls surrounded them. Black globes, housing video cameras, lined the ceiling. "I don't know. Once you've forgotten something, I guess you can't remember what you've forgotten."

"Exactly," Martin said. "So when you think you remember something how do you know it's not just another lie?"

The ghostly image of Secretary Freight appeared in the chair across the table from Martin, shoulder-to-shoulder with Judith.

"*Martin*," Freight said, drawing out his name. His voice was garbled with an echo.

"Secretary Freight," Martin said. "Long time no see."

Judith rolled her eyes. She couldn't see the secretary from her view. Secretary Freight was way above her security clearance.

"I guess I should congratulate you," Freight said.

Martin took another bite.

"You fixed the System," Freight said.

"You're welcome," Martin said, chewing with his mouth open.

Judith mouthed, "Gross."

"But it is not *actually* fixed, is it?" Freight said, rocking.

"Once the System completely reboots, and all the CBs are reconnected and reformatted, everything will be back to normal."

After a long silence, he licked his lips. "And yet the System still doesn't *feel* the same, does it?"

Martin took another bite, his cheeks bulging like a chipmunk.

"Anything you should tell me?" Freight said.

Martin glanced at the ceiling and gulped. "Nope," he said and took another bite.

"Remember the blackout virus in the early versions of Animal Farm?" Freight said.

"Nope."

Freight rocked faster, his image fading for a moment, then swelling back. "Maybe you've just forgotten." He smiled. "The first two versions of Animal Farm worked fine for a few months. After that, spots, sometimes beginning with a city block and spreading outward, rejected it. Some had nervous breakdowns, others went comatose, and a few committed mass killings. You repaired it many times, but the virus kept coming back, in a different place each time."

Martin frowned. "I get nothing. I don't know what to tell you." Small pieces of bread and meat fell out of his mouth.

"Let's hope it comes to you soon, Mr. Martin." The contemptuous tone in Freight's voice was palpable. "After you restarted the System, everything rebooted, as you said it would. But it looks like the virus—or something—is back. This time it's in the Bay Area Prefectures."

"California?"

AUSTIN REAMS

"Is there any other?"

"If there were a problem with my reboot it would have manifested here, at the source."

"Any problems there?"

"Not that I know of. Ask Charlie."

"I did. He doesn't know anything."

"What's new?" Martin said.

"I want you to recheck the System, right away," Freight said. "Double-check everything's working properly. But I don't think you're going to find anything wrong."

"Thanks."

"That wasn't a compliment. I think the source of the problem originates with the Sundogs. After all, the System crashed after they showed up. We need to find out what they are and what they want as soon as possible."

"What's the rush?"

"Shortly after you reactivated the System, all of the CBs in the Bay Area went dead, like an infection growing from one spot outward. The virus isn't limited to the coast. It's growing eastward."

"Towards us?"

"Remember Tabitha … the girl with the video who crashed the System?"

"Don't make me lose my lunch."

"Yeah, he'd better remember me," a soft voice said in Martin's ear said.

"Her video crashed the System," Freight said. "She had to have some connection with a Sundog."

"Why do you say that?"

458

"The Sundog tried to protect her when a group was sent for her."

"And what did she have to say?"

Freight rocked methodically, as if he were was grinding bones under his heels. "She escaped. Do you know anything about it?"

"It's reassuring to know you think so highly of me, Mr. Secretary. Are there any other intergalactic conspiracies I'm responsible for? Maybe you have some plumbing problems there at the Pentagon you'd like me to fix?"

"Don't tempt me. But before that, you can help us with some answers elsewhere."

"Pray tell."

"There is another girl in Oklahoma City whom a Sundog was protecting."

"More girl problems."

Judith shook her head. "Be careful," she mouthed.

"The Sundog moved off to the northwest toward Colorado. We have the girl and her twin sister in custody."

"Their names?"

"Irene and Edith Song. Their father quit his job just to find them."

"So ask the girl some questions."

"That's where you come in, Martin. You have some experience with polygraphs from your early days at the Company. The Sundog girl, Irene, isn't talking, but her twin, Edith, may know something. You're leaving for 29 Palms within the hour."

Chapter 72

I'LL REMEMBER YOU, TOO. DILLON.

The vault door closed behind me. The tunnel, bathed in dim purple light, curved into blackness to the right. To my left, it intersected with the train tracks.

Out of sight, near the tracks, a guard paced in front of elevator doors. Fiddling with his gun, the other guard hung back at the opposite end of the tunnel where it started down to Level 5.

I sprinted into the tunnel to my right, following the loop until it intersected with the train tracks again, closer to the tunnel entrance leading to Level 3.

As the guard turned his back, I ran into the ascending tunnel and followed the tracks. Since there was no lighting, I fell out of sight, though I could see him.

After I'd gone a hundred yards, a hint of ambient purple light lit my way, seeping across the glassy walls and ceilings from behind me. *I might as well be trapped in an Antarctic glacier.* I rubbed my arms. The air cooled with each step, the tunnel turning pitch black. I reached out for the wall to my right. My index finger caught a sharp edge. A bead of blood felt warm between my finger and thumb.

Well, this is great! I thought. *Now I can't even see anything and the next level is another eight hundred yards.*

I fast walked and nearly tripped on one of the train tracks. Stepping to the left of the tracks, I sensed the ground sloped to a narrow path a few feet lower. I jogged, following the slope with my right foot as a point of reference.

After I'd gone another hundred yards, it dawned on me that there was nowhere to hide if a train came. And I had another seven hundred yards to go—too far before the next train. Floodlights and cameras were attached to the fronts and backs of the trains. The image of a girl with suicide-fringe bangs in a neon-orange jump suit, running barefoot through the tunnel, would automatically trigger the alarms.

My mind raced with questions. There was a niche about a hundred yards ahead. I ran as fast as I could. Asking questions, I knew the train was stopping at Level 6. The only passenger, Carey, got out with a smile. *Yeah, Carey!* The doors closed and the train moved up. *Damn you, Carey!*

With another fifty yards to go, the train faintly hummed behind me. I sprinted faster, pushing myself as hard as I could. *Run! Run! Run!* The sound grew. *I'm not going back to the cell!* I could hear the electric hum. *Faster! Faster! Faster!* Lights flickered behind me. *Run faster!*

If someone had reviewed the train video with forensic precision, they could have seen a faint glimmer of reflective orange ahead of the train. But it wasn't enough to stop the train or trigger any alarms.

Catching my breath in the niche as the train passed, I climbed a few iron rungs, bumping my head against a metal hatch. It could only be opened by a laser-cut hexagonal key. I tried the mysterious key in my pocket. No luck.

I curled up for warmth at the bottom of the ladder and wondered what to do. I fingered the grate over a small drain on the ground, asking questions. Not counting Level 7, I was in the middle of the six levels of Talos. Even if the train stopped at Level 1, the highest, or Level 6, the lowest, it was impossible for me to run over five hundred fifty yards to the next tunnel before the train caught up with me, even assuming it stopped at each level. I might make it if the train shuttled several times between two upper or lower levels before it continued up. But I got no read on the future, no matter how many questions I asked. *Damn the unknown!*

As I sat there asking questions in the dark, I noticed in my mind's eye that I could see what the security cameras on the train were showing in real time.

I can see what any camera or CB is seeing! I pulled up a view of Irene. Wearing a soiled bra and panties, she hung by her wrists from heavy chains attached to the ceiling of a cell like mine, lined with those metal ladybugs, minus the floor, kitchen, living room, or other creature comforts. Her ankles were cuffed to short chains on the rounded floor. The room was full of water up to her knees, draining out through a small hole in the floor. She appeared to be unconscious.

She raised her head weakly at the sound of a bullhorn, then dropped it again, her hair dripping wet. They'd been waterboarding her.

Where is she?

No answer.

What is that cell?

In my mind's eye, a schematic appeared —29 Palms, Talos, Level 7.

Damn! She had been just one Level below my cell. I could have helped her!

"I'll come back for you, Irene, I promise," I said aloud.

She raised her head. "Edith?" she said. "Is that you?" She wasn't so weak after all.

My mind snapped back to the cold niche. An empty train was coming. *I'm getting out*, I thought. Then it dawned on me: *There are no cameras on the sides!*

As the train passed, I impulsively leaped out and up at it as high as I could. With both hands, I caught hold of the gap between train cars. I wedged my left knee and caught hold of a small metal ledge with my toes. Palms outward on either side of the train, my cold hands were stuck to the metal. Since I was lying over the metal exterior outside, I was out of sight from the security cameras on the inside.

As the light at the end of the tunnel swelled, approaching Level 3, I asked more questions, learning that the station and security desk were empty. Two resident Talon guards were walking their rounds. When the train stopped and doors opened, a red light above an empty elevator lit with a soft tone. I ran to it, making it inside just as the doors closed.

Next stop: Level 1. When I'd stepped into the elevator, the corridor at the top was deserted. Since then, two people had come along. My mind raced. All I could think of was being caught. As the elevator slowed, I curled into a ball in the corner. I squinted my eyes shut, thinking, *Don't see me! Don't see me! Do not see me!* In my own childish way, I hoped sheer luck would make them go away.

The elevator sounded again and the doors slid open. *Don't see me ... Don't see me ... Do not see me ... I'm invisible!* I thought. Two guys, Bob and Ken, entered the elevator chatting. Gritting my teeth, I waited for the tone of their voices to turn to shock when they saw the pathetic-albino-muskrat-girl curled up in an orange ball of sweat. Instead, Bob kept mumbling something to Ken about how many couplings he had to do. Ken kept grunting, "Um hm," with different inflections each time.

"I don't know who they think I am," Bob said. "I'm not Superman, Ken."

"Um hum," Ken said.

"You know what I'm saying, Ken?" Bob said.

"I know what you're saying, *Bob*," Ken said. Ken sounded like he was sick of listening to Bob.

As Bob kept griping, I opened an eye. There was a faint green hue around me. I rose in slow motion, holding out my hands as if walking a tightrope. Ken was leaning against the elevator door with crossed arms, staring a hole into me. He rolled his eyes at Bob. I waved. Ken didn't see me.

The doors opened. Bob and Ken left and the elevator went up. When the green hue faded, I thought, *I'm invisible! I'm invisible!* and green came back. When I reached the top, I eased out and stood next to the tunnel wall.

Ahead of me, the twenty-foot corridor was plugged up by a large metal wall with a vault door in the center. A woman dressed in a white smock and lab coat stepped through the vault door and walked inside a long Plexiglas tube toward me. At the end, she held her face over a flat panel and a clear door opened into a short tube segment, sealed off on either side by two doors. Her lab coat and hair ruffled in a torrent of wind. The last door opened and she stepped out. She said, "Phil 1," to the guard.

"Rebecca," Phil 1 said.

The elevator behind me opened. A middle-aged, fit-looking redheaded woman exited. Rebecca walked past me and entered the elevator. The redhead approached the end of the tube. *This is my chance.*

"Phil 1," the woman said.

"Phyllis," Phil said.

I wondered if Phyllis was responsible for all the Phils in Talos.

Yes.

I tiptoed behind Phyllis as she held her face to the security panel. The entrance to the tube opened again, and I slipped in behind her as she entered. There was barely enough room for us both. I held my breath.

After a gust of wind, a mechanical voice said, "Clear."

I crept behind her through the tube, which led through the metal wall into a boxy white room with a sealed doorway at the other side. Phyllis peeled off her clothes and threw them into a small trapdoor in the wall. An incinerator roared. She approached a narrow window in the door at eye level, and put her face to a security panel. I stayed close, ready to shadow her out. The door swung inward. She stepped back and nearly ran right into me. As she turned to pass through the door, the fingernail of her right index finger brushed against my orange jump suit with a zipping sound. She spun around, wide-eyed, not seeing me. She ran her thumbnail under her index finger, and turned to the door. Relieved, I released a breath.

I should have given Phyllis more credit. She was smart. And strong. She jolted to a stop and landed a perfect back-kick into my solar plexus, knocking me on my back. I was still catching my breath as Phyllis screamed, "Lock down! Lock down! Lock down!" A cold mist sprayed from nozzles that sprang out of the ceiling walls. That's the last thing I knew for a while.

Chapter 73

MARTIN WATCHED ME ON THE SYSTEM. I'D JUST WOKEN UP IN MY cell for the first time after being snatched from the school with Irene. I was checking out my new jumpsuit and poking around the room as if everything was spring loaded.

I flipped the bird at the mirror in the small bathroom.

"You think *this* girl has answers?" Martin said.

Freight's image fluttered with static, his voice echoing, "You have the questions to ask. We're sending her grandmother in now. The girl's scared, and if she knows what's good for her, she'll tell us everything."

"She may not."

"You're going to find out."

Chapter 74

HOME SWEET HOME. NOT.

I woke up in pretty much the same predicament Irene had been in – hanging by chains from the ceiling. At least they left my orange jumpsuit on. Its filth smelled too familiar to notice. The hems at my ankles were shredded. A gash ran across the back shoulder blade of my suit and the seam down the front zipper was smudged with a greasy black tar.

My head fell back over my chest when I tried to raise it. I was drooling from my mouth and nose into a small puddle at my feet. My arms and upper chest were numb, and my knees were hanging about a foot from the ground. I pulled up my left leg, pressing my foot to the floor. Pain shot from my wrists down my arms and shoulders. I grunted as I pressed myself into a hunkered standing position.

The pain in my shoulders and upper body was excruciating. But I didn't care. I mean, I *really ... just ... didn't ... worry ... about it*. I didn't feel particularly displeased about anything actually. I felt much the opposite—*pleased* with everything. I vaguely looked around the new cell. Like Irene's, it was stripped bare to a round metal ball. As usual, those metal ladybugs were all over the place.

As I swooned, the ladybugs spouted thin legs and crawled around the walls. The whole room fractured into a kaleidoscope of circles, each metal bug emerging from a larger one, then flowing into another. I smiled and chuckled, waving the chains attached to my wrists like I was conducting a drugged-out scene on a psychedelic stage.

Martin came in, walking down a ramp from the door.

"Martin," I said with a grin. "So nice to see you again. Have you met my little friends?"

Martin was not happy, not sad, just intently stoic.

"I guess you don't want to tell me what you're thinking, huh?" I said.

A long silence. As far as I was concerned, it could have been minutes or hours.

"Are you ready to come clean?" Martin said.

I ran my jittery eyes over myself. "I'm certainly not clean, am I?" I raised my head. It wobbled back and forth. "You gave me something didn't you?" The answer came. "Yes, well, they did. What was it?" The answer. Snot shot out of my nose as I chuckled. "I can't believe it! LSD! You guys!"

Martin stiffened. Sticking to script, he said, "Will you truthfully answer all of my questions?"

A feeling of love toward Martin welled up to my chest. I felt no need to lie. "Sure," I said.

Martin waved his hand in the air. A holographic screen appeared, showing me at the vault door, pressing buttons. Although not a feeling disappointment exactly, it occurred to me for the first time I'd forgotten to ask the most basic question during my escape attempt – *Was I being watched?* The answer - *Yes*.

"How did you learn the passkey?"

"I asked," I said.

"Who did you ask, who told you?"

"Just asked."

"What do you mean?"

"I asked for the passkey, and as soon as I asked, I knew the key."

"You just asked and knew the answer?"

"Yep. Ask and you shall receive. Haven't you ever heard that?"

"What's the passkey to leave this room?"

I told him the passkey; it was different from the one I'd used before.

"How did you learn the other passkeys?"

"The same – I asked."

"You used a key, the one from your pocket. Where did you find that?"

"On the table."

"What do you mean?"

"You left a small box on the table. It turned into the key."

"How did you do that?"

"I didn't do that."

"Ask my questions. Where are you now?"

"I'm in a cell at Level 6 of Talos, a subsection of the Deep Underground Military Base of 29 Palms. It's called a DUMB. Isn't that stupid?" I grinned.

Martin rubbed his fingers over his eyes. "How many people are occupying Level 6?"

"If by 'people,' you mean human beings, including you and me: nineteen."

"Are you a human being?"

The question had never occurred to me. I asked, and said, "No answer."

"Is Irene human?"

"No answer."

"But you're not one of the nineteen?"

"No."

"Are there any non-humans in 29 Palms?"

"No answer."

Martin took a small step away from me.

"What are the Sundogs?"

"They're UFOs." I said smoothly.

"Yes, but what are they?"

"No answer."

"Are they from another planet?"

"No answer." I gleamed at him like he'd just proposed marriage.

"Who or what is driving them?"

"I don't know." *He's really kinda cute*, I thought.

"What is their interest in calderas?"

"What's a caldera? Oh … a *super* volcano! No answer."

"Did they make the calderas erupt?"

"No answer."

"Are they trying to destroy the planet or save it?"

"No answer."

"Can the Sundogs be stopped?"

"No answer."

"Will the Sundogs stop the eruptions?"

"No answer."

"Can the Sundogs stop the eruptions? Where are the Sundogs from?"

"No answer. You know, you really are kinda cute."

"Are the Sundogs real or imagined?"

"No answer ... Where did you get that tie?"

"Are the caldera eruptions real or imagined?"

"Oh, they're real, all right!" I grinned.

Martin paused, listening to instructions through his earbud. The video scanned forward to show me huddled in the elevator. Then, suddenly, I disappeared.

"Do you have the power of invisibility?" he said.

"I guess I do! Cool. eh?"

"How do you do it?

"No answer. I can only say that I can do it when I want."

"Do you have any other special abilities?"

"I'm not sure, but I think I have a shield, too."

"What do you mean?"

"I can be invisible because I can shield myself from vision and other things."

"Anything else?"

"I can project myself through the System, pretty much see anything it sees."

"Anything else?"

"Can you stop the Sundogs?"

"Stop them from what?"

"Whatever they're doing over the calderas?"

"I don't know what they're doing."

"What would happen if the calderas erupted without the Sundogs over them?"

I thought for a moment. "I don't see the future but I bet we'd all die, like … you know … everyone on the planet." I smiled like I'd just won a Hawaiian vacation on a game show.

"How many others are there like you?"

"Well, there's actually twenty-three other girls in the world with black hair and platinum fringe bangs who listen to Lady Gaga, but only one is about my height."

He jutted out his cute chin. "I mean, how many other people in the world have special powers like you?"

I shrugged. "You mean, like knowing everything and being invisible?"

He nodded.

"No answer."

"Does Irene have special powers?"

"I don't know … but if she does … I pity y'all."

Martin stepped closer. His eyes bore into mine. "Edith, if you don't cooperate this time, I don't know what they will do with you." For the first time, he sounded sincere.

I smiled happily at him. "I'm being perfectly honest with you, sweetie. I'll tell you anything you want to know. It's just I cannot tell you things *I don't know*. Sometimes I ask questions and answers are provided. Sometimes the answer is *not* provided. There's no response. I don't know why."

"But most of the time, when you ask a question, an answer is provided."

"Yes."

"Who is Luciano Santo?"

"He was the president of Brazil."

"Did you know that before I asked you just now?"

"No."

"Who shot him?"

"A guy named Lucas Branco."

"Where is he now?"

"Parts of him are at the bottom of the Atlantic Ocean."

"Was a foreign government responsible for hiring him?"

"Yes, China."

"Did you even know the president of Brazil had been shot before I asked you?"

"No." His assassination had not been public knowledge.

"Who shot John F. Kennedy?" he said, squeaking the question out like he was scared of the answer.

"Lee Harvey Oswald and Richard Marino. David Lima also took a shot at Kennedy with Marino from a grassy knoll, but he missed."

"Who was responsible for having them shoot Kennedy?

"A group at the Central Intelligence Agency and other G-men types in other sections, helped by some mobsters. You want all their names?"

A booming voice yelled in his earbud. "Enough of this!"

He went silent.

I smiled at him and gently jostled my chains. "You're asking all the wrong questions, Martin."

"What are the right questions?" he asked.

477

"The locket in your pocket, the one with the picture of your daughter ..."

His eyes widened. "Don't," he whispered.

"You shouldn't beat yourself up about it, Martin. You were holding her hand. That's what you were supposed to do. You're her *dad*. You protected her like you always did. You couldn't help it if she shook her hand free. You couldn't stop her from running out in the street."

"Please stop."

"What you should really be asking yourself is ... *Whose* funeral did you attend?"

The color drained out of his face.

"It wasn't an open casket funeral was it?" I said.

"They said her injuries were too great."

"They say a lot of things, don't they? They didn't tell you the casket was empty ... Brandy's still *alive*, Martin. They're just waiting to use her against you if the need arises. You *know* too much."

"Tell me where she is!"

A deafening siren blared through the cell room. I thought for a moment my brain would burst and ooze out of my ears. The noise made it impossible to talk. Martin ran for the vault door, glancing over his shoulder with a mixed look of concern and rage.

478

Chapter 75

A SUNDOG MOVED INTO YELLOWSTONE NATIONAL PARK FROM the south, centering over the Sour Creek area toward the east side. As it halted, the ground jolted with a bang. Gas-laden steam snaked from the earth in a circle. Magma shot up, flowing outward over the surface of the Sundog until it curled around the rim, encapsulating the UFO into the shape of a fiery teardrop. The burning rock gathered into a pillar, shooting toward the halo around the sun.

The Sundog that had followed Irene arrived over the La Garita Caldera in the San Juan Mountains of Colorado, which erupted into the blazing pillar of lava, hitting the Sundog, rising onward toward the sun.

The Valles Caldera over Los Alamos erupted, a Sundog centered overhead.

Paired with Sundogs, other calderas erupted around the world:

La Pacana, Chile
Cerro Galan, Argentina
Pastos Grandes, Bolivia
Bennett Lake, British Columbia
Aira, Japan
Mount Aso, Japan
Kikai, Japan
Lake Toba, Indonesia
Tambora, Indonesia
Baekdu Mountain, China & North Korea
High Island, Hong Kong
Kurile Lake, Russia
Siberian Traps, Russia
Maroa and Taupo Volcanic Centers, New Zealand
Macauley Island, New Zealand
Chabbi, Ethiopia
Laacher See, Germany
Campi Flegrei, Italy
Snowdon, Wales, United Kingdom
Lake District, England, United Kingdom
Glen Coe, Scotland, United Kingdom
And elsewhere.

A Sundog moved over the Midwest plains from the southwest. It passed over downtown Oklahoma City and stopped directly over our house, waiting.

Chapter 76

"AH ... MR. GADDIS," I SAID DREAMILY.

His smug face appeared on the window screen.

"Ms. Song," he said. "Are you ready to answer some questions *now*?"

"Did you look in the mirror this morning?"

Cold water pulsed over me with a surge of electricity. My neck, jaw, shoulders, buttocks, and lower back were washed in pain. I could hear my teeth grinding. My back fought against my stomach, compacting every vertebra.

The horror stopped.

I only heard mumbling as my senses recovered.

Mr. Gaddis laughed. "Edith, I gotta tell ya, I don't care how long this takes. I've got all the time in the world. You don't. You know some things. And you're going to tell me everything you know, even if this takes the rest of your life." He laughed again. "And that may not be very long."

Under the influence of LSD, I felt blissfully indifferent.

Distinctions between truth and lies, win or lose, live or die – those were concepts on a lower plane of consciousness.

Electrified water fell over me again, but where there had been indifference, somewhere, buried deep in my subconscious, the unbearable pain reminded me I did care about what happened to me. A pure, concentrated sense of selfless compassion swelled inside me with thoughts of Irene and La-La. Papa and Mama. My friends. Mrs. Blakely. Martin and his daughter, and others. This compassion was small but powerful. While my mind was still controlled by drugs, my heart said, *Shield.*

I could hear Mr. Gaddis' half-muted voice in the background of my mind. He was asking questions about the Sundogs again.

"Why are they all gathered over calderas around the globe?" he said. He wanted to know whether the Sundogs had any weak spots, whether it was possible to destroy them. As he spewed out a stream of questions, the small protected place in my heart pressed outward. And I remembered. I cared about whether I lived or died, whether Irene, La-La, and Papa were okay.

The growing clarity reached my conscious mind. *Shield! Shield! Shield!* In the form of a perfect sphere, the green protection pressed outward. I felt stronger, my mind more pure. Yellow sweat poured from my skin. The saliva from my mouth also turned yellow. Mr. Gaddis' image momentarily became blurred with green ripples, and then cleared. I felt a sharp pain in my hip. A metal slug worked its way out of my flesh, slid down the inseam of my orange jumpsuit, and fell into the muck of yellow sludge pooled at my feet. I thought, *Gross! I should have asked more questions about my hip pain.*

I was still hanging by my wrists from the chains, but the pain was gone. Mr. Gaddis was still wound up with anger, going on at me about something. But I didn't pay much attention. I stood and arched my back like a cat stretching from a morning nap.

"You know … Mr. Gaddis … you *really* are starting to *bore* me," I said. His screen switched off. Another screen came on. I could see Irene in her cell. She was still shackled to the ceiling, hanging motionless.

"Irene?" I said.

No response.

"Irene, it's Edith. I know you're awake. I know you can hear me."

Her left eye fluttered as though she was half awake, struggling to comprehend.

"Fine, play these games if you want. Just listen, I don't have much time. And remember, when you see me later, I figured everything out first. You *owe me!*"

Her eyes opened wide.

"First, you're in Deep Underground Military Base, more than a mile underground. It's called Talos, which is a sub-level of 29 Palms located in southern California. The whole sub-level is protected by multiple levels of security. You are at the lowest level of Talos, Level 7. The only way out for you is through a three-mile train tunnel leading up to Level 6, where I am now. From there, a train tunnel circles upward to each of the other levels. But in the connecting tunnels there are some niches with ladders leading up to other levels. Once you find one of those niches, you can pretty much make your way to the top.

"Second, you have powers, Irene. Remember all those stories you used to tell, the characters? I'm pretty sure you have all of those powers you imagined. *For real.* Just think it and you can do it. Trust me. If you have half of the abilities I have, then you can leave this place anytime you want. *No one can stop you. Believe me.* Try it out. You'll see.

"Third, Papa is in a place called Freedom Colony in Kansas." I told her the location. "He's alive, just like we thought, and he's in a lot trouble." I told her why he'd gone there, and that he'd tried to get out and find us.

"Finally, I'm getting out of here. I'm going to get La-La. I'd help you, but frankly, you don't need my help. I can't communicate with you unless you're on the System. Once you're out, meet up back home. Take care, *Sis-ta!*

The screen in Irene's cell switched off. Mr. Gaddis' face reappeared on the window screen before me. He was still going on about his expectations. He hadn't heard a word of my talk with Irene.

Far off, in another DUMB, a screen flickered to life in a room stuffed with comfortable sofas, side tables, and a kitchen table. An attractive Hispanic woman was there, dressed in a white jumpsuit. Her long black hair was up in a bun like she'd slept several days without taking a shower. She sat alone at the table, cupping her forehead in one hand.

"Madam President?" I said.

President Sophia Martinez raised her pale face.

"Madam President, I don't have long to explain. I'm Edith Song. I'm nobody you've ever heard of before. Let me just say I know you are a prisoner and the government has been taken over by the military. I will also say things are going to *change.*"

Her face flushed red.

"You probably don't believe me, but I'm telling you ... I know where you are."

She fell into the back of her chair and laughed. "Okay, where am I?"

"You're in an underground military base at Peterson Air Force Base in Colorado Springs."

"And why should I believe anything you say, *kid*?"

"You don't need to believe me. Just remember me when I come to break you out."

Chapter 77

MR. GADDIS WAS SHOUTING WHEN MY PRESENCE OF MIND RETURNED to my body in the cell. "This is your last day on earth if you don't start cooperating!" he said.

I arched my back with arms stretched toward the ceiling. I clenched my eyes, envisioning my shield thickening outward. Shackles broke from my wrists and ankles with a loud pop, bolts ricocheting around the cell. The metal ring around my waist broke. The chains from the ceiling bulged out, lying over an invisible ball.

Feeling power surge through my nervous system, I opened my eyes and smiled. "Mr. Gaddis, I think I've heard just about enough of you!"

"I know what you mean," he said with a leer.

Machine-gun bullets poured over me from the ladybugs. Those watching the video of the inside of the cell could only see a burning green ball where the bullets hit in the center of the cell.

The hailstorm stopped. A cloud of white smoke wisped in

the silence. Untouched, I stepped into view of his video. "You were saying?"

Another volley of bullets hit me as I dug my toes through the piling layer of spent lead like a child searching for seashells on the beach. Finding it, I closed my eyes and imagined a thin string snaking down. In my mind's eye, I could see from the end of the string, and anchored it below. The image was clear, like being awake, but more like night vision in green. Forcing myself like a basketball through a garden hose, the drain chasmed open with a horrible moaning sound. Metal and rock expanded and crushed away from me as I slid down the drain.

The sewer of Talos was the lowest place of 29 Palms. A transparent green sphere encapsulated and moved with me as I pushed through chest-high black sludge for dozens of yards until it intersected with a tube at forty-five degrees, leading to another parallel to the first. Realizing the tunnel was a mile long, I jogged.

It should have required great force to push a ball down a half-filled tube of muck, but it was effortless for me. Black sewer water and debris sloshed around and over my green shield. After a few hundred yards or so, I found a drain in the ceiling, a thin green sliver anchored at the top, and I pulled upward, forcing myself through earth, concrete, and metal.

Like an angry groundhog, I dug up from the floor in the center of a large domed room as big as an aircraft hangar. Signs painted on the wall read, "Talos—Level 1." Rows of combat-ready Talon and Talos soldiers stood at attention behind twenty Marines standing at attention. Mr. Gaddis was shouting orders at the formation, pacing with his hands held behind his back. He glanced over his shoulder and took a double take at me, posing with my hands on my hips just feet away.

I ambled across the concrete floor toward the exit, spun towards him on my heels, and saluted.

Gritting his teeth, he pointed, "Kill her!"

I ran to an exit, secured by a vault door. The concrete around my feet. Bullet holes riddled the wall ahead around a perfect circle of untouched concrete, protected by my shield. The Talons and Talos surged after me.

I jumped to my right, rolling head-over-heels, and sprang to my feet. Something whiffed past and gouged a chunk out of the wall next to vault door.

I shot a sliver into a keyhole in the vault, expanded a crevice, and I repeated, until I could force a sliver though, stretching open large round passage. I leapt through the hole and sprinted down the tunnel, bullets chasing after me.

Just as I thought I was in the clear, the corridor exploded, dropping the ceiling on me. *Uh oh!* Darkness.

Standing outside the collapsed entrance, Mr. Gaddis updated Secretary Freight on the System. Four Talos soldiers guarded the collapsed entrance. Carey's Wanda was one of them. A sliver of my shield had shot out the corridor and anchored itself to the exterior of her exoskeleton suit. Pulling hard, I yanked Wanda against the rubble and she dropped her gun. I expanded the tunnel, allowing me to emerge from the rubble. As I reached for her weapon, a deafening roar of gunfire erupted in my face from the other Talons. Even at point-blank range, the heavy-caliber bullets bounced off my shield.

Mr. Gaddis took cover from the ricochets. Wanda had been protected on the other side of my shield. I sauntered over to one of the Talos soldiers and put my hand over the muzzle as he pulled the trigger. A small transparent pocket of my shield captured bullets. Once full, his weapon exploded, throwing him on his back. With a grin, I turned to the soldiers, who stopped firing and stepped away.

"Good idea," I said, and sprinted across the large room. The soldiers watched me in silence as Mr. Gaddis pried himself from the floor.

I busted through a vault door. On the other side, I recognized the security checkpoint where Phyllis had kicked me. As I hurried toward a larger vault to my right, the lights went out. Faint light filled the room. At first, I couldn't find the source. I realized I was turning bright green. From two torpedo tubes in the ceiling over the vault door, lasers lit me up.

My shield turned into an intense ball of green fire, reflecting heat equal to the strength of the lasers. Slowing to a fast walk, asking a few questions, I moved toward the metal wall. When I reached it, I just kept going, passing through like white-hot steel through a sheet of plastic, molten metal dripping from the edges of the hole. My shield cooled as I walked past the wall, out of the laser beams' sights.

The train station was the largest tunnel I'd seen so far. A light rail tube intersected and paralleled with another twice its height, the ceiling between them supported by rows of concrete columns. An aerodynamic speed train with two cars and a flatbed at the end sat on heavier rail tracks next to the light rail.

On the platform, opposite the speed train, a platoon of Talos and Talon soldiers had taken defensive positions along the columns. From the next room, Mr. Gaddis told them to hold their fire. I closed my eyes and connected with the System into each of the Talos and Talon units. These soldiers could simultaneously see me standing before them and my transparent close-up face on their integrated visor screens. I silenced Mr. Gaddis' voice. A few of the soldiers tensed but held their fire.

"Somewhere deep inside, where you remember who you were before, you know something is wrong," I said. "You know you've forgotten something. You can't remember what, but the question is there, constantly, like a whisper that they can't delete. Sure, I know you'll follow orders today. But remember what I said tomorrow, when we meet again. Because I'm leaving this place and you are not going to stop me." I sauntered to one of the columns, thrummed my fingers on it, and smiled. "These are load bearing. If one goes, this whole cavern will collapse. If any of you are lucky enough to survive, you'll still be trapped down here and starve to death before they dig you out again. So listen to the still small voice deep inside and do the right thing."

I was bluffing on those last two threats, since I couldn't tell the future. I also didn't know for sure if they cared whether the entire Talos sub-complex was buried and forgotten. Despite everything I've seen of human evil, I still believe that our essence is good. On that day, I hoped they weren't trained to be suicidal.

I cut off my connection with the soldiers and approached the speed train engine. As the soldiers were passing on my message, I pressed the passkey and opened the door to the cockpit. Once inside, I buckled myself into a five-point harness in the driver's seat, asked a few questions, and started the engine. Sealing the doors to the other passenger cars, I revved forward, leaving the train station upward to the next station, three miles away to Level 9 of 29 Palms,

Chapter 78

THEY'D PLANNED TO BURY ME ALIVE. ONCE THE TRAIN REACHED the mid-point, a mile and a half away, the explosives would cave in around me. Like everything, I'm impermanent and with limits. My shield might protect me from being crushed but I'd have no way out.

I pulled up a holographic keyboard and typed. Once the train had travelled a mile, all power in the train except the cockpit shut off, and the train coasted to a stop. Then it creaked backwards and picked up speed. Pressing more buttons, the train engine decoupled and stopped as the cars rolled backward towards the lower station I'd just left.

I climbed out of the engine and squeezed through the narrow space along the tracks to the front. Stepping to a heavy metal coupling connection at the nose of the engine, a sliver of shield extended down the tunnel a mile and a half ahead. Latching onto the engine, I thought, *"Pull! Pull! Pull!"*

I didn't know my own strength. Like I'd been released from

a giant slingshot, the train and I broke the sound barrier. The sonic boom set off the explosives buried mid-way. The blast traveled through the tunnel air vents and tore the roof off an electric and heat and air facility on the surface.

As I raced ahead, the train cars were crashing into the station below. I didn't know it at the time, but explosives had also been hidden on each segment of the train. Most Talos and Talons were dug out alive later, after many hours in utter darkness.

Explosives on the engine ignited as I reached the station. Washed in fire, I bounced around in my shield, unable to perceive the order or manner of destruction. As the initial chaos slowed, I rolled to a stop near metal elevator doors and pushed hard against them. I pried them open, anchored a sliver at the top of the shaft, and forced my way up.

Upon entering Level 7 of 29 Palms, I hurried down a passage to the large domed hangar. Hundreds of empty Talons and Talos models circled the perimeter of a running track, framing the expansive room. There were high jump and pole vaulting stations near shot put, discus, and long jump stations. In the middle was a stairwell to a sunken shooting range, its lanes reaching under the running track. A rack of weapons was locked in barred cabinets behind shooting booths.

I inspected the rows of empty exoskeleton soldiers and found one marked "Talos III," designed for a person my size. I climbed in and zipped up the form-fitting suit around my feet, calves, and thighs. I secured the vest to my chin and laid both of my arms into metal casings. Typing a few keys on a mini-keypad at the end of my right arm, the fabric of the suit came alive, pressing snugly against my body. A few more buttons pressed and a scaled-metal sheath poured around my body inside the suit up to my neck just below my chin. I gasped helplessly for a moment, thinking it would climb into my throat. Once relaxed, I hit the power. Lest someone try to track me, I disconnected the CB, System connections, GPS, and anything else transmitting in or out.

I took a few cautious steps and bounced like I was on the moon. Hopping on my mechanical toes, I easily jumped up and down on the track. Feeling confident, I bolted into a sprint, circled the race track, and skidded to a stop. "Sweet!" I said.

I bounded into the shooting range and busted open the gun rack. Asking a few questions, I grabbed the scariest-looking weapon with openings for expelling bullets, grenades, and other projectiles I'd never even heard of before. Handling the gun, which felt completely foreign to me, I said, "What the heck would I need this for?" then slung it down the range like a baton.

Reviewing the schematics of 29 Palms again in my mind, I jumped up from the shooting range over the track, and forced open a vault door leading to a tunnel. Mid-way through, I bored a hole in the wall with a few thudding punches made more powerful by the combination of my shield and the Talos suit, until I reached the drain line. Forcing myself up, I exited from the floor of the domed hangar of Level 5.

That level was dedicated to security, processing of people and things in and out. The powers that be had planned, if I tried to make it to the main levels of 29 Palms, I would have to pass through Level 6, where a massed army of Talons and Talos awaited me. But by following the drain line, I'd surpassed Level 6 upward to the Level 5 hangar, which was filled with rows of waist high cubicles and desks, manned with uniforms, lab coats, and dress suits. From the looks on their faces, the last thing they were expecting was to see a Talon, driven by a mad teen with platinum bangs, burst out of the floor.

"It's her!" a Marine in uniform said.

"It's me! It's me! It's me!" I laughed and ran to one of the connecting tunnels. It was blocked by a transparent Plexiglas tube, so I tore through it and busted into a sealed room, finding a naked guy being processed there. He held his hands over his crotch and yelled, "Hey, you!"

"Hey, yourself!" I said, laughing.

The room flooded with clouded gas and mist as I extended my shield. The naked guy passed out right away. From my perspective, I could only see a round area of clear air immediately surrounded by white smoke and moisture. I approached the small sealed door and saw several eyes peering in. I tapped on it with my mechanical hand. Their heads yanked back as I punched through. When I kicked through the door, I was met with steady gunfire from a Marine in standard issue uniform and a flak vest. The bullets bounced off a bright green spot on the exterior of my shield and ricocheted around the room. The Marine's clip emptied. I grabbed the gun and wadded it up in my hand like papier mache.

"You can cut that out now," I said.

He nodded and stepped back. I kicked through another security door opening to an empty light rail station. I ran into the train tunnel going up. A half mile seems like a long distance when trying to escape from a secret underground military base. But with a super-charged exoskeleton suit that runs nearly thirty-five miles per hour, it takes a little less than half an hour, which gave me time to ask questions and think.

They were ready for me when I reached Level 4. Cannon fire hit me as I came out of the tunnel. The exploding heavy shells bounced off my shield and dug huge chunks out of the curved black walls and ceiling, pushing me back. I willed my shield to form an aerodynamic wedge. As I pressed forward, the shells slid past and exploded behind me, collapsing the light rail tunnel.

The firing stopped when I was nearly parallel with the gun turret. I inserted a sliver into each barrel and expanded, peeling them open like bananas.

A large speed train had left the station and gone a mile down the tracks, picking up speed toward another underground base many miles to the north. A light rail train waited nearby. I climbed in and drove forward. As it entered the tunnel up to Level 3, I disconnected the video cameras and jumped out.

From where I stood in the darkness of the tunnel I could see the opening of the larger speed train tunnel. A sliver shot down and connected to a railroad tie on the tracks ahead of the speed train more than a mile away. I went invisible and yanked hard, shooting out of the light rail tunnel, through the station, and down the tracks.

The back of the train caved in like a wrecking ball when I hit it. The wheels screamed against the tracks. The video cameras on the train had already been turned off. Curious. I wasn't alone. The train rocked with each step forward. I entered the next train car and found Martin.

I was in a bad mood, to say the least. I hadn't slept. I'd been drugged, tortured, and lied to. My family had been taken from me. My hair was unwashed and uncombed. I didn't even have clean underwear. And I was armed to the teeth with superpowers and no limits as far I knew.

"Get off my train!" I said.

"Where's my daughter?" he said.

"I'm done with your questions," I said, taking another step toward him.

A little girl appeared next to him, materializing out of thin air. She held out her open palm. "Hi," she said, her happy calm attitude out of place.

"What the hell!" I was more irritated than surprised.

"I'm Tabitha," she said.

I leered at Martin. "Yes, I'm sure you are." I thought the girl was just one of Martin's diversions. I took another step toward him.

Tabitha turned right. I followed her line of sight. There was nothing there. She held out her hand. "Don't hurt him. He's trying to help you."

"Just tell me where she is," Martin said. "Where's Brandy?"

I stepped forward with a hammer fist raised over my head. My exoskeleton suit burst into small pieces cascading across the floor.

I stood bare-footed in my orange jump suit. A moment of silence passed. Martin was relieved but determined.

I shot a look at Tabitha. She smiled. I raised my fist like a cannon pointed at Martin. A shield swelled around my arm, growing from my fist into a long slender spike an inch from Martin's eye. The small pieces of the exoskeleton-left-overs coalesced into a large mechanical arm, grabbed my shield, and tried to pull it away. My shield didn't budge.

I smiled at Tabitha. "Knife over fist, I guess," I said.

She frowned into outer space again. She nodded and turned to me. "Just listen," she said.

I asked a few more questions and expanded the scope of Martin's System view. A beautiful bald woman, dressed in a simple form-fitting dark blue jumpsuit, appeared next to Tabitha. She was whispering something in Tabitha's ear.

"She sees you," Tabitha said to the woman, who straightened herself and blinked around like a blind person. "I'm Oxana," she said.

"I'm tired of listening," I said. "I'm tired of answering." I twisted my fist at Martin.

"They've got your papa," Martin said. "And they've got my daughter, Brandy."

"He's trying to help," Tabitha said. "I want to help."

"Make it quick," I said. "This looks like more tomfoolery to me, and I'm losing patience."

Tabitha blurted out a string of phrases and sentences of choppy facts. She told me how she'd crashed the System, how the Sundog protected her, how she and her family had been rescued. She'd helped Martin rig the System to prevent it from coming back online, or at least, from becoming fully functional again. She had some special powers, too. They were different from mine, but some were similar.

Martin told me what he knew about the Teardrop and everything that had happened to him since the Sundogs showed up. I already knew some of it. I hadn't known he was trying to find the president, too. I hadn't asked. I'd assumed he was with the coup plotters.

499

To Martin, I said, "If you've been trying to help me all this time, why didn't you just break free?"

"I'm not that powerful," he said. "If not me, they would have sent someone else to ask the questions. This way, we know what you've got to say. It was only a matter of time before you helped yourself. Besides, they've got my daughter."

That, I could understand. I lowered my hand. I told him where they were keeping Brandy, making him more disturbed and unsettled. "Please, help me get her out of there!"

"You know our priorities," Oxana said.

"The president's at Peterson Air Force Base," I said.

"Yes, we know that now, thanks to you," Oxana said. "We're moving in on Peterson as soon as you're ready."

I asked a few more questions about Martin, about the hours, days, months, and years before I met him, satisfying myself about his loyalties, his priorities. "Martin, you're the reason the System exists."

"I know that now," he said.

"You're the one who made it possible for the president to be kidnapped, for the coup to take over, for my papa, and your daughter, to be sent away, unaware."

His eyes swelled with pain. "I *know*!"

"Then why should I help you? How do I know, once the president is freed, once you feel like things are back the way they were, you won't just restart the Teardrop, keep the world plugged into the System?"

"Your questions say more about you than about me," he said.

"What do you mean?" I said.

"You can't know the future," he said. "And neither can I. But I do know what's best for my daughter, and it's not the System world. More to the point, you're still not asking the right questions. There's a problem with the System, and it's growing."

"Not my problem. It's your demon child, Martin. You deal with it."

"That's just it," Martin said. He stepped closer. "I tried to break it. But something else is controlling it now. We need your help to shut it down for good."

"If I'm anywhere near the System, the Teardrop, I won't be flipping switches. I'll be destroying it."

"Good," he said. "What can you tell me about the Teardrop?"

I asked several questions. "I get nothing."

"What is it? Where did it come from? How does it work? What is it doing to the System? You asked those questions?" he said.

"Those and more," I said, shrugging. "I only know things you already know. I don't know what the Teardrop is, just like I don't know what the Sundogs are."

"What is the virus in the System? What's causing it?"

I shook my head. "Nothing. I don't even know if it's a virus. The only thing I know is it's a superunknown, an unknowable question. Again, it's like the Sundogs—I get no answers. All I see is a growing black hole of information out east. Maybe I'm not asking the right questions. You tell me."

Martin rubbed his eyes. "This is why you need to help. I'm afraid if we don't figure out what these Sundogs are doing over the calderas, we'll be out of time. Let me ask you this … Is your papa still at Freedom Colony?"

"I can't tell anymore," I said.

"There's a black hole there, too, right?"

I nodded. "He was there last I asked. Now I get nothing, like the whole area doesn't exist."

"And there are more viruses, spreading like cancer, right?"

"Yes, but some of it is unknown, which just means time is running short for me to help my papa. Then I'm going after La-La. Just like you don't know what's happening, I don't know if helping you first will make any difference. If I know anything, I know where my priorities are. And the people who got us into this mess are not top priority. I mean, *hello?*"

"Then why aren't you helping Irene?" Martin said. He was incredulous.

"She doesn't need my help. For your sake, it's probably best you stay out of her way."

"Are there more like you and Irene, like Tabitha?" Oxana said.

"I get nothing," I said, "but after hearing Tabitha's story, knowing about the reports of other Sundogs, I'm guessing there could be one of us for each Sundog. But that's just a guess."

"Cool," Tabitha said.

"Nice eyeliner, by the way," I said.

Tabitha smiled at Oxana and back to me. "She helped me," she said.

"Well, I guess she's good for something," I said.

"Or there could be one of you for each caldera," Martin said.

"What do you mean?" I said.

"Ask for yourself, whether there are calderas erupting right now?"

"You're right," I said. "There are."

"Where are they?"

"They're in Colorado, Wyoming, New Mexico, and California." I hesitated, considering the information at it came to me. "Actually … there're many others around the world."

"Are there Sundogs over them all?" Martin said.

"There are a few reports of that, but I can't see for myself."

"We already know about the ones near Los Alamos, New Mexico, and Wyoming," Martin said.

"That's the one which was following me around," Tabitha said.

"It's over Yellowstone National Park now," Oxana said.

"That's confirmed?" Martin said.

"We sent a scout out. It's confirmed," Oxana said. "The super volcano is erupting up and around the Sundog."

"That's what the one in Los Alamos is doing, too," Martin said. "The eruption looks like it just keeps going into space toward the sun. If those Sundogs weren't there, we'd all be dead right now."

Silence.

"What if those Sundogs go away and the calderas keep erupting?" Martin said. "What if the virus keeps spreading? What if you, Irene, and Tabitha can help us now, but not later?"

"What if I can't?" I said. "I don't know what's going on, and neither do you. In fact, I have some questions for you."

"What, don't you know everything?" Martin said.

"Who is Richard Freight?"

"What do you mean?" Martin said. "He's the Secretary of Defense."

"Have you ever met him?" I said.

"Many times, more times than I care to remember," Martin said.

"I mean, have you met him *in person*?" I said.

Martin's face turned white. "I don't recall."

"Now that's a well-trained answer," I said. "I *know*, as a matter of absolute fact, you have never met Secretary Freight in person. But when I ask a simple question like, *Who is Richard Freight?*, I get nothing ... and nothing about Sundogs, the Teardrop, the black hole, Irene or myself."

Martin and Oxana looked uneasy.

I said, "So, the real question is: *Who's in control here?* And I get no answer. I don't know why on earth I should help you rescue the president first, when you don't even know why you're doing it. I'm not saying I won't ever help you. I will. After all, she's apparently real. There're answers about her. But I'm damn sure going to help my own family first while I still can. Get that into your head."

"Then at least help Brandy, too," Martin said.

Chapter 79

A DISPLAY OVER THE TRAIN CAR DOOR READ: "SPEED: 190 MPH. Next station: China Lake. Time to Arrival: 30 minutes."

I asked a few questions. Mr. Gaddis was talking to the Secretary of Defense.

"Wait until it's half way," Freight said.

I asked more questions. A short flatbed car was attached to the nose of the engine. It could barely be seen over the front nose from the cockpit. They were planning to cut power and trigger the bomb, which was about six kilotons of explosive – nearly half the size of the bomb dropped on Hiroshima. Not nuclear, but it was big enough to make me worry, even with my shield. My mind raced.

I told Martin about the bomb. "You didn't know?"

"I'm not suicidal," he said.

"Can't you just shield you and Martin from the blast?" Oxana said.

"Probably, but then what? I'm not sure I can free us once we're buried this deep."

I told them my plan. I interrupted Martin before he could object, told him he didn't have much choice. Tabitha reassembled the Talon exoskeleton for me. "It's pretty much the same, but I added a couple of *extras*." Reflecting on her modifications to the Talon, I thought, *Little girls ain't all sugar and spice, nor everything nice.* She was starting to grow on me.

Martin jumped on my back. "This had better work."

"Or else what?"

I dove headfirst out through the cockpit windshield, landing on the ledge of the flatbed car with the bomb, an elongated silvery cylinder. Securing the foot of my shield to the nose of the platform, I stretched a sliver ahead, attaching to the tracks at the China Lake station.

"Hold on Martin," I said.

I pressed my shield outward, securing him to my back, and expanded it backward, attaching to the rest of the train. I pulled as hard as I could think.

The consecutive sonic booms collapsed the train tunnel behind us as we rocketed at three times the speed of sound toward the station. The wheels of the train melted off of their housings; any slower and it would have fallen apart before slamming into the station.

Four platoons of Talos soldiers had set up defensive positions in the hulled out station of China Lake. Several Talos were checking the ammunition in their weapons; others sat at their stations, staring at the ceiling. They heard nothing before we hit.

The train slammed into the station exceeding Mach three. The bomb ignited upon impact. The explosive pressure doubled, angrily finding a way up and out.

Level 6 of China Lake collapsed as the blast careened through the light rail tunnel leading to Level 5, bathing prototype assault aircrafts in fire and violent chaos, setting off loads of explosive ordinances, demolishing everything and everyone on Level 5. While some of the destructive forces of heat weakened, the shock wave caved in many of the tunnels on Level 4, since it was underneath Level 1, where the fury had begun.

The underground floor of the hangar at level 3 jolted back and forth like a fun house. The ceiling cracked. Debris fell over the wings and bodies of an assortment of secret flying machines. The structure held at that level. But security was compromised. By me.

Martin clinging to my back, a storm of shells hit me as I walked in flames out of the fire-filled light train tunnel at Level 3. I leveled my weapon and pulled the trigger. Rapid fire blasts thudded out of the large muzzle. Before hitting their targets, the projectiles exploded, and cascaded in a web of smaller explosions, shredding everything in their wake. Trains, floors, ceilings, and walls, ripped apart . The train station had been armed with batteries of Miniguns and rapid fire cannons. I shot out a sliver, and hooked onto the top of one of the batteries of swiveling barrels. I ripped it off its foundation, and slung it into another battery tower, and another, until all the towers laid on their sides, shooting aimlessly upwards and sideways. After another cannon volley, the ceiling over one of the towers collapsed, burying them under craggy rock. One of the other batteries kept firing to the side, tearing down a wall. Making my way across the rubble, I shot a sliver down the center of the barrel and expanded, breaking it apart. Crumbling debris was the only sound.

I ran into the hangar and stopped, stupefied. All I could think was, *Wow!* There were rows of exotic aircraft. Some of them reminded me of flying saucers, others looked like nothing I'd ever imagined. I asked. Almost all of them were man-made, others were superunknowns. *Well, well, well,* I thought. *Secretary Freight has been busy.* Walking down one of the rows, I almost forgot where I was and what I was doing. Martin patted me on the shoulder. "That one," he said.

"You're reading my mind," I said.

"You're the mind reader."

"Hardly."

A platform rose from Level 3 to Level 1. It hissed to a stop. From the cockpit of the craft, I could see the hanger doors ahead.

As the canopy closed, Martin yelled at me, standing outside on the platform. "Promise! If anything happens to me, don't forget Brandy! Tell her I love her! Tell her I didn't forget her!"

Without asking, I knew Papa had felt the same. "I won't forget, Martin!" I said.

He ran off the platform as I triggered the engines. Then, between me and the hangar doors ahead, fluorescent light drew a wall of white light across the hangar floor. Colonel Gaddis and five Talos soldiers barged out into my path. The soldiers raised their weapons. Gaddis waved them off.

Asking a few questions, I flipped a switch.

"Mr. Gaddis!" My amplified voice boomed. "You look like you could use some shut-eye."

"Power it down now, Edith. Stop and they might still go easy on you."

The ground shuddered. Mr. Gaddis raised his hands, trying to catch his balance with worried eyes.

"I almost feel sorry for you, Mr. Gaddis," I said.

Another shudder.

"You think I'm trouble?" I said. "Wait until you get a load of Irene."

I snapped a switch on the stick between my legs. A roar fired off from my right and a stream of smoke shot over Gaddis' head. As he ducked, the hangar doors exploded outward. Sunshine fell into the hangar.

I flipped a visor over my face, took a deep breath, and closed my eyes, reflecting on the blue sky ahead. I said, "All hail Lady Gaga!" my voice echoing through the hangar. I rammed the stick of the IX-1000-SCRAM forward and shot out of the hangar. Three XC-130 hovercrafts hit me with missiles and Mingun fire. The bombs thudded against my shield, bouncing me like a basketball over the desert floor. I pulled back hard and circled up and over the XC-130s, asking more questions as I unleashed heavy gunfire and missiles.

The IX, or Nine-scram, was shaped like a fish. The cockpit— a clear ball encasing a control seat—was centered in the craft's body. Two large tubular scramjets were attached to the rear fins. Multiple air intakes and exhausters swung the fuselage around, bouncing and bobbing like a mad bumblebee, as the cockpit remained steady and level, allowing me to stay on target and keep my bearings.

I swung over the first XC-130, and fired the first missile. The hovercraft moved out of the way. More guided missiles hit me from different directions.

"Crud!" *I'm not asking the right questions*, I thought.

As I flew circle eights to buy time, I remembered one of my

strengths. Keeping my sights on my attackers while whipping the Nine-scram's body every which way, I realized the XC-130s could anticipate my guided missile attacks, even if I triggered them while invisible. So I circled in behind an XC-130, and released another missile at point-blank range, slicing it in half. Bellowing black clouds climbed out of the fuselage, the divided hulls spinning away and smashing into debris across the desert.

I rocketed north over dry lakebeds between the barren mountain ranges, passing Bolder and Sawtooth Peaks to my left, Red Hill on my right.

I hugged deserted Highway 395 into the heart of Death Valley. The tops of Joshua trees waved in my wake. Far to the north, a pillar of fire rose upward to the sky, disappearing over an invisible horizon.

Something hit at my left. I shot up and faced off three X-24 hovercrafts beading in on me from mountains crests. I spun my tail in random loops, then I aimed and pulled the trigger. A missile shot out just when a hailstorm of bullets hit me from the south. Two more XC-130s had caught up. I pushed the stick forward, flying into an inverse loop. As I raced in front of one of the X-24s, the Minigun fire from the XC-130s sliced it in two.

Maybe they've forgotten what I'm capable of, I thought.

I gunned the stick and aimed at one of the XC-130s, ramming it head on. Protected by my shield, the Nine-scram bored into the nose of the XC-130, goring it inside out, and broke out through the tail. More debris crashed to Death Valley's floor. The last XC-130 still kept coming. The other two X-24s hit me with the rest of their missiles.

This seems like a waste, desperate even, I thought. *They can't win. But they keep coming anyway.*

I nosed the Nine-scram upward and gained altitude. North, I could see the lava flow erupting from the Long Valley Caldera, engulfing the Sundog above it, flowing upward into a column rising into space.

"Now I've seen it all," I said, looking westward toward the ocean horizon in the far distance. Remembering that Martin had said there were more of those things, I asked a few questions, flipping switches. The scramjets on either side of my cockpit leveled out and locked into place.

"Let's see what this thing can do!"

I pushed the multifunction ignition on the center stick. The scramjets roared to life. I tinkered with the headset in my helmet.

With Motley Crue's *Looks that Kill* thumping, the Nine-scram shivered and jolted forward with bone jarring speed. The scramjets pulsed me upward and forward to the west. It felt like something had pulled the craft's tail back and released it like a sling shot.

I broke the speed of sound, quickly doubling it over and over. Each time the Nine-scram approached another Mach barrier, it shook with such violence my teeth rattled with a clenched jaw. Everything blurred, the beat of the music the only constant. I kept thinking —*Is this thing going to come apart?* What I didn't know at the time was my shield made the Nine-scram faster than it should have been, protecting it from airflow that would have otherwise melted away the fuselage and burned me to a crisp. Before long, I was speeding around the planet in excess of thirty-three thousand miles per hour. I leveled off in the stratosphere at one hundred and ten thousand feet above the Pacific Ocean, where I could see the curvature of the earth. Overhead, the sky was black.

I arched toward Japan. Racing south of its shores, I could see three more pillars of light flowing upwards into the sky. Farther north, a faint pillar gleamed over North Korea. Continuing to the west, I could see another to the south at New Zealand. Reaching the southeastern shores of China, just north of Taiwan, a pillar approached off my left at Hong Kong. I passed over Southeast Asia and India in minutes.

Upon reaching the expansive empire of Iran, I thought about Papa. I asked about him again. Still, no answers came. Before, he was at Freedom Colony in Kansas. Asking questions, I could still confirm its location. Just no confirmation whether Papa was there. The whole area was a black hole of information and growing.

As I plotted a course to Freedom Colony, I passed over Europe. A pillar of lava rose over Germany and Italy, and there were three in the United Kingdom. I asked again about calderas and Sundogs. No answers as before. I reached the southern United States over mid-Texas. To divert my course from returning to Death Valley, I re-plotted to circle back to Kansas.

Slowing to fifteen thousand miles per hour, at thirty thousand feet over northern New Mexico, my controls went crazy, the cockpit flashing red. A proximity alert. Something was tracking me. I asked a few questions. A missile was honing in.

I gunned the Nine-scram again, picking up speed but not altitude. A white flash as bright as the sun lit up behind me and faded out. *Thermonuclear bomb!* I tried to dodge the craft to the right. It was too late. With a trajectory toward Mammoth Mountain, the second nuke went off in my face.

Seen from the floor of Death Valley, a blinding light washed out everything, followed by a growing ball of flames. From the center, a black hole fell toward the base of the pillar of lava, the fabric of space-time rippling inward toward darkness.

Chapter 80

A Marine private leaned against the shaded metal wall of a hangar baking in the desert. He lit a cigarette and blew rings into the sunlight. Rows of eighth generation F-85 Ajax stealth fighters lined the faded blacktop of the adjacent airfield.

"They just let the old stuff bake," he said, whispering to a drifting smoke ring, watching it wilt in the sun.

Sticking the cigarette butt in the edge of his mouth and pulling up his loose camouflage fatigues, he flipped off his cap and waved it in the air, trying to dry out the sweat. He wiped his forehead with a freckled forearm, taking a deep drag on the Blue Pall Mall.

Something grumbled. He felt his stomach with bony fingers. When he tapped his boots, the sand vibrated as if there was a silent jackhammer nearby.

"Earthquake!" the private said.

He thumbed his cigarette aside and bolted into the scrub brush, losing his hat. The hangar blew apart. The walls flattened out and down like an oversized jack-in-the-box had been let loose. A billowing fireball belched out from within. A raising plume of black smoke rose upward, in an inverted mushroom cloud, knocking the private into a pile of tumbleweeds. Looking up, a contrail raced out of the top of the pillar and arched away over the horizon.

"No more bark juice!" the private said.

Chapter 81

A BLACK FIGURE APPROACHED THE FRONT GATES OF FREEDOM Colony. With a wave, the gate rolled back. She strolled across the circle drive and stepped up onto the end of a long cobblestone causeway that ran down rows of broken pyramids. Beyond chain-link fences and an ocean of barren ground, pillboxes topped slender guard towers lining the outer wall.

Wind whistled around the buildings. In full kendo fighting protectors, the *wakizashi* blade sheathed at her left hip, Irene passed the processing building and continued down the causeway. As she came to the sidewalk leading to the administration building, a grey figure exited double doors at a distance. Dressed in her standard suit, red lipstick, and hair in a tight bun, Coralee slinked toward Irene and stopped twenty yards away. Her bloodshot eyes glistened.

"Like your sword," Coralee said. Jeremy was really speaking through her. "Gives you flare."

Irene's eyes, barely visible through the metal grill of her *men*, burned at Coralee.

Coralee slipped a silver case out of her jacket pocket, fingered out a cigarette, and tapped it on her wrist. "There's been a lot of talk about that sword," she said. "I do believe I've seen its sister around here somewhere." She lit the cigarette and took a long draw. Holding in the smoke, she examined the filter as she exhaled. "Nothing to say, sugar? You came all this way to give us the silent treatment?"

Irene's left hand clenched.

"Well, I'm glad you're here," Coralee said. "I could use your help."

Silence.

"You see, I'm tired of this head. So, if you don't mind, help me out ... take that sword and cut it off!"

Irene's eyes narrowed. She stood unmoved. More silence.

Coralee shivered with rage. "Didn't you hear me?" she said. "Cut my head off ... now!"

"Bring me Rory Lawson. Now," Irene said, her voice silky smooth.

"I'll bring it to you, all right!"

Machine gun fire hit Irene from three of the pillboxes atop the distant watchtowers. She was blown back into the side of the processing building. A load of heavy cannon rounds followed, knocking the walls over, toppling into the theater pit inside.

Covered with dust, Irene walked out of the rubble. As bullets and bombs hit her again, she leaned into them. Yellow sparks spidered back from her raised forearms.

She kneeled down and then soared upward through the blue sky. Her contrail came down in the middle of one of the pillboxes from the top. The slender pyramid unzipped on all sides from the top down in a lightning strike. Debris was hurled away, revealing Irene standing at the bottom, her left hand on her sword.

When gunfire from another pillbox found her again, she leapt up, beelined into it, and yanked the cannon and machine gun with her out the other side, hurling them into wheat fields beyond the Colony walls.

Another pillbox fired. She flew around in an arch and landed in the middle of the causeway toward the factory. Unsheathing her sword, she held it over her head and sliced down in a long arch. A blue vertical blade flew out from her, streaking the ground as it cut through the air, rippling the space behind like a heat wave, hitting the guard tower with a shocking thud, halving it in two pieces. She jumped into the air and beamed through the middle of the administration building. The windows in the sixth and seventh floors shattered.

Irene circled back around and landed in front of Coralee, who was still smoking her cigarette. "Impressive," Coralee said.

"Where's my papa?" Irene said. Her amplified voice rattled the ground, echoing across the plains.

"Sugar, you *are* impatient."

Irene held out her right hand as if taking a snake by the neck. Coralee choked and clawed at her throat.

"Bring him to me!" Irene said.

"Your wish is my command, sweet soul sister!"

Swarms of green jumpsuits rose into the air from the pyramids lining the causeway, and massed towards Irene. She took to the air, racing around the perimeter of the outer Colony wall.

As she approached the factory, the swarm flooded out of its doors. When she turned back, she could see the green jumpsuits better. They were inhuman, literally. With the beaked heads of gargoyles, their elongated ears were cropped back beside curled horns. They had the forearms of tigers with the taloned hands of dragons. Their bat wings were scaled, the tips armed with pointed hooks.

And they were fast. Two gargoyles grabbed Irene from each side and yanked the *men* from her head. They bit at her neck with razor teeth. She tore one off and knocked the other away with a flick. A gargoyle dug into her from the back and shredded her *kendogi* jacket into tassels hanging around her waist, exposing a white linen undershirt.

She picked up speed, outrunning them, and circled over the far end of the causeway, doubling back under the swarm, low over the causeway. She stopped, landed, and turned, crossing her arms over her chest, leveling her fists forward as dual blasts of blue light hit the approaching gargoyles, knocking gobs of them to the cobblestone.

"That's the spirit!" Coralee said, who'd walked to the causeway. "Destroy them all, why don'tcha!"

As the remainder of the gargoyle swarm regrouped and massed at the other end of the causeway, she noticed a man nearby, covered in blood. He struggled to his feet in a state of bewilderment.

"Where am I?" the man said. "What's going on?"

The CB around his neck had been broken in half. Several other people, back to human form, were stumbling around in their tattered green jumpsuits. Their CBs were either shattered or cracked.

While Irene had been distracted, Coralee had unsheathed the *katana* sword and swung at her face. Irene stopped it in mid-air with a glance. Coralee yanked at the sword handle.

Coralee let go of the handle. She shrugged with a smile. Irene reached towards Coralee's neck.

"Do it!" Coralee said, leaning back her neck, "Squeeze the life out of me!"

As Irene gripped her fist, the CB hanging around Coralee's neck crushed into crystal dust.

Coralee blinked wildly. Blackness faded from her red-veined eyes. The *katana* sword fell from the air into Irene's open hand. With a flip of her finger, she yanked the *katana's* sheath from Coralee's hand, sheathed it, and slid it into the left side of her *hakama* with the short blade.

"All new arrivals must go through processing," Coralee said, speaking for herself again. Aghast, she twisted toward the swarm dive-bombing at her.

Irene jumped into the air as the gargoyles poured over and destroyed Coralee.

Irene circled back, over the causeway, landing at the end near the factory. The gargoyles followed in a green wave. As its crest neared, she grasped the air with both hands, twirled an invisible lasso, and snapped it to the ground, squeezing her hands. Thousands of CBs shattered. The gargoyles fell and rolled, returning to human form.

Irene flew low over the battered and confused Employees. "Papa! Papa! Papa!" she yelled, her voice booming.

"Irene!" a man yelled. "Over here!"

She flew to the voice. Buddy Caprock was leaning over a bloody figure. She thudded to the ground next to them. Papa's back was crushed. His lung pierced by a broken rib. And he was bleeding from his mouth.

"He's hurt pretty bad," Buddy said.

Irene pulled him to her chest. "Papa! Papa! Papa!" Her cries rippled from the causeway through the surrounding fields.

"He helped us escape, Irene," Buddy said. "You should have seen him. You'd have been proud. We got home but you were gone."

Papa was fighting for his life. She looked into his bleary eyes.

"Irene?" he said, forcing a smile.

"Papa? You're going to be okay, you can't die!"

"I never forgot you, sweetie," Papa said. "I never did. I never forgot you."

"I know, Papa!" cried Irene. "I know!"

Papa reached out weakly, touching the *wakizashi* blade at her waist. "I will find you again in mountains," he said.

"We got it, Papa, we got it. Edith … she told me where you were. She knew! She woke me up, too. I'm here. I got you."

Papa arched his neck in agony. His body shuddered.

"No! No! No!" Irene said.

Buddy held his hands to his ears, wincing.

Irene snatched Papa and beamed into the sky. Heading west, she broke Mach 10, passing the Long Valley Sundog, bathed in lava. With Papa's body held tightly to her chest, she landed at the bald granite crest of Half Dome in Yosemite National Park. She lowered him to the grey rock and cried his name, over and over.

Jeremy was there, too, behind Irene, hovering several feet away. He frowned up at the Sundog, just beyond its rim. Irene rubbed the top of Papa's hair back, over and over again, oblivious of Jeremy.

"We're here, Papa," Irene said, her words muddled, her mouth twisted in agony.

Papa caressed her cheek.

"It's Yosemite ... we're here ... on the mountain," Irene said.

"I love you. Take care of Edith," Papa said. "Tell her I love her." He stopped breathing. His focus fell to nothing.

Irene screamed. "Papa, I'm sorry, I'm sorry!"

"Well, well, well, if it isn't the sweet soul sister," Jeremy said.

Chapter 82

Hatred washed over Irene's face. She turned to Jeremy.

"You've got quite a temper," Jeremy said, "I don't even need to tell you what to do. You just do it …. You killed your *papa* … Pity … and you actually loved him." He shook his head at Papa's lifeless body. "You and I have a lot in common, except, I *hated* my Dad."

Like a bullet, she hit Jeremy's chest, unleashing a flurry of barrel punches. He laughed as they flailed over the Half Dome ledge under the rim of the Sundog. The power of her punches waning, Irene held her fists in pain. Her lift failed.

"Well, ain't that the damnedest thing," Jeremy said into her ear.

She latched onto his shirt, tearing away his right sleeve, and fell head over heels into Vernal Falls. Jeremy swooped down and caught her in the cascading water. She struggled in vain. Tugging her by the waistband of the *hakama*, his shadow drew down over the mountains from the meadows, circled over Mono Lake, and headed toward the lava pillar rising from the Long View Caldera.

Chapter 83

L<small>YING ON MY BACK IN A CRATER OF BLACK GLASS,</small> I <small>OPENED MY</small> eyes to a column of lava rising above me, pouring up over a Sundog in the blue sky far off.

Jeremy stood halfway down the berm, wiggling his fingers at his sides. A ramshackle collection of silhouettes outlined the rim. Some had the form of men and women, others animal-like.

Are those horns, wings? I thought. The exoskeleton whined when I lifted my neck, and dropped it, exhausted.

"When you make an entrance, girl, you make an entrance!" Jeremy said. His white shirt was unbuttoned to the chest, sleeves rolled up to knobby elbows. Kind of a nerd, really.

I made fists with mechanical hands, the only working parts.

"Like the suit," he said.

His casual attitude struck me as out of place, flippant with a hint of danger.

"It was the only thing in my closet," I said.

"Get out of it. I want a look-see."

Something inside wanted to obey. Resisting the urge, I tensed. "Thanks, but I'm comfortable for now."

He came near and stood over me with impatient eyes. "*I said get out.*"

Electricity flowed over me. Instead of knotting my muscles, it felt like euphoria. Everything was perfect. Everything was beautiful. And the most wonderful sound in the world was Jeremy's voice. Nothing pleased me more than the thought of following his orders. Every fiber of my body and mind just wanted to make him happy, my only purpose in life.

I pressed a button. The Talon released me and I climbed out, smiling with glee. But deep down, in a place beyond his reach, I felt ridiculous. Something called out from the depths of my conscious mind. *No self*, I thought. *No mind.*

"That wasn't so hard, was it?" He walked closer to the Talon unit. "Step away." I complied, giving him an exaggerated smile.

He kicked the Talon. "Crude," he said. "Those Talos units are *so* much better. Still ... too bad to lose this one. Without something ... extra ... bodies are too fragile."

He stepped away from the Talon with his back to me, fiddling with something I couldn't see.

"A lot of people are taking about you, Edith, at least, they *were*," he said. "Now, they're listening to me. It seems you and your sister are special ... like me ... but different ..."

He turned, spreading arms wide with scales extending to the huge green and blue claws of an eagle. My horror was buried behind that infernal smile.

"The thing is, Edith," he said. "There's only enough room for one of *me* around here."

528

Like milking applause, he hefted his arms at the figures lining the crater.

"Call me old fashioned, but I believe in *one* true god," he said, "and he's me!"

He wound his claw-fist around my neck, and held the other back to impale me.

Thunder split the sky from the edges of the Sundog.

He smirked. "Your sister. Right on cue."

I just kept smiling like an idiot.

"She's feeling a little emotional just now … I'm sure … about your papa. She's killed him, you see. Pity. I should go and hold her hand. Be right back."

Chapter 84

NICHOLAS SAW THE WHITE FLASH FROM INSIDE THE CAVE. HE jumped out, barefoot- and shirtless, looking eastward. A mushroom cloud rose on the horizon, north of Los Alamos.

To the west, a pillar of lava gushed up at the Sundog, obscured by the molten rock, which blocked out the sky.

Skinner leaned out of the cave, squinting up at the lava. "Now I know what that preacher meant by 'lake of fire.'"

Nicholas pointed to the thermonuclear cloud. "I have the feeling strange things are afoot."

Skinner squinted one eye at the cloud, gnawing a dried piece of rabbit from the end of a lock-blade knife. "You have a knack for understatement, son."

Another explosion ripped through the northwest sky, followed by rumbling earth and another mushroom cloud. A white contrail arched from a black dot, rippling the clear sky as it fell.

Nicholas walked out into the scrub brush. "I can't see where it went," he said.

"Trouble's moving away from us," Skinner said. "All the better."

Nicholas walked to the river, overflowing from the ice melt since the caldera erupted. He rolled up his pant legs and waded into the cold water. Through the glimmering red surface, he watched fish dart upstream. A startled deer leapt through the air over a wall of reeds. Nicholas bent over and, with both hands, splashed cool water over his face. His reflection was distorted in the turbulent waters. He ran his fingers through white locks at his temples.

When he made it back to the cave, Skinner was still gnawing on the same piece of meat. "I've seen that look in your eye before. Like you made up your mind and there ain't no unmaking it."

Several more sonic booms cracked east to west.

"Something's going on," Nicholas said, "and I'm part of it. If I don't go and see, if I don't get involved, then who am I?"

Skinner folded his knife and slid it into the back pocket of his jeans. "You're asking the same question all men ask of themselves. Anyway, you don't have to convince me, son. I owe you my life."

The wind gusted over Papa's vacant eyes, flipping torn fringes of his jumpsuit. A buzzard circled overhead. Snow melted from crusted mountaintops to the north. A bear swiped a trout from the top of Vernal Falls. Below, in the Yosemite Valley, the river roared.

Faint arpeggios whispered in the wind, dancing with swooping mockingbirds. *Here Comes the Sun* by the Beatles warmed the cold air across the mountaintops, growing louder.

A swirling river of twinkling blue light flowed through the sky, gushing over Papa. His pale skin rippled with golden pulses, flushing from purple to pink. His pupils dilated and focused. He gasped, coughed, and rolled over on his stomach, holding both hands to his throat.

As I've always said, *I love the Beatles!*

Chapter 85

I STILL HAD THAT STUPID GRIN ON MY FACE WHEN JEREMY RETURNED with Irene. He tossed her into the dust at my feet, bloodying her elbows.

I felt a little relieved. It was good to see her alive. The electric signal pulsing through my body had lessened. The sense of euphoria diminished, along with the impulsive desire to obey Jeremy. Although I wanted to frown, my face wore a Charlie-horse-smile.

Back to his normal self—which is to say he appeared human but didn't act like it—Jeremy landed behind Irene. Several of the dark figures made their way into the crater, making a large circle around the three of us. Many of them were Talos and Talon soldiers. Their torsos and mechanical arms and thick legs were the same, but their visors had been pulled back, exposing vacant bloodshot eyes and wicked grins. The soldiers had several appendages not designed by the Department of Defense: gargoyle horns sprang out of their heads in long arches over their helmets, and huge bat-like papery thin wings hung off their backs.

"How do you like my new friends?" Jeremy said, patting a Talos on the shoulder. "It's because of you that I found them." He kicked Irene in the back. "With those big shots on the System speaking so highly of you, I had to find out what mischief they'd been up to at 29 Palms." He laughed. "Well, they certainly didn't have any beaches there, but then, you know that already."

He cocked his head and pointed at me. "By the way, before we get down to business, I have a few questions for you, since you're little-miss-know-it-all. What is the Teardrop thing – as they call it – over there at Los Alamos?" He waved an open hand at the ground, smiling at me. "I know, I know, I know, you haven't been there. But just ask the question and tell me the answer."

I shrugged awkwardly.

He frowned. "Tell me what it is," he said, nodding like it would coax out an answer.

"I don't know."

"Why not?"

"Some things are unknown to me. That's one of them."

He pointed up. "What are these UFO things?"

"I don't know."

"Why are they here, where are they from, why do I have these powers?"

"I don't know."

He ground his teeth, boring his eyes into mine like he was mulling over a puzzle. "Why did my dad hate me?"

"He loved you," I said. "So did your mom."

A vicious scowl arose from his neck and crawled over

his face. "You're lying!" He stretched his neck. "You know ... I shouldn't waste any more time with this. You two have got to go, and the sooner the better." He pointed at Irene. "Bite her head off."

The smile on my face washed away. I slowly shook my head.

"Do what I tell you!" He jabbed his finger at Irene like a child demanding a cookie in a glass jar. "Kill her, kill her, kill her, now!"

"No. Don't think so, little man. I just don't think that would do." I turned to the blank faces of the Talon and Talos soldiers behind him, then to the dark figures standing around the crater, and found Jeremy's face again, which was boiling with anger. "Why don't you just hot-foot it back to your room, Bucko, and have a time out? Do it! Do it because I'm *telling* you to do it."

Jeremy's skin burst apart like he'd been made with papier maché. A bird of prey emerged, covered in black and red scales. To say his head resembled an eagle is to say it was exactly the same, except mechanical, with elk horns on top, its beak glimmering like metal with jagged dagger teeth, its head covered with scales instead of feathers. His taloned dragon hands swelled as he grew a height of over forty feet. He wrapped both talons around me and squeezed.

I'd miscalculated. He could still hurt me. I thought my guts were going to shoot out of my throat. Before my head popped, the pressure subsided.

"Let go of my sister, you little punk!" Irene said.

Irene understood, too. As best we could piece it together, the caldera and its Sundog were somehow paired to one Superunknown. For some reason, when Superunknowns came within the rim of the Sundog paired with another, they lost their powers. However, Irene and I were different. Maybe it was because we were twins, sort of like Yin and Yang, I don't know. Whatever the reason, we still had limited powers under Jeremy's Sundog, *as long as we were together*, except that our powers were reversed: she had some of my powers, and I had some of hers, but they weren't at full strength.

Jeremy swung at Irene, bouncing off her shield, flailing and knocking over one of the Talons behind him.

Eager to try on some of Irene's tricks, I raised both of my fists at Jeremy's face.

"Thunder fists!" I said.

For a moment, my forearms came off my elbows and rocketed into Jeremy. They exploded with a thunderous roar. And that was exactly the problem. I was trying to smash him into smithereens, but had only blown him against the side of the crater, unscratched.

He dusted off his shoulder and dove into me, snaking his talons around my neck. I tried to push him back on my own, but he was too strong.

The pressure lessened before I lost consciousness. Irene was standing nearby, watching us struggle. She'd extended her shield (my shield lent to her), as best as she could, around my neck.

Jeremy's enormous head turned. To the soldiers, a guttural voice growled, "Kill her! Kill her now!"

The Talon and Talos units tackled Irene, covering her in a rolling ball of twisting mechanical arms and legs. The pressure returned to my neck.

Up to then, I must admit, I'd been pretty cocky. Once I'd learned I had some special abilities, I'd acted like nothing could touch me, like I could do whatever I wanted. Jeremy had been doing the same thing, and, at that moment, what he wanted was to kill me.

As my awareness faded into regret, I thought this was it. I was dead. And when a guitar echoed through the air with uneven reverberations on muted strings, I thought I was really gone, delivered to my own private Woodstock heaven.

The tune was immediately recognizable, even in pain. Since then, when I'm in the mood to kick some butt, I think of it, always, and of Nicholas ... *My sweetie!*

The riff transitioned into lead guitar with vibrato and soul, shaking the earth. Stevie Ray Vaughn's live rendition of *Voodoo Child* blared down into Jeremy's chest at the end of a silver tube that slackened and stiffened with the ebb and flow of guitar licks.

As the guitar tone dive-bombed into a reckless abandonment of hammer-ons and pull-offs, the tube drilled into Jeremy. He squealed and roared, trying to escape.

The soldiers released Irene in confusion. Jeremy took flight, but there was no escaping the Stevie Ray Vaughn barrage. Jeremy raced to the outer eastern rim under the Sundog and swooped back toward the column of lava, searching for an angle on the source of the attack. The tube bit like an electrified snake into his back, raking sparks and fire across his spread wings.

With the lead notes, I could hear an expansive voice singing lyrics about standing next to a mountain.

The guitar lead broke into an unrelenting flurry of riffs, splashing blistering energy over Jeremy.

While Jeremy was receiving his comeuppance in the air at the hands of some Stevie Ray Vaughn on a surfboard, I rushed to Irene and peeled her off the ground. The soldiers were still looking quizzically at the sky, unsure what to do.

Holding her to my chest, I jumped into the air. Like I was on the moon, I bounded out of the crater, falling gently to the charred ground. I jumped again, this time gaining more height. Jeremy's legions snapped out of their confusion and came after us.

"You'd better hurry," Irene said.

I looked over my shoulder. "Crud!"

A swarm of Talos and Talon soldiers were gathering in the air behind us, flanked by hordes of other gargoyles, dressed in human clothes.

"Just think speed," Irene said.

"Just think shield," I said.

We sped up some but I still didn't have full powers. Neither did Irene. For when the first wave of soldiers hit us, their gouging hands wrapped around my neck. Irene's shield was just enough to keep them from crushing my spine. The next wave hit us and we were pulled to the ground by the sheer weight of the dog pile of demons.

All I could see was pressing mechanical hands and talons gnawing at us; too much weight, too many soldiers, to fight against.

The sound of Stevie Ray Vaughn broke them off in a flood of silver beams. Nicholas surfed by, the air curling behind him. With platinum blond hair and sunglasses, he saluted me. I knew it then. I loved him.

Chapter 86

With Irene holding onto my neck, I bounded through a lush landscape of trees and meadows. A mother grizzly bear with cubs tried to chase after us when I spanned a stream. We were nearing the rim of the Sundog. Blue sky never looked so beautiful.

"Hurry it up," Irene said.

"What do you think I'm doing?" Over my shoulder, a tsunami of gargoyles rushed after us, the mystery man just ahead of them.

Speed! Speed! Speed!

Reaching the edge of the Sundog rim, where lava fell upward like an inverted waterfall, power washed over us as if passing through a curtain of ice water. Irene latched onto me and slung me over her back. I curled my arms around her chest, thinking, *Shield!* as she lifted us into the air. Nicholas went past us.

"This way, girls!"

Who's he calling "girls?" I thought.

We raced over the desert of lower Nevada, reaching the Utah

border, and turned south over the Grand Canyon, heading towards the caldera at Los Alamos. The southern and eastern skies were speckled with pepper that thickened to solid black, a mass of unfortunates who'd come under Jeremy's control through the System.

We turned to the northwest, darting through scattered showers and rainbows over Bryce Canyon National Park. Clouds cast shadows over valleys of tan and orange, eroded by water, sun, and wind, taking the shape of squadrons of ancient soldiers, waiting for a command. Boulders sat atop jointed rock towers, raising their heads into the sky. Above, another dark mass headed toward us from the north. We turned east. As we reached the crest over Mount Ellen, we could see the blackness rising from the east. We were trapped.

Nicholas slung his axe around his back and waited over the mountain, taping his boots on air. Pushing up his wrap-around sunglasses, he said, "I'm Nicholas."

"Edith," I said, and before Irene could get in a word, added, "nice riffs — Stevie Ray Vaughn on Hendrix."

"You know it!" he said with a grin. To Irene, he said, "You were on top of Half Dome a little bit ago."

Irene's face crumpled in anguish.

"Well, what then?" I said.

Sobbing, she said, "Papa's dead."

I nearly fell off her back but caught myself before plummeting to the mountaintops beneath us.

"But he was *alive*!" I said, crying into her back.

"He was," she said. "He didn't make it."

"Jeremy?" I said.

"There's something ..." Nicholas said, interrupted by rolling thunder from the north. Blackness approached from all directions.

I did a double take at the approaching mass from the north. I asked a few questions, zooming in on my sight. It was *very* different.

"That's with us," I said, pointing to the north.

"Come again?" Nicholas said.

"They, those things, whatever they are, coming there, they're with us."

From the west, half-dozen or so sonic booms sounded off, descending one right after the other. A red and black bird of prey with scaled wings and sharp elk horns growing out of its head, dive-bombed at us.

"Jeremy," I said.

"I'll handle him," Irene said.

She drew next to Nicholas. Taking his hand, I stepped onto a transparent ledge of faint blue and white waves under his feet.

To Irene, I said, "Remember what Papa said. 'No self. Victory is survival. Defeat is death.'"

She gave me a wry smile, which worried me, and sped away.

I gave Nicholas a bear hug from behind. "I've got a few tricks of my own," I said.

Ripping off a few licks, we riffed northward on his wave of music.

The sides of her head shaven, Tabitha's hair was tied in a short ponytail. With sunglasses, she sat in a cockpit seat above and behind Oxana, the pilot. They were riding a hovercraft, armed with bundles of machine guns and missiles. The structure's back arched up and back, with four huge rotors encased in black metal. Thousands upon thousands of smaller versions of the same craft flanked her left and right, above and below, blacking out the sky behind them.

As we neared Tabitha's craft, I projected myself onto the screens of her cockpit, updating them on what had happened since I'd escaped from China Lake.

"Sounds like you could use a new ride," Tabitha said.

A souped-up version of the Nine-scram rose between us, similar to the one I'd crashed in California, but bigger, and with more accouterments of mass destruction.

"Aw, you shouldn't have," I said.

"We're going to need all the help we can get," Oxana said.

The hatch on top of the Nine-scram opened up. "I think I'll christen it Berlin." I kissed Nicholas' cheek and jumped into the cockpit, which fit like a glove.

Darkness fell upon us.

Irene slammed into Jeremy's neck. She dug her fingers into small crevices between his scales and swung his hulking body at the ground. He lurched out of control toward the ridge of Mount Ellen, and spread his wings before impact, swooping back up.

Irene hit the center of his back, driving his chest into the surface of the mountainside. He skidded, neck first, down the rocky slope. She threw a burst of terrible punches into his upper side, causing a high-pitched elk scream.

Irene somersaulted over his head, hooking her hands onto his horns, and planted her feet on either side of his beak. Jeremy bucked up with his forearms, knocking her off him and up against the mountain. He shot back into the air and circled back at her, streaking red smoke.

Braced on the loose rock of the mountain, she drew out her *katana* sword, holding it ready. A sound like an angry raven screeched out of her.

As Jeremy closed in, Irene's sword flashed back, then pulled through and a wide-arching blue blade of light bowed the air, hitting Jeremy across the upper chest with a shock of thunder, slamming him into a deep valley. Irene dove after him.

As they clashed, we had our own problems to worry about.

The first waves of Talon and Talos soldiers were upon us, all armed with heavy machine guns and rocket launchers. I put up my shield.

When the faint green ball encircled Nicholas and me in the air, he flinched. "What the hell?"

I patted him on the back. "Sorry," I said, "Just a little hug. I should have warned you."

Nicholas readied to release a rampage of musical licks.

"Let me handle this," Tabitha said.

"Now's the time," I said.

As missiles rained over my shield, Talon and Talos soldiers broke into clumps like dice, taking on a new form: metal cage balls encapsulating each of them. They fell out of the sky by the thousands, bouncing across the ground, the cages protecting their passengers from otherwise mortal impacts.

Jeremy soared out of the valley, Irene on his tail, dodging falling cages. She was nearly on him when he dove below a ridge. On the other side, she ran into him face first.

"Gotcha," he said.

He clawed down over her face, slicing three diagonal lines from her forehead, across her left, ending at her check. She beat back with a fury but he didn't let go. Blood flowed across her face and down her neck.

"If you can bleed, you can die, little darling," Jeremy said.

A black wave crested over us from every direction. There were simply too many of Jeremy's minions for any one person to handle at once.

Tabitha saluted with three fingers and the first salvo of her unmanned flying creations bolted forward, catching gargoyles by the thousands, their rotors morphing into steel nets upon impact, wrapping around the demons' backs, holding down their wings, then dropping them out of the sky in droves. Flightless, and still under Jeremy's control, the gargoyles ran around in angry circles, shaking their fists at the sky.

Tabitha pointed to an opening of blue sky to the east. Oxana throttled their hovercraft.

Her foot on Jeremy's neck, Irene saw the opening. She glared at Jeremy and raised her fist to take off. He latched onto her leg as the swarm washed over them.

Chapter 87

I screamed, "Nooooo!" and started to pull Berlin up and back.

Nicholas cut me off.

"There's no time!" he said. The blue sky ahead was closing fast.

Breaking out past the blackness of the waves of gargoyles was about the same as jumping barefoot off a bed of nails onto razor blades. Hurt, hurt, and more hurt. A gauntlet of XC-130's, tenth generation jet fighters, and stealth bombers were waiting for us.

I understood later Jeremy had sent the gargoyles at us first because he figured I couldn't get answers out of them. If I asked questions about gunships and aircraft, I got answers, ones that didn't matter.

I expanded my shield around Berlin, Nicholas, and Tabitha and Oxana's hovercraft. The gunfire hit us hard, grinding across the surface of my shield, followed by air-to-air missiles.

The swarm held back behind us in a wall of darkness,

watching how the aircraft fared. It quivered with the force of an underwater explosion. A bubble pushed out. Irene broke out and thousands of gargoyles fell away, their CBs shattered, twirling towards the ground on retracting wings.

Back in the fight, Irene threw a fastball of blue light at a XC-130 that was closing in on Tabitha. A heat wave blasted out of her hand at a hovercraft on my tail, tearing it apart with thunderous billows of black smoke.

Following Irene's lead, we picked up speed, weaving our way around the confused armada across the sky.

To my right, Nicholas unleashed more licks: *Seek and Destroy* by Metallica! Shooting rays of orange, yellow and red out the end of his headstock, connecting with their targets. Two XC-130's exploded and spun to the ground as she ripped on, focusing on a triple-group of diving fighter jets. One was shredded into pieces, and another lost its wing; the last one hit me dead on, breaking apart over my shield.

A group of ten more jets were diving at Nicholas. Irene went at them, crisscrossing in their path. Taking *katana* swings with each dodge, blue blades halving their hulls.

The onslaught of aircraft grew. More jets, hovercraft, bombers, and even old helicopters and cargo planes, were diving at us like kamikazes. A hideous roar emerged from behind. Jeremy, as a massive bird of prey, came out of the blackness toward us. He'd grown beyond prehistoric proportions, as big as a fifty-story building.

In the distant east, we could see another pillar of lava forming against the surface of a Sundog, rising into the sky.

Irene flew into my shield with the rest of us. The arsenal of aircraft continued to pummel us, as we pushed on.

"Do y'all see that?" I said, pointing to the mountains.

"Looks like another caldera eruption," Oxana said.

I told them about the Sundog-caldera-Superunknown connection.

"So whose caldera is that?" Oxana said.

I asked some questions, gathering only a few crude facts. "It may have been the one following Irene, but I'm not sure. Could be somebody else's."

Jeremy was closed in.

"At least we know it's not his," Irene said. "If we can make it past the rim, it may be our only chance."

"But we'll lose powers?" Nicholas said.

"And so will he," Irene said.

"And if there's another one like Jeremy there waiting for us, what then?" Oxana said.

"We'll just have to assume the best of people," Irene said.

She spun around in the air and pointed her head and shoulders at Jeremy like she was a linebacker.

"I've got this one," Tabitha said.

Irene turned her head. "Are you sure?"

"She's sure," Oxana said with a smile. "Just go on to that caldera."

Tabitha's craft rocketed at Jeremy as the masses of aircraft around us came undone. Their broken parts streamed through the air after Tabitha like smoke flowing *into* a flame. Her craft grew, changing form, as it gained mass. Still kept in their metallic nets, the downed gargoyles rose from the desert floor and mountains. The cages of metal bars that had been strewn across Ellen Mountain were sucked towards the swelling figure in the form of a one-hundred-story grizzly bear; probably the scariest thing Tabitha could think of.

Jeremy's wings cupped backward. Tabitha's bear was on him. Even without human eyes, his fowl head betrayed fear.

The bear's head yawned at the cloud-strewn sky and bit down, swallowing Jeremy's head and twisted as Jeremy's hind claws curled under the bear's neck and dug in, ripping open gashes down its body. Metal parts, mixed with tires, windshields, wires, rotors, jet engines, and sheet metal, poured out, exposing the bear's hallow core. Jeremy sliced his left fore-talon and wing across its snout.

Shaking off shrapnel, Jeremy took flight again, speeding up from the ground, leaving the bear behind. Millions of pieces regrouped. Black demon clouds fell on the bear from all directions.

"It's time to move!" Oxana said.

All she and Tabitha could see, pressed against the domed overhead glass, were hundreds of wrestling teeth, horns, sharp ears, and glaring red eyes.

As chunks of the bear were being torn away, the remaining mass of parts twisted into a fortified tube, which began to drill.

Inside, Oxana throttled their hovercraft towards an opening of light miles away; the tube snaked in every direction. With the side of the tunnel spinning, Oxana struggled to maintain a point of reference on the moving light at the end.

A gargoyle broke through ahead of them. A hand formed out of the wall, grabbed its neck, and pulled it out. The walls behind them were shredded by the masses. Before the gargoyles could close in, the tube bowed up in a loop, connecting two points, cutting off the demons, giving the craft a way out.

Sunlight again. The craft hurled itself out of the end of the tube just as it was being ground to pieces, inside and out, by the swelling waves of gargoyles, with Jeremy at their lead. His right talon curled around the hull of Tabitha's craft and squeezed, letting out a shriek. The pillar of lava, pressing up from the La Garita Caldera, glowed orange and red in his face. He was well under the rim of the UFO along with Irene and the others. Irene pounded into his face, pushing his elongated neck between his shoulders. He released the Tabitha's craft, which spun out of control toward the base of the lava pillar. Pieces reformed as a new, but smaller, hovercraft took shape, and glided to the sloped mountainside south of the pillar.

Irene kept hitting him with exploding thunder fists and flying blade strikes. Regaining his wits, he double backed, and flew low over the mountain ridges, trying to escape. For a moment the swarms of gargoyles subsided, retreating with Jeremy away from the pillar of lava. But it seemed to dawn on him; although he was well within the encirclement of the outer rim of the overhead Sundog, he and his minions still had power. And so did we.

Jeremy turned on Irene with renewed determination. The swarm of gargoyles gathered behind him from all directions, forming a point behind him as if an invisible dark hand was pulling the dark curtain. He had her. She twisted in his grip as the *wakizashi* blade pierced his gut. His roar of pain echoed for miles. His claw loosening its grip, she drew out the sword, and held it above her head, readying it for a final blow when a thudding crack jolted everything – the ground, the air, the sky, my bones. *Everything.* It felt like Zeus had triggered a lever at an amusement park called "Earth," and brought it to a sudden stop. My powers left. Everything I knew, my shield, my sight – gone. My hovercraft fell apart. Gravity took hold of me. Nicholas, Oxana, and Tabitha were falling, too, and Tabitha's craft came apart.

Deep underground at Los Alamos, in the chamber, jagged lines crazed across the surface of the Teardrop, emitting light from within. A piece of shell chipped away and thudded to the ground.

Everything came back. Nicholas was breaking his fall. The pieces of my ship snapped back into place. I wrestled with the controls. When I pulled the hovercraft back up nose first, I could see something swelling under the Sundog where its underside met the pillar of lava, pressing through the shaft of molten rock towards the earth.

As it reached the bottom, the lava flow cut off, spraying a thin burning sheet of liquid rock around the caldera. Nicholas and I dodged to the south. Near Tabitha and Oxana, a splash of lava was flung across a swath of the gargoyles, encapsulating them in balls of hot rock. The demons had also regained their force, and went on with their dark mission.

I leveled off again and caught sight of the caldera. The lava flow had been completely plugged by a black tower that had slid out of the center of the Sundog. What had looked like a lens to me before had instead been a cylinder, its shaft hidden in the body of the Sundog. The Sundog above was again exposed, untouched but for an open shaft in its middle, giving a glimpse of blue sky above.

The Sundog rose and picked up speed, leaving the tower plugged into the caldera. The tower appeared to be hollow and filled to brim with churning lava.

"There's only enough room for one of us," Jeremy said, wrapping Irene in his claws. A swarm of gargoyles washed over her and curled into a long tentacle upward, spitting Irene into the pool of lava at the tower's top.

Jeremy circled the tower, looking for signs of life. A howling elk's call of victory blanketed the mountainside, his minions rippling with delight. The Sundog continued toward the halo around the sun, others gathering with it from a distance, and disappeared over the invisible Sundog horizon around the sun.

Chapter 88

THE SUNDOGS WERE GONE, AND SO WAS IRENE. MY FATHER, DEAD. La-La, fate unknown. I thought of my mother. I cried her name, needing her more than anything, wanting to hug Papa, tell him how hard we tried, tell him I was sorry for failing him. Hatred took root in my heart, along with reckless malice towards the jubilant bird of prey circling above at the edge of the tower.

I aimed my craft at Jeremy and ignited the souped-up scramjet. Protected by my shield, I bounced off Jeremy's underbelly, both of us unharmed. Nicholas drew to my flank, and we joined Tabitha and Oxana low over the mountain. Jeremy dove at us from the sky, gargoyles gathering behind him.

The tower shuddered, rocking the earth around it. A white-hot star shot out of the top and beamed at Jeremy, cooling to the form of a black samurai warrior, slashing into Jeremy's back with a *katana* sword. Jeremy shrieked in horror and agony. The gargoyles scattered, and the samurai hit again, lashing into Jeremy's scales.

Watching Jeremy flee above, the samurai sheathed the sword,

raising a copper half-crescent moon that gleamed over the brim of its helmet. A butterfly was stamped into the chest armor. It held its hand to the sun and clenched a fist, drawing it down like an invisible hammer. Jeremy was yanked from the sky and slammed into the side of the barren mountain, sliding neck first to the base of the tower. Falling on Jeremy, the samurai dug its fists into his shoulder blades between the scaled wings, and hurled his large body back and forth on the ground, pounding out deep craters.

Jeremy shrank with each impact until he'd returned to human form. The samurai flung Jeremy across the shale rocks. Covered with bruises and gashes, he curled into a ball, whimpering. The samurai stood over him with fury. A mask, with openings at the eyes, nose, and mouth hid its face, revealed only darkness within. The samurai unsheathed its *katana* and put its foot on Jeremy's neck.

"Do you yield?" it said.

Gasping in pain, Jeremy nodded. "Yield."

As he curled tighter into a fetal position, a transparent grey shell formed over him, then clouded into solid black, forming a Teardrop.

The samurai lifted its mask, revealing Irene's face.

Chapter 89

The caldera and its dark tower had been paired with Irene. Although that is not a fact known to me, at least not when I ask questions about it, the answer seemed obvious enough. I also know enough to say, at the time of this telling, a superunknown, like Irene and me, and Nicholas and Tabitha, for that matter, who owns a tower and its surrounding real estate stretching the distance of the reach of the Sundog's rim (past and present), may take away the powers of other superunknowns who trespass too near another's tower. When we'd been under Jeremy's Sundog, he'd intuitively wanted our powers gone. It seemed Irene hadn't figured that out until her foray into the fiery depths of her new home, the tower on the La Garita Caldera.

In her new form Irene also knew that once another superunknown is beaten or submits within another superunknown's tower zone, the vanquished is encapsulated in a Teardrop until the ending of the age and beginning of the next, or by other means. But I'm getting ahead of myself.

After Irene's victory over Jeremy, people aimlessly walked around the mountains. They called out to each other, banding with other hapless souls, trying to figure out where they were, how they got there, and how to get back home.

The sky was clear above the tower. Miles away, peppery dots spun around us, dropping slowly, like flakes in a dark snow globe. Zooming in, I saw the flakes were people, not gargoyles, cascading around the perimeter of the tower, at the barrier where the Sundog's rim had extended.

A question tickled my mind.

"I don't believe it!" I said, shouting.

I throttled Berlin, hurling to the southeast, bearing down on Oklahoma City.

A hovercraft was sitting in front of our house. A Sundog menaced overhead; no lava, no tower, just the stupid UFO there, mocking me. Flying low, I circled around and landed in the street. The neighborhood was deserted. The entire city was empty. People were lost out in the Wild, having been drawn out by Jeremy as demons, trying to find their way back home by foot.

I ran from Berlin to the side door. Irene and the others arrived as I entered the *dojo*. With his back to me, dressed in a kendo uniform, a man was sitting on his knees.

"Papa!" I said, beaming with joy.

As I stepped towards him, he stood and turned.

Confused, I said, "Martin?"

"Call me 'Papa'," he said. He smiled broadly, revealing his teeth.

"You're not *my* papa."

"Is it really so hard to believe?" he said. "Don't I look and act like your papa? That's why I was sent to talk to you, Edith ... to get you to remember the truth." He smiled.

I wanted to throw up. I looked around the room, questioning whether everything I'd remembered, everything I knew, was a dream. Still dressed in a neon orange jumpsuit, I scraped my fingers through my filthy hair, and pulled it from my face. I noticed the CB around his neck glowing green. *He's not my papa*, I thought.

Irene broke the awkward silence as she entered, with Nicholas, Tabitha, and Oxana behind her. Still dressed as a samurai, she half bowed, which Martin returned. They advanced towards each other three paces and simultaneously drew their swords. Irene normally wielded her *katana* sword. This time she had the *wakizashi* sword, leaving it sheathed. Standing on the balls of their feet, their knees out to the side, they squatted to the ground with the tips of their swords touching and stood. Martin didn't know kendo, as far as I was aware.

Holding the butt of her sword with her left hand, she tilted the sheathed blade toward Martin.

"There's something written on this blade ...," she said coolly. The sound of her voice sounded off.

"So there is," he said, his eyes unflinching.

"What does it say?" Irene said.

"Don't you know?" he said.

I knew right then and there, for sure, he wasn't Papa. I felt a twinge of guilt for ever doubting.

"Who are you?" Irene said.

"What is this, Martin?" I said. "I thought you unplugged the System!"

"I've changed my mind several times over the years. I'm pretty fickle that way." He cocked his head to one side and smiled.

Irene clenched a fist, shattering the CB around his neck. Pulverized crystal salted the floor.

"Name yourself! Who's in control of the System?" Irene said.

Martin looked at the remains of his glasses and laughed. "She's a much faster study than you, Edith." He shook his head. "I'm afraid it's too late for Martin, although, I must say I owe him a round of gratitude. He's the one who made all this possible. Once he gave me access to the System, I befriended the minds of every person connected to it. I'd been trapped for an age, with little to no hope of escape! And then, like a miracle, I was free to do anything I wished. It took a little learning, true … but soon I had complete control, even though I was still imprisoned. But … things change."

"The Teardrop," Tabitha said.

"Yes, that's what they called it," Martin said, "the Teardrop. And how suiting the title is, for it is a prison of pain and suffering. I only hope the one who put me there suffers the same." He brought his attention back to the moment. "In any event, I have some presents for you all." He reached in his pocket and produced a handful of CBs. "There's one for each of you."

"I'd rather die," Oxana said.

"That can be arranged," Martin said. "Whether you like it or no, you're all going to call me 'Papa' in the end!"

"Honey?" a voice said from the kitchen.

A chill ran up my spine. The voice reminded me of an impossible dream, the kind you wake from in the dead of night and sob back to sleep wishing it as true.

Mama came to the doorway. "Honey, you didn't say we were having company."

"I'm sorry, honey," Martin said, giving us a toothy grin. "I didn't know either. Do be a peach and make some green tea for everyone. They're going to be staying for a while."

My mouth twisted in pain, eyes swollen. "Mama! Mama! Mama!" I screamed.

She held her head to one side with a vacant smile.

Irene tore off her helmet, clutching it under her right arm. A tremor ran though her and I felt it jolt the foundation.

Martin stepped toward Irene on the wood floor of the *dojo*. "In fact, they'll *never* leave." He raised his hands like he was about to throw a boulder at us.

"A voice outside the back door said, "Oh, come now, don't lose your temper."

"Oh, come now, don't lose your temper," Mama said.

With a serene smile, La-La entered the *dojo* from the back door behind us.

Tears streamed from my face. "La-La?"

She half-bowed to Irene and me. She winked at Nicholas. Passing Oxana and Tabitha, she rubbed them across their shoulders, and stopped with crossed arms at Martin. His face was red and turning purple.

"*You!*" Martin said.

"*You,*" La-La said, her voice, filling the room with a low growl. She lowered her chin, her eyes, glimmering faintly gold. "*You* ... keep your scaly hands off...my...family!"

The spin of the Earth slowed. The gravity of the room shifted to one side with the sound of a slowing freight train. The light dimmed. Martin let out a chestful of air. He gasped and fell to the ground, unconscious.

Something the size of a redwood tree trunk cut the house in half, smashing into the center of the *dojo* floor between La-La and Martin. The roof and ceiling tore away. Shouldering his guitar, Nicholas sprung into the sky. Oxana pulled Tabitha out the side door into the front yard, where a ten-story Typhon stood over us, tossing the remnants of what was left of our roof into a whirlwind of debris.

The Typhon had legs like two coiled rattlesnakes leading up into the muscular torso of a human. Its humanoid chest, shoulders, and arms led to dragon wings covered with shimmering lime-green scales. Dragon forearms extended at the ends of its wings with hands like frayed ropes of twisting cobra heads. The neck of the beast had the long body of a serpent, leading to the bearded face of Secretary Freight. His diamond-shaped eyes burned red coals.

I grabbed Martin by the shoulder and pulled him into the front yard. The Typhon swung its left arm down, smashing the hovercraft and Berlin in a single blow, blocking my path.

Through all the chaos, Mama kept talking from the kitchen as thought her pleasant conversation had continued. The Typhon reached for her. Stepping in the way, a gold light burst around La-La. She squatted, lowered her head, and pushed her right fist toward the sky. Her form swelled and a shock wave of light coursed from her, pushing the Typhon back, crushing Mrs. Caprock's old house. I turned my head. La-La's skin turned to gold. She wore a crown of flaring crests. In her right hand, she wielded a double-edged golden sword with a glowing tip of fire.

La-La hit the Typhon between its neck and shoulder, sparks

flying from her blade. He roared and whipped around one of his snake legs. It caught her in the side and knocked her crosswise, plowing through a swath of homes.

Irene rose out of the rubble of our house. Floating in the air in front of the Typhon, she held her hands in a choke hold and snapped down. The Typhon lifted from the ground forward and flipped, landing on its back, flattening dozens more homes. Its right hand entwined her in a mitt of cobras and threw her. Several blocks away, her body tore into a blacktop street, grinding a long gash of a crater in the ground.

La-La hit the Typhon in the back with circling blows, the end of her sword exploding in waves of sparks with each blow. She kept on it with full fury.

The Typhon headed for the cover of the downtown skyscrapers. Nicholas picked me up, and we surfed from overhead, leveling off behind it. Nicholas unleashed *One Vision* by Queen, Live at Wembley '86. Pulsing light flared from his headstock and pounded into the Typhon's back, peeling into flames. The Typhon let out a soul-curdling roar, crashing through the tenth floor of the Will Rogers Building. The eighty-story glass tower wavered and crumbled to one side, shattering into a cloud of powdered concrete and glass.

The Typhon darted westward down I-40 and doubled back into downtown. Nicholas poured white-hot licks over his back with *Blue & Evil* by Joe Bonamassa, burning off a rattle from the Typhon's left snake-leg and setting the right wing on fire. For reasons that are still unclear to me, Nicholas had the upper hand with the Typhon, maybe because he'd touched the Teardrop at Los Alamos.

But Nicholas' edge was not absolute. The Typhon turned,

faced Nicholas, and brought its left arm around into a punching motion. Nicholas hit an invisible wall, and me with him. When the punch hit us, I felt like I'd been riding on the back of a super-sport motorbike when it smashed into a train head on. Nicholas was nearly knocked unconscious.

La-La caught us with her left hand. She put us down on the roof of the Woody Guthrie Tower. Before she could turn, the Typhon broadsided her with cycling fireballs from its eyes, blowing her over into the Oklahoma River. Sheets of steam rose out of the water as she rolled downstream.

Irene hit the Typhon, helmet first, in the center of its back, knocking it chest first into the Chavez Tower. Grabbing me, Nicholas streaked north. Irene circled back and careened into the Typhon again. Hovering in the air to its right, she made another wood-chopping motion. Invisible arms lifted the Typhon up by its right arm and body-slammed it into the ground. She slung it back and forth, smashing the convention center and some vacant hotels into sawdust. Catching sight of her, the Typhon beamed dual blasts of red fire, hitting her in the chest, knocking her back through the last downtown skyscrapers.

La-La gathered herself and lunged at him. The Typhon's head shivered, it coiled its legs, and reached into the sky. Lightning rose from its viper fists with a clap of thunder. The wind picked up as the Typhon circled its arms and bent at the waist.

The strength of the wind grew to hurricane force. Nicholas dropped to the ground and brought us under an overpass, the worst place to go in a tornado.

In all the chaos, while homes and businesses blew away and trees were stripped of bark, an earthquake hit. Magma pushed up under the Oklahoma City metro area and erupted under the house, hitting the bottom of the Sundog, following its staggered surface outward towards its rim, and gathering into a pillar in the sky. Wrapped in hurricane winds, the ground under the Sundog rose upward, forming a mountain. A tower dropped down from the Sundog, pressed into the pillar of lava, cutting off the flow. As the top of the tower decoupled from the Sundog, the earth shuddered, and the wind ceased. A shower of sunlit debris fell to the earth. A massive cracking sound echoed across the sky.

The Typhon pushed itself up with both arms, disoriented and uncertain. Nicholas and I climbed to the top of the bridge as the Sundog sped toward the sun. Irene head-butted the Typhon's face helmet first, grabbed its beard, and slammed its body face first into the ground. She snagged its left leg by the remaining rattle and dragged the whole beast into the sky, chasing the Sundog. The Typhon kicked with its rattle-less leg but couldn't reach her. Catching up to the Sundog, with the Typhon in hand, she flew into its hollowed-out center core where the tower had been. Once she was inside, the Sundog reached the invisible horizon around the sun and disappeared. The solar Sundogs faded. Debris settled across the city. Silence fell across the world.

"No!" I said.

Back to her usual size and appearance, La-La floated from the sky. She landed on the bridge next to me.

"La-La, go get her!" I said, crying.

Seeing her pale sadness, I knew there was nothing she could do. I fell to my knees. A hovercraft approached from the north and landed on the nearby roadway. Tabitha hopped out and pushed her glasses up with a smile.

"She's gone, Tabby!" I cried. *"She's gone!"*

"Not everyone is gone," she said.

Papa hopped out of the hovercraft, holding Mama's hand. "Papa! Mama!" I yelled. I rushed to hug them before anything else could happen. Gripping them tightly, smelling their clothes, touching their faces, I knew, really knew, it was them.

"Irene!" I said, burying my head in Papa's chest.

"I know," he said. "I know." The tremble in his voice made me cry harder. We knew she was gone forever. Even though I had no answers, I just *knew*.

As Mama cupped the back of my head, thunder split the sky and shook the ground. The sun shrank and turned black. Darkness engulfed the world. My mind raced with thoughts too fast to comprehend. I fell to my knees, clutching my head with both arms, trying to keep it from popping off. The amount of information running through my brain made me feel like it might turn to jelly and press out my eyes. Pain! I screamed.

The earth shuddered and the sun burned to life from inside out. The solar halo returned and swelled with a thump as if it had swallowed something. A tiny black hole broke the invisible horizon, warping the space around it, and sped toward us. A black samurai approached, gripping a long-pole sword with its blade pointed down.

Irene landed on the roadway before us on her knee and fist. Her facemask was pulled down, and dents, gashes, and burn marks covered her armor. The cutouts over her eyes and mouth were dark pits. She straightened, hesitated, and tore off her helmet and mask, tossing them to the blacktop with a thud.

"Papa! Mama! La-La!" Irene cried. Looking older, she

limped into us.

Pulling me close, she said, "Edith! I thought I'd never see you again! You saved us!"

We held each another tightly, swearing to ourselves, *Never forget the ones you love.*

"Where's Dillon?" said Irene.

Chapter 90

THE VAULT DOOR WAS PRIED OPEN. PRESIDENT MARTINEZ STOOD up and pushed back the kitchen chair. Her hair was disheveled. She was hungry, thirsty, and short on patience.

Dressed in a clean neon orange jumpsuit, with pig-tailed platinum blonde hair, and black highlights at the fringes, I stepped barefoot through the vault door, a black stripe painted over my eyes in a straight line. I pulled white headphones down around my neck and smiled. The president smiled back and pointed.

"You're *that* girl," she said.

I put my hands on my hips. "I told you so, Madam President."

Ken 6 woke up. His eyes fluttered.

"Ken 6," a voice said, shining a penlight into his pupils and slapping his face.

"Carey, do you think he's dead?" a woman said.

"He's not dead, Wanda, just dehydrated," Carey said. "Ken 6!"

"Okay, okay, okay!" Ken 6 said, "I'm awake." He squinted into the face of a nerdy bald guy with gold-rimmed glasses.

"Good. You're awake," Carey said. "State your name and rank!"

He shrugged. "My name's Dillon," he said.

"He asked for your rank!" Wanda said.

He shook his head. "Just Dillon."

The shout went out of her voice. "Well, *okay,* then. Things are back to normal ... sort of."

Dillon looked down, seeing he'd been cupped inside a fifteen-foot exoskeleton. Carey was standing on a stool in front of him; Wanda, still wearing a Talon suit, stood behind Carey.

Dillon examined his mechanical arms and looked at Wanda. "Are you the ... the ..."

"The what?" Wanda said.

"The Superunknown."

"No," Carey said, twisting a screw near Dillon's jaw, "but she sent us ... said not to forget Dillon. She also said you're going to help us dig out of here. Her little friend made this special suit for you."

"And ... Irene?" said Dillon.

"She's waiting, said Wanda. "Can you imagine?"

"More than I ever hoped," he said.

A little girl sat in a sandbox with a green plastic bucket, digging with a red shovel. Her blonde hair was braided in small buns, cute in a mousy way. She patted the top of the sand-filled bucket, and dumped it out, making a castle.

"*Brandy*," a voice said.

As she turned, Martin stepped from a grassy playground into the sandbox. Other children swung in the sunlight behind him.

"Daddy!" Brandy said. She dusted the sand off her white dress, stitched with pink and purple flowers, and limped into his arms.

Brandy dug her head into his neck. "Where have you been, Daddy?"

Martin smiled at the imprints of my bare feet in the sand. I drew a smiling face with an invisible finger.

"Looking for you, sweetie," he said. "Looking for you."

What is nothing?

What is nothing?

MIMBREZ

Order Form

Orders may also be made on the Web at www.mimbrez.com.

Mail Orders for *The Superunknowns*: Mimbrez Publishers, P.O. Box 13508, Oklahoma City, Oklahoma 73113, USA.

Please send the following number of copies of *The Superunknowns*: _____.
Please ship to the following address:

Name: _____

Address: _____

City: _____ State: _____ Zip: _____

Telephone: _____

Email: _____

Each book price: $29.95 U.S.D.
Shipping in United States: $3.95 for first book and $2.00 for each additional product. Please contact Mimbrez Publishers to request discount if purchasing in bulk.
International Shipping: $15.00 for first book and $5.00 for each additional product. Up to ten books maxium. Contact seller for pricing of larger orders.
Total enclosed, including price of book(s) and shipping: _____.
Please include payment by check or cashiers check, made payable to "Mimbrez Publishers."

What is nothing?

Made in the USA
Charleston, SC
28 April 2016